BOOK THREE
*The Souls of Aredyrah Series*

# The Taking
*of the*
# Dawn

Tracy A. Akers

First Edition Paperback, Ruadora Publishing
ISBN-13: 978-0-9778875-4-5
ISBN-10: 0-9778875-4-5

ISBN-13: 978-0-9778875-1-4 (series)
ISBN-10: 0-9778875-1-0 (series)

Library of Congress Control Number: 2010913730

Ruadora Publishing
P.O. Box 3212
Zephyrhills, FL 33539
ruadorapublishing@msn.com

Front Cover Illustration and Interior Art: Annah Hutchings; ©Tracy A. Akers

# TABLE OF CONTENTS

# PART ONE

## FACING THE FIRE

# CHAPTER 1: OBLIVION

Dayn stood atop a rocky outcrop, silhouetted against an iridescent palette of molten fire. As far as he could see, a mesmerizing splendor stretched, a great river of lava from which sparkling channels crept down the mountainside in brightly braided patterns. Trees in the paths of melted rock ignited like thousands of flaming candles. Some evaporated into white-hot oblivion; others were turned to ebonized shapes, gruesomely posed.

Dayn reached for his sister's hand, squeezing it so tight the tips of her fingers turned white. But she didn't complain. She probably didn't even notice.

"Have you ever seen such a thing," Alicine whispered.

"I'm not sure I'm seeing it now," Dayn replied.

Alicine frowned. "Now what are we going to do?"

"I don't know. Maybe I took us the wrong way." Dayn shook his head. "We'll have to go back."

"You don't mean *all* the way back."

"No...I don't know. But we sure can't go this way."

"But Reiv said—"

"Well, he obviously didn't know about this...or maybe I misunderstood him. Don't worry, we'll get home. I probably just didn't take us far enough north or something."

Dayn pulled in a breath, then released it slowly. It didn't matter whether his cousin Reiv had told them wrong. It didn't matter whether they had gone too far one way or the other. The vale before them was impassable, or would be by the time they reached it. Turning back was not a difficult decision. Where they went next was.

The wind shifted in their direction, wrapping them in a veil of vapor that reeked of sulfur and smoke. Dayn covered his nose with his free hand and pulled his sister along with the other. "Come on," he said. "The horses are getting nervous, and we can't afford to lose them."

Dayn scrambled down the slope, but a stab to his heel suddenly sent him hopping. He cursed the ground, the rocks, and everything else he could think of at the moment. His feet were already aching, and this was yet another in a long series of attacks upon them. It was time to put his boots back on, and he dreaded it.

Where he and his sister were from, no one ever went without their boots. And for most of the past fifteen and a half of Dayn's sixteen-year-old life, he hadn't either. The terrain in Kirador was mountainous and the temperatures almost always cool, if not downright frigid. To go with bare feet was something no sensible Kiradyn would do. But Dayn had not worn his boots for months now, preferring to go barefoot. That was what the Jecta of Tearia did. And that was what he considered himself now—Jecta.

He pulled up his foot to inspect it, finding an indention with a tiny white pebble lodged within. He picked it out, then limped to the horse, grumbling as he yanked a bundle from its back.

"Don't tell me," Alicine said with amusement, "you're actually putting your boots on."

"Well, I have to some time, don't I? I'm tired of having to dance around every time I get off the horse. It's a lot rockier here than back home—I mean, back in Tearia."

"A lot rockier *and* a lot colder. I'm surprised your feet aren't blue." Alicine scolded him with her eyes, once again acting as if she were the older, then pulled her shawl tighter around her shoulders. It was the last defense she had against the decreasing temperatures, other than the ratty blanket she had been using as a bedroll.

Dayn glanced at his sister, noting the cold-swept features of her face and the stiffness of her body. The dress she wore should have been warmer; it was long sleeved and high collared, its full skirt reaching to her ankles in yards of gold-colored material. But the fabric had been selected for its beauty, not its practicality. It was a dress embroidered with hundreds of tiny white flowers—a dress for a Summer Maiden, not a girl trudging through the mountains. No, its weave wasn't enough to stave off this kind of cold. Even the molten fire on the other side of the ridge did little to warm the environment.

"Where's your coat?" Alicine asked.

"In my pack. But one thing at a time. Boots first...coat later," Dayn said.

Alicine sighed. "Suit yourself, but that tunic of yours is not going to keep you warm for long."

Dayn shrugged his shoulders against the rough, green wool of his tunic. At one time he had worn it in comfort, but it felt itchy to him now. For too many months in Tearia he had gone bare-chested, with nothing against his skin but a kilt around his hips. Now he had on long sleeves and thick trousers, the scratchy material pressed against every part of his body.

He pulled the boots from his pack and plopped to the ground, frowning with annoyance at his feet. They were stained with dirt and rough with calluses from months of going barefoot. But the boots, he knew, would bring blisters to his toes no matter how tough his feet had become. He scowled and yanked on his socks, then the brown leather boots, shiny new when he had left Kirador, now scuffed and worn with travel. He snaked the long laces up his calves without regard to pattern and tied them in a knot, then stood up and groaned. The things were miserable.

Alicine laughed. "You loved those boots when you first got them. Couldn't wait to wear them as I recall. Worked extra chores at home and helped Jorge at the smithy to earn the coin to buy them. And now..."

Dayn cocked his brow. "And who is it that keeps tugging at her collar? Hmmm?"

Alicine arched her neck and ran a finger beneath the lace of the collar that stopped just below her jaw line. Ever since she had donned the dress for the return trip home, she had tugged and fidgeted at the material almost as much as Dayn had his.

"I don't know how I ever thought this dress was comfortable," she said. "But I guess we'd better get used to dressing like Kiradyns again. I doubt the climate *or* our neighbors' icy attitudes will allow us to go around showing our arms and legs."

Dayn turned away and checked the strapping of the packs on the back of his horse. "There's a lot of things we won't be allowed," he muttered.

"What'd you say?" Alicine asked.

"I said, won't Father and Mother be pleased that we're bringing two horses back with us?" He stepped over to his sister and lifted her onto one of the horses. "Come on. There isn't much daylight left, and I want us to get as far away from here as possible before we set up camp for the night. I'd hate to wake up and find us in the path of that," he said, motioning to the glow of roiling fire on the other side of the ridge.

Dayn mounted his horse, a broad-backed chestnut with a patch of black on its face. It was a beautiful animal, nothing like the old hag of a horse their father owned. But then again, their father probably didn't own a horse anymore. Alicine had ridden out of Kirador with the only one he had when she'd gone looking for Dayn the day he ran away. They'd left the animal grazing near the cave that had taken them to the other side of the world, and it was doubtful the old gray had found its way home. The poor beast was probably still wandering the mountains somewhere, or else dead by now. Regardless, Father would be pleased to see his children riding home after all these months. Perhaps the new horses would settle his temper, once the happy emotions of the reunion faded and the reality of what Dayn and Alicine had put him through set in. But it wasn't likely.

Dayn took the lead and urged his horse down the embankment to an open space near the trees below. There wasn't exactly a path to follow, no humans had been there for centuries, but he and his sister had learned to navigate the rugged terrain by working their way through only the barest patches of landscape. The going had been slow, and they'd oftentimes found themselves having to retrace their steps. As a result, it was taking much longer than expected to make their way to the other side of the mountain range. The shortcut through the cave that had taken them to Tearia was no longer an option. It was destroyed by the violence of an angry mountain, taking evidence of Kiradyn and Tearian history with it.

It had been several days since they had left Tearia, a great region with a namesake city in the southeastern region of their island world. It was a place Dayn and Alicine had not known existed until recently. The eastern side of the mountains was supposed to have been destroyed long ago, plunged into the sea by an angry god, or so the Kiradyns believed. But now Dayn and Alicine knew the truth of it, though the people of Kirador would not likely welcome that truth. Of even more concern was the fact that they would not likely welcome Dayn either.

They turned their horses northward, neither of them saying a word for quite some time. There wasn't much to talk about; all best and worst case scenarios regarding the reunion with their parents had already been discussed. Dayn felt certain the homecoming would be an unpleasant one, at least for him, but Alicine refused to see it that way. As a result, their conversations had begun to end in more and more arguments. *Father will be so glad to see you he won't even care that you ran away or that I left with his horse,* Alicine said over and over. But Dayn knew there was more to the issue than that. While his sister imagined hugs and kisses upon their arrival, Dayn expected only angry words and accusations. Someone would be storming out of the house when all was said and done, and it would probably be him. His father owed him an explanation, as did his mother, but there weren't enough words in the world to explain it all to him. What words could explain why a man would steal a child and claim it as his own? What words could justify why two people would lie to that child and everyone else about who he really was?

"What are you thinking?" Alicine asked.

Her question yanked Dayn back to the present. His mouth compressed, then he said, "I was thinking about what I'm going to say to Father and Mother when I get home."

Alicine turned her attention to the path in front of her. "Do you have to hang onto all this anger, Dayn? Can't you just start over? I mean—"

"No. I can't just start over. It'll never be right for me there and you know it."

"It could get better. When we tell them what we know and..." Alicine paused, the scowl on Dayn's face a clear indication that he was not receptive to her suggestions. "Well, there's always Falyn to look forward to," she offered cheerfully.

"I don't want to talk about it anymore," Dayn grumbled. He kicked his heels into the horse's ribs, urging it ahead.

"I'm sorry, Dayn. I won't mention it again," Alicine said to his back.

"Good," he retorted.

That night they camped in a gully beneath an overhang of willows. Bright moonlight distorted the surrounding landscape into patterns of black and silver and gray. Trees creaked and swayed, morphing from ghostly shadows to skeletal shapes. At one time, Dayn would have been terrified to be in a place like this after dark. He had been raised to believe demons lived in the mountains and that they would make a meal out of a man if so inclined. But now Dayn knew the truth of things, and he wasn't afraid anymore. There were no demons, at least not the kind he had read about in the Written Word. That was another thing he looked forward to telling his parents.

Dayn strolled over to Alicine who was sitting and staring into the campfire. He sat down cross-legged next to her, but she didn't acknowledge his presence and continued to stare at the fire.

Dayn stabbed at the coals with a stick. He shifted his gaze to her. "So…" he said, waiting for a reaction. But there was none coming. "So…" he repeated slowly. "Do you think Reiv has—"

"I miss him," Alicine said.

"We'll see him again."

"No we won't."

Dayn stiffened his spine. "Yes we will. I will anyway."

Alicine flashed her eyes at him. "What's that supposed to mean?"

"Listen, I don't want to argue anymore, but you know full well I'll be going back to Tearia eventually."

"If you hate it so much in Kirador, then you shouldn't have come," Alicine snapped. "You've done nothing but complain ever since we left Tearia. Why didn't you just stay there?" She turned her eyes back to the fire and wrapped her arms around her bent knees.

"Because I promised to get *you* back home, that's why. And because—"

"And because you want to make a play for Falyn. What do you think is going to happen when you do, Dayn? Do you think she'll leave Kirador for you? I wouldn't put my hopes there if I were you."

Dayn felt the heat rise to his cheeks. *She's baiting you for another fight. Don't fall for it.* He forced a look of indifference and shrugged his shoulders. "Well, if she doesn't want to go back with me, then I'll go without her."

Alicine snorted. "You mean to say that even if Falyn said she loved you, you'd go back to Tearia without her? Ha! That I'd like to see."

Dayn glowered in Alicine's direction. She knew as well as he did that he would never leave Falyn behind, certainly not if the girl told him she loved him and wanted him in her life. He would suffer in Kirador for the rest of his days if Falyn would only say the words. But he also knew that wasn't likely to happen. Her father would never allow it. Lorcan, as well as all the other Kiradyn fathers, had already decided no daughter of theirs would ever court him. Dayn was strange, they said, too different, too dangerous, too demon-like in his appearance. His hair was pale and his eyes piercing blue; nothing like the swarthy Kiradyns; nothing like the girl Dayn called sister who sat beside him now, her brown eyes studying him, her thick, black hair plaited down her back.

"You heard me," Dayn said in a lame attempt to convince his sister as well as himself. "I'll go back without her if I have to."

"I heard you, but did you hear yourself? You know what Falyn said, what she told me at the festival. You've only asked me to repeat it a hundred times. No, I don't think you'll be leaving Kirador—not with Falyn feeling the way she does about you."

Dayn jumped up and kicked the fire with his foot, sending white-hot sticks and orange sparks flying. "It doesn't matter what she thinks of me!" he shouted. "Her father won't allow her to see me anyway, so there's no sense in arguing about it!"

"Things could change," Alicine said, rising to face him.

"Why do you keep saying that? They won't change, so you'd best get used to the idea that I'll be leaving one day—alone if I have to." Dayn shot her a contemptuous look. "Why do you think it will be so hard for me to leave without Falyn? You left Reiv behind didn't you? *That* didn't seem so hard."

Alicine threw her hand up to cover her mouth. But it didn't stop the sob that escaped her throat. She wheeled around and stormed to her bedroll, then threw herself upon it, keeping her back to him. "It...it *was* hard," she said between muffled sobs.

Dayn folded his arms and stared at the ground, then at Alicine's back. He could see her shoulders rising and falling to the rhythm of her grief and regretted that he had been the cause of it. His sister knew how to manipulate him with her tears, but these, he knew, were sincere. When it came to the subject of Reiv, their conversations were always emotional ones. During their time in Tearia, they had both come to love Reiv. Once a prince, Reiv's personal tragedies had thrust him into their lives in a most unexpected way. And while Dayn had come to embrace him as friend and cousin, Alicine had come to embrace him as so much more.

"I'm sorry, Alicine," Dayn said softly. "I shouldn't have talked about you and Reiv like that. I know it wasn't easy leaving him." He knelt beside her and placed a hand on her shoulder. "But he said himself that we would see each other again. And you know Reiv has a way of knowing things."

Alicine looked up at him. "He does, doesn't he."

"I don't think he would lie about a thing like that would he? I mean, you did manage to straighten him out on that little issue of his lying, didn't you?"

Alicine smiled. "That I did."

"There, you see?"

She nodded. "I'll see him again," she said with a sniff.

"Get some sleep," Dayn said, pulling the corner of the blanket over her.

He rose and made his way back to what was left of the campfire, pushing the wayward sticks and coals back onto the pile with his foot. With fresh kindling and a few gentle breaths, the fire billowed back to an orange glow that radiated a perimeter of warmth and sent a trail of smoke into Dayn's face. He wiped the sting from his eyes with the back of his hand, then curled up on his bedroll. But he found he could not sleep, and he could not stop the tears from trailing down his cheeks.

෮෮

# CHAPTER 2:
## JEWEL OF THE VALLEY

Dayn and Alicine traveled for three more days before finding the pass that led them between the mountains. As Dayn had suspected, they'd simply not gone far enough north. Reiv had told Dayn to look for the pass between the two peaks east of the smoking mountain. But the closer they got, the more difficult it was to tell where one peak began and another ended.

At last they found the passage they were seeking, but when they reached its end, they could only stop and stare. Below them was a vast green valley, its wild grasses rising and falling like waves on an emerald sea.

"I swear, if I wasn't so tired I'd gallop right into it," Dayn said. He twisted around in the saddle to look at his sister. Her grin was stretched as wide as his was.

They wound the horses down the mountainside until at last they were standing at the edge of the vale. It spread across the landscape like an endless palette of teal upon teal, spotted here and there by patches of red and white and yellow. A ring of snow-capped mountains surrounded it, rising like a great crown tipped with sparkling jewels.

Dayn pulled a breath through his nostrils, relishing the sweet scent of clover mixed with early autumn wildflowers.

"It's so beautiful," Alicine said, gazing out. "Think of the crops Father could grow in a place like this."

"Anyplace would be better than that rocky patch of ground he struggles with year after year," Dayn said. Then his hopes lifted. "Do you think he'd consider moving the family here? I sure wouldn't mind it. Then we could live closer to...oh, never mind."

"Closer to Tearia?"

"Well, if we lived halfway between..."

"I don't think that's going to happen, Dayn, so you might want to put that little fantasy to rest."

"Just a thought," he said.

The valley proved to be rich with life, and it soon drew Dayn into a sense of contentedness he had not felt since they had left Tearia. But he knew better than to linger. If what Reiv told them was true, and it probably was, they had only to make their way between the two ridges directly ahead of them and they would be in Kirador. From there they had only to go west, then—

"What's that?" Alicine asked, pointing to the ground in front of them.

Dayn squinted in the direction she was indicating, toward a patch of faded pink flowers with pale yellow leaves. A reflection could be seen glinting in the sunlight, appearing and disappearing with every step he took.

"Where did it go?" Alicine asked, rising in her saddle.

"There...over there," Dayn said, his arm outstretched. "See it?" But he didn't wait for a reply and dismounted his horse.

The glimmer vanished, and Dayn searched the area in slow circles. Alicine dismounted and joined him, but whatever it was they were looking for was no longer in sight.

Dayn shrugged. "Probably just a rock or something."

Alicine halted. "No," she said, and reached down to gather something that lay at her feet.

Dayn took several strides toward her. "What is it?"

Alicine thrust out her hand. Dayn gazed into it, his heart skipping. He would have been less astounded if she had been holding a serpent under his nose. Cradled in her hand was a brooch of silver, a purple amethyst set at its center. It was a brooch surely made for a royal, much like the ones they had seen Whyn, Reiv's brother, wear. But Whyn's jewels were emeralds, not amethysts, and he would never have had cause to be in this place.

Dayn took the ornament from Alicine's hand and inspected it. "This can't be Whyn's."

"It's Reiv's," Alicine said. "I'm sure of it."

"Reiv's? But when would he have—oh...of course. But I didn't think he'd actually *been* here. I mean, when he transcended and the goddess gave him visions of the valley, I thought they were just visions."

Alicine's eyes sparkled as she gazed at the brooch. Dayn handed it back to her. "Here, you keep it. Something to remember him by, 'til you see him next time. Won't he be surprised you found it?"

She smiled, then pinned the jewel to her dress, low enough at the breast so she could look at it with ease. "The color reminds me of his eyes," she said, running her finger over the stone. Then she gazed at the shell bracelet draped around her wrist, its iridescent swirls competing with the elegance of the brooch. Both were precious in her eyes. Reiv had given her the bracelet and now, in a way, he had given her the amethyst as well.

∾

The pass into the valley from the southern side was not difficult, other than the finding of it, but the pass into Kirador to the west proved to be more treacherous. There was evidence of recent landslides all along the canyon-like passage they had entered. Dirt and massive boulders were tumbled into precarious mounds on either side of them; trees, once towering giants, lay toppled with root balls exposed; a fresh mountain stream was now a river of mud and debris.

As Dayn and Alicine slowly made their way through, an uneasy silence surrounded them. There was no sign of life, no birds or insects, no song of the wind, no fluttering of leaves in the trees, not even the dry ones. They glanced nervously at the towering walls of stone on either side of them. Perhaps it was just as well there were no sounds. The slightest vibration seemed as if it could bring the mountain down on top of them.

A landslide of pebbles trickled down the slope, bouncing and echoing off the larger rocks below. The horses responded with nervous neighs and dancing hooves.

"We need to get out of here," Dayn whispered. "This place gives me the chills."

"Do you think it'll be like this back home?" Alicine asked in a worried tone.

"I hope not, but let's not talk about it now. I'm afraid anymore noise might bring something unpleasant down on us...like that," he said, motioning to an overhang of granite above their heads.

They continued on as quickly and quietly as the terrain would allow, and before too long the scenery changed from that of potential entombment to a place to soar and breath free. They paused atop an embankment and stared at the forest that stretched down the mountainside. They had finally reached it—Kirador—the place Alicine called home, but that Dayn no longer could.

"We're there, Dayn," Alicine exclaimed. "We're finally in Kirador!"

But Dayn remained silent. He was happy for his sister, but couldn't bring himself to share in it.

"I can't believe you actually got us here," Alicine said. "You did it!" She began to laugh, then cry, then leaned over to Dayn and threw her arms around him, almost tumbling from her horse.

"Whoa, hold on there girl," Dayn said, straightening her onto the saddle.

"Why the face?" Alicine asked, realizing her brother's gloomy expression. "Can't you be happy at all? Surely there's room in your heart for the happier memories. You do have some—don't you?"

Dayn focused his eyes on nothing as he contemplated an answer to her question. Then he said, "Well I remember it felt pretty good to sleep in a real bed. I do look forward to that."

"That's it? That's all you can say? This is your home. You grew up here for goodness sakes!"

"No, I grew up in Tearia." Dayn searched her face for a hint of understanding. To his surprise, he found it.

"I guess we both did," she said. "Come on, let's go."

Dayn forced a smile. "You're right; we still have a long way to go. No sense sitting here arguing about whether I'm happy or not. I promised I'd get you home to Mother and Father, and that I'll do. At least *that* will make me happy."

༄

It took two days for their surroundings to appear more familiar. As Dayn surveyed the peaks growing distant at their backs, he began to chart in his mind approximately how much further they had to travel. He had spent most of his life looking up at the mountains. Now he just had to look at things from a different perspective.

The cabin of their childhoods would be nestled just below the high forests of the clan lands. Only affluent citizens were allowed to own property in the fertile bottomlands or live near the thriving coastal city of Kiradyn. It was there that the Vestry council met, and it was there that the political and religious powers of Kirador were firmly entrenched.

Located on the southwestern border of Aerie territory, their family's cabin was closer to the thriving city than the others of their clan. They visited Kiradyn frequently; his mother's healing potions were popular, and his sister had been one of the few chosen by the Spirit Keeper for private tutoring. Unfortunately, Dayn was frequently forced to tag along. More than anything his parents wanted him to be accepted in spite of his differences, so had worked hard to assimilate their ways with Kiradyn customs and speech. But though Dayn may have sounded like a Kiradyn, he would never look like one. As Dayn thought on it now, he was grateful his parents had never moved closer to the city. Though the rocky soil of their homestead had caused them nothing but grief, at least he and Alicine wouldn't have to pass any Kiradyn homes to reach their own now, and there was little chance of running into anyone other than a fellow clansman along the way.

They continued their descent through a seemingly endless landscape of firs and aspens and pines. Dayn had expected them to reach home by late afternoon, but the bright autumn sun had turned dim with a thin layer of clouds moving in from the north, slowing their pace with the arrival of an early season cold front.

The wind picked up, sending a rush of frigid air whipping through the branches. Dayn tightened his collar around his neck.

"I'm freezing," he muttered.

"You've grown weak," Alicine said.

"I suppose I have," he replied. "Well, Mother will have the fire going, and I plan to plop down in Father's chair whether he likes it or not and plant my feet right down in front of that hearth."

"Oh, so you think Father will give up his chair for his run-away son? I don't know...you might not have a backside to sit on when he gets finished with you."

"I'd like to see him try," Dayn grumbled.

ᖇᓚ

They did not reach the house as soon as they had hoped. A veil of mist had descended upon them, followed by storm clouds that ushered in stinging rain. They sat hunched on the horses, their bedrolls wrapped around their shoulders, praying they wouldn't have to sleep another night on the blankets that were now soaked through. But night was upon them before they knew it, and they found themselves huddled against the cold bark of a tree, wet blankets wrapped around them, their bodies seeking one another's for warmth.

In the morning they plodded on, stiff from the dampness that penetrated their bones, their moods as dreary as the weather that surrounded them. The horses slowly lumbered through the woods, barely needing guidance. It was as if the animals knew where they were going, or maybe they sensed a nice, warm barn up ahead.

Dayn gazed through the mist. The landscape would have seemed dismal had it not been spotted here and there with bright orange leaves clinging to branches and blanketing the dark forest floor. A sudden opening in the trees caught Dayn's attention. "There it is," he said, unable to disguise his excitement. "The house—there—through the trees!"

Alicine jerked her head up, her eyes wide. "We're there—we're really there!" she said. She kicked in her heels and urged the horse forward.

Dayn followed behind her, but realized she was getting too far ahead. "Wait," he called.

Alicine stopped and twisted around to face him. "Wait for what? I've waited long enough! Come on. You're too slow."

Dayn caught up to her. "Are you planning on running through the door with me still back in the woods somewhere?" he said. "Don't you think we should ease into this a bit? I mean, Mother will keel right over if we just barrel in. She's probably going to keel over anyway, but..."

Alicine sighed, but resumed her place by his side as they rode toward the house.

When they reached the edge of the clearing, Dayn sensed that she was about to take off again. But then he realized something was wrong. He threw out a hand. "Stop," he ordered.

"What do you mean stop?" Alicine said with indignation.

"Something's not right. It's too quiet. Where are the chimes?" Dayn's eyes darted back and forth along the eaves of the front porch. There had always been chimes there, dozens of them in all shapes and sizes. Their mother had placed them there to ward off demons. All Kiradyns did.

"Why would Mother have taken them down?" Alicine asked, scrutinizing the house.

"I don't know," Dayn replied. "And you know that nice warm fire I was looking forward to? Well, there's no smoke coming from the chimney. Mother and Father always have a fire."

Suddenly the house did not seem inviting at all. Was this the home they had left all those months ago? Once it had been a place full of light, but now it was dark, like a shadow of its former self. Dayn shivered. He thought he had gotten his sister home, but now he wasn't so sure.

"I'll go first," he said. "You stay here while I take a look."

"No," Alicine said. "We go together."

Dayn frowned, then nodded. There was no sense in ordering his sister to stay. She wouldn't do it anyway.

The closer they got, the greater the knot in Dayn's stomach became. The front door was ajar, like a mouth howling the wind whipping the eaves. The windows were opaque with fog, and the gray mist made the structure's cedar appear dark and ominous. Memories of summers sitting on that porch swept through Dayn's mind. Happier times—no, he hadn't forgotten.

Dayn dismounted and glanced up at Alicine. She no longer looked as if she would leap off and run to the door with excitement. Her lips were compressed and her brow was furrowed with worry.

He reached up to lift her from the horse. "Come on," he said. "We have to go in sometime."

Alicine allowed him to help her down, and together they made their way toward the house. They hesitated at the doorway, staring at the portal as though it would swallow them whole. Then they entered, and any thoughts they had of returning to what they had left evaporated.

∽

# CHAPTER 3:
# DARKENING SHADOWS

Dayn and Alicine walked across the floorboards of the cabin, their footsteps echoing the emptiness of it. The place felt spiritless, as if the life-force of their family had been drained out of it. Most of the furniture was missing, the few remaining pieces either warped by dampness or scattered about in pieces. Kitchen cabinets were left ajar, dangling on their hinges, contents raked out. Flour-sodden debris mixed with shards of glass blanketed the floor. The wind whistled through a kaleidoscope of broken windowpanes; rain-stained curtains slapped against their frames.

Dayn could read the anxiety on Alicine's face. "I'm sure Mother and Father are all right," he said assuringly.

"How do you know?" Alicine asked, her voice rising. "Where are they? And just look at this place! Mother would never—"

"They've probably gone to stay with relatives."

Alicine crunched across the kitchen floor and opened the pantry closet. A broom sat propped in the corner, along with a pail and a few cleaning utensils. "You're right," she said. "They probably just left for a while, until the mountain settles down. They're coming back...definitely coming back."

She pulled out the broom and began to sweep, slowly at first, then more vigorously. Glass mixed with dirt scraped across the floor. "Mother would have a fit if she saw the state her kitchen is in. Dayn, why don't you get those windows boarded up and—"

"It doesn't look like they've been here in a long time," Dayn noted. "And why did they take so much furniture? I mean—what if they're not coming back?"

"Don't be ridiculous. Of course they're coming back."

Dayn looked at the fireplace that spanned the wall, longing for the heat that should have been radiating from it. The hearth was empty, the memory of its once cozy embrace evaporating with the air moaning through the half-open damper. He recalled the last time he had gazed into that hearth. There had been flames in it then, and mounds of white-hot logs that looked like imaginary mountains. That day he had been sitting in his father's high-backed chair, dreading the Summer Fires Festival, wondering if the charred landscape in the fireplace was like that where the demons lived. And wondering if he could live with the knowledge that he was one.

"What if they didn't leave because of the mountain?" he asked hesitantly. "What if it was because of something else?"

"Like what?"

Dayn turned evasively. "Nothing...you're right. Maybe we should look around some more, before we come to any rash conclusions."

Alicine leaned the broom in a corner, then nervously wiped her palms down her skirt. Her attention shifted toward their parents' bedroom door located on the opposite side of the living area. Taking her cue, Dayn headed in that direction. He pushed the door open a crack and peeked inside. His nerves were beginning to take over his common sense, and he didn't want Alicine to witness the worst-case scenarios that were playing in his head.

"The room's empty," he said with relief.

Alicine poked her head beneath his arm. "The wardrobe's gone. If they were coming back, why didn't they just take their clothes?"

"Speaking of clothes...I sure could do with a change," Dayn said. "Let's check our room. Maybe something was left behind."

Dayn moved to the bottom of the stairwell and lifted his eyes toward the darkness at the top. "I'll go up first," he said.

"Why?" Alicine asked.

"I have a funny feeling, that's all." But the feeling really wasn't so funny; he had never told Alicine about the threat that Sheireadan, the neighborhood bully, had made against their family at the Summer Fires Festival. It was a threat made when Dayn attacked Sheireadan over a remark the boy had made about Alicine. And it was a threat made when Dayn revealed himself as a demon to get his point across.

"What *aren't* you telling me, Dayn?" Alicine demanded. Her brows arched, a clear indication she expected an honest answer.

"Nothing, I–"

Alicine planted her feet on the step above him and thrust her hands to her hips. "We've been through too much for you not to be upfront with me."

Dayn closed his eyes in a brief rehearsal of how to tell her. Then he said, "Before I left the Summer Fires, Sheireadan threatened our family."

"He *what*?"

"He said since our parents had harbored a demon, his father would see to it our family was never allowed around decent folk again."

"Oh, Sheireadan's just full of hot air."

"His father is a member of the Vestry, and you know his reputation. Besides, I *did* sort of go out of my way to make Sheireadan think I was a demon."

"But you're not a demon, so it doesn't matter what he thinks."

"Listen, Alicine, the truth doesn't always matter. Sometimes all that matters is who's in power. And you know that around these parts it's Sheireadan's father—Lorcan, 'Lord Almighty' of the Vestry."

"Well, he's Falyn's father, too. Maybe she said something in your defense."

"Do you really think it matters to him what Falyn says? Why would she risk it, anyway? Lorcan's a dangerous man, even to his own children." Dayn sighed heavily. "I always thought I'd save her one day. Now it's probably too late."

"What are you talking about?" Alicine asked.

Dayn cast her a bewildered look. "You don't know?"

"Know what?"

"That he—you know—hits her."

Alicine gasped. "*What*?"

"God, where have you been? You've known her practically your whole life. She never told you?"

"No, of course not. She told *you*?"

"She didn't have to. I drank in the image of her every chance I got, remember? Never missed a single detail if I could help it. Besides, some bruises can't be hidden, even with long sleeves and high collars."

"So that's why..." Alicine's voice trailed off.

"Why what?"

"Why she never came to your defense when Sheireadan—"

"I'm glad she didn't. I would rather die than have Falyn suffer on account of me."

"I didn't know, Dayn."

"Don't worry. I told you—I always wanted to save her—maybe there's still a chance."

"Of course you'll save her," Alicine said, placing her hand on his arm. "And then you'll both live—what's the term Reiv used—happily ever after?"

Dayn grinned. "Yeah, happily ever after." He turned his attention to the stairwell and stepped around his sister. The boards creaked beneath his weight, but he continued up, Alicine following at his back.

He paused at the top, scanning the large attic room sprawled before him. Half the size of the house, it was the sleeping quarters he had once shared with his sister. With drapes pulled, they'd had plenty of privacy from one another, but the room had also provided a place for long talks, peppery arguments, and stories told with laughter. But as Dayn looked at the room, the happy memories disappeared, replaced by his worst fears. No longer was it a haven for rest and contemplation; now it was a place transformed by sorcery and hate. There was no furniture left in it except for the beds. Strangely, Dayn's had been shoved to the center of the room. Dozens of candles surrounded it, melted into blobs on the floorboards. Incantations written with an unknown substance were scrawled across the timber walls. A trail of feathers led from the bed to a pile of bird carcasses in the corner. A bowl stained brown sat nearby.

Dayn moved slowly toward his bed, staring at the misshapen lump beneath the quilt. The once cheery patchworks were now turned to depressing shades of brown, the same dark color as the words scrawled across the walls. He reached his hand toward it.

"Don't touch it!" Alicine cried. "You don't know what's under there and—"

"I think I know," he said. He threw off the quilt, then staggered back. It was an image of himself, fashioned from wax and wood and feathers. Its hair was of pale straw, and its eyes were bright blue river stones. His name was carved deep into the face, and long splinters of wood were pressed into every limb.

"Don't look at it!" Alicine sobbed, covering her face with her hands.

Dayn threw the quilt back over the image. "It doesn't mean anything, Alicine," he said. But he knew that was a lie, and was sure she did, too.

"What do you mean it doesn't *mean* anything?" Alicine practically shouted. "Of course it means something! It means—"

"It means we need to get out of here."

Dayn grabbed his sister's hand and headed down the staircase. He pulled her out onto the porch, then marched them both toward the horses waiting nearby.

"Where are we going?" Alicine asked, struggling to keep pace.

"The closest place I can think of—and it's not all that close."

"You mean Aunt Vania's and Uncle Haskel's? But it will be dark before we get there."

"Would you rather stay here?" Dayn asked.

"No, but you know they don't like unexpected company. Their place has been off limits ever since—"

"Eyan's the least of our problems." Dayn lifted Alicine onto her horse, then took his place on the other. "Besides, that's the most logical place Mother and Father would have gone."

"But Dayn, you know what they say about Eyan."

"That he's dangerous. I know. But as long as Haskel's around, what's he going to do? Listen, there's no time to dicker about Eyan. We're not going to make it there by nightfall as it is." He kicked in his heels and commanded the horse forward.

Alicine steered to his side. "I'm not dickering. It's just that the last time we saw Eyan we were only children, and we only glimpsed him from a distance even then. He must be what...nineteen years old now? And if he's as big as his father..."

"Stop worrying about it, Alicine. So Vania and Haskel have a son who's not right. They've done well to keep him away from everyone haven't they? I mean, the last few times we visited, he wasn't even around."

Alicine pursed her lips, then nodded, but she clearly wasn't satisfied with Dayn's reassurances.

∽

It was nearly dark when they arrived at the remote farmstead of their father's brother, Haskel. Most of the clouds had moved on, leaving a few feathery wisps to drift across a cold evening sky. They advanced the horses slowly, watching the cabin as it came into view.

"Look, smoke from the chimney," Dayn said. He smiled, but Alicine continued to look worried.

"They're here. . .safe and sound. You'll see," Dayn said. He nudged his horse ahead, then urged it to a trot. He twisted around and grinned. "You'd better hurry up, or I'll tell them the whole story before you even get there!" He flicked the reins and took off, Alicine galloping behind him.

They had barely reached the house when they leaped off their horses, dashed to the door, and banged. "It's us! Mother...Father...open up—it's us!"

Alicine was bouncing on tiptoes, giddy with excitement. "Look Dayn...the rockers...they're here." She nodded toward the two rockers their father had carved, both swaying to the rhythm of the chimes that clanked along the eaves of the front porch.

Dayn knocked again. "Anybody home?" he called more loudly.

"Just go in, Dayn," Alicine said impatiently. "We're family."

"I know," he said in a hushed voice, "but you know how Vania and Haskel have always been about their privacy." Alicine glanced over her shoulder at the shadowy yard behind them, while Dayn leaned his ear against the door and listened. "I don't hear anything." He pushed on the handle. "Come on," he said. "We're going in."

The door opened with a *creak*. Dayn and Alicine stepped inside. A fire was crackling in the hearth, a pot brimming with stew was on the spit, and candlelight was bathing the walls in a flickering glow. Dayn walked toward the table that dominated the center of the room, then scanned the rest of cabin. Privacy drapes had been pulled back and tied, revealing the contents of every area. He moved his focus to the sleeping quarters. Three beds could be seen: one for Haskel and Vania, a narrower one against the wall, probably for Eyan, and the third—yes, Father's and Mother's bed! Relief swept over him, but it quickly lapsed into trepidation when he realized his parents were sleeping in the same room as crazy Eyan.

"Well, the bed proves they're here," he said, "but I sure don't see any of the rest of their furniture."

"Probably in the barn," Alicine said, but she sounded distracted. She strolled into the kitchen area, her eyes in contemplation of the chopped vegetables littering the countertop. She cast a sideways look at the dining table. A single bowl, spoon, and mug sat upon it. "Why is there only one place set?" she asked. "Why not five?"

"I don't know," Dayn replied. "Listen, let's get the horses settled. Maybe everyone's in the barn." Alicine moved toward him, but her attention lingered on the place setting.

They exited the house and led the horses toward the barn a short distance away. Large and two-storied, it was three times the size of the cabin. When they reached it, they realized its double doors were slightly ajar. Dayn shoved them open and stepped inside. The interior was dark and musty and smelled of hay mixed with manure. A lantern hung on a peg inside the doorway; fire sticks were tucked into a box nailed to the wall next to it. Dayn lifted the lantern and lit the wick. Holding it out before him, he surveyed the shadowy room.

"They've gone somewhere," he said. "The wagon and horses are gone."

"Then who's fixing dinner?" Alicine whispered nervously. "Maybe it's Eyan."

Dayn handed Alicine the lantern, then pulled out the short sword he kept secured in the scabbard at his waist. He'd had little use for it since leaving Tearia, but he was more than grateful to have it now.

A sudden rustling in the hayloft above sent Alicine clinging to his side. She held up the lantern with a shaking hand. For a moment all was quiet, but then another rustling sounded. Their horses whinnied and danced about. Dayn took a step back with Alicine still glued to his hip.

"Who's there?" Dayn asked, struggling to sound brave. If it was Eyan, there was no telling what the boy might do. They had been told their whole lives that Eyan was dangerous. How he was dangerous, Dayn never understood; it was a topic not spoken of freely. Nevertheless, Haskel and Vania had worked hard to keep their son hidden from everyone, even family, so their reasons must have been good ones.

"Eyan? If that's you, we mean you no harm," Dayn said. "It's us—Dayn and Alicine. You know—your cousins."

Again they heard a rustling, but this time it was accompanied by a moving shadow. Dayn and Alicine jumped and backed away, inching closer to the exit.

"Eyan," Alicine said in a quivery voice. "We came looking for Mother and Father. Do—do you know where they are?"

The shadow grew taller, then darted to the side. Dayn lifted his sword. "We tire of your cat and mouse game. Show yourself, or—or I'm coming in after you!"

Alicine's eyes shot to Dayn's. Clearly she thought he had lost his mind.

"I'm tired and hungry," Dayn said to her defensively, "and I no longer have the patience to be kept from bodily comforts by a shadow in a corner!"

He pried his sister from his side and took a determined step forward, positioning himself between the shadow and the doorway. "I said show yourself!"

The dark form suddenly ran in his direction, but whether it was heading for Dayn or the doorway behind him was hard to determine. But Dayn gave it no choice in the matter; he threw himself upon it and knocked it down, pinning it to the ground with the tip of his sword pointed at its throat.

The young man stared up at him, panting like an animal caught in a snare. Dayn drew a sharp breath, then eased the sword back. The young man was handsome enough, with dark hair and skin the same coppery color of every other Kiradyn. But it was the eyes that left Dayn very nearly stunned: they were blue, the same forbidden blue as his own.

"Eyan?" Dayn said.

The young man did not respond. His eyes darted around for rescue, or a quick escape.

"Eyan?" Dayn repeated. "It's me, Dayn. I won't hurt you, honest. Don't run...all right?"

The young man calmed somewhat, then said, "Aye, I–I'm Eyan."

Dayn eased the sword further back. "See? I'm removing the weapon. I–I didn't mean to scare you. I just–" Dayn felt ashamed. This was his cousin, and he'd pressed a blade to his throat. But then again, Reiv had done the same thing to him at their first meeting. Dayn smiled at the recollection.

Dayn lifted his weight off of Eyan and stood over him. He held out his hand. Eyan stared up at it, not sure whether or not to take it. After a moment's contemplation, he reached up and allowed Dayn to pull him to his feet.

"Please don't tell 'em ye saw me," Eyan said anxiously. He glanced toward the doorway. "No one's supposed to see me. Father'd be furious if he knew."

"But we're family," Dayn said. "Don't you remember us? I know it's been a long time..."

"Aye, I remember ye. You're the one everyone thinks is a demon. That's why I'm not allowed to see anyone."

"What? Because of me?"

"Aye, *and* because of me."

Alicine stepped toward Eyan, her attention fully upon his eyes. "We were always told it was because you were dangerous," she said hesitantly.

"Oh, I *am* dangerous," Eyan replied. "If others saw me they might hurt my family, or me. Father says Gorman was a fool to let people see ye. He said ye should never have been allowed outside." He backed toward the door. "I have to go now. If they see me with anyone…"

Alicine followed, then reached out and placed her hand on his arm. Eyan stopped in this tracks.

"Please don't go," she said. "I don't think your father would be angry once we explained. We know all about the demons now—why Dayn's eyes are blue and his hair is blond. Don't you ever wonder why your eyes are blue, Eyan?"

Eyan stared at her hand upon his arm, then pulled away. "No girl's ever touched me except my mother," he said, sounding younger than his age. His head swiveled toward the sound of wagon wheels in the distance. "They're home early! I have to be gettin' dinner on the table. Don't come inside yet—and please don't tell 'em ye saw me." Then he bolted to the house and disappeared through the door.

☙

# CHAPTER 4: EYE TO EYE

Dayn and Alicine stood in the doorway of the barn, watching as Eyan sprinted toward the house. An approaching wagon could be heard in the distance, the jangle of horses' harnesses and the thud of wheels clambering up the road.

"I'm scared," Alicine said.

Dayn grabbed her hand and gave it a squeeze. "Don't be," he said. "This whole thing was my fault, not yours."

"No, I mean about Eyan."

"Eyan? I don't think we have anything to fear from him."

"I'm scared *for* him, Dayn, not of him."

Dayn considered her words. Eyan had clearly been in terror of being discovered with them. But why? He suddenly noticed the amethyst brooch still pinned to Alicine's dress. "You might want to tuck that away," he said, nodding toward it.

"Why?"

"I just think it best not to show it off yet. We have enough explaining to do."

"Fine," Alicine said with irritation. She removed the jewel and tucked it inside her collar, where it slid down her chest and settled at her waistband. She gave Dayn a smirk. "What about that *thing* on your ear?"

"It's only bronze and a bit of stone. Not worth much."

"That's not what I mean."

The wagon came into view, and Dayn and Alicine stepped slowly toward it. They heard a startled cry, followed by the wagon lurching to a halt. A woman was struggling to leap off the side, but a man up front had twisted around to hold her back. He managed to stay her attempt, then he hopped down from his seat and lifted her off. The moment her feet hit the dirt, she limped in Dayn's and Alicine's direction, her arms extended. "My children...my children!" she cried.

In an instant Dayn and his sister were in their mother's arms. She smothered them with kisses and hugged them until the breath was nearly squeezed out of them.

"Where have you been, where have you been?" she sobbed.

Haskel and Vania rushed toward them, the ashen hue of their faces obvious even in the darkness.

"My god—Dayn–Alicine!" Vania exclaimed as she joined the reunion. But Haskel stood back, his expression stiff.

Dayn felt the muscles of his own happy expression droop; Haskel was obviously not thrilled about their unexpected arrival. Dayn's eyes met his uncle's, but the man turned away. "Vania, get everyone into the house and out of the cold," Haskel said over his shoulder. "I'll tend to the horses."

"Shall I help you, uncle?" Dayn asked.

"No need," Haskel replied gruffly, and headed for the wagon.

The rest of them moved toward the house. As they walked, Dayn noticed how thin and sickly his mother looked. Even the smile gracing her lips could not disguise the gloomy circles under her eyes. She hugged his waist, but it was as if she had placed her arm there for support rather than affection. At her other side, Alicine walked hand-in-hand with her, chattering about how happy she was to be home and how nice a warm, clean frock sounded. But Dayn could only think one thing at the moment: Where was Father?

They entered the house and were greeted by a cozy fire, the tantalizing aroma of stew, and a long plank table now set for dinner. Eyan was nowhere to be seen, and neither was their father. Dayn thought to ask, but decided against it. Eyan was a touchy subject, he knew, and he wasn't keen on bringing Gorman into the conversation just yet. His father was probably off on some errand, a blessed relief, at least in Dayn's opinion. He wasn't looking forward to the altercation that was sure to explode between them.

Vania helped Morna remove her coat and hung it, along with her own, on a row of pegs by the door. She then ushered Morna to a bench at the table and helped her sit. Alicine settled next to her mother, hugging her close. "Oh, Mother," she said. "I've missed you so much."

"Here, Dayn," Vania said, "let me take your coat." He pulled it off and handed it to her without a word. She looked him up and down. "Goodness, child," she said.

"What a state you're in. And this coat..." She frowned and shook her head. "I'd best give it a wash."

Dayn nodded, but remained silent, his eyes scanning the room for a sign of Gorman. Strange how no mention of him had been made. He turned his attention to the place-settings. He counted five. Surely Eyan wouldn't have included him and Alicine in the count. That would have given away the fact that he knew they were there and had possibly met up with them. No, five would be the right number without them, but including Father. Seven would have meant that Eyan–

"Sit Dayn," Vania said, breaking his concentration. But he remained standing.

"Alicine...shawl," Vania said, holding out her hand. Alicine pulled it off and handed it to her without a glance, chatting on happily with her mother.

Vania tossed the coat and grubby shawl on top of a basket piled with laundry. "Missed my wash day because o' the rain," she said to Dayn. "Maybe tomorrow if the sun's out. We'll need to give those clothes o' yours a good scrubbin'." She waddled her chubby body over to the hearth and gave the stew a stir. "And baths...ye'll both be gettin' 'em, no arguments. I'll heat ye some water after dinner. I'll bet you're both starved, poor dears." She chattered on about baths and empty stomachs as she grabbed a towel, wrapped it around the handle of the stew pot, and lifted it to the table.

"Sit Dayn," she repeated. "Haskel'll be in in a bit. No need for formalities."

Dayn took his place on the bench across the table from his mother. She turned her attention to him. "Words cannot express my joy at the sight of you," she said, then she cocked her head. "What's that on your ear?"

Dayn reached to his ear, fingering the small bronze earring that dangled there. Body mutilations such as this were forbidden in Kirador, but he refused to remove it. It was a symbol of his bravery in the battle against the King. Though the war paint he had drawn on his face that day had only been temporary, as far as he was concerned, the earring was permanent.

"Have you been well, Mother?" he asked, changing the subject. "You look—"

Morna continued to study the earring, then smiled. "I'm well, now that my children are home," she said. Recognizing Dayn's expression of doubt, she patted his hand. "Just had a bit of the cold in my bones, dear, that's all. Haskel and Vania have been taking me to the hot springs. It helps ease my aches. I'll be fine."

"To Marvel Springs? But that's so far."

"Oh, no. We can't go there anymore."

"Why not?" Alicine asked.

Morna hesitated, then said, "We tried making the trip, at night, but it was too hard on me. Besides, the last time we went, Lorcan's children showed up and–"

Dayn perked up. "Falyn and Sheireadan?"

"Yes, and we knew only too well what that meant: their father would soon find out about us being there."

"So what if he did?" Alicine said.

"A lot has happened since you left." Morna shifted her gaze, as if contemplating whether or not to continue.

"Mother," Dayn said. "We went by the house before we came here. The place was a mess. And we found something while we were there: a spell-curse—of me. Is that what this is about?"

Anxiety creased Morna's brow. "Dayn," she said quietly. "The day you disappeared, word spread that you'd revealed yourself as a demon. The Vestry met that very afternoon to discuss what to do with you."

"Do with me?"

"I suppose it's a good thing you did leave, because they intended to bring you to judgment—and your father."

Dayn rose slowly from the bench. "Where is Father?" he asked.

Alicine blinked. "He's on errand. Right, Mother?"

Morna remained silent.

Vania turned and hustled toward the door. "I'll fetch us some more wood," she muttered. But before she could open it, Haskel blew in and met her head-on.

"Where are ye goin' without your coat, woman?" he bellowed.

"To fetch some wood," she said, eyebrows raised. "Maybe ye should come with me."

"What's wrong with the stack I brung in earlier? Have ye lost your senses?"

"I'm sure we have plenty, uncle," Dayn said, annoyed at the interruption. "Mother. Where's Father?"

The room went quiet. Dayn accessed everyone's expressions: Morna looked grave, and Vania and Alicine were as pale as mist. But Haskel—was the red rising from his neck that of embarrassment or fury?

"Well, someone say something!" Dayn demanded.

Alicine rose from the bench, her uneasiness now matching his. "What is it?" she asked. "Mother?"

"Children, I—" Morna buried her face in her hands.

Alicine looked at Dayn, then at her mother. "Please. We have to know."

Morna pulled Alicine into her arms. "Oh my dear child, I don't know how to tell you." She kissed the top of Alicine's head and held her close, then held out her hand to Dayn. "Son."

But Dayn did not take her hand. He knew he was about to learn some unhappy news, but there was one thing he already knew: this woman was not his real mother and the man in question was not his real father. They had stolen him, and just as bad, they had lied to him.

Morna lowered her hand, her eyes recognizing the look of hesitation staring back at her. "Your father loved you very much, Dayn," she said. "When you and Alicine went missing, he set out to find you. He never came back."

Suddenly the past and all its implications seemed irrelevant. Fear for the man that Dayn had called Father for sixteen years was all that mattered to him now. "What do you mean, never came back?" he sputtered. "He just disappeared?"

"Aye. That's right," Haskel said, marching toward him. "My brother left without a word to any of us because o' you. And we haven't seen him since."

"But you went looking for him, didn't you?" Dayn asked, already knowing the answer.

"Of course we went lookin' for him!"

Dayn felt his legs itching for the door. "Where did you go? Did you follow the river? What about the cave? We left the horse there. Did you find it? "

"Forty clansmen scoured the mountainside from Kiradyn to the mouth of the cave and back," Haskel said. "We found nothin'."

"You went inside the cave—right? Inside—not just to the mouth."

Haskel took a threatening step and moved his face inches from Dayn's. "The cave's forbidden, boy—ye know that. If your father went inside it, there's not a thing any of us could have done for him. The demons would've had him for sure."

"There aren't any demons!" Dayn said. "You should have gone in—you should have looked!"

"Who are you to judge, boy? While you were off on some ridiculous folly, your father was out searchin' for ye. Did ye give a single thought to his well-bein' when ye left, or anyone else's for that matter? No, and ye never did!"

Dayn felt his blood begin to boil. His uncle was acting like the whole thing was his fault, like Alicine wasn't involved at all, like Father's deceptions were irrelevant. "What do you know about me?" Dayn blurted. "You were never around! You were hiding out here with your own blue-eyed son!"

Haskel's face went gray. "What are ye sayin'?" he said.

"I'm saying that I know about Eyan, and that you've kept him hidden away like you're ashamed of him!"

"I am ashamed of him!" Haskel practically shouted.

"Eyan's not the one you should be ashamed of, uncle— you should be ashamed of *yourself*!"

"Dayn!" Morna said, rising.

"No!" Dayn said. "It's true!"

"What would ye have preferred I do, boy?" Haskel growled. "Prance him around for all to see?"

"Why not?" Dayn retorted. "He is who he is."

"And what is that?"

"A boy like any other."

"He's not like any other. He has the demon blood in him! Just as you do!"

"I'm not a demon—I'm Jecta!"

"What nonsense are ye talkin', boy?"

"My real parents are from the other side of the mountains. I know because I've been there and I've met them. Alicine will tell you—she's met them, too. My mother is Brina, and my father was Mahon, and they're people just like you—only better! There are no demons, you fool—they're just a myth fabricated by superstitious Kiradyns."

"How *dare* you speak to me in such a tone!"

"I'll speak to you however I wish," Dayn said, though he couldn't believe he was actually saying it.

"Dayn!" Morna said sternly. "You'll not show disrespect in this house."

"Disrespect? Let's talk about disrespect, shall we?" Dayn forced a laugh. "How about the fact that neither you nor Father respected me enough to tell me the truth? How about the fact that you stole me from my *real* mother and lied to me!"

Morna collapsed back onto the bench. "Dayn," she whispered.

"Dayn—*ha!*" he continued. "That's not even my real name! My name is Keefe! It means cherished. My *real* mother told me."

Dayn knew he should show the woman before him some sympathy; she had raised him, after all. But the gate was finally open, and years of pent-up emotion were flooding through. "Did Father even *ask* what my real name was?" he ranted on. "Did he even care? No, sounds to me like–"

"Stop it!" It was Alicine now, standing in front of him, tears streaming down her face. The sight of her made him realize how cruel his words had been, how horrible a person he had become.

"I—I'm sorry," he stammered. "I—"

"It's too late for sorry," Haskel said. "It won't bring your father back."

"Haskel, enough," Vania said. "It's not the boy's fault."

"Of course it's his fault. Who else's could it be?"

"Maybe the brother who was too afraid to go into the cave," Dayn said.

"Ye'll apologize this instant for that remark," Haskel said.

"I won't!" Dayn shot back. He wheeled toward the door.

"If ye walk out that door, don't bother comin' back!" Haskel said.

"Don't worry—I won't."

"I mean it, boy. And don't expect anyone to go after ye either."

"Fine!"

Dayn swung open the door. The last thing he heard before he slammed it behind him was his mother shouting, "Dayn, no," and his uncle declaring, "No one's to leave this house to go after him." But Dayn didn't care. He hated them all. Even Alicine. She hadn't defended him one whit. She'd just stood there. Fine, he would leave and never come back. He'd only returned to Kirador for her sake. Well, she was back; he hoped she was happy. Now he could go back to Tearia where his *real* family was.

But then he realized, there was still Falyn to consider; his love for her hadn't changed. Maybe if he found her and confessed his feelings. Yes, that's what he would do. He'd always been afraid to talk to her before, but no longer. He was a man now, not a child. He had, after all, killed a guard in Tearia. True he hadn't meant to, but what about his leading an army to rescue Reiv? That meant something, didn't it? And what about standing up to his uncle just now? He would never have been able to do that before.

Dayn set his teeth with determination. He would find Falyn and proclaim his love for her. He would prove to her that he was brave and strong. He'd face her father to prove it if he had to, even Sheireadan. Maybe then she would love him back. Maybe then she'd agree to go to Tearia with him. Yes, he had a plan now. And the girl of his dreams was about to learn of it.

∽

# Chapter 5: Hope Springs Eternal

Dayn crunched through the forest clearing, steam puffing from his nostrils and dissipating into the cold night air. He thrust his hands into his pockets and hunched his neck into his collar, then noticed a coppice of trees up ahead. It was just the sort of place a demon would hide. Dayn's feet slowed, but he scolded his own stupidity and picked up his pace. He had enough problems without succumbing to the whims of an overactive imagination. There was no such thing as demons, at least not the kind he had been raised to fear. He would do better to set his worries on a predator of a more human nature.

He turned his thoughts inward, focusing on that which was utmost on his mind—the argument he had had with his uncle. It stoked the fire still burning in his belly, the only warmth he could feel at the moment, but it was just the fuel he needed if he was to continue his reckless quest.

He had detoured from the main road early on, determined not to be met by friend or by foe. If Haskel came looking for him, not that he would, he'd expect Dayn to have taken the more-traveled route. But there was only one path Dayn had his sites on at the moment, and that was the one that would lead him to Falyn. Haskel would never suspect his destination; he couldn't possibly understand the longings of a young man's heart. If his uncle had ever felt such a thing for a woman, and Dayn could not even imagine it, he surely would have forgotten it by now. Why, Haskel had to be at least forty years—far too old for a man to think of such things. Only Alicine would have a clue as to where Dayn was heading and why, but she wasn't likely to reveal it. She wouldn't risk placing new worries on their mother's frail shoulders. Guilt trickled into Dayn's belly, threatening to extinguish the flames that burned there. Had he really spoken to his mother so cruelly?

A gust of air whipped around him, sending chill bumps across his skin. He hugged his arms, no longer able to fight the cold with anger alone. His muscles tensed. His stomach rumbled. But what was he to do? The home he had grown up in was gone; his father was missing and probably dead; his own sister had not defended him; and his uncle thought him a demon—a demon! Then there was the issue of Falyn. Was it wrong to feel about her the way he did? Surely it was no sin, though a few thoughts in her regard might be classified as such. But he loved her, and wasn't love the greatest gift of all? That was what the Written Word said, and though Dayn now knew that words set to parchment were not always true, he was confident that at least that much was.

He marched on, the springs couldn't be much further, and if fortune smiled on him, Falyn would be there when he arrived. It wasn't likely, of course, but his mother had said she'd seen Falyn at the springs with Sheireadan and... Dayn felt his insides wrench—*Sheireadan*—the very thought of him sent Dayn's teeth to grinding. The boy had tormented him for as long as he could remember. And for what? Because Dayn looked different? Or was there more to it? Dayn twisted his mouth as he contemplated past events. Yes, why *had* Sheireadan always taken such issue with him?

Dayn glanced ahead. A blanket of fog could be seen hovering along the forest floor, a sure sign of the springs, but it was the pungent smell of sulfur that assured him he had arrived. Dayn turned his icy thoughts from Sheireadan. The waters would be hot and steamy, and his feet were in need of a good soak.

The healing properties of the springs bested every medicinal known in Kirador. It was through them that individuals eased their joint pains, lung ailments, and various wasting diseases that no one could name. It was unfortunate that the distance was such a burden on his mother, and that the presence of others at the springs made her feel unwelcome. But then Dayn recalled a time when he had been little; his mother had brought him to the springs to heal an infection in his lungs. Other Kiradyns had been there that day. He remembered how they had looked at him then gathered their things and scurried away. The memory crawled under his skin, but it also stoked his determination. *I have as much right to be here as anyone else,* he told himself.

Dayn picked up his pace, suddenly aware of two pillars towering before him—the gateway to the springs. He walked between them, working to focus his eyes through the fog. To his right, statues broke through the mist, their stone-cold faces watching him as he passed. But their gazes caused him no fear; at least their eyes didn't judge. He stopped and looked around, detecting no movement other than the slow ramble of mist at his feet.

A gurgle sounded to his left, and he stepped in that direction. A layer of haze hid the waters that rippled beyond the stone-lined edge of the pool. Dayn squatted and dipped in a hand, relishing the sting of warmth upon his fingers. He rose and wiped his hand across his shirt as he trained his eyes across the pool. It was as large as he remembered, able to accommodate hundreds of people at a time. On three sides of it, structures were situated: one a temple to Daghadar made of smooth pink marble; another a series of wishing springs draped with arbors of leaf and vine; the third a dressing area, constructed of carved cedar and sectioned off to provide privacy.

Dayn scrutinized his surroundings. No sign of Falyn, but what did he expect? He felt disappointed, but most of all a keen sense of despair. What was he to do now? Wait here until he starved, or trudge back to his uncle's farm with his tail between his legs? He could fathom neither, but right now a decision could wait. There were warm waters to consider, and ten throbbing toes trapped in miserable boots.

He bent to unwrap the leather straps that coiled up his legs, but an unexpected sound gave him pause. His mind raced–perhaps it was Falyn! But then another thought shoved its way in. What if it was someone he would rather not meet up with, like Sheireadan, or even worse, their father Lorcan?

Dayn eased toward the nearest pillar and ducked behind it, then directed his attention toward the sound of hushed voices on the opposite side of the pool. Two forms could be seen emerging from the temple, picking their way toward the waters. At first Dayn could barely make them out; they looked more like apparitions than humans. A chill prickled his scalp, telling him to head in the other direction, but the power of his curiosity rooted him where he stood.

As the images came more into view, Dayn realized that one was much taller than the other. Both wore long cloaks, and their faces were hidden by the shadows of their hoods. The taller one was hunched and limping, perhaps an old man come to take a healing. The second appeared to be a woman guiding the man toward the pool.

Soft words were spoken between them, but Dayn could not decipher them. The couple stopped, and the man turned to face the woman. His back was to the pool, as well as to Dayn on the other side of it, and his silhouette all but swallowed the woman standing on the opposite side of him. A slight movement of the woman's elbows was all that Dayn could make of her, but it soon became apparent that she was unclasping the man's tunic.

Dayn slid from his hiding place, his curiosity goading him for a better look. He worked his way from pillar to pillar, pausing behind each as he made his way nearer to where the couple stood. He stepped lightly, praying his footsteps would not betray his presence, but the careless snap of a twig froze him in his tracks. His eyes darted toward the strangers, but the casual murmur of their voices indicated they had not heard it. He released a slow breath and settled his attention on a stone half-wall nearby. It was an ideal place for viewing, and near enough to the forest that Dayn could make a quick escape should he need to. He wasn't sure what there was to fear from a woman and a crippled old man, but he had long since learned that people were not always what they seemed.

Dayn reached the wall and slunk behind it. He peeked over the ledge, his eyes alert. The man was still standing before the woman, but now he was completely undressed and shivering from the cold. The curves of the man's backside were thick and muscular, and his long dark hair was braided down his back. Clearly this was not an old man, but a young one—and a badly damaged one at that. His back, legs, and buttocks were mottled with angry bruises, and his spine was angled in such a way as to suggest he had been wounded. His hands were discreetly placed, and as he worked his rumpled pants legs from his feet, his movements were slow and stiff.

Dayn swallowed with uneasiness. For an unclothed man to be standing before a woman was simply not acceptable, especially not out in the open like this. Perhaps such things were allowed in the privacy of a marital bedroom, but never in a public place. Dayn felt shame as his attentions lingered on the man's nakedness, yet he could not turn his eyes away. His masculine pride demanded a comparison.

The woman pushed back her hood and guided the man to the pool. Dayn spun and threw his back against the wall. "What sin is *this*?" he gasped. He rose to look upon the couple once more, determined his eyes were playing some sort of trick. But to his roiling discomfort, he realized they were not. The woman by the pool was Falyn, and the shameless young man who stood naked before her was none other than Sheireadan.

❧

# CHAPTER 6: SINS OF THE FATHER

Dayn felt as though he had been kicked in the gut. The image of Falyn standing in front of her brother like that, the boy's nakedness flaunted before her, was more than Dayn could stomach. A part of him wanted to purge it into the bushes. The other part wanted to beat Sheireadan into a bloody pulp. And yet, from the look of things, someone had already beaten him to the punch.

Dayn eased his gaze back over the wall. Sheireadan was working his way into the water, his battered body turned in Dayn's direction. Dayn kept his focus on Sheireadan's face, ordering his own eyes to roam no further. From the pain in Sheireadan's expression, and the angry bruise painted across his cheek, his abuser had done a thorough job.

Sheireadan lost his balance for a moment, and Falyn plunged into the water to assist him. Her skirt ballooned on the surface as she grabbed his elbow to right him. "This is far enough," she said, her voice amplified across the water.

"What are you doing!" Sheireadan snapped. "Father will know for sure now."

Falyn looked distressed, then set her face with resolution. "I'll just shove my wet clothes under the laundry pile before he has a chance to see them."

"What about the smell of the water? How are you going to disguise *that*? I swear, Falyn—what was the point in me stripping down to nothing if you're going to plunge into the water like a fool."

"Enough. It's done," Falyn said crossly.

"Well you're going to freeze before we even get home. Did you think about *that*?"

"I'll wear your cloak," she replied. Then she grinned. "Did you think about that?"

"*Fine*," Sheireadan grumbled. He turned away from her and took a step. "I need to go deeper."

"No need," Falyn said. She cupped the water in her hands and trickled it over his shoulders and back. "There, see?"

Sheireadan winced.

"You really did it this time," Falyn said. "Will you never learn?"

"I'd say I've learned more than my share," Sheireadan replied. Then he mumbled something that Dayn could not hear.

Dayn watched them cautiously as he inched along the wall. He ducked behind the nearest pillar, then peeked around to see if he was in Falyn's and Sheireadan's line of vision. Confident that he was not, he leaned around the column, far enough to spy on them without being detected, yet close enough to hear their conversation.

"Fool," he heard Falyn say. "Would you have him kill you next time?"

"Better me than you," Sheireadan replied.

Falyn smirked. "He wouldn't dare. I wouldn't be worth much to him dead, now would I?"

"Maybe not. But after he's handed you over and gotten what he wants, what then? Will Zared treat you any better?"

"I'll not go with Zared."

"Then you *will* be dead, sister, and all the blows I've taken for you will have been for nothing."

Dayn sucked in a breath. Sheireadan had received the injuries in defense of his sister? For a moment a hint of admiration threatened to weaken Dayn's distain of the boy, but then he remembered the hundreds of blows he had received from Sheireadan, and all thoughts of charity dissipated.

But what did Zared have to do with anything? Zared was a deacon of the Vestry. He was an elderly man, with narrow, beady eyes that leered whenever the girls were around. Dayn had heard the gossip, but just like everyone else, would never bear false witness against someone he knew little more about than that. Besides, Zared was not just any member of the Vestry; he was a man whose wealth gave him more power than most. His wrath could make anyone's life miserable, and Dayn's life had been miserable enough.

Falyn cupped more water into her hand, spilling it over Sheireadan's purpled shoulders. "No sense worrying about it now. I'll not come of age for two more years. Father can't do anything until then anyway."

"I wouldn't be so sure. He's been known to bend the rules."

"Hmmph! I'd like to see him try to bend *that* one. It's a mortal sin to wed before the proper time. Even he can't override that law."

"Since when has morality stopped him?"

"Let's not talk about it anymore. There's nothing we can do about it tonight, is there?" Falyn sighed and shook her head. "The bruises are really bad this time," she said. "I'm sorry I got you into this."

"Nothing to be sorry about," Sheireadan said. "I wish Father'd just hit me and leave the pit out of it though."

"At least I found a way to get you food and water. That's something at least."

"If he ever catches us…"

"He won't."

"He will. And when he does, it will be the death of us. Well…the death of me anyway."

"Don't say that," Falyn said. "I would never let that happen. Never."

Sheireadan turned to face her. It made Dayn more than a little uncomfortable. But what Sheireadan said next made him even more so: "I did everything I could to keep Dayn away from you, Falyn. I don't think I can keep Zared away from you, too. Dayn ran. Zared won't."

"And you won't either," a voice boomed.

Falyn's and Sheireadan's heads spun toward the voice. From out of the shadows a dark figure emerged, its hair and clothing so black, its face looked like that of a decapitated skull floating toward them.

Falyn gasped. "Father...we were only—"

"Save your breath, daughter," Lorcan said. "It's clear what you're doing. You're defying my orders."

"I made her come," Sheireadan blurted. "We meant no disrespect."

"I'll be the judge of that."

"I only came to take the healing. I–"

"Who gave you permission?" Lorcan asked.

"Father, please," Falyn pleaded. "He's hurt."

"Hurt?" Lorcan whipped his walking stick from beneath his cloak, slapping it against the palm of his hand. He laughed, a laugh so cruel it sent a chill down Dayn's spine. He couldn't imagine the fear it must be sending Falyn's and Sheireadan's way right now. How many times had they been forced to endure it over the years?

"Out. Now," Lorcan ordered.

Falyn and Sheireadan hesitated, but then slowly worked their way to the edge of the pool. Sheireadan reached it first. Lorcan yanked him by an arm and pulled him out, flinging him to the ground. Sheireadan groaned and curled into a ball, hugging his ribs.

Lorcan picked up Sheireadan's clothes and tossed them on top of the huddled form at his feet. "Get dressed," he said with disgust.

Falyn clambered out of the pool, her skirt weighted with water and clinging to her legs. She shuffled over to Sheireadan, but her father grabbed her arm and jerked her away. "He will dress himself," he said.

"But Father, he can't. He—" But the backside of Lorcan's hand sent her sprawling.

Dayn stepped around the pillar before he could think what he was doing. "Touch her again and I'll kill you with my bare hands," he said in a tone that even he did not recognize. He stood, hands fisted at his side, glaring at Lorcan with a rage so intense, he wondered if he truly possessed demon blood after all. Dayn's legs felt like pudding quivering on a plate, but at least his words had come out sounding like those of a demon.

If Lorcan's expression had turned any darker it would have disappeared into an abyss void of color. All Dayn could see of the man were the whites of his eyes, but then a cruel flash of teeth sent a message of hatred across the spans of the pool. "Demon," Lorcan hissed.

"That's right," Dayn said, trying to sound as sinister as the creature he was facing. "Lay another hand on her and you'll feel me tear your soul out by the roots." Dayn forced his feet forward, slowly making his way around the perimeter of the pool. As he drew nearer, he kept his focus on Lorcan, knowing that Falyn was watching him, yet daring not a glance her way.

He stopped within feet of her, and only then did he turn to her. He reached out a hand. "Are you hurt?" he asked.

Her eyes darted to Lorcan, then back to Dayn. She shook her head. "No," she said.

"No you aren't hurt, or no you won't take my hand?" Dayn asked.

Falyn looked at her father once more, her face awash with fear, but then, hesitantly, she reached up her hand to Dayn's and took it.

Dayn pulled her up gently and ushered her over to Sheireadan. "Help him get dressed," he said. "It will be all right." But he wasn't so sure. Lorcan was watching him like a snake poised to strike, and Dayn didn't know how much longer his own façade could last.

"How dare you interfere," Lorcan said, but he did not make a move to stop Falyn from assisting her brother, nor did he make any attempt to tighten the distance between him and Dayn.

"Even a demon would not treat their own children so cruelly," Dayn said.

"You should know," Lorcan replied.

"Yes, I suppose I should."

Lorcan inclined his head toward Falyn and Sheireadan. "The disciplining of my children is my affair, not yours."

"Discipline? I wouldn't call this discipline."

Lorcan's nostrils flared. "I do what is necessary. Sin must be purged from their souls."

Dayn laughed. He could not help it. "Sin?" He laughed even harder.

Lorcan's face flushed with fury, all hesitation in Dayn's regard tossed to the side. He raised his cane to strike, but from out of nowhere a hand grabbed his wrist, stopping it in midair.

Haskel leaned his face to Lorcan's ear. "Touch my kin," he growled, "and ye'll find a hundred clansmen at your door."

Lorcan glared at Haskel with an expression that went beyond hatred. "Your *kin* is interfering in my business."

Haskel glanced at Falyn, her lip swollen and bleeding, and Sheireadan, panting from fear and injury. "Ye call this business?"

Lorcan's eyes narrowed into slits. "Yes. *My* business. Now get your hand off of me, or you and your *clansmen* will be hearing from the Vestry."

Haskel stared at him a moment longer, then let go his hold. He turned to Dayn, without regard to the cane still clutched in Lorcan's hand, and said, "Come, boy. We're leavin'."

"But uncle, what of..." Dayn looked at Falyn and Sheireadan. "We can't just leave them!"

"I said we're leavin'. Now."

Dayn opened his mouth to argue, but before he could utter a word, his uncle had grabbed him by the shoulders.

Haskel forced Dayn's gaze into his. "For *their* sakes, as well as yours," he said, "we go—*now*."

Dayn knew there would be no debating it. He might have been able to hold his own with Lorcan for a time, but there would be no winning with Haskel. He felt himself suddenly spun around and shoved toward the woods where two horses waited. Dayn glanced over his shoulder at Falyn, but she had faded into the fog.

Haskel handed Dayn the reins of one of the horses. Dayn hesitated. "But what will happen to Falyn and her brother?" he asked anxiously.

Haskel did not answer.

"Uncle, there must be something we can do!"

"Not here."

Dayn watched his uncle's face, searching for a sign of hope, but the man's expression bore no sign of it. Dayn mounted the horse, then looked toward the pool one last time. All he could see was a blanket of mist, and the lingering image in his mind of Falyn being slapped to the ground by her father.

"How can the Vestry condone Lorcan treating his children like that?" Dayn asked when they were some distance from the springs.

"They don't condone it. They simply turn a blind eye to it."

"Isn't that the same thing?"

Haskel drew a deep breath and released it slowly. "You're too young to understand how things work."

"I understand more than you know."

Haskel raised an eyebrow. "Do ye?"

"I have to help her," Dayn insisted. "Maybe if we talked to the Vestry…told them how bad it was for her and—"

"That we'll *not* do!" Haskel barked. He steered his horse in front of Dayn's, stopping him short. Haskel drew his already large frame into an even more impressive height. "We'll not talk to the Vestry, Dayn. Not about this or anythin' else."

"But—"

"Ye heard me, boy. Since your little performance at the Festival a few months back, things have gone bad for the clans."

"What do you mean?" Dayn asked, but he was sure he already knew.

"It didn't take much for the townsfolk to buy into Sheireadan's rantin's that ye'd revealed yourself as a demon. Talk grew from ye bein' one, to the role your family and the clans played in it. We were harborers of evil, they said, so were breakin' the law."

"But, I'm not a demon," Dayn insisted. "I give my word—"

Haskel scowled. "Your word's not good for much around here. And now neither is mine, or anyone else's in the family."

"So the clans won't believe me either."

"Listen, most of the clans support ye and your mother—even though it's put 'em in danger. All the clans left the Festival early that day. Several members stopped by your folks' place on the way home, along with me, your Uncle Nort, and a few others. By the time we arrived, your father'd already taken off, and your mother...well, let's just say she was in no condition to be left alone. Vania and some of the women folk stayed with her, while me and the men headed out to search for your father. We gathered other members along the way and searched for days. When we reached the cave..." Haskel paused, his expression grim. "Ye know the rest." He kicked his heels and reined his horse back to the path.

Dayn urged his mount after him. "What does that have to do with the Vestry?" he asked.

"The Vestry sent some men the next day to fetch ye and your father for a hearin'. When they discovered neither of ye were there, they threatened to take your mother instead. But Vania..." Haskel's lips curled with satisfaction. "Well, let's just say she told the bastards what's what.

"When we got back, we had a tough time talkin' your mother into goin' to our place with us. Ye'd been gone nearly five days, but she insisted ye'd all be home soon, and that she needed to be there when ye did. Vania reminded her that the Vestry's men might be back, that she wouldn't be safe there on her own. Only when I promised to check on your place every few days did she agree to go with us. We told her to pack as much as she could so it would look like she'd taken off for good. We knew if the Vestry returned, they'd think twice before headin' further up the mountain huntin' for her. But we also figured if Gorman, or you and your sister, returned and didn't find anyone at your place, the next thing any of ye'd do would be to go to our place. It was the best ruse we knew of to get your mother to agree to go with us."

Dayn felt a wave of regret for all the suffering he realized he'd put them through. "Thanks…for looking after Mother," he said, "and for—"

Haskel grunted. "No need."

They rode on without speaking for a time, until at last Dayn broke the silence. "How did you know where to find me, tonight I mean?"

"Your sister told me."

"What did she tell you—exactly?"

Haskel cleared his throat. "That ye have affection for Falyn and had likely gone to find her. Since your mother mentioned we'd seen her recently at the springs, it seemed the most likely place to start."

"I have more than affection for her, uncle. I love her."

Haskel looked surprised, then frowned his disapproval. "Ye'd do better to turn your heart elsewhere," he said.

"If you'd been told to turn your heart from Vania, would you have?"

A hint of humor played on Haskel's face, then he cleared his throat again. "No, I s'pose not."

"Then why is it so wrong for me to love Falyn?"

"It isn't wrong, it's just—dangerous."

"I'd risk anything for her."

"Even her life?"

"Her *life*?" Dayn said with alarm.

"If she's caught with ye, she'll be more than disciplined. Ye heard what her father said about purgin' his children's souls."

"You heard that?"

"Aye. And Lorcan takes his children's souls very seriously. From the look of the injuries on his son's back, I'd say Sheireadan's soul was Lorcan's primary concern tonight. No father should do what Lorcan does, and no son should have to endure it."

It occurred to Dayn that although Haskel had not, in Dayn's mind, been the best of fathers, at least he had never had a reputation for violence. If anything, he had only tried to protect Eyan from people like Lorcan and the members of the Vestry.

"Uncle?"

Haskel gave another grunt.

"What I said to you about Father, I'm sorry."

Haskel's expression relaxed somewhat, but his tone remained stiff. "I'm sorry, too."

"Did you try to enter the cave? I mean—"

"Aye. But a landslide had blocked the path, and we could go no further. I feel certain that's where your father met his fate."

Tears stung Dayn's eyes as he realized it was his own fault that his father was dead. Gorman would never have gone back to the cave if Dayn had not run away and entered it.

"You and your sister'll have time to grieve," Haskel said in response to Dayn's obvious anxiety, "but right now your mother needs your courage."

Dayn swallowed thickly. "She's grave ill, isn't she?"

"Aye."

"Am I the cause of it?"

"Aye." He glanced at Dayn. "And no."

Dayn remained silent, sorting through his remorse.

"You and your sister are back now. There's no better medicine for her than that. But soon there'll be more pressin' issues to deal with."

Dayn did not have to ask what his uncle meant. Memories of spell-work done at his parents' house, and his own recent altercation with Lorcan, made the meaning clear. "What are we to do?" he asked.

"We must call a gatherin' of the clans. Lorcan'll not let this go. He's the one that started the crusade against you and your parents to begin with. The anger of the mountain gave him more leverage. Now that he knows ye've returned...well...let's just say he wasn't bluffin' when he said the clans'll be hearin' from the Vestry."

"But what can the Vestry do?"

"They can demand we turn ye over for trial."

Dayn reined his horse to a halt. "Trial? For what?"

Haskel stopped in response. "Demon craft. Taintin' wells. Fire on the mountain. Take your pick."

"There are no demons, so how can I be one?" Dayn cried.

"Of course there are demons. The Word tells us so."

"No uncle. I know the truth of it. I do."

"You'd best watch your words, boy. Blasphemy'll not endear ye to the clans *or* the Vestry."

Dayn inched his horse to Haskel's side. "I swear, it's not blasphemy. Alicine and I went to the other side of the mountains, to a place called Tearia. There are people there. And they're not demons."

Haskel's mouth twitched, but he said nothing.

"The Word says that pale-haired demons survived after the Purge," Dayn continued, "and roamed the mountains as a message to us. But it was pale-haired people that roamed the mountains, not demons. They were Tearian guards, sent to keep the Kiradyns on their side of the mountain, even if it meant killing them. Before the Purge, Tearians and Kiradyns were friends, and visited back and forth, but when the mountain sent the fire, the Tearians blamed the Kiradyns, so they stopped them from crossing over."

"Enough," Haskel warned. "To speak such things is to declare the Word a lie, and believe me, the punishment for that would be far greater than any penalty for bein' a demon." Haskel sounded angry, but not as angry as Gorman had been all those months ago when Dayn had suggested there could be others living on the island of Aredyrah. It gave Dayn hope that he could convince his uncle, but he knew he would need to approach it from a different angle.

"Did Father tell you he found me in the cave when I was a baby?" Dayn asked.

Haskel's lips compressed. He kicked his heels into his horse's ribs, urging it onward. Dayn followed, keeping pace.

"Did he?" Dayn persisted.

"I was there when he found ye," Haskel said stiffly.

For a moment Dayn thought to rein his horse to a halt again, but if he stopped every time Haskel said something shocking, they might never reach home.

"We were young then, and foolish," Haskel continued. "Your father was desperate to save your mother. She'd lost so many infants that he feared she would either take her own life or die tryin' to bear another one. He prayed—we all did. But Daghadar didn't answer. Your father grew angry, and in a moment of desperation decided that if his own god wouldn't help him, he would find one who would."

"What do you mean?" Dayn asked.

Haskel shook his head. "Your father confided in me—god, I wish he hadn't—that if Daghadar wouldn't help him, he'd turn to the underworld to bargain for your mother's life.

"I tried to stop him—but that stubbornness of his. I followed him to the entrance of the cave, then confronted him and tried to reason with him. He would have nothin' of it, so I did what I had to do—I followed him in."

"That's what happened with me and Alicine," Dayn said. "She found me and tried to get me to come home. When I wouldn't, she went with me into the cave."

"She has your father's stubbornness in her."

"And I don't."

Haskel smiled sadly. "No, I s'pose not."

"So when he found me...what then?"

"He took ye home to Morna and told her that Daghadar had given ye to 'em as a gift for their devotion. O' course, he'd not really thought through the fact that ye had demonic features. All he cared about was that for the first time in months your mother was happy. That was all he needed. He did worry for a time that the witch might come lookin' for ye. He lost a good bit o' sleep over it, I'll tell ye that. He eventually headed back to the cave and hung chimes in front of it. He figured she wouldn't trespass beyond 'em."

"*He* hung those?" Dayn thought back on all the ragged chimes he and Alicine had seen draped around the entrance to the cave. Never in his wildest dreams would he have imagined that it was his father who had placed them there.

"Aye, he hung 'em, and it must have worked, too. Never saw any more sign of the demon. At any rate, as ye grew older, he was determined to treat ye as his own. I honestly think he came to believe ye were. I warned him against takin' ye to town and pretendin' ye were anythin' but what ye were."

"Is that why you never took Eyan to town?"

"Aye."

"Did you find Eyan in a cave?"

"Of course not!" Haskel sounded genuinely offended.

"Then why do you think he is demon-kind."

"Because he is...he must be."

"How? You and Vania have always been faithful to each other I'm sure. How can Eyan be a demon?"

"His blood is tainted by the ancient seed, o' course."

"Ancient seed?"

"Aye. Planted through the rapes of long ago."

"*What?*"

"There are tales of it amongst the clans. Your father never told ye?" Haskel's expression grew puzzled. Then he explained. "As ye know, we Aeries live in the high regions, those closest to the dwellin' of the demons. Many generations ago, after the Purge, but before the demons were driven back into the mountains, they did despicable things. Since then, the taint of their deeds has been watered down, but a few children are born now and then with their features. Usually—" He stopped mid-sentence, as if realizing he had crossed into a subject he did not wish to discuss.

"What happens to the children with those features, uncle?" Dayn asked.

"Never ye mind. It's none o' your concern."

"Of course it's my concern. I have those features, don't I?"

Haskel frowned. "Very well. The children are put to rest most times."

Dayn reined his horse to a halt. "They are *killed?*"

Haskel stopped alongside him. "Most times, aye. But not always."

"You mean Eyan."

"I argued that he had to be weeded out, for the sake o' the clan, but Vania refused to consider it."

"That's what my mother did for me, too."

"What?" Haskel asked with confusion.

"My real mother is Brina, and my father was Mahon. In Tearia, the people strive for purity, just like the clans are doing here." Dayn pulled back his collar, revealing his birthmark. "This mark made me impure, so I was sentenced to die. Brina was a royal and had no choice. She told Mahon she would kill me herself, but instead she smuggled me to the mountains to ask the gods to cure me. When she met Fa—I mean Gorman—she thought he was a god. He made her think he was by saying he would cure me and return me to her in a year's time." Dayn paused. "But you know all that, don't you."

Haskel nodded.

Dayn felt resentment resurfacing. "So Gorman lied to her, and stole me, and never took me back like he promised. And while he was happy, and his wife was happy, I was miserable, and my real mother was even more miserable. What right did he have?"

"Sounds to me like he saved your life."

"What?"

"I said, it sounds to me like he saved your life. What would have happened to ye if Brina hadn't turned ye over to him in the cave?"

"I—I don't know."

"I think ye do."

Dayn clenched his jaw, fighting the chink that Haskel had just put in his mettle. But before he could form a retort, Haskel said, "We're home, boy. Best not say anythin' about all this, at least not yet."

Dayn's eyes shot forward, surprised to see the house just ahead. It had seemed to take an eternity to reach the springs when he'd stormed out earlier, but strangely, only moments to get back.

As they drew nearer, he noticed a glow radiating through the foggy windowpanes. No doubt the family was waiting up for them. How in the world was he going to keep what he had learned tonight a secret? His mother would be easy to fool, and Vania and Eyan were Haskel's problem, but Alicine? She could read him like parchment, and he knew the moment he entered the door, the events of the evening would be written all over his face. How could he keep from her the fact that he was even less welcome than he had originally anticipated, and that now, more than ever, he had to leave this place, and leave it for good.

∾

# CHAPTER 7: AFFAIRS
# OF THE HEART

Haskel shoved open the door and ushered Dayn inside. Vania and Morna rose from their chairs by the hearth, while Eyan sat upright in his bed, blinking at the sudden commotion.

"Good, we can go to bed now," Alicine mumbled. She lifted her head from her arms that were resting, criss-crossed, atop the table.

"Dayn—" Morna began, but Haskel silenced her with a wave of his hand. "Let the boy get some rest," he said. "There'll be time for talk later."

Morna pointed Dayn to a pallet that she had arranged for him near the fire. "Here son. You can settle yourself here."

"I'm not tired," Dayn said.

"I'll heat ye some tea," Vania said, hustling over to the kitchen counter. She lifted the lid from the tea kettle, then reached up and pulled a tiny vial from the shelf. "A little somethin' extra to take off the chill," she said with a wink. After adding a dash of its contents to the kettle, she hung it over the fire and motioned Dayn to a chair by the hearth. "There now, sit yourself down. You're both half froze. Haskel...get those wet boots off your feet, and Dayn...yours, too."

Haskel yanked off his boots, then grabbed up Dayn's, which were now in a wet heap by the fire, and took both pairs to the front porch.

"Back in a mite," Vania said as she turned to follow Haskel out the door. "Oh...Alicine, would ye watch the tea? And Morna, dear, ye look exhausted. Why don't ye take yourself to bed? Dayn's home now. We'll hold off any talk 'til ye get up." She glanced at Dayn, then back at Morna. "The boy just needs some warmth in his belly. He'll soon be ready for the pillow."

Morna nodded, but after the door clicked shut, she stepped to Dayn and placed a hand on his shoulder. "I'm glad you're home, son," she said softly. "We'll talk later, all right?"

Dayn did not respond. His eyes were focused on the flames in the hearth, but his mind was somewhere else entirely.

Taking his cue of silence, Morna headed for her bed.

Eyan slid off his mattress and shuffled slowly toward Dayn. His long hair was in a wild disarray, and his dressing gown was a rumpled mess. "Where'd ye go?" he asked. "I mean, if ye don't mind me askin'."

"Nowhere," Dayn muttered.

"Well, ye can't have gone *nowhere,* eh?" Eyan said. "Otherwise Father would've found ye standin' outside the door."

Dayn turned to Eyan, expecting to see humor, but Eyan looked completely serious. "I went to the springs," Dayn said, then returned his gaze to the hearth.

"Why'd ye go there?" Eyan asked. Then his face grew concerned. "Are ye sick?"

"Something like that."

"Let me get your tea then," Eyan said. "Mother says it can cure any ill. I've been sick plenty o' times and it always made me feel better."

Dayn sighed, then nodded. Eyan grabbed a towel and lifted the tea kettle off the spit. "Mother knows lots o' things," he said. "Like what herbs can cure a fever, or help ye sleep, or ease the aches." Eyan poured the brew into a mug. "Here," he said, holding it out to Dayn. "It'll make ye feel better."

Dayn accepted the tea and drank it down. It hadn't been over the fire long enough to get hot, but it sent a flood of warmth to his bones nonetheless.

Eyan took the mug and refilled it. "Where do ye hurt? Is it your head?"

Dayn forced a laugh. "My heart."

"Your heart? Hmmm…I don't know anythin' about that," Eyan said quietly. "Father says I should avoid the affairs o' the heart. I don't know what that means though."

"It means love," Alicine said.

"Love?" Eyan fixed her in a bewildered stare.

"Yes," Alicine said. "You know, like when you love someone."

"Ye mean like for a mother and a father?"

"No. It's more like *between* a mother and a father."

"Oh." Eyan paused for a long moment. "Is that kind o' love better?"

"No. It's just different. Right, Dayn?"

"I don't want to talk about it," Dayn said.

"Why?" Eyan asked cautiously. "Is it bad?"

"Yes," Dayn replied.

Alicine slapped Dayn on the arm. "Is not," she said.

"No? Tell us how it's *good* then."

"You know how it feels. Don't you dare put me on the spot."

"Well Eyan doesn't know how it feels. Why don't you explain it to him."

Alicine glanced toward their mother's bed across the way. Morna's steady breathing indicated she was fast asleep, but Alicine lowered her voice, just in case. "It's like you love someone special...someone you want to touch or–" Alicine blushed. "—or kiss on the mouth. You know."

Eyan looked away awkwardly. "I haven't been around enough people to feel that way about any of 'em."

"Be glad of that," Dayn said.

Alicine slapped his arm again. "Don't say that!"

Dayn laughed.

"Is that kind o' love...funny...like a joke?" Eyan asked.

"Sometimes," Alicine replied.

"Never," Dayn added.

Eyan shook his head. "I don't understand."

"Didn't your parents ever talk to you about love?" Alicine asked. "I mean, you do know what happens when a man and woman have special feelings for each other, right?"

"They get married. But I won't be allowed to, so I guess that's why my parents never told me much about it."

Dayn rose abruptly from the chair, then realized his body was screaming to lie down. "I can't talk about this anymore," he said, and moved toward the pallet. He curled up on the patchwork pile and yanked a quilt over his head.

Alicine stood over him. "Don't you want to get out of your damp clothes first?"

"No."

"I'll leave the room if you want me to."

"No."

"Ye really should put on somethin' dry, ye know," Eyan said. "Mother says that if ye stay wet, ye'll catch a chill, and if ye catch a chill, ye'll catch the fever, and if ye catch the fever—"

Dayn threw off the covers. "All right—*fine*! But I don't have anything else to wear."

"Your mother packed up your and Alicine's clothes when she left and came here, but right now they're all in a trunk in the barn. I've got plenty o' stuff, though," Eyan said. "Here, let me find ye somethin'." He walked over to a cedar chest at the foot of his bed and lifted the lid. "How about this one? No, wait...this one'd be better." He held up a wool sleeping gown in one hand and a large faded work shirt in the other. "Which one do ye want? This one's the softest, but this one—"

"I—don't—care," Dayn said between gritted teeth. He sat up and thrust out a hand. "Just *give* me something."

Eyan handed him the gown, while Alicine secured the drape to their mother's sleeping area and walked toward the door. "We'll wait outside. You coming, Eyan?" she asked.

Eyan looked at Dayn as though requesting permission. "Can I stay? I can help ye if ye want."

"I don't care," Dayn replied.

Alicine sniggered. "You wouldn't have said that a few months ago. You used to hide your body like it was the biggest secret in Aredyrah."

"You're one to talk. Who just said the words 'kiss on the mouth'?"

Alicine's face grew noticeably red.

"Besides, it's just Eyan, and he's a boy," Dayn said. "Trapped in a cave with Reiv forced me to adapt."

"What do you mean?" Alicine asked.

Dayn chortled. "The cave wasn't exactly designed for privacy, and you know how Reiv is."

"Oh," Alicine said. For a moment her attentions seemed to drift, but then she hastily added, "Well, Eyan can stay if he wants, but I'm sure not." She turned and slipped out the door.

Dayn tried to pry off his damp tunic, but the thing was glued to his skin. Eyan reached out and grabbed hold of it, helping to pull it up and over Dayn's shoulders. Dayn then rose and peeled off his pants. Stripped down to nothing, he yanked the nightshirt over his head. When he looked up, Eyan was staring at him like he'd seen a ghost.

"What's the matter?" Dayn asked.

"Nothin'...I...nothin'." Eyan gathered up Dayn's wet clothes and hurried to the door. "I'll hang 'em on the porch rail 'til mornin'. Mother'll want to wash 'em...they're very dirty...and..." His voice trailed off as he hurriedly exited the room.

❧

# CHAPTER 8: GREAT EXPECTATIONS

It was late morning when Dayn finally awoke. He knew by the angle of the light beaming in through the open windows and the warming breeze rustling the curtains. He threw off the covers and sat up, rolling the stiffness from his neck and shoulders. The pallet had not been comfortable, but at least it was better than the rocky ground he and his sister had been forced to sleep on for the past two weeks. But it was not the pallet that had him feeling less than rested; it was the thickness behind his eyeballs.

He scanned the room. No one was there. Even Alicine, who had surely required as much rest as he had, appeared to be up and about. He rose and looked down at the night shirt that hung to his knees, trying to recall where he had put his trousers.

The door burst open. "Mornin' dear," Vania chirped as she made her way to the table and lifted a cloth napkin from a plate of food. "Saved ye a bit o' lunch—too late for breakfast. Hope ye don't mind that it isn't warm."

"It's fine, auntie," Dayn said as he trudged to the bench.

Vania filled a mug from a nearby crock. "Here's some milk to give your body a go."

Dayn took a swig, then dug his fork and knife into a slice of meat, wild pig by the looks of it, and sawed it into a more manageable piece. He shoved it into his mouth and chewed it down. It was tough and had a gamey taste, but he was half-starved and couldn't seem to fill his stomach fast enough.

"Lands, boy. Ye'll choke if ye don't slow down a mite."

"Sorry," Dayn mumbled through a mouthful. He gulped down the rest of the milk, then held out the mug for more.

Vania scampered to refill it.

"Where's Alicine?" Dayn asked, his eyes still focused on the plate.

"Gone to help Eyan with the horses."

Dayn crammed a chunk of bread into his mouth and sawed another piece of meat. "Wha 'bout Mother?"

"She's in the root cellar; won't be long, and your uncle's gone to meet with the clans."

Dayn's jaw stopped mid-chew. "The clans?"

"Aye, went to give 'em an invite."

"An invite?" Dayn forced down the bread that had lodged in his throat. "What kind of invite?"

"A Gatherin', here, in two weeks time."

Dayn set down his eating utensils, his appetite all but vanished. "So we're here alone? I mean..."

"Now don't ye go worryin' yourself about it," Vania said, bustling over to pour the last of the milk into his mug. "It would take a calamity to tempt the Vestry to venture *this* far. Besides, Eyan's well skilled with a bow."

"Why is Haskel calling a Gathering? I mean, he said he intended to meet with some of the members, but a full Gathering?"

"All the mountain clans will be needin' to know you and your sister are back. The Aerie clan, bein' our own, should know first, o' course. But we figured might as well tell everyone, before any rumors filtered up from Kiradyn."

"But why here? You and Haskel never had the clans meet *here* before."

Vania set the crock aside, then pulled out the bench from the other side of the table and sat facing him. "We never had 'em here before because of Eyan."

"So how is it different now?"

Vania folded her hands on the tabletop and lifted her chin. "We've decided to introduce him to the clans," she said. Her expression, though somewhat pinched, showed signs of a hard-won victory. "It's been a long time comin', Dayn. We can no longer deny our son his rights as a member o' the clan. Besides, after what ye told Haskel—"

"I thought he didn't believe me," Dayn said.

"He didn't, until Alicine confirmed it this mornin'."

"So he believed her, but not me?"

Vania patted Dayn's hand. "It's not like that, dear. It's just that she told him the same thing you did, and he figured there wasn't likely a conspiracy between ye."

Dayn slanted his eyes toward the door, worried that his altercation with Lorcan was just the sort of calamity the Vestry needed to make their presence known. "How long will uncle be gone?" he asked.

"Oh, ten days, no more."

"Ten *days*?" Dayn nearly choked.

"He's got several homesteads to visit, Dayn, so he can get the message movin' down the line. Then he's headin' down to tell Eileis. She'll be wantin' to come, too, I expect."

"Eileis? The Spirit Keeper? But she lives near Kiradyn!" Dayn's voice began to rise. "What if Haskel's seen there? What if—"

Vania cocked her head. "What's driven such fear into ye, child?"

"Didn't uncle tell you?"

"You mean about Lorcan?"

"Of course I mean about Lorcan!"

Vania patted his hand again. "He's an evil man, there's no denyin' it. But I don't think he'll be wantin' everyone knowin' about the treatment of his children. Haskel could easily use that bit of information against him. And he knows it."

"So Haskel is going to keep it secret just so Lorcan will leave us alone? And what about Falyn and her brother? What happens to them?"

"No worries, dear. Haskel intends to tell Eileis. Figures she can help without involvin' the rest of us. I'm sure she'll figure somethin' out."

The door opened and Morna swept into the room, her arms loaded with tubers, jars of spiced meats, and a strand of dried onions. Vania rose to help her. They set the items on the table and sorted through them.

"Well, it's enough for a stew and a couple o' mince pies," Vania said. "But it won't be enough to feed all the folks that'll likely be comin'. We'll have to do some gatherin'. There should still be some blackberries on the vine, and there's a spot where we always find fine mushrooms. I'll send Eyan out later."

"There's plenty of preserves in the cellar," Morna assured her, "but before we pull any more out, I guess we'd best wait to see what Haskel says when he returns. There's always a chance some of the clans won't come."

"Why wouldn't they come?" Dayn asked.

"Some aren't so forgiving," Morna said. "They'll be more concerned with what your return means to the Vestry than what it means to your family."

"Maybe this isn't such a good idea," Dayn said. "I don't want to cause anyone any more trouble."

"What isn't a good idea?" Alicine asked as she entered the doorway. Eyan followed at her heels.

"Vania said Haskel has gone to invite the clans here for a Gathering," Dayn said.

"I know," Alicine said cheerfully. "Isn't that exciting?"

"Well," Dayn said, "what if the clans aren't happy about us coming back and telling what we learned?"

"Oh, pooh. They'll be fine once we explain it. Besides, it's a chance for everyone to meet Eyan."

"And how well do you expect *that* to go over?" Dayn said.

"It will be fine, won't it Eyan?" Alicine smiled at Eyan assuringly.

"I...um...guess it'll be fine," Eyan said.

"Of course it will, dear," Vania added. "It'll be a celebration of Dayn's and Alicine's return, and your comin' out."

"I'm not so sure I want a celebration," Dayn said.

"This isn't just about *you*," Alicine said haughtily.

"Well, maybe *you* like being the center of attention," Dayn shot back, "but that doesn't mean Eyan and I do."

"Since when are you Eyan's spokesperson?" Alicine placed her hands on her hips and turned her eyes to Eyan. "*You* don't mind a celebration...*do* you, Eyan?"

Eyan glanced back and forth between the bickering siblings. "Um...well...I've never been to anythin', so I guess it'll be all right." Dayn threw him a glare. "I mean... maybe Dayn's right. Maybe it's not such a good idea."

"All right, enough," Morna scolded. "The clans are invited for the Gathering and that's that. As for a celebration...Dayn, if you don't want to be included in it, fine, but at some point you're going to have to show your face and verify what you told your uncle. As for Eyan, how his introduction to the clans is handled is for him and his parents to figure out. And if Alicine wants to be the center of attention, she'd best find something decent to wear." She turned her eyes to Alicine's startled face. "Don't look to me for help on that, daughter. I've enough to do."

Alicine gawked down at her own well-worn dress. She had already spent part of the morning pulling her and Dayn's rumpled clothing from the trunk that Eyan had dragged down from the loft in the barn. The stored clothes had not been dirty, but in need of a good airing, so she had shaken them out and pinned them to the line that was stretched across a sunny patch of yard beside the house.

Alicine spun and headed out the door. It was still cool, but warming fast. As she rounded the house and crossed the yard toward the line, lady beetles spiraled from the grass, clattering noisily around her. She waved them aside, then stopped, surveying the clothesline. To the left, a row of Dayn's trousers and tunics could be seen, lifting and falling with the breeze. She moved her eyes along the line toward two homespun skirts, an oatmeal colored blouse, and a few discreetly placed undergarments. On past, three dresses hung shoulder to shoulder, their modest Kiradyn style in such contrast to the skin-revealing clothing she had worn in Tearia. Originally dyed in rich earth-tones, the dresses now seemed dull and tired, but even worse, confining. At the end of the line, her Summer Maiden's gown was pinned, clean but tattered. Alicine heaved a sigh. Everything she owned was either faded, patched, or inappropriate for the Gathering.

"I don't suppose you packed the sarong," Dayn's amused voice said at her back.

"Funny," she retorted. She turned and noted the dressing gown he was still wearing. "Your legs are showing."

Dayn looked down at himself. "Maybe I'll wear this to the Gathering. It sort of looks like something a Jecta would wear. *That* would certainly make an impression."

"Hmmm....looks more Tearian, I think." Alicine walked around him, assessing him up and down. "If you belted it, it would resemble one of Reiv's tunics."

"And I wouldn't have to wear my boots!"

They laughed, but then Alicine turned back to the line. She sighed again, and shook her head. "Nothing. I have absolutely *nothing* to wear."

"Don't be ridiculous," Dayn said. "You've got what... four dresses. Just pick one."

Alicine rolled her eyes. "You don't understand. I haven't seen these people since the Festival. I'd at least like to look presentable."

Dayn stepped between her and the line and crossed his arms. "Why do you even care? I thought...I mean, after all that's happened, I figured you'd have moved beyond all that."

"Beyond all what?"

Dayn hesitated, then said, "Before we left, you always cared so much about how you looked and what people thought of you."

"What's wrong with that?"

"It's one thing to try to look good for yourself, it's another to do it for people who don't really matter. Like the townsfolk." He gave her a condescending look. "When I think of all the times you hobnobbed with them...I just think it's beneath you, that's all."

"I did *not* hob–"Alicine grew flustered, then annoyed. "You don't know what you're talking about! You were never in town enough to know how things work. You have to play the game, Dayn."

"Which game? The one where my face gets rubbed into the dirt? Is that the game you're referring to? If it is, then believe me, I played that game plenty of times."

"That's not what I mean and you know it! It's just that people from Kiradyn are different. They have certain expectations, and if you don't abide by them, then you're nobody."

"You mean like me?"

"Of course not! You're putting words into my mouth."

"Am I?"

"It doesn't matter what they think of you, Dayn. You're—"

"So it doesn't matter what they think of *me*, but it matters what they think of *you*?"

"Yes. I mean...well...yes."

Dayn stiffened his spine. "I see. Well, that's beside the point anyway. The people coming to the Gathering aren't *from* town, so they won't care one whit about your clothes."

"Well, I care!" Alicine snapped.

"Why? So you'll look better than them?" Dayn cocked his head. "That's it, isn't it? You don't want to be like them; you want to be *better* than them."

"What's gotten into you? You're making it sound like I'm a snob or something!"

"No, but you sure have your priorities twisted around."

Alicine stomped her foot. "You're the one doing the twisting! I just wanted something nice to wear to the Gathering."

"Well, I guess it doesn't matter what you want. You've got four dresses hanging there. I suggest you pick one."

Dayn grabbed a pair of trousers and the first shirt he could lay his hands on and snapped them from the line. He turned and headed for the house, storming past Eyan who had just stepped off the porch. As Dayn's heavy footsteps hit the porch boards, Eyan paused to watch him disappear through the door.

Eyan walked toward Alicine. "He's angry *again*?" he said when he reached her. "Why is he always so angry?"

Alicine blinked. Eyan was right—Dayn *was* angry a lot. Before, when he was just Dayn, before he had gone to Tearia and learned his true name, he had been mild-mannered, at times almost docile. But now...

"He hates it here," Alicine said.

"Why?"

"He wants to be someplace else."

"Where? That place ye went to before?"

"Yes."

Eyan tilted his head. "I don't see why. It's nice here. But I don't know very much because I've never been anywhere but here."

Alicine studied Eyan's face. "You really haven't been anywhere else, have you. That's—" She shifted her attention to the line. "Never mind."

"That's what?"

"That's...sad is all." Alicine felt uneasy at having said it. Eyan's exile from society *was* sad, but did he think so? He had been protected, but as a result knew little of the things a young man his age should know. He was innocent, almost childlike, and could easily be wounded by those who might not understand him. Maybe Dayn was right. Maybe the Gathering wasn't such a good idea.

❦

# PART TWO

## PARTING SEAS

# CHAPTER 9: THE BIG SHELL

Reiv stood in the doorway of the hut, gazing out through a drape of cockles toward the beach dunes beyond. The sun was high, casting a dazzling light upon the sand's golden crests, and soft gray shadows along their drifts. Waves clapped against the shoreline. Distant voices stirred with the hum of a late-morning breeze. Reiv pulled the salty air through his nostrils, relishing the musty ocean scent. It had not been that long ago that he had feared the vast waters, but since coming to the seaside village of Meirla a few months prior, he had come to love the sea as his own.

He arched his back and stretched his arms, working the tightness from his muscles. He'd slept hard that night, and his joints felt achy and thick. Bedding on a pallet had a way of doing that to a prince raised with down comforters and plump feather pillows. But he was no longer a prince; now he was a Shell Seeker living with four other people in a palm-frond hut, missing the comforts of a real bed, and longing for the privacy he once knew.

The people Reiv lived with all had cots, but he didn't really mind. He had, in fact, acquired one of his own recently, much to his delight at the time. It was constructed of reeds and strapping, layered with piles upon piles of soft palm fronds. In the brief time he'd slept on it, he'd come to think it every bit as nice as the royal bed he'd once owned. But then his aunt Brina had come to live with them, and he'd had no choice but to turn it over to her. Brina was a strong woman, but her royal disposition was not accustomed to a mat, and Reiv's pride would never allow a woman to sleep on the floor while he slept on a cot.

He lifted a hand to his eyes and scanned the sunny landscape. Brina could be seen marching toward him, returning from the fresh-water springs beyond the palms. A large reed basket was clutched in her arms, and an expression of distaste was plastered across her face. Even through the distance, Reiv could see that her lips were primed for a reprimand. But he wasn't concerned. Brina was more a mother to him than an aunt, and he was accustomed to her frequent lectures. When he had been Prince, her terse words were usually rebukes of his youthful rebelliousness. Now they were focused more on his work ethics, or what she considered his lack of them.

"Well, I see you are *finally* up," Brina said as she brushed past him to the drying line. She plopped the basket onto the ground, then pulled out a wet garment and flung it across the line. She shot him a look. "Sleeping all morning, lazy child. You will not find many shells reclined on a bedroll."

Reiv strolled toward her. "I find plenty of shells, in case you have not noticed," he said. "Besides, it is not that late. Look...it is barely high sun."

Brina scowled and snapped another garment in her hand. "High sun indeed. While you slept like a prince, I tended your horse, hung fish to smoke, washed your clothing—"

"Fine...fine," Reiv said, raising his hands in defense. "I will go right now if that will make you happy. I certainly would not want to interrupt your martyrdom. You are so good at it."

Brina spun to face him. She tossed the garment back into the basket and thrust her fists to her hips. "Martyrdom? I will thank you to reconsider that remark!"

Reiv could not help but laugh. "Very well," he said. "It is reconsidered."

"Well it had better be! And while you are at it, you might reconsider a few more things...those sleeping habits of yours for one...buried under the blankets 'til all hours of the morning...you should be ashamed."

Brina shoved a strand of white-blonde hair from her eyes and swept it behind her ear. She had never been meticulous about her hair, but since coming to live with the Shell Seekers, it had gotten downright undisciplined. It didn't help that she now had a multitude of daily chores to do, chores that servants once did for her. Nor did it help that she no longer had a dressing table of hair clips and grooming tools at her disposal. But still, considering everything, she had adapted well to the more earthly realities of life.

Reiv gave her a hug. "I am sorry, Brina. You are right—you are always right."

"Humph!" She turned and reached into the basket, then hung another piece of laundry over the line. "Well I am certainly right about this much—Kerrik will bring in the best shells today, and I will hear no complaints from you when he does."

"Ho, no," Reiv said with a chuckle. "The sprite will not beat *me* today. I am feeling lucky."

"It will take more than luck to beat that boy. He's been diving since dawn."

"We shall see who beats who," Reiv said, turning and ducking back into the hut. He stepped toward the grooming table and raked a comb through his long, red hair, then, after binding it at his back, leaned toward the reflective plate to outline his eyes with kohl. It was a Shell Seeker custom to decorate one's eyes, and though Reiv did not wish to waste time with it now, he at least made an attempt. He grabbed his belt, knife, and hunting bag and secured them at his waist, then before leaving, scrubbed his teeth with a leaf of mint.

He tossed the leaf aside and hustled out the door.

"How many shells will you be finding today, Brina?" he asked as he walked past her.

"More than you at this rate," she said. But in truth she had never dipped a toe into the sea and likely never would.

Reiv laughed and continued on, his feet crunching across the sand as he made his way toward the water. He scanned the teal surface for a sign of Kerrik, but saw no hint of him. The boy always headed out early, an advantage when it came to finding the nicest shells. But Reiv usually managed to hold his own; he had a knack for finding those hard-to-reach treasures tucked between the rocks. Jensa, Kerrik's older sister, would also be out and about. She and her older brother Torin were always the first ones up. As the accepted leaders of the household, Jensa and Torin were surprisingly generous in regard to

Reiv's need to sleep late; he seemed to require it more than the average person. But they still expected him to work late in order to catch up. And there was a lot of catching up to do.

During the earthquake weeks before, the sea had become violent and unpredictable. Many huts were dragged into its depths, while others were shaken to the ground or crushed beneath the weight of falling palms. For a while the Shell Seekers dared not venture into the waters; the tides were swift and unforgiving. But now the sea was finally calm and most of the huts rebuilt—except for the one Reiv hoped to have for his own one day. But there was no time for dreaming of huts; there was only time for seeking.

Reiv spotted Kerrik's head bobbling offshore, then saw his feet kick into the air as he dove beneath the surface. Reiv could not help but beam. It had not been that long ago that the boy lay bleeding on the sand, his wounds from an encounter with a monstrous sea snake so severe that recovery was doubtful. But now there he was, diving as if he had never been injured at all.

Kerrik bobbed back up. He turned his grinning face toward Reiv. "Oy, Reiv," his high-pitched voice shouted. He hoisted a large shell out of the water and flaunted it in the air.

Reiv waved and continued his approach. "So... you have a fine one already, do you," Reiv muttered. "Well, we shall see who comes out with the greatest catch today." He stepped into the water, determined not to waste a single moment more, but angry voices suddenly diverted his attention. He stopped to look down the shoreline. Jensa could be seen in the distance, facing a dark-haired young man about her age. Her arms were waving as her mouth contorted angrily.

Reiv considered staying out of it—Jensa was a girl certainly capable of defending herself–but then he saw the man grab Jensa's arm, and a surge of fury bubbled in his throat.

Reiv sloshed out of the water and stormed in their direction. As he drew nearer, he saw Jensa try to work her arm free, but the young man gripped it even tighter.

"Get your hands off of her," Reiv ordered upon reaching them.

The young man glared at Reiv, but did not let loose his hold on Jensa. "This is none of your concern," he growled.

Jensa turned her eyes to Reiv. "I can handle this, Reiv," she said.

"No doubt," Reiv said. "But I will see no man put his hands on you like that."

The man scoffed. "Your hands have been on her often enough!"

"That was out of line, Lyal," Jensa said.

"Was it?" Lyal retorted. "I've heard the talk."

"And what talk would that be?" Reiv asked.

"As if you don't know," Lyal replied.

"As a matter of fact, I do not." Reiv took a threatening step forward. "Now, you had best tell me or—"

"Or what?" Lyal said. "Will you assault me with those pitiful fists of yours? Or will you simply transcend and have Agneis do your fighting for you."

"Enough!" Jensa said. She wrenched her arm free. "Lyal. You would do well to ignore the idle gossip of a few old women."

"It's not idle," Lyal said. "And it's not a few old women. Everyone is talking about it."

"Talking about what?" Reiv asked.

Jensa rubbed her arm and averted her face from Reiv's probing gaze.

"Jensa?" Reiv said, commanding a response.

"There is talk that you and I are…mates. You are an unrelated male living in my hut. Naturally people think the worst."

Reiv was taken aback. *The worst?* The thought of her being with him was *the worst?* True, he didn't think of Jensa in that way, at least not since their first meeting when he thought her the most beautiful girl he had ever seen. But that had been months ago and since then he had come to think of her only as a friend. But for him to be considered *the worst?*

"That's right," Lyal said. "Everyone knows what's going on between you."

"That is the most ridiculous thing I have ever heard," Reiv said.

"That's what I've been trying to tell this arrogant oaf of a Shell Seeker!" Jensa said.

"Then why has Reiv not yet taken another woman?" Lyal demanded of her. "Enough feminine heads have turned his way. Why has he not responded to them? I'll tell you why—because he has you!"

"Have you no sense at all?" Jensa said.

"What? You think a man who's had as many women as the prince would take no notice of you?"

*Had as many women as the prince?* Reiv's pride swelled. So Lyal thought he had been with a lot of women, eh? Fine…let him think it. No sense confessing that he was still pure in that regard. That would be more humiliating than being described as "the worst."

"And you, Jensa; why do you avoid me?" Lyal ranted on. "You act as if I never even existed for you!"

Reiv eyed the young man with distaste. He was obviously jealous of Reiv's supposed relationship with Jensa, yet Reiv had never witnessed the two of them together until now. He had seen Lyal around, of course, and was well aware of the handsome Shell Seeker's charisma. Perhaps Reiv had turned a few girls' heads, but if Lyal happened to be anywhere around, the heads always swiveled from Reiv and instantly turned to Lyal.

"Who *are* you, anyway?" Reiv asked.

"You know full well who I am," Lyal practically shouted.

"No, fool. I mean who are you in relation to Jensa? I do not recall seeing you with her, nor do I recall her ever mentioning your name."

Lyal's face went blood red. "Why...she is my woman!"

"I am no such thing," Jensa said coolly. She turned to address Reiv. "Lyal and I knew each other for a short while, before you came to Meirla. But he is not the sort of man who can be with only one woman. I will have no man who cannot be faithful to me."

"Well, Lyal," Reiv said, "since I am acquainted with so many women, Jensa obviously would have no interest in the likes of me."

Lyal remained silent, sorting through the defense Reiv had tossed his way.

"There you have it," Jensa said. "The prince is too much of a ladies man for my taste."

Reiv felt like beaming, but he kept his expression in check. "I will not lie to you Lyal. I did find her attractive at first. But after seeing her every morning for that past several weeks, I can honestly say she no longer appeals to me."

Jensa shot Reiv a look, but he winked at her, aware that Lyal's eyes were turned momentarily elsewhere.

"Well," Reiv said with a pretended yawn, "if you will excuse me, I have some seeking to do. You know, with all this talk about women, perhaps I will do my seeking outside the waters today." He turned to leave, but paused to look back over his shoulder. "But if I see your hands on her again, Lyal, you will learn that my scarred fists are not as weak as you think."

As Reiv sauntered off, he could not help but replay his own snappy comeback. *After seeing her every morning I can honestly say she no longer appeals to me.* He laughed to himself, but then he thought of Jensa and how she truly looked in the morning. Her long, light brown hair would be a tumble of locks, and the thin dressing gown she wore would barely conceal her feminine curves.

He shook his head, trying to fling the image of Jensa from his mind. There could never be anything between them; he knew that. Besides, what about Alicine? She was the one he wanted—wasn't she? But Alicine was gone now, returned to Kirador and not likely to come back. It was true that Shell Seeker girls had expressed an interest in him, but Reiv had remained faithful to Alicine, just as he had been faithful to Cinnia before that. But saving himself for true love did not seem to be paying off. How long was he expected to wait?

He suddenly became aggravated at the state of his love life, or lack of it. Cinnia had abandoned him when his hands were burned, Alicine did not think him worth staying for, and Jensa thought him "the worst." Lyal and the others thought Reiv a man. But Reiv did not feel like a man at all. Right now he felt like a boy—a pure, stupid, inexperienced boy.

He marched on furiously, turning his anger toward the women who had rejected him, and funneling even more of it toward Lyal who had more than his share of partners. What made Lyal so special? Reiv wondered. The bastard was good looking enough, but that arrogance of his. It wasn't fair that girls turned their eyes from Reiv when that conceited rooster named Lyal strutted by. Maybe it was Lyal's confidence; he did have a confident walk. Perhaps Reiv could practice his walk...and his talk. Reiv ground his teeth. Women were so much work. Why were they so much work? Regardless, he would save himself no longer. He would be more like Lyal. He would strut and brag; he would be a rooster, whatever it took. Yes, he determined, he would have his way with the first girl that came along.

And then she came along.

Reiv recognized the young woman strolling toward him; she had commented to him once that she liked the kohl design he painted around his eyes. She wasn't beautiful, not the type he was normally drawn to, but at least she was female. And right now any female would do.

"Hello, Reiv," the girl chirped as she drew near.

He stopped, facing her, and smiled his most charming smile. But his charm evaporated in a hurry when he realized he did not remember her name. "Hello, um...hello."

"Cora," she said. "My name is Cora."

"Oh yes...of course...I knew that–Cora," he said.

He ran his eyes over her, assessing her features. She was an unusual looking girl, with a friendly, freckled face, and hair the color of straw. Her body was round and ample, especially her breasts, and Reiv found his attentions lingering on them for a moment.

"What are you staring at?" Cora asked, her expression indicating she knew full well what.

Reiv felt his face blush. "Nothing...I mean...sorry...I was just going to my hut. Would you like to—would you like to—" His words froze. Gods, was he insane?

"*Join* you?" she asked with a playful arch of her brow.

Reiv's heart raced. Yes, that was what he was going to say, but now that she had said it in his place, he could not help but wonder what she meant. Did she mean she wanted to join him, or join *with* him? And what if he misunderstood? The way the village gossiped about him, why, he would be a laughing stock. Reiv felt a case of nerves gurgle in his belly. "Would you like to see my bump?" he blurted.

"Your what?"

"My hump...I mean, my hut."

"Well, of the choices you've offered, I would have to go with the hut," Cora said.

*Take her to the hut. Just do it.* Reiv grabbed her hand, pulling her behind him as he marched on. Perhaps this really was going to be his lucky day. But as he headed in the planned direction, he realized he didn't have a hut to take her to. Not one to call his own, anyway. And what did he expect to do with her when he got her there? He didn't have a proper bed, but even if he did, there was little chance for privacy. Brina would be there, and probably

Torin with his second haul of the day. No, the most Reiv could hope to offer the girl was a mug of tepid tea.

"Reiv! Reiv!" Kerrik came bounding up, his hair wet and plastered against his head, his feet frosted with sand. He grinned and flipped a large pink shell into the air. A bag filled with even more was clenched in his other hand. "You'll not find one bigger than this, Reiv!" he said, beaming. "No sense in you even going out today."

Reiv's mind scattered to retrieve a response to the challenge (and prepare for a defense of his rushing along with Cora in hand.) But he had no time to respond before Kerrik asked, "Are you two heading to the hut?"

Reiv felt flustered. "Wha—I mean…uh…no, of course not," he stammered.

"We're not?" Cora asked, turning her eyes to Reiv. "I thought it was either the hut or the bump, and we chose the hut."

Kerrik laughed. "What do you mean, bump?"

"I'm not sure. Perhaps it is a Tearian term." Cora tilted her head. "What *did* you mean by bump exactly, Reiv?"

"I misspoke. That is all." Reiv felt his throat go dry.

"Well, I'm going to the hut whether you two are or not," Kerrik said. "I'm thirsty." He trenched up the sand toward home, leaving Reiv and Cora behind.

Reiv folded his arms and stared at his feet. Then he lifted his eyes to Cora, surprised to see amusement on her face. He studied her, realizing he had never really looked at her that closely before. She was not what a typical Tearian would consider attractive, but neither was she an ordinary girl. Her hair was bleached stiff with sun and salt water, and though an attempt had been made to pin it, it sprang from her scalp like a spiky sea urchin. Her eyebrows were white, and her eyes green…or were they blue? It was hard to tell; the color of them seemed to vacillate like the shades of the sea. And her figure, so round, so feminine, so…Reiv felt his stomach flutter and his groin ache. He hated to admit it, but he quite liked the look of the girl.

"Well," he said, glancing at Kerrik in the distance. "I suppose we could go somewhere else."

Cora sighed and shook her head. "I'm sorry, Reiv, but you're too beautiful."

"Thank you…I think," Reiv said awkwardly. He wasn't sure he should be thanking her at all; girls didn't usually say those things, did they?

"I have to be honest with you," Cora continued. "I do find you attractive, but there can be nothing between us."

"What do you mean?" he asked.

"I know what you were thinking when you grabbed my hand and started marching this direction. But all the while I was trying to think my way out of it."

"Think your way out of it? But you were the one that asked if you could join—"

"If you'll recall, that's not exactly how the conversation went, and if I understand things correctly, there is a big difference between a hut and a bump. You really meant to say "bump", didn't you?"

"No, of course not." Reiv suddenly felt confused. The girl was twisting this all around, or maybe it was him doing the twisting. He readied a quick defense. "You are mistaken, Cora. I was only taking you for tea. I knew my aunt would be there…and now Kerrik of course. I—"

Cora placed her fingers on his lips, silencing him. "Please, Reiv, do not try to explain. Thank you for inviting me, but I fear that for me you would just be a big shell."

"A big what?"

"Shell. A big shell, Reiv." Cora sighed again. "You and I are too different. You hunt for big shells, I hunt for small ones."

"I do not see the relevance in that distinction."

Cora pulled a necklace from around her neck and draped it around his. Then she kissed him on the cheek. "I'm sorry, Reiv, but it was not meant to be." She turned and walked away.

Reiv stared after her, his jaw slack. What had just happened here? What was not meant to be? And what was all this about him being a big shell? Was that better than being "the worst?" His skull ached. Gods, girls were so much trouble.

He headed home, but the image of Cora stayed with him. He fingered the shell necklace she had placed around his neck, and lifted it to take a look. There were spires of peach-colored cockles and fan-shaped shells as transparent as tiny fingernails. There were swirls the hues of the sea and starburst shapes the color of the sun. He grinned in spite of himself.

He entered the hut, muttering to no one in particular, and went about preparing a robust stew of mussels, shelled crab, and seaweed. Brina and Torin watched Reiv silently, the two of them obviously afraid to break the spell that had enchanted him. Finally Brina placed a hand on his forehead. "Are you feeling ill?" she asked. "You do not seem yourself."

"Very amusing," Reiv said as he tossed another handful of seaweed into the pot. "I am quite myself, thank you. Now, you just sit down and drink some tea. This will not take long to cook." He hung the pot on the spit over the fire pit and gave the stew a stir.

"I think Reiv's in love or something," Kerrik said. "He didn't even go in the water today. All because of that girl Cor-ra."

Torin's usually rigid face perked up. "What's that? Cora?" he said. "Buxom Cora?"

"Torin—please—the boy," Brina said, motioning her eyes in Kerrik's direction.

"What's wrong with buxom?" Kerrik asked.

"Nothing," Reiv said sharply. "And I will have no more talk of it in Cora's regard."

All went quiet.

Jensa swept through the drape and into the hut. She stopped, surveying the group that was now sitting in awkward silence, then turned her attention to Reiv who was pouring refills into mugs.

"What's going on?" she asked suspiciously. "Why is Reiv cooking?"

"Gods, you all act like you have never seen me cook before," Reiv said.

"We haven't," a round of voices replied.

"It seems a girl named Cora has left Reiv feeling somewhat domestic today," Torin said.

"A girl?" Jensa said, shocked. "But–but what about—" Reiv's eyes darted to hers.

"–Alicine?"

"Listen, I was with Cora barely any time at all. We spoke less than a dozen words. But even if I had brought her here and had my way with her—"

"Reiv please...not in front of Kerrik," Brina said.

Reiv's annoyance flared. "At the pace I am going, Kerrik will know the touch of a woman before I will!"

"He's right you know," Kerrik said. "There are plenty of girls who like me."

"See...even a seven-year-old has better luck with the women!" Reiv said. He threw the ladle into the pot, sending the stew splattering. "I am tired of being surrounded by people all the time. I was a royal...a prince accustomed to having his own room...then his own apartment. Now I live in a one room hut with four other people and I never have a moment's privacy!"

"What are you saying?" Brina asked, rising to face him.

"I am saying I want my own place!"

Reiv wheeled toward the doorway.

"Reiv!" Brina called after him.

But he continued on, determined not to listen to a word of protest, determined not to waste any energy arguing about it. He had plans to make, a hut of his own to build. But even more importantly, there was a girl named Cora to consider. She had tickled his senses and toyed with his mind; she had sent desires to the primitive regions of his body, then had simply walked away, calling him a big shell, or some such nonsense. He refused to accept her rejection or her excuses. Why should he? After all, he had been born a prince; he had even transcended to the gods. No, no girl would call him a big shell and get away with it. He could be as small as the next man. And he intended to prove it.

෴

# CHAPTER 10: GUILTY SECRETS

Reiv tromped across the sand in the direction of his only sanctuary, a calm inlet pool bordered by a semi-circular wall of glistening rocks and pocked coral. On the other side of it waves crashed, sending sprays of water fountaining into the air, then settling in fine mists upon the pool. It was the perfect place for Reiv to contemplate the problems of the world. For a while now he had been considering his future, or trying to, and this was the only private place he knew of. Kerrik had introduced him to it when Reiv had first arrived in Meirla. Back then, Reiv had been about as far from being a Shell Seeker as any person could be. As a prince, he'd had plenty of opportunities to swim, but in Tearia the pools were free of sea creatures, and you could always see your feet at the bottom. When Kerrik first took him to the pool to teach him to dive, it had been more than a little intimidating. There were crabs and fish, and salt water that stung his eyes and tasted bitter on his lips. Over time, Reiv grew to love the swift currents and dark recesses of the sea. But it was the calm of the pool that always drew him back.

As he approached, he heard voices followed by laughter just over the rise. The pool was on the other side of it, and he wondered if someone had dared make his private sanctuary their own. He crept to the top, crouching in an attempt to stay hidden from view. In an instant he spotted Cora, and he dropped to all fours. He crawled across the sand until he was safely concealed behind a large clump of shore grass.

Cora had been in Reiv's thoughts ever since his mind boggling conversation with her that morning. He'd seen her only once since then, and that had been from a carefully calculated distance. He was determined not to speak with her, yet there were a thousand things he wanted to say. He was not sure if he was performing the ritual properly—he had never played such games as a prince—but people usually wanted what they could not have, so he hoped his pretended disinterest would make her realize she had made a mistake in his regard. He and Alicine had acted out a similar version, but they'd never ignored each other entirely; circumstances had not allowed it. As he thought back on it now, he recalled how the romantic misunderstanding with Alicine had left him feeling like a fool. His cheeks burned at the recollection. He could ill afford to let that happen again—especially with Cora.

Reiv ground his teeth as he peeked over the rise toward the pool. What was he doing groveling in the sand like this? Where was his pride? Cora was just a girl, a girl like any other. But he knew that wasn't the reason he was hiding behind a clump of vegetation. That strutting rooster Lyal was with her, and Reiv felt the raging need to spy on them.

Cora was swimming in the pool, paddling slowly as she skimmed across the water. Lyal was on the shoreline, walking along it as he followed her from one side to the other. He said something to her, and she laughed and rolled onto her back, floating backwards. She was clothed, but even through the distance Reiv could see there was no real point in it; her peach-colored skin was clearly visible beneath her clingy attire. Reiv felt jealousy rise to his throat as he watched Lyal's lusty eyes roam over her. What right did that arrogant stud have to be in Reiv's place of solitude? What right did he have to look at Cora like that?

"That's not his sister, if that's what you're wondering," Torin's amused voice said.

Reiv jerked his head over his shoulder to see Torin towering behind him. "Shhhh! Get down," he whispered. "Do you want them to see you?"

Torin chuckled, but got down as instructed and lay on his belly next to Reiv. "What have I missed?"

"Nothing to miss."

"Why are we hiding then?"

"We are not hiding!"

Torin raised a brow. "So we are prone on the sand because...?"

Reiv scowled. "Fine. I saw Lyal arguing with Jensa this morning. I just wanted to see what he was up to. That is all."

"No interest in Cora, I suppose?"

"Of course not. Why should I care?"

"Because she's an attractive girl," Torin said. "You could do worse for a mate."

"I am not looking for a mate," Reiv snapped.

"I thought you wanted a hut of your own. Young Shell Seeker men normally stay with their families until they are ready to start one of their own. You are clearly thinking in that direction. I would suggest–"

"I do not think I need advice from a man who shows no interest in women," Reiv retorted.

"What is that supposed to mean?" Torin asked.

Reiv hesitated. Maybe he should not have said anything. It was Torin's business if his attentions did not turn in that direction. "Nothing. I have just never seen you with a girl, and you are attractive enough."

The veins in Torin's neck bulged. "Are you implying that I'm attracted to *men*?"

Reiv wished he had just kept his own mouth shut. "I am sorry—I did not mean to offend."

Torin leapt up, red-faced. "I have known the touch of a woman," he said heatedly. "Can you say the same?"

It was then Reiv's turn to leap up. "Gods, Torin! Do you want them to *hear* us?"

Torin leaned in threateningly. "Take back what you said."

Reiv glanced toward the pool, then back at Torin. "Fine, I retract my words. We will speak of it no more. Satisfied?" Torin spun and stormed away, leaving Reiv to stare after him.

Reiv's conscience scrambled for an excuse, but then he realized, perhaps he was wrong about Torin, but Torin sure wasn't wrong about him. He returned his attention to Cora and Lyal, but his mind was no longer on the subjects of his spying eyes. The argument with Torin was gnawing at him, and he couldn't help but cringe at the callousness of his own remarks. He and Torin already had an uneasy friendship, and this certainly wasn't going to help things any. Perhaps if he offered the man an apology, said it like he meant it. But he knew Torin's acceptance wasn't likely, at least not until Reiv had suffered enough.

Reiv plodded down the beach, rehearsing various versions of what he might say. Before long he found himself well past the village. He gazed out toward the horizon. The late afternoon sun was growing dim behind a bank of clouds moving in from the north. He sighed and turned back, then quickened his pace toward the icy reception he knew was awaiting him.

As Reiv approached the hut, he noticed Jensa and Torin arguing beneath a nearby palm. Their voices were rising and falling with obvious emotion, and for a moment Reiv wondered if it involved his earlier altercation with Torin. It occurred to him that maybe it had something to do with Dayn and Alicine; they had departed from Meirla over two weeks ago, and Reiv knew their journey to Kirador was a dangerous one. Could word of tragedy have filtered back so soon? Fear mushroomed in his throat as he hurried toward them. He dreaded whatever news there might be, but couldn't wait another moment before knowing it.

Torin did not see Reiv approaching; his face was buried in his fists.

"What is wrong?" Reiv asked upon reaching them. "It is not Dayn and Alicine, is it?"

Torin raised his eyes to him, and Reiv was shocked to realize they were red with tears.

"No, Reiv," Jensa said. "It's Farris. He's dying, and now Mya has fallen ill also."

"Gods," Reiv replied. His chest felt as if it had suffered a blow. Farris was only nine, a clever, inquisitive boy, and Mya's only son. Reiv had spent a brief time with them in Pobu, and now regretted the last words he'd said to the child had been a lie.

"What of Mya's girls?" Reiv asked.

"No sign of sickness in them yet," Jensa said. "Torin wants to go to them, but Nannaven will not have it."

"But why?" Reiv asked. "He could help look after them until…"

"Nannaven sent word that the fever is spreading. A messenger came bearing the news about Farris and Mya, but kept a safe distance. He was told not to come near the village. We need to call a clan meeting as soon as possible. Nannaven fears the sickness will spread to Meirla and wants travel between us to cease."

"Well, I don't care what she wants!" Torin said. "I will be at their sides no matter what she orders."

"You cannot risk yourself, Torin," Jensa said. "If Mya and Farris are ill, there is nothing you can do. Nannaven will take care of them until they are better."

"And if they don't get better?" Torin said.

"Of course they will," Reiv offered.

"How can you be certain?" Torin said. "Word is that people are dying in droves. The dead are being piled upon pyres." He shook his head. "No—I will be there for Mya and I will see that Farris is held in my arms before he is returned to the earth!"

Torin pivoted toward the hut, but Reiv grabbed him by an arm, stopping him short. "Torin, think what you are saying. Mya would not want you to risk yourself, not for her or for Farris."

Torin jerked his arm away. "My son is dying, Reiv. This may be the last chance I have to tell him I love him."

Reiv took a startled step back. "Your *son*?"

"Yes. My son. Will you keep me from him now?"

"No, of course not. I—I did not know."

"It is not something we speak of."

"What of Eben...did he know?" Reiv asked, wondering if Mya's recently deceased husband had been a willing participant in the deception.

New regret swept Torin's features. "Eben was a good father to Farris. That is all that matters." Then he turned and continued toward the hut.

"What about Kerrik?" Reiv asked, struggling to keep pace.

"He does not yet know about Farris, though he always suspected my affection for Mya"

"How is he going to handle you leaving like this?"

"He will understand," Torin said.

"Understand what?" Kerrik asked from the doorway.

Jensa rounded Torin to scoot Kerrik back inside. "Torin is taking a little trip to New Pobu," she said. "It is none of your concern."

But the boy would have nothing of it. He planted his feet in front of Torin, barring his path. "Why are you going, Torin? Why?"

"Nothing to worry about," Torin said.

"You must think I'm as stupid as a snail," Kerrik said.

Torin sidestepped him and headed to the trunk at the foot of his cot.

Kerrik followed him with crossed arms and a disgruntled face. "I'm a member of this family, too," he said. "Just because I'm seven doesn't mean I don't have a right to know if something's wrong."

"It can wait, Kerrik," Reiv said.

"You too?" Kerrik said. "You should be on my side."

"What side would that be?" Reiv asked.

"The side that says we're family and family shouldn't keep secrets from each other! I sure don't keep secrets from you, Reiv."

Brina swept into the room. "What is wrong?" she asked with alarm. "It is not Dayn, is it?"

"No, Brina, it is not Dayn," Reiv assured her.

Reiv turned his attention to Torin who was gathering up personal items and shoving them into a bag. "Torin... you may as well tell the boy. There is no way to keep it from him."

Torin paused, his back rigid. He tossed the bag onto the cot. "Very well," he said. "Farris is dying of the fever, Kerrik. And Mya is very ill. I'm going there to take care of them, and Nely and Gem."

"Farris...dying?" Kerrik's eyes filled with tears. "Will you get sick, too?"

"I have every intention of coming back safe and sound. Mya and Farris need a friend by their side, and Nely and Gem need someone to keep them safe. They are scared little girls right now. They have lost their Father, their brother is sick, and now their mother. Nannaven is old, Kerrik; she cannot handle them by herself."

"I don't see why you have to be the one to do it," Kerrik said. "Aren't there others who could help?"

"A lot of people are sick right now," Torin said.

"Then I'll come with you. And I'll help you make them well."

Torin pulled Kerrik into his arms and held him tight. "You are a brave warrior, little brother," he said, then released him. "But you cannot go with me."

Torin grabbed the bag, slid his short sword into the belt at his waist, and headed for the door. Once outside he stopped to say his goodbyes. He embraced Jensa and kissed her on the cheek, then did the same with Kerrik who was trying very hard to be brave.

Brina hugged Torin's neck. "Be safe," she said, "and please get word back to us if you can. We will not sleep a wink until you do."

"Torin," Reiv said, "take Gitta at least. She is swift and will get you there safely." He turned to fetch the horse, but Torin stopped him.

"No," Torin said. "I may not have time to see to her needs when I get there, and there is too much risk of her being stolen."

"But—"

"Listen, Reiv. I expect you to take care of things in my absence. If you need me, you will be glad to have the animal. I have traveled the road many times at night and on foot—you haven't. I want you to be able to reach me quickly if need be."

Reiv nodded reluctantly.

Torin disappeared up the path, leaving them all to pray for his safe return. But Reiv did not know if prayers would be enough; some things in life, and death, were already fated. He could only hope that this was not one of those things.

# CHAPTER 11: THE TORCH

Torin hustled up the dirt road, working to outstep the nightfall that would soon be upon him. The road between Meirla and the encampment could be treacherous for the unseasoned traveler; it wound unevenly throughout the hills between the city and the sea. But Torin was well-acquainted with its unpredictability—he had made the trip to Pobu often enough—and his legs were strong and his eyes keen. But on this day he was oblivious to the pits in the road, the occasional washed-out rut, and the sudden dips from the grooves of carts and wagons. For that matter, he was barely aware that he was putting one foot in front of the other.

He turned his focus from the dark corners of his mind toward the vivid colors of an evening sky. To the west, the horizon cast a golden glow that blended to shades of pink, then to the rich indigos of night. To the north, the direction he was heading, a blackening sky flashed an occasional white, revealing the approach of an early autumn storm. Torin quickened his pace, praying the lighting of the funeral pyres would not be hastened on account of it.

He turned his thoughts to Farris, and the surrounding landscape all but disappeared. It occurred to him that Farris could be on one of those pyres, his body just moments from the reach of a torch. An image of his son's laughing face blossomed in his mind, then dissolved into charred ruin. A groan escaped Torin's throat. "I won't let you down," he said. "Not this time."

But Torin knew he had let Farris down, many times. He recalled how Farris had often begged to go to Meirla with him. "Teach me to dive, Torin," he would say. "I want to be a Shell Seeker like you." But Torin had always refused him, insisting the boy's duty was to follow in his parents' footsteps and become a potter. Farris, however, had no interest in clay. He had other interests, and one of those was the sea, a place he had never been to but knew well from Torin's tales. *Why didn't I take you?* Torin lamented, but he knew the answer. There was too much risk that the truth would be revealed, too much risk that his own feelings would be laid bare for all to see.

Torin's and Farris's true relationship had been a carefully guarded secret, but the boy was the pride of Torin's heart, a secret he now regretted more than any other. Their resemblance to each other was undeniable, though Torin had at first tried very hard to deny it. Mya and Eben were fair-complected for Jecta, and Farris was tawny-skinned and black-haired like Torin. That in itself was not enough to call paternity into question, but as the boy grew older it was all too clear that his handsome features, as well as the telltale cock of his right eyebrow, were not traits he shared with Eben, but with Torin, his father's best friend. It was never spoken of between them, but there was no way Eben could not have known.

Torin swallowed the regret, but memories of the past clawed through him, tearing open old wounds. Eben and Torin had been friends since childhood, both having been orphaned at an early age. They, along with Torin's younger sister Jensa, and Mya, a girl they had met on the streets, were a ragtag group of urchins until Nannaven, the Spirit Keeper, took them in. They had grown up together, but over time Eben's and Torin's feelings for Mya evolved beyond friendship. There was jealousy and rivalry between them, each trying to separate the other from the object of their affection. But when an incident with a Tearian guard left Mya scarred, both boys united for her welfare and put their differences aside.

Torin was sixteen when he and Mya became lovers. But it did not seal their future together. Torin was prideful and quick tempered, and in a jealous fit at having seen her with Eben, packed his belongings and headed to Meirla. He had not really meant to stay there, had not intended to become a Shell Seeker. It was only an attempt to trick Mya into choosing a mate once and for all. And choose she did. But it was not him. Two months later she was married to Eben and blossoming with child.

Torin closed his eyes, trying to suppress the pain. There was nothing he could do about the past. Eben was dead, it was too late to make restitution with him, and now maybe Farris was as well. All Torin could do was hold his son for the first and last time; all he could do was beg Mya's forgiveness and promise to be at her side now and for always. He clung to the hope that it was all a mistake. Perhaps it was another child that was dying, not Farris. Perhaps it was another woman who lay ill, not Mya. He fabricated a scenario of arriving to find his loved ones safe and sound, of them laughing at his foolishness. But then reality bullied its way in, shoving hope aside, and he knew the fantasy was only that.

He reached the last rise. The encampment was just below him now; it would not be long before he knew. He hurried down the hillside, all the while scanning the landscape before him. Hundreds of campfires dotted the darkness, throwing orange glows upon a field of makeshift tents and the slow moving shapes of people working their way between them. Torin's eyes moved over the area as he sought a sign of familiarity. It had been too long since he had been there. How in the world was he going to find Mya and Farris in all this sameness?

The entire Jecta population lived in the encampment now, except for the Shell Seekers who lived on the coast. The first city of Pobu had been leveled during the earthquake weeks before. There had been a great battle between the Jecta and the Tearians that day, but the gods had sent their wrath and cut the fighting short. Torin knew the gods were wise; their vengeance had proved to be a blessing. The Jecta could never have hoped to defeat the Tearian Guard. Only the total destruction of the city of Tearia had given the Jecta freedom from their enslavement. Afterward, a peace treaty had been signed with Reiv's brother, Whyn, who was the King of Tearia. There was singing in the Jecta encampment then, and laughter and hope for a future. But now with the plague taking so many, Torin wondered if such joy would ever be felt again. He certainly did not think he would ever feel it.

On the hillsides beyond the encampment, great bonfires glowed in a semi-circular pattern. Pyres, Torin realized, though he had not expected to see so many. He whispered a prayer that his son was not amongst them. If only the gods would allow him time to tell Farris he loved him, to say it with Mya as witness, perhaps then he could find some forgiveness. But Torin knew that even if he reached Farris, it was probably too late. Farris was dying. Perhaps he was already dead. The thought filled him with anguish, and his mind scrambled for relief from the pain. He envisioned his own sword, pointed at his chest by his own hand, pressing through his ribs, piercing his heart, freeing him from his guilt. Only then would he be truly united with his son. Only then would he be able to say the words he never had the courage to say to him in this lifetime.

Torin felt tears of weakness prick his eyes, but he brushed them aside and lifted his chin. He could allow no one to see him like this. It was bad enough that Reiv had witnessed it, but here no one knew his frailties. He slid his usual stoic mask into place. Here he was Shell Seeker. And being Shell Seeker meant strength.

He wound his way into the encampment. It was nothing like he remembered. It was quiet now, except for somber voices and an occasional wail of grief. The faces staring back at him were haunted and dull, and the air no longer held the scent of venison roasting on spits. Now it held the stench of death. He glanced at the people he passed, ignoring their soft pleas and outstretched hands. There was no time to offer help or condolences—what could he do for them anyway? But it was hard to ignore the inner voice telling him to turn and run in the opposite direction.

"Torin!"

The voice spun him around, and he was relieved to see Nannaven hustling toward him. He smiled in greeting, but then the smile slipped from his face.

The old woman planted herself in front of him. "Gods, boy," she said. "I told you not to come. Why didn't you listen?"

"Where are Mya and Farris?" Torin asked, scanning the tents beyond her.

"You shouldn't have come. There's nothing you can do."

Torin felt a lump of dread. "Where are they, Nannaven?" he asked. "Please...tell me."

She sighed and shook her head. "Very well. What else can I do."

Torin followed as the Spirit Keeper turned and led him to a nearby tent, but when they reached the portal, he found himself immobile and staring at the canvas. It was as if it had become a wall of rock, and his common sense refused to walk him into it.

Nannaven pushed back the flap. "Did you expect it would be easy?" she said. "Go on now."

Torin pulled in a breath and ducked into the tent. The interior was warm and thick, and smelled of urine and sweat. A lantern hung in the center, its solitary flame casting a feeble glow.

Two little girls lying on pallets in the far corner sat up with a start. Nely and Gem stared wide-eyed at Torin. Nely, the youngest, began to cry.

"There, there," Nannaven said as she moved to her. "It's all right." She knelt and gathered the child into her arms. "It's Torin...come to check on you." She smiled and nodded at Torin. "You see? It's not the Torch...not the Torch."

Gem rose and shook her tiny fist. She was only five, but her determination seemed well beyond her years. "I will kill the Torch," she said defiantly. "I will kill him with my knife."

"Hush, now," Nannaven said to her. "Do you want to scare your little sister?"

"What's this talk of the Torch?" Torin said to Gem. "You're too little to concern yourself with such things." His eyes moved over the room toward a pallet where he could see Mya. Her eyes were closed, and her breathing was slow and labored.

"I'm not too little!" Gem shouted, drawing Torin's attention back to her. "The Torch will try to burn Farris, but I won't let him!"

"Farris…," Torin whispered. His eyes shot to a nearby blanket, and he instantly recognized the form beneath it. He rushed over and reached down to throw back the cover.

"Torin—no," Nannaven said. But it was too late.

Nely buried her face in the old woman's shoulder, but Gem marched over to Torin's side.

Nannaven rose and moved to usher her back. "Come, Gem," she said softly. "Torin needs to say his goodbyes."

Gem took a step toward Nannaven, then turned to Torin and said, "Don't let the Torch take him, Torin. Don't you dare."

"Never, Gem. I promise," he replied.

Torin stared at Farris as though in a dream. He searched the boy's face for a sign of life, but it was gray and still. He knelt and ran his thumb over Farris's pale lips, then along his eyelids and brows. "What a fine man you would have been," he said. He placed his palm on the boy's chest, determined to feel it rise and fall. But there was nothing.

Torin shook his head in disbelief. "This cannot be."

The world came crashing down around him. Everything became a blur. Torin pulled Farris into his arms, sobbing like no man had ever sobbed before. "Give him back to me!" he cried to the gods. "Give my son back to me!" But the gods had already taken possession of the child's soul, and there would be no returning it.

"Torin," a voice croaked.

Torin turned to Mya, who was now awake.

He rose with Farris still in his arms and moved to her side, then laid Farris next to her and settled beside them. He smoothed back Farris's hair. "You are my son," he said to him.

"He loved you," Mya whispered. "Very much."

"And I him." Torin moved his gaze to Mya. "I love you, too. You know that, don't you?" He leaned over and gathered her face into his hands, then brushed his lips against hers. It was the kiss of death, he knew, but it no longer mattered to him. Death would be welcome if it took him to that place where Mya and Farris would soon be dwelling.

Their lips parted. "Torin," Mya said. "Please, no." Tears spilled down her cheeks.

"You are my heart, Mya," Torin said. "Now and for always." He drew her into his arms and held her close, the heat of her body radiating through his, the salty taste of her sweat lingering on his lips.

Suddenly there was loud shouting outside the tent, and the rise and fall of shadows darting past it. Screams rent the air; the sound of horses thundered in the distance. Torin eased Mya back onto the pallet, then rose and rushed toward the exit.

He glanced back at Nannaven who was still standing with the girls at the far side of the tent. "Stay here," he ordered. He stepped through the flap and surveyed the commotion going on around him. People were screaming, running, and pushing, but no one seemed to know where they were going. In the distance a fiery glow filled the night sky. Darks silhouettes of horses and riders flashed across flickering palettes of orange.

Torin grabbed a man running past and stopped him short. "What's happening?" he asked.

"Guards!" the man said, trying to catch his breath. "The King's guards!" Then he pulled from Torin's grasp and stumbled into the thickening crowd.

An explosion of thunder reverberated through the air. Lightning crackled like skeletal fingers across an ebony sky. Torin's eyes shot upward, then toward the bonfires that dotted the distant hills. A line of torch fires could be seen snaking from the pyres toward the encampment, winding like an iridescent serpent around its perimeter.

Guards on horseback lumbered between the rows of tents, their long swords cutting a bloody swath through the crowd. Others, torch in hand, followed behind, igniting tent after tent into billowing flames.

A whir of arrows sounded overhead, their sinister shapes all but invisible in the darkness. One *thunked* an inch from Torin's foot. He jumped back as more sailed across the sky.

Torin realized the Guard were drawing near, their torches and weapons just moments away. He pulled his short sword from his waistband and rushed toward the advancing soldiers. The arrow-riddled bodies of men, women, and children littered the ground, but he leapt over them without hesitation. A guard on foot barreled in his direction. Torin sank his sword into the man's chest then shoved him aside. Two more moved in, but Torin stopped them with a shout and a determined swipe of his blade. Others approached, but Torin aimed his weapon, daring any man to come nearer.

The guards continued toward him. Torin backed away slowly, keeping his blade ready. The line of soldiers stared at him with steely expressions, but their smirks were nothing compared to that of the horseman riding toward him through a swirl of lurid smoke.

The young man on horseback was no guard. His clothing was pale and fine, not dark and metallic like the Guard, and the color of his hair and the shine of the glitter painted around his eyes were as bright as the mid-day sun. But his eyes bore no warmth. They were icy blue and cold as the deepest sea, and seemed in such contrast to the boyish features of his face.

Torin drew a sharp breath. "Whyn!"

The young man barked for the guards to stop their approach and urged his black stallion to the front of the line. "Well, we meet again," the young King said as he looked Torin up and down. "Torin, isn't it?"

Torin stared at him in silence.

"I believe the last time we met you were at my table, signing a...what did we call it...peace treaty?" Whyn laughed.

"Why are you doing this?" Torin asked angrily. "The Jecta have done nothing to you."

Whyn's pale eyes flashed crimson. In that moment Torin realized he was not looking at the same young King he'd met at the negotiating table. That king had been beaten and vulnerable. This one was fiendish and cruel, armed with sword and bow, yet strangely feminine in his persona.

Whyn tossed his blond head. The gold painted around his eyes and upon his lips glinted in the fiery darkness. "Ah, Torin...of course they have done something. They have brought impurities to our door, and now they must be purged."

"What do you mean, *purged*?"

Whyn nudged his horse closer. He glared down at Torin. "You know of what I speak. It is impurity that has brought sickness to our land. It must be stopped before it reaches those not deserving of it."

"So you would kill *innocents* for the sake of your own?" Torin exclaimed.

"Of course. The gods demand it."

"Whose gods?"

"*My* gods! The only gods!" Whyn snapped. Then he smiled and glanced around. "Is my brother with you?"

"No," Torin replied. He stepped back, his weapon still raised.

Whyn looked toward the tent at Torin's back. He motioned to a guard. "Let us see what the Shell Seeker is trying so hard to defend."

A guard swept a blade to Torin's throat before he could react. Torin lowered his weapon slowly as his eyes darted amongst the guards. One snatched the short sword from his hand and tossed it aside. Another threw back the flap to the tent and thrust his torch-bearing hand inside.

In the flickering light, Nannaven stood with her arms around Nely and Gem. Mya lay in the shadows, embracing Farris's body, her eyes white with fear.

"There is no one here of concern to you," Torin said.

"Is that so?" Whyn threw an order to the guard who was holding the torch. "Bring the old woman out...and the girls."

The guard did as instructed, dragging out Nannaven and the little girls who were still clinging to her skirts.

Gem pushed away from the Spirit Keeper, clenching her fist at Whyn. "You leave us alone!" she cried.

Nannaven pulled Gem back. "Hush, child," she commanded. "You hush now."

Whyn eyed Gem up and down. "Is this your woman, Torin? Or is it the old crone?" He laughed. "My, but your taste does run in opposite directions."

Torin took a threatening step toward Whyn, but a guard stopped him short. He glanced into the tent.

Whyn followed Torin's gaze. "Ah, my mistake," he said. "Clearly that is where your affections lie. Was the boy yours?" He shook his head. "Pity."

"What do you want?" Torin demanded.

"What do you think? I want Tearia brought back to her grandeur and the impure ones wiped out once and for all."

"You're insane," Torin said.

"Perhaps, but that is not relevant. I have the Lion on my side and you have, well, nothing."

"We have the Unnamed One, and the Transcendor!" Torin said, though he knew the Unnamed One had returned to Kirador and would not likely be back.

"Do not bore me with your myths." Whyn turned his attention to Nannaven. "Guard, bring the old woman closer."

Nely and Gem were yanked from her grasp, and Nannaven was shoved before Whyn.

"You are a Memory Keeper," Whyn said.

Nannaven did not respond.

"Your silence does not hide the truth. I met another of your kind not so long ago. Tenzy I believe her name was."

Nannaven stiffened.

"You knew her then," Whyn said.

"She was my sister," Nannaven said. "She defeated your Priestess, I believe."

Whyn's face seemed to morph momentarily into that of a woman, beautiful, yet sinister. "The Priestess cannot be defeated," he said. "She is eternal."

"Where is she then?" Nannaven asked.

"She is here…in me."

Nannaven scoffed. "I see no Priestess here. Only a boy who has confused his identity with that of a woman. If the Priestess has a future, then I fear that you, Whyn, do not."

"You are in no position to speak of futures, old woman." Whyn whipped his sword from its sheath so quickly that Nannaven had no time to flinch. He plunged the blade into her belly as she gasped in disbelief.

Nannaven ran her eyes over the golden lion at the sword's hilt, then over the blade as it was pulled slowly from her gut. She lifted her fading gaze to Whyn's face. Blood dribbled from her mouth as she spoke. "You may have taken my life," she said, "but there will be another to take my place." She fell to the ground, dead, but her words lingered in the air.

"Nannaven!" Torin screamed. He reeled toward her, but soldiers grabbed his arms and dragged him back.

Whyn flicked his hand toward a guard. "It is time for this place to be purified," he said. The guard stepped forward and handed Whyn a torch.

"No!" Torin cried.

Whyn eyed him, then glanced from the girls to the tent. "Very well.  I will give you a choice." He pointed the sword toward Nely and Gem with one hand, the torch toward Mya and Farris with the other. "What will it be, Shell Seeker? The living? Or the dead?"

Torin's heart pounded. "Wh—what?"

"You heard me. Choose."

"You are letting us go?"

"Only you, and the two you feel worth saving. Who will it be, I wonder? The girls...or the corpses?"

Torin looked to the tent, then back at Whyn. "But Mya is not dead," he said.

"She will be. Now make your choice. My patience wears thin."

Torin glanced between the two small girls cowering in the grasp of the guards, then at the forms of Mya and Farris in the far reaches of the tent. His mind raced. "I can't—I—"

"Choose!" Whyn shouted.

Torin thought the contents of his stomach would spill into the dirt. He stepped slowly toward the girls.

The guards let go their hold, and Nely and Gem ran to him. Torin gathered them up into his arms, but his limbs were so weak he did not know how he could hold them, much less carry them to safety. Tears filled his eyes and shame filled his heart. But the sorrow of what he was doing to Mya and Farris filled him even more.

Whyn smirked. "Now, Shell Seeker, you may cart your rubbish back to Meirla. When you get there, give my brother a message. Tell Reiv I expect him to leave Tearia once and for all."

"Leave? But where would he go?"

"I do not care, but he has three days time in which to do it."

"But if I return to Meirla, I risk spreading the fever."

"It is too late for that," Whyn said. He waved his hand toward the south. "You see? The rabble is running in that direction as we speak. They will likely reach Meirla before you do. How unfortunate. Regardless, if you wish to see the sea again, or anything else for that matter, I suggest you run."

A chill raced down Torin's spine, telling him to flee, but strangely his feet refused to obey.

Whyn narrowed his eyes. "Perhaps some incentive then." He tossed the torch into the tent. More guards surrounded it, their flames pressed to the canvas.

"No!" Torin screamed. He made a move toward the tent, but a line of guards blocked his path.

Whyn removed his bow from his shoulder, then slid a gold-tipped arrow from the quiver hanging at his back. He notched the arrow and pulled it back slowly, aiming it at Torin. "I suggest you run, shell-rabbit," he said with a grin.

Torin spun before he could think what he was doing. With a girl in each arm, he dug his toes into the dirt and pushed his legs forward. Nely and Gem pressed their knees into his sides and clung to his neck, screaming in high-pitched terror. But before he had gone any distance at all, a pain as hot as fire tore through his back. He staggered, and looked down to see the tip of an arrow protruding from his shoulder. Blood spilled down his chest, smearing the legs of the girls still pinned to him.

"I suggest you run faster," Whyn's voice shouted after him.

Then Torin heard the clank of the black stallion's harness, and the pounding of its hooves as Whyn commanded it forward. Gem began to struggle, sending a burst of pain radiating down Torin's arm. "He's coming!" she shrieked.

Torin grimaced, but dared not look back. He tightened his hold on the wriggling girl and ran as best he could, but his speed was nowhere fast enough. For a moment he thought to give up. He could not hope to outpace Whyn who was now on the hunt. Would it not be better to stand and fight, regardless of the outcome? The loves of his life were gone and his pride all but demolished. What did he have to live for?

But then he realized he still had Nely and Gem, and he couldn't let them down, not like he had Farris and Mya. If he saved the girls, then Mya could live on—in them—with him. He summoned every ounce of strength he could muster and pushed on harder. But as fast as he was running, he could not shake the stallion at his back, nor the taunting words of its rider: "Run, rabbit. Run."

Gem continued to struggle, and Torin felt certain he would lose his grip on her. He barely had the strength to hold the girls, much less run with them. Why was Gem fighting him so? She cried out, and Torin felt the hot breath of the horse at his back. He changed direction and dodged between two tents, barely navigating a heap of flaming debris.

He stumbled into the main corridor of the encampment and slid to a halt. People were running all around him, shouting and shoving and blocking his path. Which way? Which way? Dozens of eyes darted in his direction, then turned as one to stare beyond where he stood. People screamed as the crowd scattered in various directions, leaving Torin standing in the emptiness of their wake. The clank of a horse's bridle sounded at his back. He slowly turned his head. The sky exploded like a thousand drums. But it was the sight of Whyn that sent a start to Torin's heart.

"Ah, there you are," Whyn said with amusement. "I thought you would be better sport."

Torin turned and ran. One by one bodies dropped around him. One by one tents burst into flames. Guards approached from every direction, some on foot, others on horseback. Torin managed to outmaneuver them, but he could not evade Whyn who was not far behind. He veered into a passageway too narrow for any horse to navigate. When he reached the end of it, he deviated in yet another direction. His eyes darted back and forth, expecting to see Whyn around every corner.

Torin wasn't sure where he was or which way to turn; he only knew that he had to escape the encampment. A flash of lightening illuminated the landscape, just long enough for him to gain his bearings. Then his hopes lifted. The last row of tents was just ahead. If he could make it to the foothills beyond, perhaps he could hide the girls and find refuge from Whyn.

Torin sprinted past the perimeter and up the hillside, struggling to keep his footing on an increasingly slick terrain. The landscape had become a blur of rain, and the steep incline of the hill felt treacherous beneath his feet. As Torin plunged deeper into its shadows, he risked a glance back. The orange glows within the camp were turning to steamy hues of gray. Even the screams of the people were growing more and more distant.

Torin clambered up the slope, his lungs laboring so hard he felt certain they would burst. His arm and shoulder screamed with pain, and his legs were all but numb. He honestly did not know how he was moving them; they no longer seemed under his control.

The girls were quiet and still in his arms; even Gem no longer struggled. He glanced down to see their faces buried in his neck. "Almost there," he said. "Almost—" But before he could say another word, something *thunked* into his back, throwing him forward. The girls tumbled from his arms, and Torin plummeted to the ground.

Torin lay there, sprawled in the mud, unable to move, unable to think. All he was aware of was the air dragging in and out of his chest and the sound of the rain pelting the ground around him.

His pulse began to beat a rhythm in his ears, playing in unison with the wheezing of his lungs. Their tempos raced then gradually slowed, until at last they seemed to stop altogether.

Torin was not sure which sound gave out first, the beating of his heart or the rasping of his lungs, but he no longer cared. All went quiet as the world plunged into darkness, and Torin gladly followed it there.

∽

# CHAPTER 12: CONCERNS OF THE WORLD

Reiv bolted upright, his heart hammering in his throat. He scanned the room, seeking any sign of an intruder. But the only movement he saw was the moonlight flickering through the drape. He turned his gaze to Kerrik sleeping nearby. Perhaps the boy had been talking in his sleep; Kerrik's nighttime ramblings did frequently wake the household. But no, Kerrik was quiet and his breathing steady and slow. Reiv relaxed, deciding whatever had startled him from his pillow must have been a dream. But he rose from his bedding nonetheless.

He tiptoed past Kerrik, then toward Brina and Jensa. A cool breeze tinkled through the drape in the doorway, sending a melody of cockles and the scent of rain into the room. Reiv turned his attention to the shells. Perhaps that was it, the drape. But then a horrible vision stole into his consciousness, and he knew it had been neither dream nor drape.

He moved to Jensa's bedside and shook her shoulder. "Jensa…wake up," he whispered.

"Wha–?" she mumbled. She swept a mass of curls from her forehead and squinted up at him.

"I think Torin is in trouble."

Jensa threw her legs over the edge of the bed and rose. "What—what are you talking about?"

"Something has happened," Reiv said. He turned and reached for his tunic and pulled it over his head.

Brina, now awake, sprang to her feet. "What is it?"

"I am leaving to find Torin," Reiv replied.

"What? Why?"

"He may be injured."

"*Injured?*"

Jensa clutched Reiv's arm. "How can you know this?"

Reiv eased his arm from her grasp and secured his belt around his waist. He turned his attention back to Brina. "Fetch Gitta for me, will you?"

Raindrops began to pelt the hut. Brina grabbed her shawl and pulled it over her head, then raced out the door.

"I'm going with you," Kerrik declared.

Reiv turned to face him. He hadn't realized the boy was awake, and cursed himself for not having handled the situation more covertly.

"Back to bed, sprite," Reiv said. "I will be back soon."

"No," Kerrik said, and threw off the covers. He scrambled up. "I have a right; he's *my* brother."

"You're not going, Kerrik," Jensa said firmly. "Reiv can handle this on his own."

"Jensa is right," Reiv said. "Gitta will get there more swiftly with only one rider."

Kerrik stomped his foot. "I'm tired of being treated like a baby."

"You're not being treated like a baby," Jensa said. "Brina and I aren't going either, now are we?" She handed Reiv a pouch of water, then another containing herbs and assorted medicinals.

Reiv rushed outside to find Brina waiting with the horse. There was no saddle on its back, but Reiv rarely felt the need for one. He leapt onto its back and grabbed hold of its mane. "Jensa, call the clan together—tonight," he said. "Something is afoot."

"What do you mean?" she asked anxiously.

"I saw things," Reiv said, "during my Transcension, things I never wished to see, things I have tried to deny. This is one of them." He nudged the horse and turned it toward the road. The rain began to come down harder. "The perimeters must be watched," he said over his shoulder. "No one can be allowed in. And the healers must be prepared."

"I will notify them," Brina said.

Reiv looked down at Kerrik, now standing beside the horse. "No worries, sprite," he said. "Torin will be fine."

"I'll hold you to that," Kerrik said. And Reiv knew he meant it.

Reiv set his jaw, then kicked in his heels and sped off into the night.

∽

# CHAPTER 13: MUDDY WATERS

Reiv reared his horse to a halt and studied the thick bank of fog creeping up the hillside below. The rain had stopped, but the downward slope of the road was steep and slippery with mud. The horse snorted and shook her head, flinging a spray of wet mane. "Whoa there, girl," Reiv said. "I'm soaked through as it is." He leaned down and patted her neck, then took stock of the descent. One misstep and the horse could be lamed and Reiv tossed into the mud.

He urged the horse down cautiously, guiding her as best he could, halting when her pace became too confident. At last she reached the base of the hill, but a dark shadow shifted in the fog, diverting Reiv's attention.

"Who is there?" Reiv called, but he was met by only silence. He prodded the horse onward a few more steps. The fog shifted again as the shadow crept closer.

"Halt," Reiv said. "State your name."

"State your own name first," a man's voice replied.

Reiv resented the stranger's tone, but there was no time to challenge it. "I am Reiv, come from Meirla, seeking a friend. He was headed to New Pobu earlier this evening."

An old man, soaked though and muddied with soot, emerged from the shadows. A woman cowered at his back. "If your friend made it there," the man said, "you'll be lucky to see 'em again."

"What do you mean? What has happened?"

"The King's what happened. Burned down the encampment and killed just about everyone in it. Some of us made it. Some of us didn't." He nodded his head toward the woman. "We were lucky I reckon."

"Have you seen others out this way?" Reiv asked. "My friend is a Shell Seeker. Torin—you might know of him."

"Shell Seeker you say? Aye, I know of him. The King himself was after him." The man spat into the mud, then eyed Reiv darkly. "Tearian filth," he said, but whether the remark was intended for Reiv or the King, it was hard to tell.

"Where did you last see him?" Reiv demanded. He moved Gitta closer. "Tell me!" Suddenly he noticed a shell necklace draped around the man's neck. Reiv leapt from the horse and whipped his dirk from its sheath. He grabbed the man by the tunic and pressed the blade beneath his quivering chin. "I said, where did you last see the Shell Seeker!"

The man's eyes went wide with fright. He flicked them toward the road. "Back a ways…off the main road."

Reiv gripped the necklace in his fist. "He gave you this?"

The man flinched, but remained silent.

Reiv tightened his grip. "I said, he *gave* you this?"

"In a manner of speakin'," the man croaked. "He'll have no more need of it."

Reiv yanked the necklace from the man's neck, breaking the leather strand and sending shells flying. He flung the rest of it into the mud, then sprang onto Gitta's back. "You had best not show your face around me again, old man," Reiv said. "I will not soon forget it!" Then he kicked in his heels and urged the horse in the direction the man had indicated.

Reiv quickened his pace, careful not to lead the horse into danger, but equally determined to find Torin and soon. Before long he noticed more bedraggled people making their way along the road. With each and every one, he stopped to inquire if they had seen a Shell Seeker. But no one had and quickly warned him against traveling any closer to the encampment. In response, Reiv advised them against traveling closer to Meirla, but they continued on, oblivious to his words. Had he had more time, he would have tried to reason with them, but as it was, he feared it was already too late.

Recalling what the man had said about Torin not being on the main road, Reiv turned off and picked his way along the rocky hillside. He saw no movement, but the moon was barely a glow in the sky. The clouds had yet to move on, leaving his vision minimal at best. Reiv grew impatient. "I will never find him at this rate," he muttered. "Torin!" he shouted. "If you are out there, make a noise—anything." He stopped and listened. Nothing. He urged the horse on slowly, then stopped again. "Torin!"

A sound of whimpering wafted toward him. He guided the horse, straining his ears to determine its location. The sobs grew louder, until at last he spotted a pale-haired child huddled near the bushes.

Reiv dismounted his horse, but before he could reach the girl, another leapt in his path, pointing a stick in his direction. Her hair was dark and her eyes wild. "You stay away!" she shouted. "You stay away from us!"

Reiv held his hands up in conciliation. "I mean you no harm, girl. I am only here to help. See...no weapon." He moved closer, then stopped. *"Gem?"*

She thrust the stick at him "Stay back."

"It is me—Reiv. Remember? Your mother tended me when—"

"I remember. You're the Tearian one."

"I am only Reiv, Gem," he said, realizing the hatred in her voice. "Not Tearian."

"Yes you are," she said defiantly. "You're like the one who killed my mother. He killed my mother, and he killed Nannaven, too!"

"Nannaven?" Reiv whispered. "Gods, no." He glanced at Nely still huddled to the side, then turned his attention back to Gem. "Where is Torin, Gem? If I am to help him you must tell me."

"No!"

Reiv rushed forward, yanked the stick from her hand, and tossed it aside. She pummeled him with her fists, but he grabbed her by the wrists, pulling her feet from the ground. She writhed and kicked until at last he released her, letting her fall onto her back. "No more, Gem! You hear me? No more!" He jerked her up by an arm. "Where is Torin?"

Tears of anger welled in Gem's eyes, then tears of defeat. She worked her arm from his grasp. "In the mud."

"Where? Show me."

Gem pointed a finger beyond Nely. "Over there."

Reiv dashed past her and discovered Torin face down. He dropped to his knees beside him. Two arrows were protruding from the man's shoulder and back. Blood-colored streams of water ran alongside him. Reiv pressed an ear to Torin's back. *Still breathing.* He shifted his attention to the shafts of the arrows and immediately recognized the royal mark. "Gods, Whyn…what have you done?" He turned his head toward the girls. "Gem," he barked, "get the pouch off the horse."

She moved to do what she was told, but was too small to reach.

Reiv rose and hurried to retrieve it. "Keep an eye on your sister. It is best you do not see this."

"I'm not scared," she declared.

Reiv pulled in a steadying breath; there was no time to deal with a headstrong child. "Of course not. But Nely is, so do as I say."

Gem stared past him, her eyes focused on Torin.

"Do not worry," Reiv said. "I will help him, and when he is well again, I will tell him how you fought to protect him. You have been very brave, but you must be brave a little longer. And right now the bravest thing you can do is stay out of my way and help your sister."

Gem nodded, then scrambled over to Nely. She sat beside her and wrapped the little girl in her arms. "It's all right, Nely," she said. "I'm here."

Reiv returned to Torin, at a complete loss as to what to do. "Agneis, help me," he muttered. "I know little of such things." But a goddess would not likely help him in this; he would have to depend on his own instincts. He scraped the mud from around Torin's mouth and nostrils, making sure the man's breathing, shallow as it was, was unobstructed. He then searched the pouch that Jensa had sent with him, finding strips of cloth, herbs, and a small bottle of liquid. Reiv opened the bottle and sniffed. Definitely not to be taken orally.

Blood pooled around Reiv's knees. *You have to stop the bleeding*, he realized. He pulled out the cloths, intent on pressing them against Torin's wounds, but then he wondered if he should extract the arrows first. He examined the shafts to determine how deeply they were embedded. They were deep—too deep. If he tried to remove them, the damage he caused would probably be worse than it already was.

Reiv felt a lump rise in his throat. "I do not know what to do!" he said. *Correct, fool. So do what you can and get him back to Meirla.* Resolved to do his best, Reiv took hold of the arrows, one at a time, and carefully snapped the shafts, leaving a shorter portion protruding from Torin's back. He then poured the mysterious liquid onto the wounds and pressed the cloths to them. He rose. "Gitta, come!" he said, and the horse came forward.

Reiv eyed Torin, then the horse. How in the world was he going to get an unconscious man onto the animal's back?

Gem rose and came toward him. "I can help," she said. "I'm strong."

Reiv looked at her with skepticism, but agreed. "Let me get the horse situated first. Then you can help me drag Torin onto her."

He positioned Gitta as close to Torin as he could, then attempted to get her to kneel. But the horse refused to cooperate.

Gem grabbed up a stick and slapped the back of the horse's front legs. "Down, horse!" she ordered.

Gitta struggled to her knees, then rolled slightly onto her side. Reiv would have laughed if the situation had not been so serious.

Between the two of them, Reiv and Gem managed to drag Torin onto the horse's back. Gitta scrambled to her feet, nearly tossing Torin off. Reiv held onto the Shell Seeker as best he could, maneuvering Torin's body until at last his arms and legs were evenly distributed on either side.

"Get your sister, Gem," Reiv said. "Time to go."

"Where are we going?" she asked.

"Meirla. There are people there better equipped to help than I am here."

"Will I see Kerrik?"

"Kerrik will be there."

"Good." A smile formed on Gem's face. "He's going to marry me, you know." Then she charged around the horse to lead the way.

꙾

# CHAPTER 14: OPEN WOUNDS

The return trip to Meirla was agonizingly slow. It had begun to rain again, and the road was becoming increasingly mired in mud. Torin, an arm and leg dangling over each side of the horse, his cheek pressed against Gitta's mane, frequently groaned and mumbled. Gem marched ahead of the horse, her pace like that of someone on a mission. Reiv walked behind her, keeping his eye on her as well as Torin, and holding fast to Nely's hand.

The closer they got to Meirla, the more refugees they met along the road. Many appeared ill, which was of grave concern, but Reiv knew there was no way to stop them. He could only hope that the Shell Seekers had made some sort of preparation for the Jectas' arrival, a separate encampment perhaps.

Their advancement slowed, then stopped. People were milling around, some clustered in groups in the middle of the road, others huddled off to the side.

"Why the delay?" Reiv asked two women standing nearby.

"The Shell Seekers have instructed us to wait while they find us accommodations," one of them said.

Reiv nodded, praying it meant none of the refugees had yet made it into the village. He led Gitta onward, weaving slowly through the crowd. The sun was just beginning to rise along the distant horizon. Clouds were tinted here and there with shades of peach filtering through the gray. As Reiv guided Gitta and the girls through the mob, heads turned to watch as they passed. Mutters were followed by hushed whispers, leaving Reiv with the sinking feeling that he was involved in this more than he knew.

At last they reached the crest of a hill and stopped at the outer edge of the crowd. Down the road a line of Shell Seeker men could be seen keeping guard, no doubt posted to prevent anyone from reaching Meirla. Several Shell Seeker women hustled back and forth, depositing bundles of food and gourds of water onto the road between the guards and the refugees. Jecta scurried to retrieve the bundles, then hurried back to transfer the supplies into outstretched hands.

Reiv pushed through the perimeter of the crowd, but stopped before he had gone more than a few steps. He called across the distance, "You there, Shell Seekers. I must get a message to Jensa of your village."

One of the Shell Seekers took a step forward, squinting at him. "Is that you Reiv?"

"Yes. I have Torin with me. He is wounded. Can you fetch Jensa?"

The Shell Seeker waved a hand, then took off in the opposite direction. Reiv turned to Torin and peeked under the bandages. The bleeding had stopped, but the rain had washed it in rivulets down Torin's arms and along his spine, staining his skin and the material wrapped around his hips. The broken shafts of the arrows still protruded from his back. Around them the flesh was puffy and inflamed.

"Gods," Reiv said.

Torin's eyes fluttered. His head jerked as he attempted to move.

Reiv placed a hand on his arm. "Be still now. Help is coming." Reiv glanced over his shoulder. Where in the world was Jensa?

"Reiv!" Jensa's voice spun him around. She was running toward him, oblivious to the Shell Seeker guards who were scrambling to stop her.

Reiv took several strides forward and raised his hand. "Stop!" he commanded.

Jensa halted, panting. "But, Reiv—"

"Torin needs a healer," he called to her, "but you cannot come any nearer. What plans have been made for the wounded?"

"The healers are tending the worst cases," she called back. "An encampment is being set up nearby, but we didn't have enough time—"

"More wounded are coming. Can you direct me and those with the most life-threatening injuries first? As for those with the fever…perhaps a separate ward could be arranged for them. Are there any volunteers to help?"

"A few," Jensa said.

"I suppose you are included in that count."

"I am now."

"What about Kerrik?"

"Brina will look after him."

"So you would risk Kerrik losing both you and Torin? No. You cannot come here."

"Torin is my brother," she insisted. "I cannot ask any-one else to tend my kin when I am perfectly able."

"You do not have to ask," a voice said from behind her. "I will do it."

Jensa wheeled around. It was Cora, and in her hand was a basket of supplies.

Reiv could hear Jensa and Cora arguing, but he could barely make out their words. Their voices rose and fell as their hands gestured in the air, until at last they grew silent. Jensa turned back to face him. "Cora will do it," she said, but she did not look happy about it.

Cora stepped around Jensa and marched up the hill. As she approached, Reiv studied her face, hoping she would acknowledge him in some special way. But when she arrived, she only had eyes for Torin. She brushed past Reiv and headed straight for the horse. Torin's face was turned toward her. His eyes were closed and his breathing labored. Cora placed her hand on his forehead, then frowned at the shafts protruding from his back. Standing on tiptoes, she rested her cheek against his. "I will take care of you," she said gently. And it was then that Reiv knew: It was Torin she would have liked to have spent time with in the hut that day, not him.

"This way," she said, and led the horse away from the group. Reiv took Nely's hand while, once again, Gem tromped ahead like an alpha leading the pack.

Reiv turned toward Jensa. "Torin will be all right," he called to her. "I will get word to you soon."

Jensa raised her hand in acknowledgment, but she did not turn away. She watched until Reiv was over the hill and out of sight.

Beyond the rise was a small encampment. Barely put together, its makeshift tents, pallets, and supply areas were still being hastily assembled. Cora pointed Gem to the nearest empty tent.

"At least we'll have shelter," Cora said, eyeing a sky still heavy with rain clouds. "But I fear there won't be enough for everyone."

She ducked into the tent where two blankets were folded on the ground. She spread one out, then returned to the horse. Without a word she lifted Torin's arm and placed it around her shoulders. She was not tall, but she was determined and clearly had every intention of carrying the man herself.

Reiv rushed over and grabbed Torin by the waist. Between the two of them, they managed to drag his limp form into the tent where they lowered him face down onto the blanket.

Gem and Nely hovered in the doorway as Reiv and Cora inspected the wounds. "How about starting us a fire, Reiv," Cora said as she dabbed Torin's wounds with a cloth. "And tell the girls to stay outside. I don't think they should see this."

Reiv exited the tent. Before long he had started a small but adequate campfire. He then instructed Gem and Nely to stay near it, but not too near. He had not forgotten that fire held no sympathy for the foolish.

"Your knife," Cora called to him through the flap.

Reiv ducked back inside and pulled the knife from his waistband. He held it out to her.

"Over the fire, fool," she said impatiently, "but just enough to burn off any contaminants."

For a moment Reiv felt annoyed by her tone, but then he realized that she was only trying to save Torin's life and had no time to dictate his every move.

He stepped out and angled the blade over the flames, then returned to the tent and handed it to her. She took the knife by the handle. "Be ready with another cloth," she said. "The wound will bleed at first, but we will cauterize it after."

Reiv felt uneasy at the thought of burning flesh. He glanced down at his own burn-scarred hands, then turned his attention to Cora. She was inserting the knife near the first shaft, trying to pry it gently from Torin's back. Torin moaned and jerked. Cora quickly withdrew the blade.

"Have you done this before?" Reiv asked.

"No," Cora said, "but I've seen similar procedures, though not removing Tearian arrows of course. More like shards of coral...things like that." She noted Reiv's expression of doubt. "Oh, just hold him still," she snapped.

Reiv moved to Torin's other side and knelt beside him. He pressed his palm against Torin's good shoulder, his other hand hovering while he determined the best location to place it. He finally decided on the base of Torin's spine, but for some reason he found it disquieting.

Cora looked up at him. "You all right?"

Reiv swallowed thickly. "I am fine. It is just—the blood." But he wasn't so sure.

Cora turned her attention back to the wound and continued to probe. Torin moaned again, and Reiv increased his weight upon him.

After a few moments, Cora shook her head. "It's too deep. We might need to shove it through."

"What?" Reiv asked, appalled at the idea. "But what if it pierces something on the way out?"

"It's either that, or I go deeper and peel the flesh back further. The prong is very wide."

Reiv swallowed down the saliva that had begun to pool in his mouth. "I—I think it would be best to draw it from his back. We cannot risk damaging anything vital."

"The pain will likely rouse him. Can you hold him?"

"I think so."

"I need more than 'think so,' Reiv. If he jerks while the knife is doing its work...Maybe if you straddle him."

"If I what?"

"Straddle him. You know, sit with your legs on either side of him."

The thought of positioning himself across Torin's backside sent a wave of nausea to Reiv's gut. Why the hesitation? he wondered. Why the fear? It was to save a man's life, nothing more. He took a deep breath and planted his knees on either side of Torin's lower back. Leaning forward, he grasped the back of Torin's neck with one hand and pressed the other against the uninjured shoulder.

Cora held the knife ready.

"All right. I have him," Reiv said.

Then it was Cora's turn to hesitate. Her hands were trembling, and her face was beaded with sweat. She swept her brow with the back of her hand, then drew a stabilizing breath. With a sudden determined slice of the blade, she cut downward from one side of the shaft, then upward from the other, making a wide groove from which to work it free.

Torin arched his back, and Reiv felt certain he was going to be bucked off, but then Torin went still.

Reiv looked at Cora with concern.

"He's only fainted," she said. Reiv moved to lift himself off, but she ordered him to stay. "He might reawaken. You'd best stay put."

Reiv felt uncomfortable, sitting on Torin like that. Heat flared to his cheeks. For a moment he thought to climb off, regardless of what Cora said could happen if Torin awoke. But what if Torin did awake? Reiv gritted his teeth, suddenly aware that he was more concerned about a man discovering him astride his backside than he was of a potential slip of the knife."

"Reiv?"

Cora's voice drew Reiv from his thoughts.

"It's out. I need you to reheat the knife."

Reiv realized the shaft was now lying on the blanket, and blood was pouring from the wound.

Cora pressed a cloth to it. "Hurry," she said. "I need to get the bleeding stopped."

Reiv scrambled up and out to the campfire. Gem was standing to the side of it, tossing in sticks. "Thank you for keeping it going," Reiv said. Gem shrugged as if indifferent, but Reiv thought he detected a hint of satisfaction in her eyes.

He returned to the tent, the knife's blade glowing red. Cora took it from him and held the hot metal to the wound. The blood sizzled with the smell of burning flesh.

"Now. The other one," Cora said. "It's already pushing through the other side. We'll have to shove it on through."

"Shall I roll him onto his side then?"

"That would probably be best."

Reiv leaned Torin toward him and braced his chest against the man's back. It made his skin feel clammy, but

Cora scooted to his side before he could think any more about it. She pressed the butt of the knife handle against the broken end of the shaft. The pronged tip blossomed through Torin's chest, and the rest of the shaft followed. Cora grabbed hold and slid it out.

Reiv dabbed the blood on Torin's back, while Cora tended the exit wound.

"Lean him against me," she said, "while you reheat the knife."

Reiv did as instructed and again returned with the metal glowing hot. "Hold him," Cora said, and he took hold of Torin while she pressed the blade to Torin's chest.

Torin moaned as the pain roused him. "Stop…" he said weakly.

Reiv tightened his hold. "Almost done," he said. "Almost done."

"Let me die," Torin said. "Please, Reiv. There is nothing left for me." Then his head lolled against Reiv's arm and he said no more.

Reiv's eyes met Cora's. "He does not mean it," he said.

Cora looked away.

"He is the toughest man I know," Reiv insisted. "He would not give up so easily."

Cora motioned for Reiv to roll Torin onto the blanket. She blotted the wound at Torin's back, but said nothing.

"Cora? Torin will live, will he not?"

"Yes," she said softly. "Now go reheat the knife."

Reiv rose and left the tent, then struggled to the nearest bush and vomited into the dirt.

∽

# Chapter 15: Wading In

"Reiv...Reiv!"

Reiv felt a hand shaking his shoulder. He rolled over and sat up, his heart pounding against his breastbone. "What!" he blurted.

"You were having a nightmare," Cora said.

Reiv blinked his eyes awake, then scrubbed a hand through his hair. "Was I?"

"Yes. You were shouting."

"Shouting?" He yawned and stretched. "I do not recall."

Cora eyed him suspiciously.

"What?" Reiv asked with amusement. "Was it that bad?"

"It seemed so. Who's Crymm?"

Reiv's amusement evaporated. "Someone I used to know." He turned his focus to Torin. "How is he?"

"Better, but he has a slight fever. Hopefully it's only from the wounds, nothing more. I gave him an herbal brew. That should bring the fever down a bit."

Reiv rose. "How long have I been asleep?"

"A while. Are you ready to take the next shift?"

"Yes, but let me tend to another matter first."

As Reiv exited through the flap, he realized the camp was now bustling with activity. There were numerous campfires scattered about, and tents filled to capacity with the injured. Many people were gathered on pallets, some sleeping, some not. Others were rushing in and out of tents, tossing medical waste onto burn piles and spilling red-tinted water into the sand.

Reiv worked his way behind the tent, intent on finding a private place to ease his bladder, when he heard Gem and Nely playing nearby. He finished his business, then stepped back around the tent and walked toward them. He paused quietly, watching as they played.

The girls had fashioned dolls from sticks held together by strands of vine. They were staging them in a make-believe world of strategically placed stones, mounds of sand, and other assorted landmarks.

"Quick! Hide in the house!" Gem's doll commanded the one held by her sister. "We can't let the Guard see us!"

The girls hopped their dolls behind a rock. "Save me, save me," Nely's high pitched voice squealed.

"Do not fear," Gem replied bravely. "I have a knife."

She grabbed another doll and leaned it in front of the rock. "No one passes through your door without passing through me first!" she declared.

Gem lifted another doll and moved it toward the first. Her voice grew deeper. "I am the King—here to kill you all. You are rubbish and deserve to die!" She snatched the doll at the pretend doorway and tottered it toward the mock king. "Not if I kill you first."

The two dolls scuffled at the command of Gem's small fists. The King fell into the dirt. "Now who's rubbish," Gem said as she smashed the other doll into it, beating it until both were nothing more than shattered twigs.

"Gem," Reiv said softly. "Is that what happened?"

Gem rose to face him, her expression a mixture of surprise and annoyance. "No," she said. "That's what I wanted to happen."

"I understand," Reiv said.

"No you don't."

Reiv sighed. "If you say so, Gem." He glanced back at the tent, then smiled at the girls. "Would you like to go in and visit Torin? I am sure your voices would bring him cheer."

Gem twisted her mouth, then asked, "Will he know we're there?"

"I do not know, but perhaps he knows more of what is going on than he lets on."

"Then I need to tell him something," Gem said. "Before he dies."

"He is not going to die," Reiv said.

Gem bared her teeth. "You don't know that. You don't know anything!" She spun and ran in the opposite direction.

"Gem—wait!" Reiv called after her, but she had vanished into the maze of refugees.

Cora emerged from the tent. "What happened?" she asked, her eyes trailing after Gem.

Reiv shook his head. "There is no talking to that child. She is so angry, so..."

"Shall I give it a try?" Cora asked. "Perhaps she just needs to talk to someone who is not Tearian."

"I am not Tearian," Reiv snapped.

Cora laughed. "Oh Reiv, of course you are. You're the brother of the King."

Reiv looked over at Nely who was staring at him. "Is that why your sister will have nothing to do with me?" he asked her.

The girl nodded.

"I suppose you will have nothing to do with me either?" he asked.

Nely stepped toward him. Her eyes sparkled as she gazed up at him. "*I* like you," she said.

"Well, at least someone does," he muttered.

"Can we go see Torin now?" Nely asked. She reached for Reiv's hand.

Reiv gathered her hand in his, then turned to Cora. "Perhaps you should see about Gem. A little girl should not be running around camp unsupervised, though I pity any man who dares cross her."

Cora smiled. "I'll see what I can do."


Cora found Gem just outside the perimeter of the camp, stabbing the dirt with a stick.

"Did you kill it?" Cora asked with amusement.

"Not yet," Gem said. "But I will." She rammed the stick into the dirt, where it stuck.

Cora leaned down to inspect the imaginary victim. "Definitely dead," she said, then turned to Gem. "Are you finished now?"

Gem scowled. "Yes."

"I was on my way to the stream for a dip," Cora said matter-of-factly. "Would you like to join me?"

Gem shrugged.

"As you wish." Cora turned and walked away. Gem hesitated, then followed.

When they reached the stream, Cora led Gem along its bank. Up and down the shoreline people came and went, some filling water bladders, others bathing or beating laundry against the rocks. She headed to a tumble of boulders shaded by an overhang of leafy branches. The area was bordered by ripples of sand and gently flowing waters, and would provide a place for sitting and privacy for bathing. "This should do," Cora said.

She picked her way along the rocks, then settled onto a boulder that was half in and half out of the water. Dipping a toe into the river, she swirled it in a circular motion, then patted the rock next to her. "Here, Gem. Sit with me."

Gem climbed over and sat, but her feet did not reach the water's surface. She slid down a bit, touching her toes to it. "It's cold," she said, and scooted back up.

"Oh, it's not so bad." Cora turned her eyes to the sky. It was still cloudy, but the rain had stopped and the sky was growing paler. "If we're lucky, the sun will be shining soon; then it will feel warmer when we swim."

"I don't know how to swim," Gem grumbled.

"Would you like to learn?"

Gem thought for a moment. "I guess," she finally said. "My brother always wanted to learn to swim. But Torin wouldn't teach him."

"Why not?"

"He said Farris had to be a potter and that potters didn't swim."

Cora smiled. "I see. Well, I would have to disagree with Torin on that one. Anybody can swim."

"I think it was because he didn't want anyone to know about Farris, so he made up stories so he didn't have to take him there."

"To Meirla you mean?"

"Yes. He didn't want the people there to know."

"Know what?"

"That Farris was his."

Cora felt her stomach clench. "What do you mean, *his?*"

"His son."

"How do you know this, Gem? Did he tell you?"

"No. I heard my mum and pada arguing about it once, and when Torin came yesterday, he said so, too."

"Torin...has a son?" Cora turned her gaze to the opposite shore.

"Not anymore. He's dead, so now Torin doesn't have one."

Cora looked at Gem, expecting to see sadness, but instead she saw only bitterness. "Oh, Gem, I'm so sorry." Cora paused, noting the conflict emerging on Gem's face. "Do you want to talk about it? Sometimes talking helps when we lose people we love."

Gem remained silent.

"How about if I start?" Cora suggested.

Gem lifted her eyes to her. "You lost someone?"

"My mother and father, and my little sister. They drowned."

Gem hugged her knees to her chest, staring at the swirling waters. "How did they drown?"

"They were very good swimmers, all Shell Seekers are, but the sea was angry that day and pulled my little sister far from shore. My mother went in after her, and my father followed. But the waters took them, and never gave them back."

"Why didn't your father save them?"

"He tried, but he couldn't."

"Then he didn't try hard enough," Gem said.

"Is that what you think? That people die because someone didn't try hard enough to save them?"

"My mum died because Torin didn't try hard enough."

"How can you say that?"

"Because he took me and Nely and let the King burn up my mother and brother."

"Why would Torin do such a thing? There must have been more to it."

"Farris was dead, and Nannaven, too. But my mum was alive and she was sick." Gem's voice grew angry. "Then the King came and told the men to burn the tent, but first he said that Torin could save her or us, and Torin picked us. But he should have picked Mum."

"Gem, please listen. The King is the bad one, not Torin. Torin was put in a terrible position. What else could he do? If he had chosen your mother, then you and your sister would be dead. Are you saying you would rather Nely be dead than your mother?"

"No."

"So how was Torin's choice the wrong one? What would you have done in his place?"

"I wouldn't have chosen anyone! I would have killed the King!"

"Well then, why didn't you?"

Gem's face reddened with anger. "Because I didn't have a knife!" she said.

"Did Torin have a knife?"

"No, but—"

"So how could he kill the King?"

"He should have hit him!"

"Why didn't he?"

"The soldiers had him and he couldn't!"

"I see."

Cora's sympathies shifted from the child sitting next to her to the man lying wounded in the tent. For Torin to have found his boy dead, then to have been forced to choose between the lives of two little girls and the mother of his son—no wonder he felt he had nothing left to live for.

"Cora?" Cora felt Gem's hand on her arm.

"Yes, Gem."

"Do you like him?"

"Who?"

"Torin."

"Of course."

"What about Reiv?"

"I like him, too." She cocked her head. "Why do you ask?"

Gem crinkled her nose. "I don't like him."

"Reiv? What possible reason could you have to dislike him?"

"He's Tearian."

Cora shook her head sadly. "Well, I guess you'd better tell him then."

"Tell him what?"

"That you don't appreciate him saving Torin, and that you wish he'd just left you and your sister back on the road. I'm sure some nice Jecta would have come along and helped you, eventually." Cora paused. "Oh...wait...didn't I hear something about a Jecta man finding Torin in the mud, and after stealing from him left you and your sister there?"

Gem's brows slid up with surprise. "How did you know that?"

"Reiv told me, and believe me, that Jecta had better stay away from Reiv if he knows what's good for him." Cora sighed. "I don't know why Reiv bothers though. I mean, he's *Tearian*. Why should he care about an injured Shell Seeker and two unappreciative little girls?"

"You're just trying to trick me into liking him."

"Am I?"

Gem rested her chin on her bent knees and stared at her toes for a long moment. "Reiv's helping you make Torin well?"

"You know he is."

"Who's going to take care of me and Nely, now that Mum is dead?" Gem asked.

"Torin, of course."

"What if he dies."

"He won't. I won't let him," Cora said. "But he has much healing to do. In the meantime, I will take care of you and your sister. Would that be all right?"

A smile teased the corner of Gem's mouth. "That would be good."

Cora nudged Gem with her shoulder. "How about we wash this grime off, then go check on Torin. Maybe he's awake, and we can tell him how brave you have been."

Cora rose and led the way to a patch of sand bordering the shallows of the shoreline. She held out her hand. "Come, Gem. Today we'll only wade. There's time enough to learn how to swim."

Gem studied the water, then set her face with determination. "Today I'll wade," she said. "But tomorrow I'll swim." Then she took Cora's hand and stepped with her into the river.

∽

# CHAPTER 16: THREE DAYS

"Three days," Torin mumbled.

Cora placed a cool rag upon his forehead, then looked at Reiv who was sitting nearby. "What does he mean do you think?" she asked.

"Probably just nonsense…from the fever or loss of blood," Reiv replied.

"I don't know. He's been saying it a lot."

"Do you think the girls might know?" Reiv glanced beyond the open flap of the tent.

"Maybe. Why don't you ask them."

Reiv forced a laugh. "Like they will tell *me* anything."

"Tell them I sent you to ask," Cora suggested.

Reiv rolled his eyes. "Fine." He rose and stepped out the tent and over to where the girls were chasing each other beneath a tree.

"Gem."

Gem stopped and glared at him.

"Cora sent me to ask if you know what Torin means when he says 'three days.' We thought it might be important."

"That's what the King said," she answered.

"The King? What else did he say?"

"I don't remember."

Reiv stepped closer. "Please, Gem. Try. Is something supposed to happen?"

"I think so."

"What, Gem? What is supposed to happen in three days?"

She scowled. "I said I don't know."

Reiv turned his attention to Nely who was several paces away. Perhaps she knew, but somehow he doubted it. Worst-case scenarios scurried through his mind. Three days—and it had already been two. What could Whyn be planning? Reiv suddenly noticed that Nely's crumbling expression was beginning to mirror his own emerging fears. "Come, Nely," he said, holding a hand out to her. "You, too, Gem."

Nely came to him readily, but Gem refused to budge. Reiv bit back his aggravation. "Gem, I have a very important job for you. I must go to Meirla and meet with the Shell Seekers. While I am away, Cora will need your help."

Gem nodded.

"You must also keep an eye on your sister, and you may be asked to help take care of Torin. It is a big responsibility. Do you think you can handle it?"

Gem nodded again, but then she narrowed her eyes. "Why are you going to Meirla? You should stay here with us."

For a moment it sounded as if she actually wanted him to stay, and Reiv's spirits lifted somewhat. "I would much rather stay and look after things here," he said, "but I must leave for a time." Reiv placed a hand on her shoulder. "Gem, I think you are big enough to hear what I have to say next. You have shown yourself to be very brave, but now you must be even more so. I fear the King is making new plans, and I will see no harm come to you and your sister, or to Cora and Torin. That is why I must meet with the Shell Seekers."

"I will look after things while you are gone," Gem said.

"Thank you...and you, too, Nely. I know Torin and Cora will take comfort in your help while I am away."

Reiv let go of Nely's hand and returned to the tent.

"Cora, I must leave for Meirla," he said as he entered. "I have already told Gem and Nely. They are prepared to help you."

Cora rose with concern. "What is it? Why are you leaving?"

"Gem said she heard the King say 'three days,' but she knows nothing more. My brother is planning something; I am sure of it. And if that plan is to happen in three days time, then it has already been two. I must meet with the Shell Seekers."

"Will they let you enter the village?"

"They will." He turned to leave, but then stopped. "Can you handle Torin and the girls by yourself, Cora? I hate to leave you, and I do not know how long I will be gone. Hopefully not long, but. . ." As the words left his mouth, he realized how very much he regretted leaving. In the brief time he had been with Cora and the girls, he had come to feel responsible for them, almost like the head of the household. It made him feel needed, but when he glanced at Torin, the feeling turned to loss. A family might be forming within these canvas walls, but it would be Torin's family, not his.

Cora stepped toward him. "Before you leave, I want to thank you for everything you've done for Torin. I love you for it, you know."

Reiv nodded stiffly.

Cora wrapped her arms around him, and as she did so he could not help but bury his face in her wild, sea-scented hair. He longed for more, but Cora was not his to take. He eased from her embrace.

"You may love me, but not the way you love him," he said, tilting his head in Torin's direction.

"No, but it's still love, isn't it?"

Reiv smiled. "I suppose it will have to do." Then he stepped toward the exit and slipped through the flap.

⚬⚬

The Shell Seekers that guarded the road stopped Reiv only briefly. They trusted that he, as one who had Transcended, was beyond the limitations of a mere mortal man; surely the fever could not touch someone who had died and returned to tell of it. But not everyone believed his former tale of Transcension, and so when he arrived at the village, he was met by a group that was far less trusting of him than the guards on the road had been.

"Halt, Tearian," Lyal's voice commanded.

Reiv bristled as he turned toward the voice, realizing several pairs of accusing eyes were aimed at him, as well as half a dozen equally sinister blades.

Reiv stopped, keeping his focus on Lyal, who was clearly the leader of the pack. He would have liked nothing more than to fight the arrogant fool, but Reiv was outweaponed and outmanned, and there were more pressing issues at hand.

"I appreciate your loyalty to the village," Reiv said, "but I have news of the King that must be relayed to the clan."

"Then you will relay it to me first," Lyal said, not lowering his blade.

"You are not the clan's leader, Lyal. I will relay it only to the person in charge."

Lyal curled his lip. "Then that, Tearian, would still be me. Torin, as you know, is indisposed."

"You have been elected in his place?"

"In a manner of speaking."

Reiv took a step toward him, shoving Lyal's short sword aside with a swipe of his hand. "What do you mean, in a manner of speaking?"

But Lyal remained nonplussed. "I was assigned to look after the village while the rest of the clansmen set up a line of defense in the surrounding area. So for now you'd best get used to the idea of dealing with me."

Reiv glared at the cluster of young men at Lyal's back. Most of them were barely older than he himself was, but he could tell by their expressions that they would welcome a chance to prove their manhood. Reiv forced self-control into his voice. "I need to speak with the entire council, Lyal, not just you. Now, would you be so...*kind*...as to send one of your boys to fetch them. We are wasting time debating the issue, time we do not have."

Lyal narrowed his eyes. "How much time *do* we have?"

"Hours...minutes...I do not know. But I am confident of this much—we will have no more than a sunset to find out."

Lyal looked skeptical, but he jerked his head for one of his cohorts to carry out Reiv's instruction. "Get the word out to the rest of the village," he barked to the others. "We'll meet as soon as all are gathered."

Reiv stepped in the direction of Jensa's hut, intending to give her a pre-meeting update on Torin's condition, but Lyal stopped him short. "Oh, no, prince. You're coming with me."

"I have had enough of you," Reiv said. "I need to speak with Jensa."

"You may speak with her later. She is cloistered."

"*Cloistered?*" Reiv said.

"The women and children have been instructed to remain inside. The Elders thought it best, in order to decrease the risk to future generations."

Reiv scanned the area, realizing only men were moving about, and most of them were too young or too old to serve any real purpose at the lines.

"Brina, then. I need to speak with my aunt. I doubt she is any threat to your future generations."

Lyal opened his mouth to decline, but then appeared to reconsider. "Very well," he said gruffly. "I'll escort you to the Place of Observance first, then I'll fetch her. But you'll wait there until I return, understand?"

Reiv growled inwardly at being ordered about by Lyal, of all people, but he realized it would do no good to antagonize him further. All that mattered was that the clan meeting was being called. He nodded reluctantly and headed to the meeting place, Lyal at his back and breathing down his neck.

The Place of Observance was a massive pavilion of bamboo poles woven together by marsh reeds and palm fronds. Thousands of iridescent shells decorated its exterior, making the place shimmer like a star. The entire compound was situated on a tor, midway between the sandy village it faced, and the dark rock cliffs that towered at its back. Though positioned to rise above the village, it did not loom over it like a master to a slave, but seemed to gaze upon it like a parent to a child. A wide path ambled up from the village to the structure, and was lined on each side by lush greenery and god-like statues carved from the local coral. A large clearing surrounded the building, which was where religious and communal ceremonies were held. Though the pavilion itself could accommodate a hundred souls within, the area that surrounded it could easily accommodate a thousand.

As Reiv was escorted toward the sacred place, he could not help but recall the first time he had been there. It sent pain to his heart and sweat to his brow, for it was there, not all that long ago, that he had been poisoned and sent to the After Place. Though he had returned intact and with great knowledge, he would never forget the agony that had burned in his belly, nor the terror that had possessed his soul. But he could not dwell on that now; he had to stay focused on the matter at hand. Today his concern was not the death of an individual, but that of an entire race.

They soon reached the clearing and marched across it toward the pavilion. As they did so, three spiritual Elders stepped through the beaded portal to greet them. The three bowed to Reiv, an honor usually bestowed only upon others within the sect. This brought an immediate scowl to Lyal's face.

"He is to remain inside until I return," Lyal said. "The King has declared war on the Jecta, and we mustn't forget this is the cur's brother."

"You go too far with your words, Lyal," one of the Elders said. "Reiv is beyond the royal blood ties. He is a Transcendor. His ties are with those of a higher order."

Lyal scoffed. "So you say, Yustes."

"So we all say," a second Elder replied.

"A clan meeting is being called," Lyal said. "Keep him here until the members arrive."

"Reiv may stay here as long as he wishes," Yustes said. "But not on your order." The old man's voice grew threatening. "Do not throw your arrogance in *my* direction, Lyal, or your own transcension may take a turn in the other direction."

"Is that a threat?"

"Call it what you wish."

Lyal glared. "My concern is for this world, not the next. Save your threats for someone else."

"And you yours."

"Your threats have no sway over me, old man," Lyal said. "You will see to it that Reiv stays." Then he turned and stormed back toward the path.

It did not take long for the Place of Observance to fill with Shell Seekers. Some were men who had previously been assigned to set up the perimeter to prevent refugees from entering the village. Though most of the Jecta had traveled the main road that led to Meirla, others had staggered toward it through the hills, and were still doing so. Rather than give up the line entirely, some of the men continued their patrols, while the rest departed for the hastily called meeting. Other residents attended also, but strangely there were no females. Reiv found this most unsettling. Shell Seeker women had never been known to sit back and let the men do all the work. They were a society of equals, so why they had agreed to such an arrangement was beyond him.

"Reiv!" The voice snapped him from his contemplations and toward Brina who could be seen shouldering her way across the room.

She grabbed him in a quick embrace. "We have been so worried," she said. "How is Torin? Jensa is beside herself. And Kerrik—"

"Torin's wounds will heal. As for his spirit. . ." Reiv glanced around, then ushered her aside. "He has said little, other than he feels he has nothing to live for."

Brina drew a startled breath. "Surely he does not mean it."

"I do not think Jensa and Kerrik should be told of it," Reiv said, "at least not yet."

Brina leaned closer. "Are his days as clan leader over do you think?"

"I hesitate to say, though it might be wise to select an interim leader." Reiv shook his head. "But it *cannot* be Lyal."

"Lyal?" Brina laughed. "Oh, I do not think it will be *Lyal*."

"I hope not. He and his little pack of lapdogs were salivating for a chance to stick a knife in me when I arrived." Reiv's eyes wandered over the crowd. "What has been happening these past two days, Brina? The confinement of the women worries me."

Brina nodded. "After you left, I notified the clan leaders and the Elders of your suspicions. That, along with Nannaven's earlier message that the fever had spread, told them all they needed to know. At first they assigned men to watch only the road. But when the first survivors of the massacre made it to the village by way of the hills, more drastic measures had to be taken. The Elders reminded the people of past plagues, particularly the one that followed the Purge. There is still the threat of the Guard of course; who knows what they have planned. At any rate, it was felt that in order for the tribe to survive, the women and children needed to be protected. Believe me, this was not welcome news for the women, but after some debate, it was agreed that some could volunteer to help the sick, but would not be allowed back into Meirla."

"Jensa volunteered to help with Torin," Reiv said, "but I insisted that she not. And when Cora volunteered in her place—"

"Jensa would have gone, though she knew the risk. She only bent to Cora's will for the sake of Kerrik."

"That was my argument as well."

"At this point, it is Jensa I am worried about, not Kerrik."

"How so?"

"The poor girl cries day and night, Reiv. I do not know how to console her. Even Kerrik brings her no solace. And it is a rare person indeed who cannot be cheered by that child."

Reiv felt new hatred surge toward Lyal for preventing him from seeing Jensa. By the gods, when the meeting was over he would speak to her, and not even that strutting rooster would keep him from it.

The three Elders moved to the dais at the far side of the room. At their backs sat an altar, so large it nearly dwarfed them. Carved from dark, well-oiled wood, the altar was covered with dozens of beeswax candles and pots of simmering incense. Behind it, the skin of a massive sea snake was stretched. Flames flickered from torches lining the perimeter of the room, sending shadows skipping along the walls, and a golden haze drifting through the crowd.

Yustes called the meeting to order, then beckoned Reiv to approach.

As Reiv stepped upon the dais, the Elders again tipped their heads. The audience followed suit, except for a few men standing in the back, and Lyal who was seething off to the side.

"Thank you, Yustes," Reiv said. He then addressed the crowd. "For my brother's actions, I have no explanation. I can only say—"

"We expect no explanation from you," an angry voice interrupted from the back. Reiv turned his attention to the voice, realizing it was one of Lyal's cohorts. "There is nothing you can say that I, for one, would believe," the man declared.

Voices mumbled, many irritated by the rudeness that had been aimed at Reiv. Few had forgotten Reiv's bravery in slaying the serpent Seirgotha, and even fewer had forgotten the miracle of his Transcension.

"Believe what you wish," Reiv responded. "I, for one, intend to find some answers."

The same man snorted. "Answers? What answers would those be? How about we start with why you came here in the first place?"

"What are you implying?" Reiv asked.

Another of Lyal's friends stepped forward. "That you were sent as a *spy* perhaps?"

The crowd rumbled. Brina burst onto the dais and faced the accuser down. "How *dare* you!" she shouted.

Lyal, who had remained quiet thus far, straightened his spine. "You should not even be here," he said. "You have no right to speak."

"I have every right!" Brina shot back.

"Enough!" Yustes ordered. "Lyal, you had best keep your corner of the room under some semblance of control." He turned to Brina. "Madam, if you will be so kind as to step aside. I believe your nephew has come with some news. Is that correct, Reiv?"

"Yes," Reiv said grimly. "I believe my brother is not yet finished with us. We need to be prepared for—"

"For what?" a young man up front asked. "Another slaughter?"

The crowd grew anxious.

"How can we prepare for something like that?" voices exclaimed.

"We can't!" others cried. "We will end up like those from Pobu. Only this time there'll be no place to run!"

Heads waggled as opinions were traded back and forth.

Reiv raised his palms to calm the crowd. "We must devise a plan. A means of negotiating with the King."

"Negotiate?" Lyal grunted.

"Yes, negotiate," Reiv said. "We cannot fight him. We are ill prepared. We must bargain with him...offer him something that he wants."

"But we have nothing of value," someone cried. "What could we possibly offer?"

"We have *Reiv*," Lyal said loudly. "Maybe *that* will appease him."

Opposing views rose and fell.

"What makes you think he wants me?" Reiv asked. "If it were me he wanted, he would have simply come for me."

"Perhaps the attack on the Jecta was merely to strike you where it hurt," Lyal suggested. "The slaughter of the Shell Seekers may be the final twist of the knife."

"You are wasting our time trying to second guess Whyn," Reiv said. "There is no way you can understand the workings of his mind."

"That's right," the man in the back called out. "After all, we're not *Tearian*."

"You are more like a Tearian than you know," Reiv said.

The man bared his teeth and stormed toward Reiv. A host of arms grabbed him, preventing him from drawing any nearer.

"I'll not be insulted by this betrayer!" the man declared over the shouts of those holding him back.

Lyal stepped to the man and settled him down with orders that Reiv could not hear. He then turned to Reiv. "Excuse my friend's ire," Lyal said sarcastically. "But he's only stating what others are afraid to say."

"And that would be?" Reiv asked.

"That we lived in peace until you showed up a few months back." Several voices muttered in agreement. Lyal ran his eyes over the crowd. "Is it not true that the day Reiv arrived, so did our troubles?" He pointed a finger at Reiv. "You–you are the one that brought this on us. If you had not come, none of this would have happened and you know it!"

Reiv felt the urge to leap into the crowd and pummel the damned fool into the dirt. But before his feet, or his temper, could carry him forward, a man burst into the room.

"The Guard," the man cried. "The Guard has come!"

࿏

# CHAPTER 17: DUAL IDENTITIES

The crowd rushed as one to the entrance. Reiv shouldered his way through and halted just outside the door. Before them stood a regiment of Guard on horseback, lining the entire perimeter of the courtyard. The soldiers were indeed an intimidating sight. Their armor was polished in shades of pewter trimmed in crimson, and banners in similar colors snapped in the breeze that ruffled the plumes of their helmets. The guards waited, silent and ready, their pale eyes staring through the slits of their visors. But none of their gazes met the kohl-lined eyes of the Shell Seekers staring back at them.

Reiv pulled in a steadying breath. "Wait here. I will speak with them," he said, and slowly stepped into the courtyard. As he approached the militia, Shell Seekers spilled out of the pavilion behind him. He stopped before a Guard that he felt certain was the Commander. Dressed in an elaborate uniform of mail and dark leathers, the man looked imposing, though not nearly as imposing as Mahon, the former Commander had been.

"Is the King with you?" Reiv asked politely. "Or have you been sent as his representative?"

The Commander stared past him and did not respond.

"Are you at liberty to take a message to him, then?"

For a moment it seemed that Reiv was again to be ignored, but then the line began to move in a motion similar to that of an awakening serpent, and from within its dark-armored realm a lone figure of white appeared.

Whyn rode toward Reiv on a horse that was as dark as he was light. He approached in an aura of brightness, as if emerging from a shimmering mirage.

"Gods," Reiv whispered. A wave of nausea swept through him. Though the figure riding toward him was the person he had once called brother, the face more closely resembled that of the former Priestess. The King's white-blond hair hung loose at his shoulders, but was braided and pulled back at the temples and twisted atop his head. Liquid gold was painted around his pale blue eyes and upon his lips and eyebrows. Even his fingernails were coated in the same glimmering shade. His tunic was white and nearly transparent, revealing peach-colored skin beneath, and his bare legs were shaven and oiled to a radiant sheen. A sword with a lion's head at its hilt was belted at his waist, and a quiver of gold-feathered arrows was nestled next to the bow at his back.

Whyn stopped within feet of him, staring down at Reiv as if contemplating an insect beneath his feet.

Reiv took a startled step back. He had met the Priestess prior to her death and was well-acquainted with the nadir of her evil. Though he was aware of the sinister hold she had once had on Whyn, never had he imagined she could have dwelt so deep.

"Whyn?" he said hesitantly.

Whyn regarded him with a cock of his head. "I have been called such."

"Are you not...him?" Reiv asked.

"I am known by many names. Whyn is one."

Reiv licked his suddenly parched lips. "May—may I call you Whyn?"

Whyn's eyes flashed. "You may not."

"What shall I call you then?"

Whyn lifted his chin. "You may call me Master."

Reiv felt his own self-control slip. How dare his brother demand servitude! *He* was first born; not Whyn. "I call *no* one Master," he said through gritted teeth.

"Oh, but you will," Whyn said. He slid from his horse and stood before Reiv. Reiv searched his brother's face, but realized there was nothing of him there.

"Let us talk of the conditions of your survival," Whyn continued dryly.

Reiv balled his fists at his side. "I have defeated far greater foes than you," he said. "Seirgotha's skin adorns the pavilion wall, just as *your* death fills my memories."

"My death?" Whyn laughed. "Do you not see me standing before you?"

"I do not speak of the death of my brother, but that of the witch defeated by Agneis!"

Whyn's eyes narrowed. "A serpent sheds its skin to be reborn. Is that not what your precious Spirit Keeper told you? Perhaps you did not listen. But it does not matter, for now you stand before me, while she lies rotting in the dirt."

Reiv gasped. How could Whyn possibly have known what Nannaven had told him at their last parting? That had been a private conversation, or so Reiv thought. He reached for his dirk, his hand moving on impulse, but before he could touch it, Whyn whipped the Lion from its sheath and pressed it against Reiv's throat.

Whyn grabbed Reiv by the hair as he held the blade to his neck. "I loathe you," he hissed. "I loathe every fiber of your being. The very beating of your heart."

He forced Reiv to his knees and glared at him, the intensity of his gaze so evil, Reiv's sense of reality began to evaporate. He felt as if he were under a spell, drawn by a darkness beyond his comprehension.

Reiv quailed as he stared into the King's icy gaze. If only he could find a flicker of his brother beyond that hideous façade! But there was no hint of the Whyn he once knew, and that flung Reiv beyond any terror he had ever experienced, and he had experienced many.

"Whyn," he said, "I am your brother. Please—"

"You repulse me," Whyn said. He angled the blade toward Reiv's jugular. A trickle of blood seeped beneath it, sending a bright red rivulet snaking toward Reiv's clavicle.

Whyn grinned. "I should love to see you drained of the *one thing* left to bind us." He teased the blade deeper.

Reiv grabbed Whyn's hand. "Please," he cried.

"Say it again," Whyn said.

Reiv tried to gather some saliva into his mouth. "Please."

"Again."

"Please!"

Whyn laughed, then tilted his face to the sky. He groaned as if in the throes of lust. "Gods, that I could savor this moment for eternity," he said. He raised the sword high into the air, where it seemed to hover for a moment. Then

the blade fell in a dazzling swath of motion, sweeping downward toward Reiv's neck.

Before Reiv knew it, he was lying prostrate on the
ground. He had little memory of what had just transpired—it had happened too fast—only the brief recollection of a flashing blade and the sound of laughter ringing
in his ears.

But then he realized his head was still intact, at least he
thought it was. He could taste dirt on his tongue and feel
gravel beneath his skin, and the laughter...yes, he could
still hear the laughter.

He pushed himself to his knees as he moved his gaze
up the looming form of his brother. The sword was still
grasped in Whyn's fist and Reiv could not seem to tear his
eyes from it.

"Did you think I would miss my mark?" Whyn asked
with amusement. "I spared you only because there is more
from you that I want."

"What more could you possibly want from me?" Reiv
asked cautiously. "You took my throne, my love, everything I once held dear. What else can I give you?"

"Your happiness."

"My happiness?" Reiv said, confused. But then he
glanced behind him and saw the Shell Seekers now gathered outside the pavilion, and realized they were his family
now, and that living amongst them had been the happiest
time of his life. His focus moved to Brina, standing with
the others, her arm in the firm grip of Yustes who was trying to prevent her from rushing to Reiv's aid.

Reiv returned his eyes to Whyn. "You want me to leave
Meirla," he said.

"Meirla is mine, as it has been since the reign of the Red King. And yes, I want you to leave it. I want no more to hear of you, or for others to acknowledge that you ever existed. But fear not; I will think of you often. For I will own your happiness and will forever celebrate the day that you gave it to me."

Brina wrenched her arm free and raced to Reiv, who was still on his knees, and examined the wound on his neck. Her eyes blazed at Whyn. "You would draw your own brother's *blood*?"

"I could have drawn much more," Whyn said. "Unfortunately, I must be satisfied with but a taste of it. Though I would prefer his death to his exile, it is not my decision to make. The gods demand the honor of that task." He sighed. "Ah well, perhaps knowing he wanders in misery will have to do."

"If he goes, I, for one, go with him."

Whyn guffawed. "Do you think I care? Two traitors can starve as easily as one." He turned to address the Shell Seekers. "Reiv is hereby exiled from Tearia," his voice boomed across the distance. "If any of you wish to go with them, you have my blessing. But know this: Never again will you be allowed within Tearia's borders." He gestured his arm toward the sea. "You will be banished from these shores that you call home, from the very waters that give you sustenance. How will you feed your families? How will you survive?"

Reiv rose shakily to his feet. "Will they survive if they *stay*?" he asked. "Or will you do to them what you did to the Jecta?"

Whyn looked astonished by the question. "I did what had to be done. As for who lives and who dies, the Shell

Seekers can still offer me service; the others could offer me nothing."

Reiv's mind scrambled. What would happen to the Jecta who had made it to the encampment outside of Meirla? And what of the sick and injured, and those tending them? His heart thumped at the thought of Cora. Would Whyn spare her because she was Shell Seeker? And what of Torin and the girls? Would Whyn finish what he had started?

"So the Shell Seekers will be allowed to live if they agree to serve you as before," Reiv said, working to piece together Whyn's meaning.

"Of course."

"And the Jecta? Will you offer them the same?"

"If they are worth the offer."

"And if some choose to leave with me?"

Whyn laughed. "Then they would be fools. What do *you* offer them?"

"Freedom."

"To do what? Starve?" Whyn shook his head. "No, Reiv, I very much doubt they will go with you. As I recall, but moments ago you begged for your life. What sort of leadership would that provide?"

Humiliation flared to Reiv's cheeks.

"I see you agree," Whyn said.

Reiv remained silent, again assessing Whyn's words. It seemed out of character for the King of Tearia to offer anyone a choice in the matter. After all, he could simply demand that they stay and serve him.

"Why do you give them a choice at all?" Reiv asked. "Why such…generosity on your part?"

"It is simply good sportsmanship, do you not think?"

Reiv's eyes slid to the gold-tipped feathers rising from the quiver at Whyn's back, the very same as those removed from Torin's shoulder. Reiv had known those belonged to Whyn, but now he could not help but wonder: Is that what Torin was—sport?

Whyn turned and mounted his horse, then squared his shoulders as he stared down at Reiv. "Tell your people I offer them a choice. They may stay, or they may go. As for those who stay, another choice must be made: who will serve me and who will not. Only this time, *I* will do the choosing."

"But that offers them little choice at all!" Reiv said.

"They will soon learn to be satisfied with what I give them." Whyn lifted his chin as he made his last announcement to the crowd: "I return at dawn. If Reiv is not gone by that time, your life is forfeit. Leave with him if you wish. It is your choice. But know this: If you stay, the quality of your life will depend on your worthiness to serve me." He steered his horse into the mass of guards that turned to follow him down the path.

Reiv watched as the Guards' backs grew distant. The Red King had returned—and with him the Purge. Reiv felt as if a cloud of doom had descended upon him. There was little hope of avoiding another massacre, especially of the Jecta. Even the Shell Seekers were in peril. But how could he convince them to leave?

"Do not listen to his lies," Brina said. "He cannot be trusted to hold his part of the bargain."

"He can be trusted to hold this one," Reiv said. "Or part of it at least."

They suddenly found themselves surrounded by faces painted with kohl and confusion and fear.

"What else did he say?" some questioned.

"What are we to do?" others asked.

"I would say a better question would be, why did Reiv bow down like that?" Lyal said as he pushed his way toward him through the crowd. "Perhaps our suspicions about you were correct."

Reiv lurched toward Lyal, but Brina grabbed hold of his arm and held him back. "Did you not see the blade at my throat!" Reiv snarled. "Or were you too busy watching the urine pool at your feet!"

"Perhaps the sword at your neck was just an act," Lyal sneered. He eyed the rest of the crowd. "I, for one, still see a head upon Reiv's shoulders."

"Would you rather see it rolling in the dirt?" Reiv asked

"Perhaps I would," Lyal said, fingering the short sword at his waist.

Reiv was consumed by rage. He curled his fists and attempted another lunge, but Brina held tight to one arm, while two men grabbed the other.

"Enough!" Yustes shouted above the swell of tempers.

Individuals stepped aside as the Elders, led by Yustes, wound their way between them and toward Reiv and Lyal. Yustes placed a calming hand on Reiv's shoulder, ordering him with a nod of his head to relent. Reiv jerked his arms free, then worked to steady the breath seething through his teeth.

Yustes shot Lyal a glare. "Remove your hand from the weapon," he ordered. "There'll be no blood spilled here today."

"There'll be blood spilled here soon enough!" Lyal responded. "How do we know we can trust this—this Tearian? Did you not see him kneel before the King?"

Voices muttered in agreement.

"Fools, all of you," Yustes said. "The only thing I saw was a boy facing death while the rest of you cowered near the doorway."

Men mumbled, realizing the truth of the Elder's words. Only one person had dared go to Reiv's defense, and that had been Brina.

"Tell us, then," Yustes said, addressing Reiv. "What does the King command?"

"He commands that I leave," Reiv said. "As for why..." Reiv thought back to Whyn's cruel words and bizarre appearance—and the Lion sword sweeping toward his own neck. It all seemed so surreal. But the more he thought on it, the more he wondered: Why had Whyn simply not killed him?

As if reading his mind, Yustes said, "Your neck was well in the path of your brother's sword. When he pulled it back, it was as if an invisible hand had forced it from its mark. Why do you think he spared you?"

Reiv shook his head, exceedingly grateful that he was still able to. "I do not know. He said it was up to the gods. Perhaps the entity that possesses him does not wish to challenge at least one of them again. Agneis was no ordinary foe."

"Agneis?"

"It was not the collapse of the temple that killed the Priestess," Reiv said. "It was Agneis." He shivered at the recollection. "The Priestess was no mere woman possessed by her beliefs; she was something more—a fiend from the underworld."

"And now she has returned," Yustes said.

"You saw her too then," Reiv said. "In my brother's face."

"I do not think she seeks to hide her identity, do you? Clearly she wants her presence known."

"I never realized how deep her hatred ran, but seeing Whyn…"

"Did he say anything more?" Yustes asked. "I seem to recall the word 'worthiness' being thrown our way."

Reiv hesitated, but realized the worst had not yet been said. "Yes. Whyn has initiated a Purge. It began in New Pobu two nights ago, and will continue here in the morning, unless–"

"But we signed a treaty with him!" someone shouted. "Does that mean nothing?"

"At the moment, little," Reiv said. "I suspect it is the plague that has motivated the King to invalidate it. The earthquake very nearly destroyed Tearia. Now the fever is entering its borders. If Tearia is to survive, Whyn must protect its citizens. And if he hopes to rebuild the city, he will require slave labor."

"But why slay the Jecta?" Yustes questioned. "Would they not have suited his needs in the rebuilding?"

"The Jecta are weak," Reiv said. "The fever has seen to that. They can offer Tearia little at this point, other than the threat of more illness. Thus far, the Shell Seekers have avoided the outbreak. Whyn knows this. But he now also realizes that many Jecta fled here. This could jeopardize his plan. He will purge whatever and whomever he must in order to see it done. That means the Jecta, and any Shell Seeker who holds no value to him."

Voices exploded, but Yustes cut them off, reminding them that the sun was already descending the sky.

"You all heard the King," Reiv continued. "He offers you a choice, though a poor one. Anyone wishing to leave may do so. But I know that is inconceivable to most of you, as seeking is all you have ever known. On the other hand, if you stay, the King will expect servitude and—" Reiv hesitated. "—worthiness."

"So," Yustes said grimly, "he will spare some. But not all."

"Yes," Reiv conceded.

"Then we must fight back!" Lyal declared. "We must strike the Tearians down!"

"Yes!" others cried. "We cannot sit back and do nothing!"

"Think what you are saying!" Reiv said. "You are ill prepared to fight the Guard. And what of the Jecta? What happens to them?"

Tensions quickly turned to the subject of the refugees and what could be done for them. The Jecta would be the first ones purged, that was clear. But was there time to relocate them, and if so, to where? Suggestions were made as to the caves in the nearby cliffs, but transporting the infirm up a precarious path would be nearly impossible. Perhaps the healthy could find refuge there, but the sick and injured would have to be brought into the village. A perimeter of spears and swords might protect Meirla for a time, but if the Jecta were brought within its borders, the Shell Seekers would be at risk of contracting the fever. And that would erode any chance they had.

"We are running out of time," Reiv said. "I for one know what I must do: I must leave, and soon. As hard as that will be for me, you have the more difficult choice, I think. Stay and serve, or stay and die."

"Or leave with us," Brina added.

"But where would we go?" someone asked.

Yes, where *would* they go? Reiv pondered. To the mountains? He had attempted that trek before, and very nearly starved for it. Up the coast perhaps. No, that led to The Black, and everything around it was still Tearian realm. Kirador? No, not possible...they would not be welcome there. But where else was there?

An image formed in Reiv's mind. "The valley," he said, startled by the realization. "Yes...beyond the mountains— I have seen it!"

Color drained from Yustes's face. "Valley?"

"Yes, Agneis showed it to me. During my Transcension..." Reiv knitted his brows. "Or did she take me there? I do not know for certain. All I know is the valley is real."

"The prophecy names this place," Yustes said, his voice hopeful.

"Names it?" Reiv asked.

"Oonayei."

The word, though spoken softly, echoed as if it had been shouted across a canyon. Many faces in the crowd brightened, while others gawked in wonder. But some scoffed at the suggestion.

"*Oonayei?*" Lyal said. "Why, that is nothing but a children's tale."

"Is it?" Yustes said. "It is named in the Prophecy of Kalei, the one that foretold the coming of the Transcendor who now stands before you!"

"You may lay your hopes on fables if you wish, old man," Lyal said. "But no prophecy determines *my* future. The gods gave me a free will, and I intend to fight for it!"

Others who had snickered at the suggestion of Oonayei joined him in similar sentiment.

"You are correct," Yustes said, addressing the skeptics. "The gods did indeed grant us free wills. But they also gave us tools to guide our lives, and Kalei's prophecy is one of them. It speaks of a great migration, of a shift in the stars. Look around you—does the evidence not point to it?"

"All I see is an outcast prince speaking hallucinations!" Lyal said. "How do we know he even Transcended? You're a fool if you think the gods mean for us to skip down some golden path with a Tearian!"

Yustes settled his gaze on Lyal. "I did not hear those words from you when Reiv slew Seirgotha. Nor did I see you dispute the truth of our histories when he risked his life to give it to you. You united with the rest of us when Dayn led us to rescue Reiv. And it was Reiv that you, and everyone else here, turned to when the time came to negotiate with the King."

"I'll not deny it," Lyal said, "but now I see the truth of things. I see a worthless treaty and a Purge in the making—and more lives in ruin if we don't do something to stop it! If we don't fight for what is ours, if we don't show the King that we will not bow down to him, we will return to the darkest part of the history that Reiv so eloquently spoke of!"

"He's right!" a voice shouted. "We cannot lie down like sheep before the slaughter!"

"Slaughter it will be if we try to fight the King," another argued.

"Death is better than servitude!"

"Perhaps you should ask those who have already died!" someone sniped. "They might have a different opinion on the matter."

"I for one would rather die on my feet than on my knees!" Lyal declared.

The air exploded in argument. Some sided with Lyal, but others defended Reiv, basing their views on his Transcension and the prophecy's promise of Oonayei. But after much debate, Reiv decided he had had enough.

"Stop!" he shouted. "I know little of your prophecy. I only know what I must do if I am to keep my head attached to my shoulders. Stay if you must. Follow if you wish. I leave tonight." He turned, pushing through the men, and marched toward the path.

"Reiv, wait!" Brina shouted, hustling to catch up. "What do you plan to do?"

"Leave," he replied.

"Will they come with us, do you think?"

"I do not know."

"What of the prophecy Yustes speaks of? Will it sway them?"

"It will test their faith, and their tempers. Of that I am certain."

Brina struggled to match his steps. "Some—some of them may be tempted to leave. But I think most will stay and fight."

"Then they will die."

A roar of voices approached from behind. Reiv glanced over his shoulder to see a wave of men sweeping around them. The meeting had clearly dispersed, and from the battle cries of the men racing past, a decision had already been reached.

"So they have made their choice," Reiv said, watching them disappear down the trail.

"Perhaps they have the right of it, Reiv," Brina said reluctantly. "We do not know for certain that this Oonayei even exists."

"I do not know about Oonayei, but I do know about the valley."

"Regardless, for us to simply bow to Whyn's demands..."

"It will be–difficult," Reiv conceded.

"What if we stayed, Reiv? Stayed and fought by their sides."

"No," Reiv said.

"So you will simply *abandon* them?"

"If that is what you think I am doing," he snapped, "perhaps you should stay with them."

Brina grabbed him by the arm and yanked him to a halt. "What are you saying?"

Reiv scowled at her fingers digging into his arm. "I am *saying,* everyone has the freedom to make their own choice, even you. You need not feel obligated to go with me if your loyalties lie elsewhere."

"You know where my loyalties lie!"

Reiv jerked his arm from her grasp. "Then why are you putting me in this position? You act like I do not care about these people! You *know* what will happen if I stay."

"By staying, you might at least offer them hope!"

"I saw little hope placed in *me* just now," Reiv said, waving his hand in the direction of the path.

"You place too much value on the actions of a few. They were only reacting out of fear. They are your people. You will see."

"They are *not* my people!" Reiv blurted before he could think what he was saying. "I am Tearian."

Brina slapped him hard across the face.

Reiv raised a hand to his flaming cheek, his eyes stinging from the blow.

"I will not hear you speak such words," Brina said harshly. "You are no longer Tearian, Reiv. No more, do you hear me? You are Shell Seeker."

Tears filled Reiv's eyes—more humiliation to heap upon that which he had already suffered. Yes, he was Shell Seeker. He knew that, just as he knew any hope he had for happiness was all but lost.

"I *know* what I am," he said, forcing the words past the pinch in his throat. "But if I must leave, I can pretend it does not matter, can I not?"

"Pretend all you wish," Brina said. "You fool no one."

Reiv looked toward the village. "Well, I cannot pretend with Jensa and Kerrik. They will need the facts if they are to accept leaving this place."

"They may still choose to stay, Reiv, regardless of your honesty."

Reiv shook his head determinedly. "No. They *must* leave. At least Kerrik must. He would not be found worthy."

৩৩

# CHAPTER 18: UNITED WE STAND, UNITED WE FALL

The village was a mass of confusion. Men, women, young, and old—all were gathered at its core to debate the impending invasion. Reiv and Brina shoved their way through the crowd. Hands clutched at them; voices cried out for answers, but they dared not stop to address them. They broke through the mass and stepped past the perimeter of the village. The air became easier to breathe, but Reiv knew it would only be a momentary respite.

They made their way toward a cluster of palms near the dunes that separated the village from the sea. Torin's and Jensa's hut came into view. As they approached, Reiv's heart grew heavy. This was probably the last time he would ever see it. It occurred to him that although he had lived there for months, he had never called it home. He had always referred to it as Torin's and Jensa's hut. Perhaps, he reasoned, he had not set his roots in Meirla after all. That would have required a hut of his own, wouldn't it? He had dreamed of having one, of course, but had he ever taken any real action? No—all he had done was plant his feet in someone else's. And now it was probably just as well.

They arrived at the doorway, and Reiv paused to gather his wits. *Give me strength,* he whispered, then swept open the drape and entered.

Jensa rushed from seemingly nowhere and threw her arms around him. "The Guard was here—in the village!" she cried.

Kerrik ran up behind her, his eyes as round as saucers. "Did you see them?" he asked Reiv. "The guards, they had *weapons!*"

"Yes, Kerrik. I saw them," Reiv replied. He released Jensa from her hold on him and ushered her to the nearby work bench. "They did not harm you, did they?"

"No," she said as she sat down. "Some stayed and searched the village, but appeared to take nothing. The rest rode toward the Place of Observance. We were so worried. But then, before we knew it, they simply rode out again. Why did they come, Reiv? What do they want from us?"

Reiv realized Jensa's hands were trembling. He grabbed a pitcher from a nearby shelf and poured a mug of herbal tea, then handed it to her. Though Jensa was one of the bravest girls he knew, fears of the plague, Torin's recent injuries, and now the arrival of the Guard had clearly taken their toll. Whether she drank the tea or not, Reiv did not care, as long as the holding of the mug helped calm her hands.

Brina instructed Kerrik to sit next to his sister. The boy huddled next to Jensa as they watched and waited.

Reiv paced for a moment, then stopped to face them. "There is something I must tell you both," he began. "It will not be easy, but there is no way around it."

Color spilled from Jensa's face. "Gods, no," she said. "Do not tell me that Torin is dead."

"No," Reiv assured her. "Cora is taking good care of him."

"Thank the gods," Jensa said. She smiled weakly. "Say what you must, Reiv. Anything is better than what I thought you were about to tell."

"You are right, anything is better," Reiv said. He opened his mouth to explain, but for some reason the words refused to leave his lips. This was going to be harder than he had imagined, though he had had very little time to imagine it.

"I am leaving," he said stiffly. "I will not be coming back."

Kerrik launched from the bench. "No," he cried. "You can't leave us. You can't!"

"I am sorry, Kerrik, but I have no choice," Reiv said.

"You *do* have a choice," Kerrik said. "Everyone has a choice!"

"You are right, Kerrik. I do have a choice. And I have made it."

"As have I," Brina said. "I intend to go with him."

Jensa rose slowly, her eyes moving back and forth between Reiv and Brina. "Why?"

Reiv looked down at his hands, realizing Jensa's weren't the only ones shaking. "Whyn has exiled me from Tearia," he said.

"*Exiled* you? But why?" Jensa asked.

"Jealousy, spite…" Brina answered. "All we know is that he has given the order that Reiv must leave. If he is not gone by sunrise, Meirla will pay."

"We could fight the King," Kerrik said boldly. "We could take our spears and knives and fight him!"

"And we would lose."

"But we fought him before and won," the boy insisted.

"No. We did not win," Reiv said. "The gods cut the fighting short, but they did not hand us a victory." He turned his attention to Jensa. "There is more that I must tell you, and I fear this will be even harder to bear."

Jensa nodded, but remained silent.

Reiv chewed his lip. How could he tell Jensa and Kerrik that they had to leave their home? What words could convey the reason for it? And what words could make them understand the overwhelming guilt he felt for it?

"I am sorry," he said, though that was not what he had meant to say.

"Sorry?" Jensa asked. "For what?"

"For everything." Reiv clenched his fists, fighting to keep his feelings at bay, but self-control was sifting through his fingers, and the words came tumbling out. "If I had never come to this place…" he said. "If I had not begged you to bring me here, none of this would have happened."

Jensa took a step toward him. "Say what you have come to say, Reiv."

Again Reiv hesitated. *Just say it…*he told himself. *Just say it.* "Whyn has reinstated the Purge. He returns in the morning to select those who will serve him and—" His eyes darted between them. "You and Kerrik must leave. There is no other way."

The mug slipped from Jensa's hand, sending tea splattering across the floor.

"I am sorry," Reiv repeated. But he expected no forgiveness.

"*Sorry?*" Jensa asked. "You are *sorry?*"

Reiv grabbed her hands in his and held them fast. "I should have stayed in Pobu all those months ago. I should have accepted my fate, not burdened you with my problems. Then everything would be as before."

"Before *what?*" Kerrik asked.

"Before I came," Reiv said. "Before I ruined everything for you and your family."

"*Ruined* everything?" Jensa threw his hands from hers. "Fool of a prince! Do you truly not *know?*"

Reiv narrowed his eyes with confusion. "Know?"

"Do you not realize how much you have given us? By the gods, Reiv. Before you came to us we were slaves to the King!"

"And will be again," Reiv said. "The Guard is coming, and there is nothing I can do about it!"

Jensa thrust a fist to her hip, waving the index finger of her other hand inches from his nose. "There is only one man that will ever enslave *me* again," she said. "And that is the man who holds my heart!"

"Well, if it is Lyal, you may find death instead of slavery," Reiv said with irritation. "He has convinced the Shell Seekers to fight."

"Is he so wrong in it?" Jensa asked. "What else can we do?"

"You could leave with *me*," Reiv said, annoyed that she had not even considered it. "Whyn said those who wish to leave may do so. Would that not be better than spilling your blood in a fight that cannot be won?"

"At least our pride would be intact!" she said.

"Oh, and mine would not?"

Jensa stomped her foot. "That is not what I meant and you know it!"

Reiv leaned his face to hers. "And what of Kerrik?" he said darkly. "When the Shell Seekers lose, and they *will* lose, what happens to *him*!"

Jensa looked at Kerrik's deformed foot, and her expression collapsed. "Oh gods," she whispered. "You're right."

"What happens?" Kerrik asked, tugging at her skirt.

Reiv and Jensa hesitated, but before they could answer, Brina pulled Kerrik to her side. "No. He is only a child. He is too young to learn such things."

"Young or not," Reiv said, "I would rather he learn it from us than witness it for himself."

The muscles in Brina's jaw tightened. "Very well. But he does not have to know everything, does he? Leave him *some* innocence at least."

Reiv turned to Kerrik and knelt on one knee before him. "Kerrik," he began. "Remember how you told me your parents abandoned you because of your foot?"

Kerrik nodded.

"And that you did not understand why, because you would have been no trouble?"

Kerrik nodded again.

"Well, in Tearia your foot would have been considered an—impurity. And impurities are weeded out."

"I know that," Kerrik said. "My parents threw me away because of my foot." His eyes glistened with tears, but he blinked them back.

"No, Kerrik," Brina said, resting a hand on his head. "They did not throw you away; they loved you very much. But Tearian law forbade them to keep you."

Kerrik turned his gaze to the floor, but Reiv crooked a finger beneath the boy's chin, tilting his face toward his. "What Brina says is true, Kerrik. Your parents saved you—through her. You told me once that Brina saved many babies, did you not?"

"Yes, that time on the beach, when I taught you to swim."

Reiv smiled. "I was a rather awkward swimmer back then."

"Awkward? Humph!" Kerrik said. "A better word for it would be *awful*."

Reiv laughed. "You are right–I was awful. You know, Kerrik, that was an especially difficult time for me. I was struggling to make a new life for myself...away from my family, everything I held dear. At first I thought I could be happy no place else but Tearia, but when I met you and Jensa and Torin, I found happiness after all. Now I must leave, and though I hope you go with me, I will understand if you do not. But if you stay only because this place holds your heart, please know this: You might think Meirla is the only place you can find happiness, but that is not necessarily true."

Reiv rose, then turned to Jensa. "You and Kerrik are free to stay, but you know as well as I do why you must leave. Even Torin has little choice; Cora and I removed two arrows from his back, and they belonged to Whyn. But there is more." He paused, dreading the words. "Mya and Nannaven are dead."

Jensa's hand drifted to her mouth. "No," she said.

"Whyn murdered them, Jensa. He is possessed by a hatred we will never understand. But there is no time for anger or grieving; we must fetch Torin and leave this place."

"Who else is going?" Kerrik asked. "Are we the only ones who must go?"

"No," Reiv replied. "Anyone who wishes may come with us. But I suspect most of the Shell Seekers will stay." He forced a smile for Kerrik's benefit. "As for who *will* be going with us, Nely and Gem are safe with Torin, so they will come, of course. As for Cora—"

"She will go, too, I suppose," Jensa said with obvious annoyance.

"I suspect she will," Reiv said. "She has no other family. I know she will be sad to leave Meirla, but—"

"She would be even *sadder* to leave *you*," Jensa said, finishing the sentence for him.

"Why do you say that?" Reiv asked, surprised by both the statement and the sentiment.

"I'm sorry," Jensa mumbled. "I know you have affection for her."

"And *she* has affection for Torin," Reiv said.

Jensa's expression lifted. "Oh...well...that answers that."

"Frankly, it leaves me rather confused," Reiv said.

Jensa laughed, but her face grew solemn as her gaze wandered over the hut's meager contents. "I suppose there can be no more debate as to whether or not we leave," she said. "But where are we to go?"

"I know of only one place," Reiv said.

"Kirador?" Jensa asked, but Reiv could not tell from her tone whether or not she wished it.

"No...no," Reiv said. "I do not think we would be welcome there. Do not forget, the Kiradyns believe in demons. No doubt we would be mistaken for them. Besides, Dayn and Alicine went home to resume their old lives. I do not think it would do well for us to barge in on them so soon."

"So where, then?" Kerrik asked. His eyes brightened. "Will it have sand and water?"

"No, not like here, but it is beautiful nonetheless. The place I am thinking of is a valley, beyond the mountains. Between here and Kirador."

"How do you know of this place?" Jensa asked suspiciously.

"I learned of it during my Transcension," Reiv said. "Yustes thinks it is a place called Oonayei, but I—"

Jensa gawked. *"Oonayei? The* Oonayei?"

"I do not know—perhaps. There was much argument about it—something about a prophecy. Yustes seemed convinced, but Lyal and his friends scoffed at the idea. I know little about it myself."

"Everyone knows about Oonayei," Kerrik said.

"Is that so? Well how is it that I do not?"

"Because you don't do Service," Kerrik said.

It was true; Reiv did not participate in the spiritual teachings of the Shell Seekers. He believed in the gods—well...the Tearian gods at least. Why, he had even met one of them: Agneis. But he had no desire to participate in any more rituals. That which he had experienced during the act of Transcension was enough for one lifetime.

"Kerrik is right, you know," Jensa said. "If you had paid more attention to your spiritual health, you would know about Oonayei."

Reiv raised his palms in surrender. "You are right, but no lectures, please. There is no time for them. We must be away from here by dark. I suggest we start packing."

Within the hour they had collected the barest of essentials: food, eating and cooking utensils, blankets, medicinals, flint, and a few personal items. There was little time to worry over the rest of their possessions; the sun was nearing the peaks of the mountains, and they still had to fetch Torin and the girls.

Reiv and Kerrik constructed a travois to transport Torin along with the bedding. The cart that they had once used to carry goods to Market held the rest of the supplies. The poles that made up the transport for Torin were fastened to Gitta's harness. She would pull the travois, while Reiv pulled the cart and the others walked alongside.

With supplies finally loaded, Reiv ducked back into the hut to survey its contents one last time. There was still one thing left to retrieve: the book that Nannaven had given him the last time he saw her.

He knelt beside Kerrik's cot and stretched an arm beneath it. The underbelly of the bed was stuffed with boyhood collections: rocks, feathers, and birdlike skeletons; shells, trinkets, and weapons made of sticks. All were crammed willy-nilly, which was why Reiv had hidden the book there in the first place. Since Kerrik rarely pulled anything out of the pile—he primarily just shoved things into it–Reiv felt the hiding place was a good one. Of course, few of Kerrik's collectables were going with them, so there was plenty to dig through.

He pushed some items aside, then scraped out even more as he tunneled to the back of Kerrik's treasure pile.

At last his fingers fell upon the burlap cloth that wrapped the book and, grabbing it by a corner, pulled it out.

He brushed off the dust, but dared not unwrap it. There was no time to look at the thing, and even less to answer questions should a member of the Guard lay eyes on it. Though the treaty had lifted the ban on books, it probably no longer held. And knowing what happened to those caught with writings in the past, he did not relish the idea of being caught with the tome now.

He crawled up from his knees and tucked the bundle beneath his arm, then headed out the hut and to the cart. "Had to retrieve one last thing," he announced casually as he walked past the others who were now waiting by the horse. He secured the book under his sleeping roll, then double-checked the ropes that straddled the cart.

Reiv turned to Jensa, Brina, and Kerrik and his spirits took a dip. Their eyes were not turned in the direction they would soon be traveling, but were gazing past the dunes, longing for the sea.

"Shall we visit it one last time?" Reiv asked. Though they were pressed for time, he realized they could not leave without saying goodbye, and knew he couldn't either.

Together they made their way toward the beach. When they arrived, they stood solemnly, drinking in the bright teal colors of the sea and the musty scent of the waters. The waves crashed loudly in the distance, but lapped the shoreline gently. One by one the four of them stepped into the water. Even Brina, who had never dared, soon stood ankle deep.

Kerrik dove beneath the waves, then sprang back up to the surface. "Look!" he announced. He grinned and thrust out a hand to display his latest prize: a shell, large and pink and spiked in iridescent shades of white.

Reiv's heart melted. "It is a fine one, Kerrik," he said.

Kerrik's grin wavered as his eyes moved past Reiv toward the tree line.

Reiv wheeled around, half-expecting to see a host of guards standing there. But what he saw sent him a very different emotion. Shell Seekers, hundreds of them, were weaving between the trees, making their way slowly toward the beach. All were adorned in their finest garb: togas and sarongs dyed in shades of the sea and the sunset; eyes outlined in kohl; shell jewelry dangling from ears, necks, wrists, and ankles. There were ancient men and elderly women, bent in stature but proud in spirit. There were mothers with children clinging to breast and skirt; young men, old men, and in between. Teens and adolescents, males and females, all approached in mass. And Yustes, the Elder, walked ahead of them all.

Yustes led the people toward Reiv, and there he stopped. His face was lined with age, but his eyes were bright with anticipation. The Elder tipped his head respectfully, and Reiv returned the gesture, but neither said a word; there seemed to be no need.

Yustes turned to face the sea, then raised his arms and began to chant. As the words left his lips, Reiv realized the man was singing in the Old Tongue, a language Reiv had heard only rarely and did not understand. But as the crowd responded in unison, Reiv understood it was a Service of sorts, a ceremony of thanks.

Reiv stood respectfully, feeling like an outsider. He had never thought of their religion as his own, and had no clue as to what they were saying. But as he listened to the love and gratitude reflected in their voices, and gazed at the water to which it was directed, he realized that he felt it too. He loved the sea, and he loved the gods, no matter who, or what, they were.

The Shell Seekers knelt, and so did Reiv. They kissed the sand; he followed their lead. As they sang, he closed his eyes to focus on the rhythm of their words. When they had finished, they prayed for a moment in silence. And as they did so, Reiv whispered a prayer of his own: *Thank you for allowing me to have known these people.*

He felt a hand on his shoulder, and he looked up to see Yustes standing over him. "It is time," the old man said.

"Time?" Reiv asked.

"Time to leave. The sea forgives us. One day she will welcome us back."

"You are—coming with me?" Reiv asked.

"Those of us here. Some have remained to do what they must. Elders Nye and Quin have chosen to stay and offer spiritual guidance."

Reiv ran his eyes over the congregation. "How can we hope to move so many so quickly?"

"Fear not," Yustes said. "You lead us to Oonayei. We will do the rest. It was foretold by the gods; they will not desert us."

But Reiv was skeptical. "How long until they can be packed and ready?" he asked. "The sun will be setting soon. We need to be well gone by then."

"Our supplies are lined up behind yours," Yustes said. "We sought you at your family's hut before finding you here. When we saw your supplies, but not the rest of you, we knew you were doing what we, too, intended—giving thanks to the sea."

Yustes's words resonated through Reiv's thoughts. Jensa... Kerrik...Torin...Brina...they *were* his family, as were every man, woman, and child now standing before him. And should they go with him, he risked losing them all.

"Yustes," he said, "we must go to the Jecta encampment first. Torin must be fetched, and any Jecta who wishes to go with us. Do the people realize that?"

Yustes smiled. "We have already prepared transports and packed additional supplies for the sick. A messenger has been sent ahead to help the Jecta prepare for the journey."

"But many are badly injured," Reiv insisted, "and others are dying of the fever. My family is willing to take the risk for Torin's sake, but these people—" He waved his hand toward the waiting crowd. "Are they sure this is what they want to do?"

"They are," Yustes said. "The gods have never turned their backs on us. Who are we to turn our backs on others?"

They all made their way back to the path near the hut. Reiv stepped toward the cart and slid the pull-harness over his head and across his back and shoulders. He grabbed hold of the pole handles on either side of him and took the first step. The load was heavy, and Reiv was not particularly strong. Torin had always been the one to pull the cart to Market, and now Reiv appreciated the man's seemingly super-human strength.

The encampment was not far, but by the time they reached it, Reiv's arms and legs were shaking from exertion. He disentangled himself from the harness and motioned for Jensa to follow him.

"You stay with Brina," he ordered Kerrik.

"But Reiv—" Kerrik whined.

"No arguments," Reiv said, and he meant it. He did not know what shape Torin would be in when they arrived, and did not want Kerrik to see something he was not prepared to see.

The rest of the Shell Seekers quickly dispersed to various corners of the encampment. Brina and Kerrik joined them as they pitched in to help fold tents, gather supplies, and lift the disabled onto transports.

"Here," Reiv said as he and Jensa arrived at the tent where Torin could be found. He pulled back the flap and ushered Jensa in ahead of him.

Reiv scanned the interior, not sure what to expect, but he was pleased to see Cora and the girls gathering up what little they had, and Torin awake and propped up on a roll of blankets.

"Torin!" Jensa cried. She rushed over and fell to her knees, smothering his face with a half a dozen kisses. He winced and offered her a weak smile, but clearly he was in much pain.

"Oh, gods, what did they do to you?" she said, looking him up and down. "Never you mind. You will soon be on your feet."

Jensa rose, then discreetly motioned for Cora to follow her to the other side of the tent.

"How is he?" Jensa whispered. "Be truthful with me."

"His wounds will heal, but his spirit is very weak."

"What do you mean?" Jensa asked.

"Did Reiv not tell you?" Cora frowned. "Come with me." She looked over her shoulder toward Reiv. "Reiv, will you help the girls finish gathering our things? I'll be back in a moment to help you with Torin."

Reiv nodded, and Cora and Jensa slipped through the flap.

"Tell me, please," Jensa said as they stopped outside the tent.

Cora compressed her lips, then said, "Your brother suffers greatly. When he was in Pobu, the King forced him to make a decision: he could either save Gem and her sister, or he could save Mya and the body of his son."

"Oh, gods," Jensa said, horrified. "And he chose the girls."

"Yes. And received two arrows in his back for it."

Jensa felt grief wash over her, not only for Torin, but for Mya and Farris. She had known Mya since childhood, and Torin had loved her since he was old enough to know what love meant. While Jensa had made many friends since joining Torin in Meirla all those years ago, Mya had always been her one true constant. Now she was gone forever, as was Torin's son. And if Torin did not recover from it, he might soon follow. "Grief could take him," Jensa said. "I fear that even more than the wounds in his back."

"I'll not desert him," Cora replied. "And neither will you. It will take time, but I think he'll heal, especially now that his family is here." She smiled with encouragement. "When you arrived, I saw a spark in him I'd not seen since I first tended him."

Jensa drew a breath of relief, then turned her gaze to her feet. She folded her arms. "I have not been friendly to you, Cora, and I'm sorry. I now realize how much you care for my brother."

Cora cocked her head. "And the reason for your previous distrust of me?"

"I thought you had affection for another," Jensa said. "But it was none of my concern."

"I see," Cora said. "Then there is no longer a reason for you to deny Lyal your affections."

"*What?* Lyal? Gods, why does everyone think I have affection for Lyal!" Jensa said.

Cora lifted a brow. "Not Lyal then?"

Jensa's face went hot. "I'll not deny I've…kissed him. But no. Lyal does not hold my heart."

"Some other man, then?"

"No…I mean…he wouldn't wish it."

"But you would," Cora said.

Jensa shook her head. "We wouldn't be a proper match. Besides, he's meant for another."

"Ah…so you were not trying to protect the *man* from me, but the other woman."

"Well…" Jensa paused, considering Cora's words. Satisfied that they would suffice, she said, "It doesn't matter. I should know better than to second guess the affairs of the heart."

"Don't be so hard on yourself. What is meant to be will be, and if not…" Cora laughed. "I don't think we have as much control over these things as we'd like to believe. I know I never have."

Jensa looked toward the tent. Cora followed her gaze.

"If there's one love that is constant," Cora said, "it's that of family. My mother always said it could cure any ill."

Jensa smiled. "Then my brother will soon be well."

Reiv knelt next to Torin's pallet, watching him closely. Torin's eyes were closed, but Reiv felt certain he was awake.

"Torin," he said softly. He placed a hand on his shoulder.

Torin's eyes opened slightly. He forced a thin-lipped smile. "Thank you for looking after Nely and Gem," he said, then coughed.

Reiv tilted a mug of water to his lips. Torin lifted his head, and with the support of Reiv's hand, took a sip. Reiv eased Torin's head back onto the bedroll. "I am sorry for what my brother did to you, and—and to the others. I am sure you do not wish to speak of it, but please know how grateful we are for you."

"Grateful?" Torin frowned. "Whatever for?"

"For the fact that you are not dead. If you had died, a piece of us would have died with you."

"Us?"

"Yes, *us*," Reiv said, but he felt embarrassed to be included in that *us*. "You know—Jensa, and Kerrik, and Brina, and Cora and Nely and Gem and—" He sighed. "Very well...and me."

Torin's right eyebrow arched. "I didn't know you had such affection for me," he said.

"Do not get any ideas," Reiv said. "Besides, there is another who loves you more I think."

Jensa and Cora swept into the room. Reiv rose to his feet. "The fever must have addled your brother's mind," he said to Jensa. "He made an attempt at humor just now, and it frightens me."

"Humor?" Jensa asked with surprise. She turned to Torin. "Shape shifter, what have you done with my brother?"

Cora made her way over to Torin and reached down to check his wounds. "Much better," she said as she secured the dressings. "Do you think you'll be able to travel? You're the last to load, and everyone is waiting."

"If you think it best," he said.

"I do," she replied, and lifted his arm and placed it around her shoulder.

Reiv helped Cora hoist Torin from the mat, then they guided him to the travois waiting outside. Brina and Kerrik had brought it at Jensa's signal, and Kerrik was now dancing around it, antsy to see his older brother.

"Reiv said you got shot with arrows!" he said as Torin and the others approached.

Torin grunted as Reiv and Cora lowered him onto the transport.

Kerrik leaned over him. "Did it hurt? Where'd you get shot? What did it feel like?"

Torin's eyes flashed at Kerrik, but then glistened with affection. "Nice to see you too."

"Sorry." Kerrik gave him a quick kiss on the cheek. "But did it hurt?"

"Of course it hurt," Torin growled. But he seemed more amused than annoyed. "Take a look at the gaping hole in my chest, if you think you have the stomach for it."

Kerrik sucked in a breath. "Oh *can* I?"

"No, you cannot," Cora said firmly. "I've only just secured the bandages and we need to be going."

"I can tell you all about it, Kerrik," Gem said. "I saw everything." She was standing next to Kerrik now, and her face was absolutely beaming. In all the time Reiv had been with the girl, he had never seen her beam about anything. But then he recalled her saying she was going to marry Kerrik someday, and realized there might be something to it.

With Torin settled, and the Shell Seekers and Jecta ready to go, Reiv motioned them to follow him. He turned to the cart, but then a huge tattooed man stepped in front of him and secured the harnesses onto his own muscular shoulders.

"Gair!" Reiv exclaimed. He had not spent as much time with the Jecta blacksmith as his cousin Dayn had, yet he could not help but be overjoyed at the sight of him. "You are alive!"

Gair nodded. "I am. You?"

"I have been better."

Gair lifted the cart poles. "This is an ambitious undertaking, Reiv," he said, "even for you."

"I had no choice. As for the rest…" He gazed back at the long line of people that would soon be following his lead. "They are either as desperate as I am, or they have placed their faith in the wrong person."

"Oh, I doubt that," Gair said. He grinned and jerked the wagon into motion.

The line of people at their backs began to move like a great waking worm, until at last it evened out and moved forward at an equalizing pace. As they reached the first rise, Reiv turned to look at Meirla one last time. But then his gaze fell upon the caravan, and a lump of realization made its way to his throat. These people had placed their future in his hands, believing he, as a Transcendor, could lead them to some sort of promised land. True, he had died and returned to tell of it. True, he'd been given visions of the past, present, and future. But what no one yet realized was that while he knew how to get them to the valley, he had not allowed himself to see what would happen once they got there.

❧

# CHAPTER 19: WAR PLAY

The encampment was deserted, and Whyn's disappointment had quickly reached a boiling point. His spies had inspected the place but one day prior and had assured him it was well-filled with Jecta. He raked his eyes over the remains of the encampment, working to steady his temper. Perhaps he should not have given the Shell Seekers warning. That was something Whyn would do. But not her. Never her.

A stab of pain shot through him, sending a grimace to his face.

*Did I not tell you to be swift about it!* she hissed. *You and your human frailties. How many more lessons must you be taught?*

"Pray few I hope," Whyn whispered. He clutched his gut, fighting to remain upright in the saddle.

*You well know how I like to give lessons. Do not test me further, boy, or your body will soon not be worth the having.*

Whyn flinched. Yes, he knew the lessons that she taught, carried out by her command, yet meted by his own hand. She could have him press his face to the flames if she wished it, even slit his own throat if that was her desire. As it was, she'd only had him flog his back until raw, carve her name upon his flesh, and perform acts upon himself so deviant, he wondered how in the world she had ever thought them up. Each time she would heal him and soothe him, then have him repeat the act over and over again, until at last she was satisfied the lesson had been learned. Perhaps that was why Whyn had come to enjoy the suffering of others so much. It gave him the power to hurt someone other than himself.

He glared at the encampment, realizing he should have purged it when he'd had the chance. But no, he had hesitated, and now it was nothing more than dying campfires and a few discarded tents. No blood, no torture. Just refuse and disappointment—her disappointment.

Whyn guided his horse through the debris. He had hoped to open some veins here today, but the remaining Shell Seekers would just have to do. Surely that would appease her. He turned his eyes toward a nearby hillside and smiled. A funeral pyre could be seen, glowing with the embers of the dead. He felt a glimpse of satisfaction. But it soon ebbed.

Whyn jerked the horse's reins. The animal snorted and strained at the bit as he steered it toward a mound of human waste and medical debris. He stared at the pile with disgust. "Torch this," he shouted to a nearby group of guards. He pulled a perfume-scented kerchief from the belt at his waist and pressed it to his nose.

Several guards on horseback galloped forward, waving torches that had been greased and lit. They tossed them onto the heap. It roared into flames, sending an acrid stench into the air.

Whyn reined his horse back. "Commander!" he barked. "Have the area searched. There might be stragglers."

"Yes, Lord," the Commander called back. He snapped a brusque order, and several guards spurred their horses into the surrounding trees, swords whacking through the underbrush.

The Commander reined his horse toward Whyn, then stopped at his side.

*What of Meirla?* she hissed into Whyn's mind.

"Is Meirla secured?" Whyn asked the Commander.

"It is, my lord," the Commander replied.

*The dead? What of the dead?*

"How many dead?" Whyn asked.

"Many. But we captured the survivors with little difficulty."

"Was my brother amongst them?"

*He was not.*

"No, Lord."

"Did they have a leader?" Whyn asked.

"Apparently. But we have him. Shall I have him brought to you?"

*Yes...Let us teach him a lesson.*

"I look forward to meeting him," Whyn said. "But later. I should like to see the village first."

The Commander shouted another order, and he and a group of guards gathered at Whyn's side to escort him to Meirla.

"Anything else I should know?" Whyn asked as they rode casually toward the village.

"Only that the structures have been torched, and the survivors await your decision."

Whyn felt anticipation surge from his breast to his loins. But this was not lust in the usual sense. No, this was lust of a very different nature. He smiled. "Then let us go to them," he said. "We cannot keep our lady waiting."

The surviving Shell Seekers had already been sorted by the time Whyn arrived at the village. The Guard were well-drilled in their duties. There were many ways a slave could serve a master, and their King expected organization and ease when making his selections.

All of the captives were on their knees, roped together at the neck, their hands bound at their backs. There were four groups of them. Girls and women made up the largest, assembled according to age and physical attributes. Those with exceptional beauty would be used to please the court. The rest would be sent to serve individual Tearian masters or to join the labor force currently rebuilding the city. Some would be housed to replenish the stock, but only those with purer features would be considered for that. The aged and infirm had already been purged, their bodies tossed upon the pyres along with those who had perished in the earlier skirmish.

Children were yanked from their parents' arms and sent to a group of their own. Infants lay squalling upon the ground, while toddlers clung to children only slightly older than themselves. Pre-adolescents were corralled, boys and girls separated. Adult males made up yet another group. They were the most heavily guarded.

Whyn eyed the prisoners from atop his horse, sorry now that he had not joined in the fray. It had not been much, the Guard had described it as little more than archery practice, but still, it might have been fun.

A chair had already been brought for him. Though Whyn had no intention of lingering in the vile place, he was not one to give up his comforts. Servants had laid out a tapestry rug decorated with swirls of red, black, and gold. Upon it sat the chair, its seat draped in red velvet, its back and legs carved from the finest mahogany.

Whyn eased out of his saddle and strolled toward the chair. The Commander followed at his back. A groom quickly gathered their horses' reins and led them aside, while a serving girl in a nearly transparent gown brought Whyn a goblet of wine. She curtsied and stepped aside as a boy offered him an assortment of fruits, cheeses, and meats, all displayed on a highly polished platter.

Whyn sat, then took a swallow of wine and handed the goblet to the nearest servant. He rested his elbows on the arms of the chair and ran his eyes over the prisoners assembled before him.

"This is *all?*" he asked.

"Yes, Lord," the Commander replied.

Whyn sighed. "Very well," he said with a flick of his hand. "The girls first."

A line of adolescent girls were marched forward and made to face him. He looked them over, but with little enthusiasm. He pointed offhandedly to one with pale hair and eyes. "That one pleases me," he said. A guard holding a bowl of dye dipped his fingers and painted a bright blue streak upon the girl's forehead.

Whyn moved his attention down the line. He gestured toward a raven-haired girl with a murderous expression plastered across her face. "She will serve the reconstruction effort well enough." Again a line was painted on her forehead, but this time it was black rather than blue. Next to her a girl was painted with a streak of green, a serving girl, and beyond her one was marked with red, a breeder.

On and on Whyn singled out girls from the line. Before long their terrified expressions came to reveal that of understanding: Those that had been painted were the lucky ones. Though their futures would not be pleasant, those that received no paint would have no futures at all.

After those chosen were separated from those who were not, Whyn ordered the group of women brought before him. When he was finished with them, he then made selections from the group of boys. He felt uneasy at the pleasure he took in it, but he knew it was her pleasure, not his.

At last the men were brought before him. He felt a surge of anticipation.

*Where is the leader? Him first.*

Whyn grinned. "Let us first guess who he is," he told her. He moved his eyes down the line, resting his gaze on each man individually. Although most made no effort to disguise their contempt, he had little difficulty selecting the leader amongst them.

"That one," he said, nodding toward a handsome young man glowering at him with kohl-lined eyes.

*Yessss, of course.* Whyn felt her delight. *Ah…but he is pretty, is he not?*

"Yes, very," Whyn said.

*I should like to play with him.*

Whyn cringed, but made every effort to disguise his revulsion. He knew all too well what she meant; she had played with *him* often enough. But what she had in mind for the handsome young Shell Seeker was different. And for the first time in a long time he felt compelled to say the one word he knew would bring him more suffering. "No."

Her fury swept through his veins like acid. *You shall pay for your disrespect,* she said. *But no need for the others to see you grovel. Later, after I am finished with the boy.*

Whyn gritted his teeth. "I will not do as you desire with this one."

She laughed, a laugh so cruel it twisted him to the core. *You will, and I shall enjoy watching you do it. Now bring him to me. The Commander may choose from the rest.*

"Commander," Whyn barked. "Escort the leader to me. You may make the selections from the rest. We are leaving."

Lyal was cut from the line and dragged before the King. With his hands still bound at his back he was forced to kneel. His face was shoved toward Whyn's feet where he was made to press his lips upon them. The young man was hers now. And there was nothing Whyn could do about it.

☙

# PART THREE

## QUICKENINGS

# Chapter 20: The Writing on the Walls

Alicine marched toward the barn, guilt gnawing at her insides. Ever since she'd learned of the Gathering, and had baited Eyan and Dayn over it, she'd felt miserable. That, along with the fight she'd had with her brother, had brought her nothing but worry. She knew she had a right to her opinion–there was always more than one side to an argument—but if she wanted to clear the air, and have the company of her brother or her cousin any time soon, she knew she would have to offer an apology.

She set her teeth, trying to maintain some resolve. If apologies had to be made, she should probably start with Eyan. He didn't know enough to take a stand on anything, and was probably more forgiving than Dayn.

She yanked open the barn door and stepped inside. It was dark and stuffy, and she couldn't imagine why Eyan would want to spend so much time there. She hadn't seen him since dinner the evening before–he'd only popped in for a quick bite, then had left to do his chores—but by morning it was clear his bed had not been slept in. Vania assured her this was not unusual; Eyan frequently chose the solitude of the barn over the comforts of his bed. But as Alicine scrutinized the barn's shadowy recesses, she could not help but wonder, was he up to something she'd just as soon not know about?

She stepped in further. "Eyan? You in here?" she called. But there was no response. She glanced from side to side, but saw no sign of him, only farm tools left to be hung and a floor spotted with horse manure. Alicine twisted her mouth. Whatever Eyan was doing, it certainly wasn't his chores.

"Eyan?"

She detected a slight rustling and turned her eyes to the planks above. "You might want to get yourself down here and finish your chores," she said. "Just because your father left doesn't mean he won't come home early."

*That should do it*, she thought to herself. She tilted her head, certain she heard a *huff* followed by the scent of an extinguishing candle.

Eyan leaned over the edge of the loft. "Ye haven't seen him, have ye?"

"No, I only meant—" She sighed. "Come down, will you?"

Eyan slid down the ladder. A cloud of dust rose from his feet as they hit the ground. He turned to face her. "What d' ye want?" he asked, but his tone sounded rather cross.

Alicine chewed her lip, then gathered her pride. She had never cared for apologies, especially when she had to make them.

"Listen," she said as casually as she could, "I'm sorry I pitted you against Dayn in this whole Gathering issue. You don't have to *want* to go if you don't want to. But if you don't, then you should at least tell your parents."

Eyan crossed his arms and studied the ground. "I d'know if I want to or not. I don't really know what it means."

"It means you're going to meet hundreds of people at once, and there's going to be a lot of scrutiny."

His eyes turned to hers. "What scrutiny?"

"Like...lots of questions, maybe some accusations about your eye color and why your parents kept you hidden these past nineteen years."

Eyan remained silent.

"Didn't your parents tell you what to expect? I mean, they talked to you about it, right?"

"Mother said I'd make friends, but Father seemed worried." Eyan creased his brow, considering it. "I'd like to have friends. I never had any real ones before, just pretend ones."

"Pretend ones?"

"Aye. I make up friends...draw 'em on parchment. But they're not real."

"May I see them?" Alicine asked. She had always appreciated paintings and sketches, mainly because it was a skill she could never hope to acquire. Though she could sew a fine stitch and was well-gifted in herbology, to take a simple writing tool and recreate a tree, or a bird, or someone's *face*, was simply beyond her.

Eyan's cheeks blushed. He dawdled for a moment, then said, "Well, I s'pose you can see some, but not all of 'em, all right?"

Alicine smiled. "All right...some then."

Eyan pointed his finger toward the loft. "They're up there," he said, and turned and led her to the ladder.

Eyan took the lead up the rungs while Alicine followed. "They're in the back," he said over his shoulder when he had reached the top. He scrambled onto the platform and grabbed a fire stick from a nearby box. "Wait here though, aye?"

Alicine perched near the top as Eyan disappeared to the back of the loft. She could hear him shuffling around, but the darkness denied her a clear view of what he was doing.

He soon returned with a lit lantern. He reached for her hand and helped her navigate the last few rungs.

With lantern in hand the back of the loft was lit in a golden glow, drawing Alicine's eyes to a plank table covered with numerous bowls of dye powders, chalk, and liquid colors. Dozens of pictures could be seen tacked to the walls, but there were a few spaces where some appeared to have been removed.

"Oh...my," Alicine exclaimed. She walked slowly toward the wall, drinking in the images as she approached. Eyan followed, raising the lantern to further illuminate the gallery.

Alicine paused, running her fingers gently over some of the pictures, leaning in to study others more closely.

"D'ye like 'em?" Eyan asked.

"Yes, but..." Alicine turned to face him. "Where have you seen people like this?"

Eyan lowered the lantern, the happy expression on his face vanishing with the light. "I know I shouldn't be drawin' demons. Does it make me a sinner d'ye think?"

"No—of course not. I just wondered where you've seen people like this, that's all."

"I found pictures of 'em on a wall in a cavern past the brook. I know it's wrong, but I like the way they look. Some I copied, but others I made up."

Alicine returned her attention to the drawings. Most were on parchment, but others were on animal skins or shavings of bleached bark. Each held the image of a different person: male, female, young and old; all were beautiful, but even more disturbing, all were blond-haired and pale-eyed.

Alicine moved down the wall, surveying more and more portraits. Eyan held up the lantern and followed along behind her.

Alicine halted with a sudden intake of breath. "What about him?" she asked, pointing to one image in particular. "Was he there, in the cave, too?"

Eyan leaned in, examining the image in question. "Aye. He's there."

Alicine felt dizzy as she stared at the image. Her mind could barely grasp what her eyes were seeing. There before her was a painting of a red-haired boy. And he was staring back at her with bright violet eyes.

Alicine barreled through the front door, letting it slam against the wall at its back. "Dayn!" she shouted. "Come quick and see!"

Dayn jumped from the bench and reached for the knife next to the potatoes he was about to peel.

"What is it?" he exclaimed. His eyes darted toward the door. "Who's here?"

"No one," Alicine responded. "Just come and see."

Dayn set down the knife with a scowl. "Don't scare me like that," he grumbled.

"Come *on*!" Alicine grabbed his hand and pulled him from the bench.

"Lands, what's goin' on?" Vania asked from across the room. An armload of laundry was in her arms, and her startled eyes were peering over it.

"Nothing, auntie," Alicine called back breathlessly.

"A lot o' carryin' on over nothin'," Vania muttered. "Bout sent me to the grave."

"Sorry…" Alicine said as she swept out the doorway with Dayn in tow.

"Let go my hand," Dayn groused when they reached the barn.

Alicine dropped it, but grabbed his sleeve and continued to pull him along.

"And let go my sleeve. God, Alicine. What's going on?"

She grinned. "You'll see." Then she led him toward the ladder.

Eyan peeked over the edge and watched as Dayn and Alicine ascended the rungs. He glanced over his shoulder nervously, then took Alicine's hand when she reached the top. After she had stepped safely aside, Eyan offered Dayn his hand as well.

"I can handle it," Dayn said gruffly as he crawled onto the platform.

"Sorry," Eyan mumbled.

"For what?" Dayn asked. He slapped the dust and straw from his pants legs. "I only meant I was at the top and didn't need any help." He sighed with annoyance. "What is it you dragged me up here to see, Alicine?" he asked. "A trunk full of dresses or something equally important?"

Alicine curled her lip, then took the lantern from Eyan's hand and marched to the back of the loft. Raising the light, she nodded toward the portraits tacked to the walls and said, "Look."

Dayn's jaw went slack as his eyes moved over Eyan's drawings. "What the—"

"Eyan did them," Alicine said.

Dayn turned to Eyan. "You—did these?" he asked.

"Aye," Eyan said meekly.

"Where have you seen people like this?" Dayn asked.

"He saw pictures of them in a cave near the river," Alicine said. "And look, Dayn; look at *this* one."

She moved the light toward the red-haired image at the far end of the gallery. Dayn stepped closer, then took a startled step back. He gawked at the Reiv look-alike, then wheeled to face Eyan. "Take me to the cave," he said.

Eyan's expression tightened. Dayn's command clearly had him rattled, or was it something else?

Dayn moved toward him. "*Now*," he ordered.

"But—but Father said I'm not to go back there," Eyan sputtered.

"I don't care," Dayn said. "I need to see what's in that cave."

"What is it, Dayn?" Alicine asked. "He told me he was only copying old cave pictures. What else do you think you'll find?"

"History. Or prophecy," he said. "I guess we'll know when we get there."

Eyan nodded reluctantly and took the lantern from Alicine's hand. He beckoned for her and Dayn to follow. They descended the ladder and headed out the barn, then made their way around to the other side of it. He motioned for them to keep quiet as he peeked around the corner toward the house. His mother could be seen heading to the drying line.

"She'll skin me alive if she knows where I'm takin' ye," he whispered. "Where's your mother right now? Do ye know?"

"Last I saw her she was heading to the root cellar," Alicine said.

"All right," Eyan said. "Let's go then."

They snuck around the back and high-tailed it toward the woods. Eyan took the lead, darting around the wood-pile, then sprinting into a nearby copse of woods. The snapping of twigs shouted their every step, prompting Dayn to glance over his shoulder as often as Eyan did. But no one appeared to be following or standing with their hands fisted on their hips as they watched them go.

Before long they were following a brook which led to a widening stream. "Not far now," Eyan said. He shoved aside a wall of brush and sidled into a narrow abutment of rock.

"How'd you ever find this place?" Dayn asked, stepping sideways as he followed.

Eyan changed direction and scrambled up an incline of gravel. "Chasin' a rabbit," he replied, then vanished into the cliffside.

Dayn and Alicine reached the spot where Eyan had disappeared and realized they were standing at the entrance of a cave.

"Come on," Eyan's voice echoed from the shadows.

"I think I'll wait here," Alicine said.

"I think I'll wait with you," Dayn said with uneasiness. "How far in does it go?" he hollered in Eyan's direction. "Do we need a torch?"

"No," Eyan hollered back. "It's shallow; plenty o' light."

Dayn drew a breath and ducked inside. Alicine followed close behind.

Dayn soon learned that Eyan was right; the cave was nothing more than a wide fissure in the rocks, eroded into a grotto of lichen and spotty mushrooms. Bright light spilled in at its mouth, but grew dim as it crept toward the throat.

"The pictures are further back," Eyan informed them. "It's not as bright there, but ye can still see 'em."

He waved for them to follow, and the three of them worked their way along a path littered with splintered bones and rocky debris.

Eyan stepped over the skeletal remains of a rather large animal, but Alicine worked her way as far from the carcass as possible. Dayn, on the other hand, stopped to lean over it. Perhaps it warranted investigation, he reasoned. The last time he'd seen bones in a cave, they had not belonged to an animal.

"What are ye lookin' at?" Eyan asked, twisting around to see what held Dayn's attention.

"Just wondering what these were," Dayn said. He squatted down to get a better look. "It's not a wolf is it?"

"No. It's a mountain cat," Eyan said.

Dayn's eyes widened. *"Mountain cat?* They haven't been seen in these parts for at least five hundred years."

"I know, but I saw a picture o' one in an old book once. I can tell by the teeth and the shape of the head that that's what this is, or was."

"How old do you think it is?" Alicine asked, glancing around nervously.

"Old, but not five hundred years, that's for sure," Eyan said. "I think this one was killed by a person."

Dayn straightened up. "How do you know?" he asked.

"See the knife marks on the bones there? But I also found the knife and—" Eyan paused, watching Alicine cautiously. "There's what's left of a person back there," he said, then motioned them toward the back of the cave.

The ceiling grew lower the further back they went, and Dayn and Eyan were soon walking with knees bent and heads ducked, though Alicine had far less difficulty.

The ceiling suddenly soared to incredible heights, and they found themselves standing in a tubular-shaped chamber. There was no exit, clearly they had reached a dead end, but above them a narrow shaft of light ricocheted in, leaving areas of the room illuminated in bright shades of gray. Eyan stopped and pointed. Slowly he moved his finger from one end of the circular space to the other.

"Those are the pictures," he said, "and that—" He turned his attention to the floor near the far wall. "—is the person I was tellin' ye about."

Dayn tore his attention from the images he had only just begun to see and turned it to the musty lump against the far wall. He walked toward it then stopped, staring at it for a long silent moment. It was a skeleton in an advanced state of decay, curled up on a tattered pallet of moldy cloth. At its side sat several bowl-shaped rocks, each with a hint of stain at their center. A writing tool was propped nearby, and next to it lay a pouch and a rusty old dagger.

Dayn knelt down and fingered the disintegrating remains of the victim's garb, then noticed a shriveled leather belt at its waist. Something about it caught his eye. He removed the belt gently, then ran his fingers along the symbols tooled into the grain. Runes, he realized, and Tearian ones at that.

"What is it?" Alicine asked.

Dayn rose with a start. He had been so immersed in his discovery, he'd not realized she'd come up behind him. "Look at this," he said, thrusting the belt toward her.

Alicine leaned away. "No thank you," she said.

Dayn shook the belt. "It's Tearian, Alicine. Tearian!"

Alicine's lips parted as her eyes gravitated to the belt.

"What's Tearian?" Eyan asked. He was peeking over Alicine's shoulder, curious as to what all the fuss was about.

"This belt has runes on it," Dayn said. "And they aren't Kiradyn. They're Tearian. Tearia is on the other side of the mountains—that place we went to after we left the festival."

"Oh…I heard ye tell your mother about it," Eyan said. "But I didn't think it was, ye know, *real*."

Dayn brushed past him, ignoring the implication, and made his way back to the paintings nearest the entrance. As he studied them, he realized they weren't just random images; they were faded petroglyphs, carved and stained upon the rocks. He stepped to the right as he slowly worked his way along the story pattern.

Alicine moved to his side. "A line of people," she observed. "One after another, walking toward the mountains."

"And Kiradyn, by the looks of them," Dayn said.

Eyan pointed to a spot further down. "That's where the demon images are," he said. "They're walkin' toward the mountains, too. I guess that's how they came to live there."

"Demons don't exist," Dayn said absently. His attention was fully focused on the images before him, not the ones down the way.

Alicine stepped around her brother, anxious to see more. "Look, Dayn," she cried. "It's like Reiv said. There was a gathering beneath the mountains, in the chamber with the altar."

Dayn shuffled down a few feet to see what she was referring to. Sure enough, beneath an exaggerated image of the fire mountain, was a cave, and within it a celebration of two very different races of people.

Eyan shuddered. "That's where the demons sacrificed people."

"No it's not," Dayn said with annoyance. "See, the people are smiling."

Eyan moved closer. "Oh. I thought they were cryin'."

Dayn rolled his eyes and stepped around Eyan, turning his attention to the line of pale-haired Tearians making their way to the mountain from the other side.

"Look here, Eyan," Dayn said, pointing to the wall. "See? The pale people there are from Tearia. And the darker ones, over there, are from Kirador."

Eyan surveyed them more intently.

"A long time ago," Dayn continued, "they were friends. Every year they'd meet in a great cavern beneath the mountain to celebrate."

"What were they celebratin'?" Eyan asked.

"I'm not sure. But one day something terrible happened." Dayn moved down, certain of what he would find: the next chapter of the story that Reiv had told him.

"See—there," Dayn pointed out. "The mountain erupted in fire and the people in the cavern died." He leaned toward it. "You're right, these *are* crying."

"So are quite a few others by the looks of it," Alicine said. She motioned her head toward the land depicted on both sides of the mountain—fire to the east, blackness to the west.

"Daghadar's Purge," Eyan whispered.

"No, no. Not Daghadar's Purge," Alicine interjected. "It just happened, like this last time, only back then it was much worse."

"Will it happen again?" Eyan asked.

Dayn and Alicine exchanged glances.

"I haven't been sick…recently," Dayn said, realizing the illnesses that once alerted him to such things hadn't visited him in a while.

"That must mean it's over then," Alicine said optimistically.

"What happened next?" Eyan asked.

"Well…" Dayn said. "At first the Tearians were afraid, but then they grew angry. They thought the gods were punishing them for fraternizing with the Kiradyns. So they started killing anyone who looked like a Kiradyn. They thought that was what the gods wanted them to do."

"Gods?" Eyan asked. "You mean they had more than one?"

"Yes," Alicine said. "They have many."

"Then that's why they were punished," Eyan said. "Because they didn't believe in Daghadar. There's only one Maker, and He's it."

"Well if you're so sure about that," Dayn said, "why did Daghadar kill the Kiradyns, too?"

"Because they were mixin' with the heathens," Eyan replied.

Dayn's impatience flared, but Alicine placed a commanding hand on his arm. "Let's finish looking at the drawings," she suggested.

Dayn expelled a huff and moved down the wall. As expected, blond-haired people were shown dying on the Kiradyn side of the mountain, dark-haired people doing the same on the other.

"Here, Eyan. See? This shows the Tearians killing the Kiradyns, and the Kiradyns killing the Tearians."

Eyan leaned in closer. "That's not people, that's demons."

Dayn growled. "No—that's Tearians."

"How do ye know so much," Eyan asked. "That isn't what the Written Word says."

"I learned of it while we were in Tearia," Dayn said. "A friend—well, cousin actually—told us. He had visions."

Eyan looked horrified. "*Visions*? That's the Dark One's work!"

"Don't be ridiculous," Alicine snapped. "If that were true, Dayn and I never would have found our way home. Reiv told us how to get here, past the valley and all that. He'd seen it in visions."

Dayn turned and crossed to the other side of the chamber, attempting to distance himself from further debate. But as new images came into view, he became more and more intrigued. These drawings held no semblance of order like the others did. They were more like a kaleidoscope, a hodgepodge of depictions that appeared to tell more than one story, or no story at all. He ran his eyes over the scenes. There were elongated swords and people tied to stakes, a sky turned black and...Dayn shuddered; these were nothing like the stories Reiv had told him. These were different—and far darker. Were they records of past events, he wondered, or prophecies of the future? He prayed they were only the hallucinations of a madman, for if there was any truth to them, there existed an evil that no one could have imagined—and it dwelt in Aredyrah.

He moved further down and discovered more disturbing images. One in particular caught his attention; it resembled a giant snake, writhing through the hills and mountainsides of the island. He took a closer look and was relieved to find it wasn't a serpent, but a line of people. Dayn stepped back, trying to gain a broader perspective, and it was then that he realized the entire painting was a map of Aredyrah. It covered so much of the wall that he had not initially recognized that the images represented events and where they had occurred. The mountains were easy to identify now, as was Tearia and Kirador. He studied the snake-like line of people. They were moving northward, from Tearia toward the valley he and Alicine had crossed. A migration of people, but how many? He tried to calculate their number, starting at the head of the line, but he suddenly realized the leader had hair of a very distinctive nature—red. Red like Reiv's.

Dayn glanced over his shoulder at Alicine. There was no need to show it to her, he reasoned, especially since there was no way to interpret its true meaning. The images could be of events that had happened in the past, not the future, and it wasn't like Reiv was the only person ever born with hair like that. No, Dayn decided; he would not tell her, not now anyway. He would steer her away from it...make some excuse...say they had to leave or—

"Where's the picture of the boy with the red hair?" he heard Alicine ask Eyan across the way.

Dayn cringed.

"There," Eyan said, "and there, and there, and..."

Dayn turned to see where Eyan was pointing and realized: The Reiv look-alike wasn't just on the map—he was all over the room.

☙

# CHAPTER 21: THE GATHERING

Dayn paced the kitchen, deep in thought. It had been fourteen days since Haskel had left to notify the clans of the Gathering, and he had said he'd be back in ten.

"Stop your frettin'," Vania said from the table. "There's nothin' to worry about."

Dayn flicked her a look of annoyance. She had uttered those same words to him at least a dozen times, but Dayn was not convinced that she meant them.

He stepped toward the kitchen window and peered through the panes.

"It's been fourteen days," he said.

"Aye, it has," Vania said. She smiled at Morna who was sitting next to her, chopping vegetables. "Was it you that taught him to count, dear?"

Dayn marched to the table. "Shouldn't we at least go to Uncle Nort's to see if he made it that far?" he asked.

Vania grabbed a turnip and cleaved it with a thrust of her knife. The blade tapped against the cutting board as she chopped it into pieces. "Of course he made it that far," she said. "Nort's homestead is the closest one, isn't it?" She rose and scraped the pieces of vegetable into a pot, then slanted her eyes at Dayn. "What are ye implyin', Dayn?"

"Well, if Nort's place is the closest, why isn't Haskel back already? I thought each family was to send the message down the line."

"The entreaties we plan to present to the Plenum of Four must be addressed quickly. That's why Haskel felt he should notify several homesteads himself. Accordin' to the calendar, if we make the entreaties tonight—on the day we planned—the stars will be in the constellation of Konyl. Hopefully the Chieftains will see it as an omen that favors us."

Dayn could not disguise his irritation. "I doubt even Konyl will be of much help tonight," he groused.

Vania stepped to the sink where she gave the pump handle a hearty thrust. "Have you and Eyan got all the tables trestled?" she asked as she filled the pot of vegetables with water.

Dayn sighed. "Yes, auntie," he said. "The tables are finished, and the stage and the benches."

"And the barn's cleaned?" Morna asked.

"Yes, Mother. Clean as it's going to get."

"And the circle of stones?" Vania added.

"Yes...assembled." Dayn moved to the window and gazed out toward the plenum location. It was highlighted by a wide circle of stones that seemed to lord over the hillside. The circle was where the plenum itself would take place, and the space within it was considered sacred for the duration of the Gathering. The stones were not large, not like those that made up the more ancient circles of Kirador, but they had been difficult to erect nonetheless.

Within the circle, Dayn and Eyan had built a stage, and at the center of the circle they had piled wood for the great bonfire that would be lit after the plenum. The pile only awaited the touch of the torch that would signal the conclusion of business and the commencement of festivities. But Dayn wasn't sure there would be much to celebrate.

"And the wood for the—" Morna began.

"Yes," Dayn said with annoyance. "The tables—the seats—the barn—the circle—the stage—the benches—the wood for the bonfire—logs and kindling for the campfires. Anything *else*?"

"You don't have to snap," Morna said. "It's not like the rest of us haven't been working day and night to get things done."

"Well what's Alicine been doing?" Dayn said. "Besides fretting about what she's going to wear, I mean."

"She's been gatherin' mushrooms and berries," Vania offered, "and helpin' your mother and me with the cookin'. Now don't ye go suggestin' your sister's not been doin' her part."

"She made some lovely decorations for the barn, too," Morna said.

Dayn rolled his eyes.

Vania gazed toward the open front door. Though winter would soon be approaching, the weather today was almost spring-like, and she had thrown open every portal in the house to welcome it in. She drew a deep breath. "I hope Eyan comes home with a buck this time," she said. "You boys've brought us back plenty o' rabbits, bless your hearts, but a buck would make a fine impression on the clans. There haven't been many around these parts lately."

"Why didn't you go hunting with Eyan today?" Morna asked Dayn.

"I don't know," he mumbled. "Didn't feel like it I guess."

"Well, maybe next time," she said.

Dayn turned toward the doorway. "I think I'll go find Alicine."

"You'll find her in the barn, dear. She's adding the final touches to the dance floor."

Dayn's insides rankled. The dances were always the part he hated most. It wasn't that he didn't like dancing, though he'd never actually done much of it. It wasn't even the issue of girls; his heart had always belonged to Falyn, so the others didn't matter. But still, that hadn't kept him from feeling even more like an outcast when he was the only boy in the room not doing it.

He exited the house and headed for the barn. When he arrived, he spotted Alicine perched atop a ladder, hammering colorful strips of cloth along a beam. In addition to the numerous streamers she had already hung, the room was dotted with crocks containing bouquets of wildflowers and dried flora. Most of the flowers from the meadows had already faded with the changing season, but the purples and golds of the grasses she'd gathered gave the arrangements a nice earthy touch.

"Looks good," Dayn said, but his tone held little enthusiasm.

Alicine jerked with a start, then twisted around to face him. "You scared me half to death," she said. She scrambled down the ladder and set the hammer aside. Smiling, she ran her eyes over the interior of the barn. "You like it?"

"I said I did, didn't I," Dayn said.

Alicine looked at him with skepticism. "You *are* coming to the dance, aren't you?"

Dayn shrugged. "Maybe."

"This'll be Eyan's first dance, Dayn. It would be nice if you came to at least give him some advice."

Dayn forced a laugh. "Like I know anything."

Alicine scowled. "Fine. You can both sit off to the side together and feel sorry for yourselves." She turned and grabbed up another handful of streamers, then surveyed the beams.

"I think you have plenty up already," Dayn said. "Add much more color and no one will get any sleep."

"Like anyone will get any sleep anyway," Alicine said with a grin.

"No, I suppose not."

Dayn gazed around the room. The barn, though primarily decorated for the main dance, would also accommodate the less-official party expected to follow. Most families had packed their own tents and bedding, and eventually crept back to them and the wagons that had brought them. But one group was known to linger at the dances well into dawn: the pre-adults. Of all the clan members, they seemed to require the least amount of sleep and the most amount of socializing, and generally conducted celebrations of their own after everyone else had retired for the night. Although they would be well outside the earshot of their parents, the barn doors would be kept strictly open, and there would be plenty of Elders on hand to keep young virtues intact.

But Dayn had no interest in any party; he was mainly interested in the bed he would be falling into early. He had never felt comfortable around people his own age, at least not in Kirador; the events of past Gatherings had pretty much sealed that sentiment. Regardless, he had no desire to make new friends. It would be good for Eyan, he supposed, but as for himself, the only friends he wanted were back in Tearia.

Alicine saw things differently, of course. She'd already made it clear that her heart belonged in Kirador, and though a part of it still remained with Reiv, she could not have Reiv and Kirador both. As for Dayn, the approaching party gave him a glimmer of hope, at least. If Alicine met a candidate for future husband, then Dayn could feel assured that there would be someone to take care of her, and maybe even Mother. And if Alicine were to meet that person tonight, Dayn could return to Tearia sooner than expected, and without the guilt of having left his mother and sister behind.

"So have you decided what you're going to wear?" he asked. Perhaps if he turned the conversation toward his sister's social interests, and away from his lack of them, he could aim her in the desired direction.

Alicine's face lit up. "Yes, I took one of my old dresses, the faded brown one, you know, the one I wore to the Harvest Festival a couple of years back, and removed the lace from the collar and sleeves. I dyed the lace yellow, it was already ivory anyway, and added it to the bodice of the blue dress, you know, the one with the red braiding at the hem. Then I—"

Dayn's mind drifted.

"—and if I add the same color of red to my hair," Alicine babbled on, "—I think Mother has some ribbon that will match—at least I hope she does because if she doesn't it just won't have the same effect…anyway, then it will look really nice I think."

Alicine grew silent.

"Sounds…uh…good," Dayn said, then hastily added, "I'm sure you'll be the prettiest girl here."

Alicine eyed him suspiciously. Dayn laughed. "I guess it doesn't matter what I say, right? But the other boys will tell you soon enough I think."

Alicine blushed, but Dayn knew from her smile that his comment had pleased her.

"So what are you wearing?" she asked.

"Me? What I've got on, I suppose."

Alicine gasped.

Dayn looked down at himself. "What's wrong with it? It's clean isn't it?"

Eyan strolled into the barn, a passel of rabbits slung over his shoulder. He halted and gawked at the room. "What'd ye *do*?"

"Decorated it, what else?" Alicine said. "The dance will be in here and I wanted it to look nice."

Eyan looked at Dayn.

"Girls like to do this sort of thing, Eyan," Dayn said.

"Oh," Eyan replied.

"Dayn and I were just discussing what we're going to wear to the dance," Alicine said. "What are you planning to wear, Eyan?"

"Uh…I…"

"Don't be so nosey, Alicine," Dayn said. "He wants what he wears to be a surprise, don't you Eyan?" He stared into Eyan's eyes, attempting to convey the message that it would be wise to just follow along.

"Oh…aye…I…uh…guess so," Eyan said, staring back at him.

Alicine glanced between the two of them. "You're neither of you fooling me with your act." She turned to Eyan. "You should talk to your mother. She'll help you pick out an outfit." With that she turned and left the barn, clearly irritated at the amusement plastering the boys' faces.

Dayn burst into laughter. Eyan joined in.

"Do we really have to wear somethin' special?" Eyan finally asked. "I don't think I have anythin'. I mean, it's not like I've been anywhere."

Before Dayn could respond, the thud of wagon wheels and the clank of harnesses redirected his attention. He sprinted to the barn door and looked toward the road leading to the house. In the distance, the first clan family could be seen rumbling over the hill. "Get to the house, Eyan," he said.

"I—I have to clean the rabbits, first," Eyan replied. But his eyes were fully focused on the road.

"I'll take care of the rabbits," Dayn said. "You go on to the house and tell your mother the first guests have arrived."

Eyan nodded and handed him the rabbits. He headed out the door and hustled to the house.

Dayn set the rabbits aside and walked out to greet the wagon now pulling into the yard. He was relieved to see that it was his Uncle Nort, but he did not recognize the attractive young woman sitting next to him, nor the little black-haired boy nestled between them. Nort, Haskel's older brother, had never married. He was a hard-working man, and a handsome one too, but he'd never shown much interest in women, and even less in the ritual of marriage.

Dayn raised his hand hesitantly, not sure how his uncle, or the woman or the boy, would react. Nort jumped from the wagon and rushed toward him. Dayn tensed, recalling the reception he had initially received from Haskel. But to his relief, Nort grabbed him in a bear-hug of affection.

"God, boy," Nort said, his voice cracking, "we were so worried." He leaned back and placed his hands on Dayn's shoulders, looking him up and down. His eyes brimmed as he grabbed Dayn in another embrace.

"Are ye well?" Nort asked at last. "And your sister? How does she fare?"

"We're well, uncle," Dayn said. "And you?"

Nort smiled, then turned toward the woman and boy who now stood beside the wagon. He gestured for them to approach. "Come, Seela. You, too, Ben."

They approached reluctantly.

"Ah, now," Nort said to them gently. "I told ye of my young nephew Dayn, did I not?" He laughed. "Ye didn't forget already did ye?"

The woman smiled shyly, while the boy, no more than five years of age, clung to her skirts. Seela pried the child from her side, then leaned down and whispered into his ear. The boy glanced up at Dayn, then down at his own feet. Then he and his mother walked toward him.

The two of them stopped, and Ben moved his gaze up Dayn's towering frame. "My mother says I'm not to be scared," he said.

Dayn squatted before him. "But you're afraid of me anyway?"

The boy nodded.

"Well, Ben. I'm just a boy—like you. Only older." He winked.

"You're not like me," the boy said. "You're different."

"And different is bad?" Dayn asked.

Ben cocked his head. "I don't know."

"Fair enough," Dayn said. He rose from his stooped position. "Well, Ben, I'm happy to meet you, and you too Seela." Dayn looked at Nort, his eyes conveying the question that courtesy would not allow him to speak.

"Ben's my son," Nort said proudly.

Dayn smiled toward Seela. "Your wife then."

"No. Not wife," Nort said, but strangely there was no hint of hesitation or shame in his voice.

For a moment Dayn felt judgment rush to his breast. Nort had fathered a child out of wedlock? And Seela—did she actually *live* with the man? If that were the case, Eyan would not be the only person facing the clans tonight.

Dayn muttered with embarrassment. "Uncle, I'm sorry...I mean—"

"Don't mask your words on my account," Nort said. "Ben's a child of my heart, not my blood. As for Seela, I love her and see no sin in sharin' my life with her, eh?"

"No, I..." At that moment Dayn realized he saw no sin in it at all, just as he saw no sin in his own desire for Falyn. It was only the voices of others that had invited judgment in. He smiled and shook his head. "No. I see no sin in it."

Nort grinned. "I thought not," he said. "Now then, where shall I park the wagon?"

Dayn pointed and directed him to the side of the house. Nort and Seela would be staying near the family residence, of course, while the rest of the guests would be directed to a field past the barn. The field was a good distance from the circle of stones and the bonfire that would eventually roar within it. It would not do well for the guests to sleep on pallets of soot, so Dayn and Eyan had planned the encampment to insure both safety and comfort.

Nort climbed into the wagon and flicked the reins, while Dayn led Seela and Ben toward the house. Vania rushed through the open front door and ran across the yard toward them. Squealing with excitement, she threw her arms around Seela.

"Goodness, I'm so happy to see ye. Ben, my how ye've grown!" Vania ruffled his thick black hair. She smiled at Seela. "And when's the little one due?"

"Late spring," Seela said, splaying her fingers across her still-flat belly.

Dayn again felt judgment rear its head, but he forced it down. Had he actually expected Nort to share his home with the woman he loved, but not his bed? For a moment, Dayn could not help but picture the scene, sending envy to his thoughts as well. But then the image shifted to Falyn, and hope joined the fray. If the clans accepted Nort's and Seela's arrangement, and the conception of a child outside of wedlock, then surely they would accept Falyn, regardless of the fact that she was not part of the clan and that her father was now their enemy.

The conversation between Seela and Vania went quiet as Seela drew a sharp intake of breath. All heads turned toward the doorway of the house where Eyan was standing.

"My son, Seela," Vania said gently. "That's my Eyan."

"Oh, I'm sorry, I didn't mean to react like that," Seela said, flustered. "I knew we were to meet him, but well… it's just, the stories I've heard." Her cheeks turned red.

"I understand, dear," Vania said. "I'm sure there'll be a variety of reactions to him in the next few days, so don't feel bad about yours. Shall I introduce ye?"

"Aye...of course. Come, Ben," Seela said, and grabbed his hand in hers.

Vania led Seela and Ben to the porch, but Dayn turned back toward the barn. He dreaded the look that would surely come to their faces when they realized the color of Eyan's eyes. Dayn had seen the look in regard to his own eyes often enough, but as hard as it had always been for him, he hated the thought of it being directed to Eyan even more. He felt overwhelming pity for his cousin, realizing that while Seela had gasped at the sight of him, others in the clan would react far worse.

At that moment Dayn decided to look after Eyan, even if it meant going to the dance and sitting against the wall with him. He groaned. This was surely going to be the most miserable night of his life.

∽

# CHAPTER 22:
# CIRCLE OF STONES

The hill sloping upward from the barn was dotted with wagons and the contrasting costumes of the four visiting clans. Those dressed in blue were from the Crests, a northwestern region that boasted mossy cliffs and magnificent waterfalls. Shades of sienna mingled amongst them; the Sandright clan had recently migrated to Crest territory when the anger of the mountain had sent poison to their wells. The Crests had welcomed the Sandrights into their fold. No doubt their colors would one day merge as one. Those dressed in green were the Aeries, Dayn's clan. And those in bold plaids of red and brown were the Basyls. Leathers and wools, tunics and trews, skirts and vests— all forms of costume could be seen representing the clans and the regions from which they haled. But though their clothing made a fine show of diversity, in truth there was little to be found amongst them. All had dark hair and eyes. And all clung to a common fear that no one dared dispute.

Chatter rose and fell as families set up their campsites, greeted other clan members, and scolded children running willy-nilly between the rigs. Vania watched from the porch rail, craning her neck to see beyond that which her abbreviated stature would allow. But her gaze was not on the hillside or the campsites; it was focused on the road and the line of wagons still making their way toward them.

"What are we goin' to do with 'em all?" she said, wringing her hands. "I didn't expect so many."

"Everything will be fine," Morna said. "You'll see. There's plenty of space for them to camp. Dayn and Eyan set up the area just fine, didn't you boys?"

"Of course we did," Dayn said from the doorway at their backs.

Eyan, peering over Dayn's shoulder, remained silent, but his breath quickened against Dayn's neck as he watched the wagon train that was *clanking* toward them.

"We've not near enough to feed 'em all," Vania said. "What'll we do if—"

"Now don't you fret," Morna said. "Goodness, they don't expect you to feed them the entire time. They always bring plenty of supplies." She laughed. "Believe me, Vania, *no one* goes hungry at a Gathering."

"I s'pose," Vania said. "Guess I haven't been to enough of 'em to know. But it just doesn't seem natural, me not bein' responsible for feedin' 'em."

"You only have to host it, auntie," Dayn said, "and provide meat for the Chieftains and refreshments for the dance. The rest of the families will add their share to the tables. It would be rude of them to do otherwise."

The women turned to face him. From the looks on their faces, they had not expected an etiquette lesson, at least not from him.

"Alicine told me," Dayn said defensively. "I thought I'd better know the finer details, since I'll be looking after Eyan."

"What do ye mean, lookin' after Eyan?" Vania asked.

"I just thought someone ought to look after Eyan, that's all, especially since...."

Vania's eyes misted. "Why...thank ye Dayn," she said, then returned her gaze to the road. "But Haskel will be home soon. I'm sure of it."

"Auntie?"

"Hmmm?" she said.

"If uncle doesn't return, how are we going to handle the introduction of Eyan to the clans and the issue of Tearia?"

"I said he'll be here," she said crossly.

Dayn turned his eyes to his feet. "Sorry. I didn't mean it like that."

"I know," Vania said, softening her tone. "But he'll be here."

"Is there anything you'd like me to do in the meantime?" Dayn asked. "All the wagons pretty much know where to go now, and I wasn't sure if I should stay out of sight with Eyan...until the plenum starts, I mean. I was thinking maybe we should start it early, so there'll be enough time."

"Enough time?" Vania asked.

"To discuss everything."

Vania glanced toward the sky. The sun was easing toward the west. "I'll leave the startin' time to Haskel," she said.

"All right," Dayn said, but he knew a decision would have to be made soon. Though most of the families were expected to arrive well before dark, it would be unwise to delay things on account of a few stragglers. In the past, the duration of the Plenum of Four had not been an issue. According to his father, there sometimes wasn't much business to discuss, so many plenums wrapped up early. That left plenty of time for entertainment, the primary reason most people came anyway. Dayn knew little else about the plenums; he had never been allowed to attend one. But this time he and Alicine would be up front and center with news about Tearia–a topic the clans would definitely not welcome. Then there was the issue of Eyan, his eyes another subject sure to explode in debate. Hopefully the information about Tearia would ease the argument in Eyan's regard, but first Dayn had to convince them the place existed and, of course, that demons didn't.

But if that wasn't enough to keep tempers roiling, there were still the issues of the Vestry's discord with the clans, the fire on the mountain, and Dayn's recent altercation with Lorcan at the springs. Dayn wasn't sure how much Haskel had told the clans when he went to notify them of the Gathering, but based on the numbers arriving, he must have said plenty. And based on the expressions of some of the guests, there were going to be a lot of raw feelings.

∾

# CHAPTER 23: THE PLENUM OF FOUR

The sky was moonless, but a canopy of bright autumn stars, coupled with a hundred or so towering pole-torches, illuminated the circle where the plenum was about to take place. The torches, evenly dispersed between the stones, threw flickering patterns upon the faces of those in attendance, and dancing shadows on the landscape that surrounded them. Most members had already taken their places within the circle, but a few remained huddled outside the perimeter, whispering and glancing toward the stage. They were well aware that once their feet touched the inner circle, personal business was required to cease.

The stage bordered the highest edge of the interior circle. There the ground rose along the hillside and allowed fine viewing for all in attendance. Timber planks made up the platform that held two sections of seating. On the right, one long bench accommodated the Chieftains who made up the Plenum of Four. Already seated, three of the leaders waited, eyeing the crowd with crossed arms and serious faces. On the left, two rows of benches were arranged for the hosting family, not only to honor them for their invitation, but to give their entreaties top priority. Dayn was seated on the front bench, in his assigned place. To his right sat his uncle Nort, staring trancelike over the heads of the crowd, and to Dayn's left sat Eyan. Eyan's shoulders were hunched, allowing a shock of long hair to fall over his eyes. He sat as if frozen, with the exception of one leg that refused to stop bouncing.

Dayn moved his gaze along the line of Chieftains, noting their appearances and recalling their reputations. At the far end was Brenainn, chief of the Basyl clan. A huge, rugged-looking man, Brenainn was dressed in thick plaids of red and brown. His long black hair tumbled down his shoulders, and a wiry beard nested atop his barrel-shaped chest. The Basyls haled from a remote northern region, a barbaric place known for its wild game and even wilder lore. The men there were famous for their hunting skills. It was said a Basyl could bring down a full-grown boar with his bare hands, not for lack of a weapon, but for the sheer sport of it.

Seated to the left of Brenainn was Ionhar of the Crests. Lean, middle-aged, and dressed in tight-fitting leathers of indigo blue, Ionhar was known as one of the finest archers in all the lands. He was also said to be the voice of reason when disagreements arose. Next to him sat Uaine, clan leader of the Sandrights, the clan which had recently assimilated with the Crests. Word was that his people had relocated because of tainted wells, but newly emerging gossip indicated there might be more to it.

As Dayn watched Uaine, he realized he knew little about the man. The Chieftain had only recently inherited the position when his older brother, Aode, the former leader, had mysteriously vanished. Still, Uaine looked well-suited for the role. Unlike most clans that held elections for leadership, the Sandrights clung to the more traditional method of inheritance. They held steadfastly to their fundamentalist ways, and Uaine's covered head, conservative tunic, and ankle-length coat seemed to amplify that lifestyle. Dayn could not help but wonder how the Crests and the Sandrights managed to get along. But they obviously did; they were, after all, now living side by side. It was then that he realized one of the Chieftains had not yet taken his place on the stage—Peadar of the Aerie Clan.

Dayn turned his attention to the crowd, searching for a sign of his own clan's Chieftain, when he noticed a conspicuous group of men still standing outside the circle. Their heads were leaned in, their voices low, and they were flicking hostile glares in his direction.

Nort nudged Dayn with an elbow. "Hot here, ain't it?" he muttered.

Dayn turned his eyes to his uncle, realizing he wasn't the only one feeling the heat. Nort's face was streaked with sweat, and his hands were clasped so tightly, his knuckles had gone white.

"Yes; hot," Dayn managed. He ran a finger along the interior of his own sticky collar.

Nort looked at him from the corner of his eye. He snickered. "Didn't think ye could get much paler, boy. Guess I was wrong."

Eyan, still hunched, gazed up at Dayn through a shock of hair. "Ye look like you're about to puke," he said.

"You don't look so good yourself," Dayn replied.

"I didn't say I wasn't about to puke, too."

Nort snorted. "Well you boys turn your heads in the other direction when ye do, eh?"

The men outside the circle stepped toward the official entrance. Dayn prayed they would be turned away. He knew entry was strictly enforced. Circles could not typically accommodate the large numbers that attended Gatherings, so families were allowed to send only one representative to the plenum itself. Anyone could watch from outside the circle, but only those within it had any say. They could be male, female, pre-adult or old, but those invited had to be familiar with the agenda and respectful of the protocol. An exception to the rule was made for the hosting family, as well as those who were directly involved in a particular aspect of the agenda, such as the formal introduction of a new member, or disputes that required intervention. The way Dayn saw it, he and his family were covered from just about every angle.

The seemingly disgruntled men were allowed to enter, they had obviously been invited, but there was no time to worry about them now. Dayn turned in his seat and surveyed the bench at his back. Seela was seated there with young Ben squirming in her lap. Dayn leaned toward Nort. "Where's Vania, and Mother and Alicine?" he asked. "I thought they were with Seela."

Nort scanned the crowd. "They're here…somewhere."

A sudden shuffling at the steps alerted them to the tardy, but welcome, arrival of the remaining women. Vania, Morna, and Alicine moved to their seats. Fluffing their skirts, they settled in and folded their hands in their laps. Thin smiles graced their lips.

Vania leaned forward and whispered something into Nort's ear. *Hopefully her apologies*, Dayn thought.

"Where have you been?" Dayn grumbled over his shoulder. "We've felt like target practice up here."

Vania patted his shoulder affectionately. "Had to attend to a few last minute details, dear. That's all."

"Like what?" Dayn retorted. "Alicine adding more ribbons to the barn?"

Eyan chuckled.

"Funny," Alicine said. "I'll have you know—"

But before she could say another word, the commanding presence of Peadar, Chieftain of the Aeries, made its way onto the stage, and behind him were Haskel and Eileis.

Dayn closed his eyes and muttered a prayer of gratitude. But as grateful as he was to see Haskel, he was even more grateful for the presence of Eileis the Spirit Keeper.

Frail and elderly, the Spirit Keeper was probably the last of her kind, at least in the land of Kirador. For generations Spirit Keepers like Eileis had been healers of body and counselors of soul, but even more importantly, they had been teachers of the mind. Their arts had been passed down from mother to daughter for nearly a thousand years, and with those arts had come hundreds of texts filled with the wisdom of the ancients. But in recent years those teachings had been silenced by Vestry laws that dictated one philosophy and one religion. No longer could the writings of one's ancestors be taught; no longer could other belief systems be explored.

It was because of their original attachment to their own ancient ways that the clans had difficulty getting along with the citizens of Kiradyn, most particularly the members of the Vestry. Their people still traded, of course, for the Kiradyns had come to enjoy the wild meat and pelts, minerals, painted potteries, and medicinals the clans had to offer. But it was an uneasy relationship. The only reason Eileis remained in Kiradyn rather than join the mountain clans was because she felt the Kiradyns needed her wisdom more, or so she said. Unfortunately, she had become little more than a figurehead to the Kiradyns, a quaint custom that was due some courtesy, yes, but allotted little power other than that which was required for appearances.

Fortunately, the clans still held her in high regard.

As Dayn watched, he realized she looked older than when he had last seen her. That had been at the Summer Fires festival several months prior, when she had made a strange entreaty asking everyone to open their minds to the truth. Her body, bent and frail even then, seemed even more so now, as if a simple puff of wind could blow her away. But Dayn knew Eileis had a strength in her that few possessed, and prayed it would carry her, and the rest of them, through the debate that was sure to take place tonight.

A rustle of clan members took their last-minute places within the circle. Peadar waited in the center of the stage, arms at his side, feet planted, while Haskel and Eileis stood at his back. Haskel looked toward his family sitting on the benches to his right. He gave them a nod and a smile, but his expression was wary.

Peadar stepped to the edge of the stage, his presence demanding attention. Dressed in the rich forest greens of his clan, Peadar looked noble and proud. His cloak was tossed back across his shoulders, revealing muscular arms encircled by bronze bands. His black hair, streaked with gray, was pulled back and tightly braided, making the planes of his face look angular and pronounced. He narrowed his eyes as he slowly ran them over the crowd.

He raised his arms, palms turned toward the audience. All went still. Only the crackle of torch fires could be heard. Even the distant campground chatter had gone silent.

"Aye, hear me brothers and sisters," he said, "clans of the air, of the soil and the rock, of meadow, forest, and stream." His voice emitted through the air, amplified by the power of the great circle and the silence of the crowd. "Welcome all to the realm of Aerie, born of the blood of Konyl who once lived in the highest reaches. Hail the blood of Konyl, he who led the clans against the demon hoards o'er ten generations ago."

"Hail Konyl," the crowd shouted in a well-rehearsed chorus. "Hail the blood spilt in his name."

"Thank ye, the house of Haskel, son of Fiach," Peadar said, "and to Vania, daughter of Yann, for their hostin' of the clans this day."

Haskel and Vania tipped their heads in acknowledgement.

"Hail Haskel, son of Fiach," the audience echoed, "and Vania, daughter of Yann."

"This day we have much to discuss," Peadar said. "Two members of our clan: one unrecognizable…" He turned his eyes to Dayn. "The other not yet recognized." Eyan's bouncing leg grew still.

"Both prepared to reveal their true selves to us," Peadar continued. "Tonight we will hear for their defense."

*Defense?* Dayn wondered. He and Eyan weren't on trial, were they?

Peadar swept a hand toward Haskel, then moved to sit with the other Chieftains.

Haskel stepped forward. "My friends," he said. "My family and I welcome you all. We come before ye today to ask recognition for our son, Eyan." He motioned Eyan to join him.

Eyan hesitated, then rose and shuffled toward his father. He stopped at his side, but kept his eyes aimed at the floor.

"Raise your face to 'em, son," his father said quietly.

Eyan lifted his head, flicking back the hair that had previously veiled his eyes.

The crowd gasped and muttered. Most had heard the recent rumors in regard to the color of Eyan's eyes, but few had actually seen them.

"Present yourself to the Chieftains, boy," Haskel said.

Eyan turned and walked slowly down the line of Chieftains. His gaze was no longer turned to the floor, yet he could not seem to lift it above the men's knees.

Ionhar of the Crests watched intently as Eyan passed, but the leader showed no emotion, only contemplation. Next to him, Uaine stared grimly. He said not a word as Eyan continued along the line, but the hardening of his face indicated a repressed desire to speak.

Brenainn's bear-like frame rose from the far end of the bench. He reached out and grabbed Eyan by the chin, stopping him short. The Chieftain surveyed Eyan's face, then let go his hold. A broad grin parted his beard. "Why the boy's a damned demon," he said, and bellowed out a laugh.

Dayn saw Haskel tense, but his uncle made no move. Dayn, on the other hand, found himself vaulting from the chair. "He's not a demon!" he cried.

The crowd grew noisy. Brenainn arched a wiry brow. "He ain't eh?" he said. The audience grew still. "Well, I be sayin' he's naw anythin' but! An you one to be talkin'." He guffawed. "A lot o' braw in ye, I be thinkin'."

Dayn worked to decipher Brenainn's garblings. "Eyan's not a demon," he managed in rebuttal. "They don't even exist."

There was a new rumble from the circle. Mutters of *blasphemy* filled the air.

"Don't exist, eh?" Brenainn rubbed his chin. "Well, mebe they do and mebe they don't. I for one am willin' to hear your piece, but I be thinkin' ye'll be upsettin' more than a few folks here iffin' ye do."

Uaine rose. "I agree," he said firmly. "We're not here to test our fellow clansmen with innuendos and propaganda, especially from two boys who may have ulterior motives."

"With all due respect," Haskel said, taking a bold step forward. "There're no ulterior motives here. Eyan is my son, comin' out to the clans, nothin' more. And Dayn... well...he has information that'll not be easy to hear, that I grant ye. But he *will* be heard nonetheless."

"I don't think you're in a position to dictate who will and will not be heard," Uaine said. "That's the decision of the Chieftains, and the last time I looked, it was Peadar that led the Aeries."

Peadar stared darkly at Uaine. "That's correct, Uaine. I speak for the Aeries. And I say Haskel's nephew will have his say."

Uaine stiffened. "Very well," he said through gritted teeth, and waved Dayn to the center of the stage. Haskel took his seat next to Vania while the standing Chieftains resumed their places. Nort rose politely, gesturing for Eileis to sit beside him.

Dayn glanced around nervously. How had the attention turned in his direction so quickly? Shouldn't more time be spent on Eyan's acceptance into the clans? But then he realized that his revelation about Tearia was the exact kind of information the crowd needed if they were to accept Haskel's son. He motioned for Alicine and Eyan to join him. If he was going to take a leap into the fire, he wasn't taking it alone.

"My name is Dayn," he said to the audience. "I was given it by my Kiradyn parents, Gorman and Morna. It was they who raised me, but I am not their blood son." Heads shook and voices whispered, but Dayn continued. "My name is also Keefe," he said more boldly. "I was given that name by my true parents, Brina and Mahon of the realm of Tearia.

"My eyes are blue. My hair is blond and my skin is pale. Yet I am as human as you are. You claim I have demon blood in me. In a sense, that's true. But the demons you speak of are not from the underworld, they are from this world, our world."

One of the men who had been glaring at Dayn earlier from the sidelines shook his fist in the air. "Stop 'im," he demanded. "Stop 'im before he says another word."

"He speaks against the Word," others shouted in agreement.

Dayn turned to Peadar, expecting to see the Chieftain rising to remove him, but the man remained seated.

"Continue, Dayn," Peadar said. "Or would ye prefer I call ye Keefe?"

"No; Dayn."

"Very well...Dayn." Peadar then addressed the audience. "We will hear what the boy has to say. Anyone not wishin' to hear it may leave the circle now." No one moved a muscle.

Dayn pushed back his collar, revealing the flower-shaped birthmark on his neck. "This stain—this is what prompted my Tearian mother to give me away. There it meant my death." Dayn felt his courage building. "But in Kirador this scar means nothing. It's only the color of my eyes and my hair that signals my differences. In Tearia, had I been allowed to thrive, I would have been a royal, someone whose family had riches and political authority. But here—"

"What is this...*Tearia* you speak of?" Uaine asked.

"It is a great land," Dayn said, "on the other side of the mountains. It wasn't destroyed, at least not like the texts say it was."

Uaine rose from his seat. "All but Kirador was destroyed during Daghadar's Purge," he said. "You'll *not* dispute that truth in this sacred circle."

"Where shall we dispute it then?" Alicine said, leaning around Dayn. "Because it *is* going to be disputed."

Uaine sputtered in an attempt to respond.

"More braw then ye know what to do with, eh Uaine?" Brenainn chortled.

"We'll discuss the subject of Tearia *now*, Uaine," Peadar said. "As Chief of the hostin' clan, I have the final word at this plenum."

Uaine's brows met, then he tilted his head in forced deference and sat back on the bench.

"Do ye have somethin' to add, Alicine?" Peadar asked.

"My brother and I went into the cave—" she said.

"The forbidden cave?" voices asked in amazement.

"Yes. And through it we wound our way to the other side of the mountains. Tearia is there. We saw it. And there are people there, fair-haired people like Dayn, and with eyes like his and Eyan's."

"People or no, d'ye not deny they'll bring nothin' but harm to us?" Brenainn asked.

"They won't come here," Alicine insisted.

"How kin ye know that fer certain, lass?" Brenainn said. "They been here before, en they?"

"Have ye seen any such creatures in your realm lately, Peadar?" Ionhar asked. "You're closest to the range. Any reason to suspect more demons are crossing over?"

"No, none," Peadar replied. He turned his attention to Dayn. "What keeps these Tearians on their side of the mountains?"

"Long ago the people of our world traveled back and forth. But the mountain erupted, sending death and destruction. Many from both sides were killed. The Tearians decided to allow no more people from Kirador to pass into their lands; and they would allow no more Tearians to pass into ours. Soldiers were sent to protect their borders. Anyone who tried to pass beyond them was killed."

"Then why did they invade us?" Uaine asked. "Why did they seize our lands and murder our people?"

"I don't know," Dayn said. "Perhaps it was rogues or some group that had broken away from Tearia."

"There was more to it than tha'," Brenainn reminded them. "Those damned cat-folk came over first."

"Aye," Peadar said. "The Taubastets. Caught between us and them." He shook his head. "Most unfortunate."

"Unfortunate indeed," Uaine said. "If not for the cats, we'd have defeated the demon hordes sooner."

Ionhar clenched his fists. He had been silent thus far, but the topic had clearly touched a nerve. "If not for what we *did* to the cats, we'd have had them as ally, not foe!"

Brenainn rolled his eyes. "Achh...here we go again," he muttered.

"That debate is not up for discussion tonight," Peadar said. He turned his attention back to Dayn. "If this place ye speak of does exist, we'll need proof. We're in no position to make a stand without it. Maybe there are Tearians, maybe there aren't. But that doesn't mean there aren't demons, too. The Taubastets of old proved the existence of cultures even our ancestors weren't aware of. And that's what caused the divide."

Eileis rose. "Divided, yes, but we shouldn't be, not from each other." She turned to the audience. "Your ancestors migrated from the higher mountains when they lost their battle with those you call demon. It was Konyl who led your kin. It was Konyl who died for them."

Voices agreed. "Hail, Konyl," many said.

"Yes," Eileis said. "Hail, Konyl. But he was fighting for more than the lands you lost; he was fighting for the convictions you've since given away! What do you think Konyl would say if he were to see you cow-towing to the likes of Lorcan and the Vestry? Assimilating values is one thing. Turning away from your beliefs is another."

A woman standing up front spoke. "I mean no disrespect to Konyl," she said. "We Sandrights appreciate him and the other Aeries fightin' the hoards for us back then the way they did. But that was a long time ago, and since then the laws o' the Vestry have become the real threat. You know what happened to those who refused to give up the old ways."

"Their sacrifices will not be forgotten," Eileis said.

"Maybe the Vestry's right," the woman continued, "and the Maker is angry with us for not listenin'. I don't know. But I do know the wells on our land have gone bad. That livestock is dyin' and crops are witherin'. If Daghadar's sendin' us a message, then we'd best pay heed to it!"

"Daghadar does indeed send us a message," Eileis said.

"No," Ionhar interrupted. "He sends us a test."

"A test?" Uaine said.

"Aye, ye know..." Brenainn retorted, "like a challenge o' sorts."

"I know what a test is," Uaine growled. "I meant what manner of test?"

"A test of our spiritual strength," Eileis said.

"A test to see if we're worthy," Ionhar added. Then he smiled slyly. "The same test, I believe, the followers of the Vestry are currently experiencin'."

"Yes," Eileis said, "but their solution is to cleanse Kirador of what they perceive to be the cause of it. And that gets us back to one of the reasons for this Gatherin'—Dayn."

"How can I be responsible for all that?" Dayn sputtered. "I only just got back!"

"Doesn't matter," Eileis said. "The Vestry means to make an example of you. They believe you've roused the demons against them and that the clans, especially the Aeries, have been a party to it."

"Ye know this to be true?" Peadar asked her.

"Yes. Lorcan paid me a visit just days ago. Asked me to persuade you to turn Dayn over."

"And you said?" Dayn interjected.

"What do you think I said," Eileis replied. "I told him what he could do with himself." She smiled at Vania. "I learned that from you, Vania."

The audience laughed.

"I see no humor in this," Uaine seethed. "Your words may well have lit a fire!"

"The fire was already lit," Eileis said. "Lit the moment the first Vestry torch was set upon those who opposed them! How long has it been since your own clansmen were staked for their beliefs? Have you forgotten their suffering?"

The audience grew solemn.

"No, Eileis. We've not forgotten," Ionhar said softly. "But we can't risk it again."

"Yet you would consider sending Dayn to the Vestry?"

Ionhar rose from the bench. "I would *not* consider it. And neither will Peadar, I'm sure."

Peadar nodded.

"Easy to say, Ionhar," Uaine argued. "But the fact is, we have no choice *but* to consider it."

"I'll agree with ye there," Brenainn muttered, his arms folded across his chest. "Don' mean we hafta send him though."

"Very well. It's been considered," Eileis said. She ran her eyes along the line of Chieftains, capturing the attention of them one by one. "So what will it be, Lords? Do you send the boy to the Vestry, or do you tell them what they can do with themselves?"

The Chieftains glanced at each other.

"Braw," Brenainn said, then he gave her a broad smile. "Ye'll not be seein' us send yon Dayn to the Vestry this day, Spirit Keeper."

"That's good to know," she said, "for we face another threat, one that is far greater than that of the Vestry: We face the mountain." She stared hard at the Chieftains. "You know Dayn is not the cause of our troubles. It is the Vestry that must be convinced."

"But how to convince 'em," Ionhar said thoughtfully.

"The only way we can," Eileis said. "We tell them Dayn's story, show them there may be more in this world than what they have chosen to see. For this to ring true, the clans must be united in it; there can be no fighting amongst you."

"No judgment of this magnitude can be made without proof and further deliberation," Peadar said.

"I can give you proof," Dayn said.

All heads turned.

"Well, let's see it then!" Brenainn said.

"You can't see it tonight," Dayn said. "But I can show it to you in the morning."

"The *morning*?" Uaine said with indignation. "What's wrong with now?"

Dayn looked at Eyan, then drew a steadying breath. "Because the proof is in a cave."

The muscles in Haskel's face constricted. Dayn saw Eyan glance his father's way, then jerk his eyes back to the floor.

The Chieftains turned to each other, muttering and discussing. In the background the crowd buzzed with discussions of their own.

Peadar rose and stepped toward the audience. The circle grew quiet.

"It is determined by the jury of your lordships that the Plenum of Four shall re-converge tomorrow." The audience gawked with surprise. "Until then," Peadar continued, "we'll take into account all evidence presented to us in the matter of Tearia and the birthrights in question, includin' young Eyan, whose request for clan rights has not yet been thoroughly addressed. We will notify ye of the time when the next plenum is to take place. Meanwhile, you're all to remain here at the Gatherin'."

People stood speechless. No plenum had ever been cut short in the history of Gatherings. The crowd began to grow restless. How long were they to wait? many could be heard asking. What were they to do until then?

Brenainn threw up a hand. "Be glad of it, ye fools," he bellowed. "Now get on with yer partyin'."

The crowd's mood lifted, but Dayn's could not help but plunge. The misery of this night was now doomed to drag into the next and maybe even the next. And then what? Only the writings in the cave held the answer to that.

∞

# CHAPTER 24: THE DANCE

The music was lively, but the rhythm of the dancers' feet was sluggish in comparison. Fiddle-bows bounced across vibrating strings; pipes chirped to the pounding of the drums. But the patrons seemed distracted as they made their way across the floor.

Dayn sat slumped in a chair against the far wall, his arms crossed and legs stretched out before him. He watched as a young man in blue ushered a female partner to the center of the dance floor. The girl, dressed in velvety shades of sienna, smiled and flicked her eyes at Dayn. Her fingertips were resting on her partner's outstretched palm, indicating they were a couple, at least for the duration of the dance. But when the young man noticed her smiling at Dayn, he threw an arm around her waist to further stake his claim. An Elder standing nearby gave him a glare that could have dropped him where he stood. The boy's Adam's apple bobbed. He knew full well it was unacceptable for a male to touch an unmarried female in such a manner. The boy tipped his head to the Elder, asking forgiveness with his eyes if not with his words.

Dayn snickered to himself. The boy looked rather pitiful, he thought, like a pup that had been put in his place. It was a ridiculous ritual, trying to keep boys and girls at arm's length like that. Perhaps the older patrons didn't mind it, but the younger ones wanted nothing more than to wrap those arms around each other. After years of sitting on the sidelines, Dayn had become a keen observer of such things. He knew the boy's non-verbal apology was merely for show; the couple had probably arranged a private rendezvous later.

"Tell me what they're doin'," Eyan said, interrupting Dayn's musings. Eyan was sitting beside him, his wide gaze bouncing around the room.

"Dancing," Dayn said.

"I know, but the other part...the fingers on the hands, the—"

"They are pretending they don't want to roll in the hay with each other."

"What?" Eyan asked.

"Never mind. Look...their fingertips are allowed to touch, but their arms keep them apart. It lets others know they belong to each other, at least for the duration of the dance. It's all part of the courtship."

"Courtship," Eyan echoed, keeping his eyes on the swirling dancers. "Explain how one does the courtship."

Dayn sighed. Perhaps Eyan was a simpleton, but if he needed an explanation, Dayn supposed he was the best person to give it to him, though he would probably do better learning about courtship from someone who had actually *done* it.

"Well," Dayn said, "courting is when a couple gets to know each other. They usually start by visiting each other at their parents' houses; then, with permission, they might be allowed to go to dances, maybe sit next to each other at festival dinners, things like that." He inclined his head toward the girl who had flicked her eyes in his direction earlier, a Sandright, and her audacious partner, a Crest. "See that boy and girl there? They're from different clans. In the past, the clans were too far apart for any real courtship to take place between them. But the Sandrights have joined with the Crests, so they'll probably mix now. I think it's good; it makes the clans seem more united."

Eyan's forehead creased with confusion.

Dayn laughed. "All right, let's just focus on the couple. They are dancing together, see? So are probably courting."

"And because they're courtin', they'll marry each other?" Eyan asked.

Dayn shrugged. "Maybe. But they're not obligated to. If you'll notice, the girl's looking at other boys, not just the one she's dancing with. The boy however—"

"He's lookin' at other boys," Eyan said, attempting to fill in the blanks.

"No," Dayn snapped. "God, Eyan, don't you know *anything.*"

Eyan winced.

Dayn immediately regretted his tone. Of course Eyan didn't know anything; he had spent the past nineteen years in seclusion. How could he possibly know about courtship? His parents had decided early on that he would not be allowed to marry. They obviously hadn't talked to him about things he could never hope to have. But if they hadn't talked to him about courting, what else hadn't they talked to him about?

Dayn glanced around, assessing who might be within earshot, then leaned in and said, "How much do you know about...procreation?"

Eyan looked startled, then his expression turned to genuine interest. "Father talked to me about it once. I've seen the horses do it. And other animals."

"Right. But people do it, too." Dayn felt like a complete idiot; surely Eyan knew all this.

"I'm not *stupid*," Eyan said. "But only certain people are allowed to procreate, right?"

Dayn felt his aggravation rise to the surface. But it wasn't toward Eyan. It was toward the way his cousin had been excluded from everything, how he had been denied a full life, and how, until recently, he'd had little hope for a future either. As Dayn thought on it, he realized it wasn't entirely Haskel's and Vania's fault. They had, after all, only done it to protect him. All too often parents were forced to make difficult decisions in regard to their children; Dayn had learned that well enough from his own mother, Brina, who had given him to a stranger rather than have him slain because of his birthmark. Dayn reached up his hand, fingering the flower-shaped stain on his neck.

"*Right?*"

Eyan's voice drew Dayn back. "Uh...no, Eyan. Anyone can procreate." But Dayn knew the statement, though easily said, was not so easily done. He himself had once been told he would not be allowed to marry. Sheireadan had rubbed it in his face at the Summer Fires festival, the day Dayn had run away several months prior. Apparently everyone had known of Dayn's impending bachelorhood, everyone except him, that is. Even Dayn's own parents knew, though they had not bothered to tell him about it. It was that, and all the other miseries he had suffered on account of his differences, that had prompted Dayn to leave Kirador in the first place. At the time, he'd felt he had little choice in the matter. But since going to Tearia and meeting his cousin Reiv, since learning of his own heritage, experiencing his first kiss, and ultimately wielding a sword in battle, Dayn had evolved into a different person. No longer was he a boy who would accept a fate imposed on him by others. He was his own master now.

He watched Eyan's face, trying to interpret his cousin's response to the answer he'd just been given. But Eyan's attention seemed elsewhere, or maybe that in itself was the response. His eyes were fully alight with excitement as they watched the couples pirouette around the dance floor. *Good*, Dayn thought. *Maybe there'll be no more questions.*

Dayn surveyed the crowd, realizing everyone's earlier reluctance to celebrate had dissipated. The place was fairly well hopping with merriment now. There were so many people on the dance floor, it was hard to follow the movements of the boy and girl who had been the subject of Dayn's courtship speech. He craned his neck, searching the room for a sign of them.

Dayn followed the swirl of flouncing skirts and colorful tunics, until at last he spotted the couple in question. He wasn't sure why he'd chosen to seek them out in the first place. Perhaps it was because of the way the girl had looked at him. Or maybe it was because for the first time in his life he'd actually made another male jealous. Either way, as Dayn watched he realized how very pretty the girl was. He glanced at Eyan, noting his cousin's eyes were realizing the same thing.

"She's pretty, eh?" Dayn said.

"Hmmm," Eyan said absently.

Alicine suddenly bounded up, her hands extended. "Come on, dance with me," she said.

Eyan and Dayn looked at each other, grimacing.

"Uh, no thanks," Dayn said. "Eyan and I will just sit here and hold up the wall."

Alicine huffed. "Very funny." She grabbed Eyan's hand. "Come on, Eyan. Dance with me."

Eyan shook his head furiously.

She tried to pull him from his seat, but only succeeded in scraping the chair, and him with it, forward an inch or two. "I'll show you what to do. Come *on*!" But Eyan had planted his heels firmly in the dirt.

"Don't you have some other poor boy to pick on?" Dayn said. He leaned around Eyan and eyed a slender youth standing nearby. "How about him?" Dayn cocked a brow in the direction of the boy. "Hey, you there," he called out. "You'd like to dance with my sister, right?" The boy's face went positively gray. He slunk along the wall and scampered out the door.

Dayn burst into laughter. "Our sentiments exactly," he said.

Alicine let go of Eyan's hand and thrust her fists to her hips. "How's Eyan supposed to learn how to dance if he doesn't get out there and do it?" she demanded.

"Who says he wants to learn how to dance?" Dayn said.

Alicine leaned toward Eyan, her hands still planted. "Well...do you?"

Eyan frowned. "Why am I always caught in the middle of your arguments?" he said. He stood from his chair. "Maybe I do want to dance. Maybe I just want to dance with someone other than my *cousin*!" He shoved past her and marched into the crowd.

"Well. He told *you*," Dayn said with a grin.

Alicine's lips compressed into a jagged line. "Hmph! He's going to make an absolute fool of himself. He doesn't know the first thing about asking a girl to dance—much less where to plant his big feet."

"Well…" Dayn nodded toward the dance floor. "I'd say you're wrong about the first part."

Alicine spun to see what held Dayn's attention. Eyan was stepping onto the dance floor, and in the palm of his hand were the fingers of a lovely young dance partner, the girl in sienna.

Alicine's mouth dropped. "That's Olwyn, *Uaine's* niece."

"Uaine, as in *Chieftain* Uaine?"

"Yes," Alicine replied. She smirked. "Well, Quillan won't be happy to see *this*. Serves him right."

"Quillan? You mean the boy she was dancing with before?"

"Yes. He's fairly well smitten with her, you know."

"Uh-huh…" Dayn rose from his seat to take a better look. "So that's Olwyn, eh? I wonder how Eyan got her to dance with him."

"He got his backside out of the chair for a start." Alicine grinned. "And now that *your* backside's out of the chair—"

Dayn plopped back into the seat and crossed his arms. "Nice attempt."

Alicine turned her attention back to the dance floor, biting her lip as she watched Eyan clumsily navigate the dance steps. But Dayn didn't think Eyan was as worried about how he looked as Alicine was. His cousin frequently stepped in the wrong direction, then would practically run Olwyn over trying to get it right. But he always apologized to her, and then she would laugh. Fortunately, she did not seem to hold his awkwardness against him and would patiently demonstrate the step again and again until he knew what to do.

"He's making a fool of himself," Alicine repeated. "An absolute fool."

"No he's not," Dayn said. "He's doing fine...sort of."

Alicine snorted. "Right. Well, let's see how fast Olwyn runs out the door when the music stops." Alicine redirected her attention. Standing on tiptoes, she gave a quick wave to a girl across the way. "I'm going to say hello to Gwynna," she announced, and skipped off, leaving Dayn to himself.

Dayn growled inwardly. The only reason he'd come to this cursed party was to look after Eyan. Now his cousin was off dancing with some Chieftain's daughter, and he himself was sitting there feeling like a ninny, as usual. It was then that Dayn's gaze landed on the refreshment table. A plate of food and a mug of cider sounded good; it would give his hands something to do besides hide under his armpits. But as he looked in that direction, he realized the Sandright girl's former dance partner was standing by it, watching Eyan intently.

Dayn turned his gaze to Eyan and Olwyn, trying to determine whether or not they were doing anything inappropriate. Their dancing seemed innocent enough, he thought;

Eyan's skills were certainly no threat. But the way the Crest boy stared at him...

"Dayn?"

Dayn rose at the unexpected greeting. "Eileis!" he said, and gave her a respectful bow.

"My boy, how glad I am to see you," she said, embracing him. She glanced around and lowered her voice. "May we speak, Dayn? Privately?"

Dayn glanced at Eyan, who was still dancing, then at the refreshment table. The boy from the Crests was no longer there.

"Of course," Dayn replied. "Outside?"

Eileis nodded and headed for the door. Dayn followed.

They stepped out and into the cool night air. Dayn filled his lungs, realizing how hot and stuffy the barn had been. The sky was canopied with a kaleidoscope of stars, and the surrounding area smelled fresh and clean and perfumed with the scent of pine needles and campfires.

Eileis motioned Dayn to follow. "Your family's at the dance, or off visiting," she said over her shoulder. "The house is the safest place to go."

Dayn began to feel uneasy. What was so important that it needed this much secrecy?

They stepped onto the porch and Dayn opened the door for Eileis. She entered and quickly surveyed the room. "Good," she said. "No one's here."

"Let me get you something to drink," Dayn said, closing the door behind them.

"No need; no time." Eileis reached into the side-seam pocket of her skirt and pulled out a folded piece of parchment. She pressed it into his hand. "For you," she said.

"What is it?" he asked. The parchment appeared to have been hastily folded, but someone had at least taken the time to seal it with a blob of wax.

"It's a letter—from Falyn," Eileis said.

Dayn felt a surge of energy. "Falyn?"

"Yes. But no one's to know I gave it to you, you hear?"

"Where—where'd you get it? I mean, when did she give it to you?"

"She was at my place when Haskel arrived. Poor child; she'd come to see if I could intervene on behalf of her brother. Lorcan's been particularly harsh on the boy lately. Falyn has reason to fear for his life."

"His life?" For a moment Dayn wasn't sure whether or not he cared. Sheireadan had caused him so much misery over the years, it was hard to feel any sympathy for him. But then Dayn recalled the bruises on Sheireadan's back and how Lorcan had treated him and Falyn that night at the springs. It was then that he realized if Sheireadan was suffering, then Falyn was, too. And that he would not tolerate.

"I'll kill Lorcan with my bare hands," he said. "I swear I will."

"You'll do no such thing," Eileis scolded. "The man's dangerous. You stay away from him." She eyed his hands that were now curled into fists. "Do you intend to crumple it before you've even read it?" she asked.

Dayn looked down. "No," he said. "Of course not." He relaxed his grip. "So what did you do?"

"About Sheireadan you mean?" Eileis shook her head. "Not much I could do. Your uncle said it was urgent that I came to the Gathering, so I came."

"What about Falyn?" Dayn asked.

"She went home, of course, but before she left she scribbled this note to you."

"What does it say?"

The Spirit Keeper scoffed. "I didn't *read* it, boy. I don't go round reading other people's letters."

"Why all the secrecy, then?"

"Your uncle didn't want me to give it to you. Said it was too dangerous. He knows how you feel about the girl. He thought giving it to you might tempt you to see her again, and he'll have none of that."

"Well it's not his decision," Dayn said.

"Your uncle's right in this, Dayn. Lorcan'll see you dead before he allows you to go near his daughter again."

"Then why'd you give me this if you don't think I should see her. Why give me hope then snatch it away?"

"I didn't give you the letter to give you *hope* boy. Falyn told me it was to thank you for helping her and her brother that night at the springs. I saw no reason to deny her the courtesy. But if it's gonna get you all riled up and fill your skull with pig-headed notions, then you can just hand it back."

Dayn stared at the note, fingering the wax that sealed it. "No, you're right. I know I can't see her. No sense wishing for things I can't have, right?" He ran his finger under the wax and flicked it open. But as he read the brief message, his pulse quickened, for her words held more than simple gratitude. She wanted to meet him at the Well of Wishes. Her father would be attending a Vestry meeting, she said, and she could slip away then and–

"Dayn?"

He looked up. "As you said…a thank you." He paused in thought, then said, "How many days ago did she give you this?"

"Why?"

"She says there's to be a Vestry meeting."

"Yes. There's been one called for tomorrow night," Eileis said. "Does she say anything else?"

"Just that I should stay as far from Kiradyn as possible. Do you think the meeting is about me?"

Eileis stroked her chin. "Hard to say. But knowing you confronted Lorcan at the springs…"

"Well it was time he was confronted!" Dayn said.

"Perhaps, but that doesn't mean you had to go and stir the pot when you did!"

"That was two weeks ago. Why would they be calling it now? I mean, it seems if it were about me, they would have ordered it sooner."

"Maybe they're beginning to see the incident between the two of you as more than just an altercation."

"What do you mean?"

"Much has been happening in Kirador lately, Dayn. Things that have stirred up fear and finger pointing. The awakening of the mountain was the first, but since then crops have been withering and livestock's been dying. And people are getting sick." She shook her head. "An entire family was found dead in their home just last week. No wounds, no sign of illness or trauma; just dead."

"The lady at the plenum tonight mentioned something similar about the clan lands," Dayn said. "About strange things happening with the wildlife and wells and such."

"That's right. What's happening to the clans is happening to the folks around Kiradyn too. We might want to strike before the iron gets any hotter. The meeting tomorrow night might be the perfect time."

"What are you saying—that you and the Chieftains might go to the Vestry meeting?"

"Yes. This evidence you spoke of earlier…is it enough to convince the Chieftains to go?"

"It should be."

"Then in the morning we'll tell them about the meeting. If the evidence is as valid as you say it is, I have no doubt the Plenum of Four will want to meet with the Vestry."

"Then I'm going with them," Dayn said.

"That you'll *not* do," Eileis ordered.

"But I know things that could help explain."

Eileis eyed him darkly. "Now you listen to me, boy. I may have said fingers are pointing, but in truth it's become much more than that. There have been executions."

"*Executions?*"

"Yes. As much as I'd like to spare you the details, I suppose I'd best tell you, especially since you've got a mind to walk yourself into a pyre."

"There have been *burnings?*" he exclaimed. "But who? Why?"

"The accusations started as soon as the mountain started rumbling. Daghadar was angry, people were heard saying. Someone had to be the cause of it. The Vestry called an immediate meeting; inquiries were made; names were taken."

"The names of *who*? I mean, how could any individual be responsible for that?"

"Your name was at the top of the list, Dayn, but the Vestry knew better than to confront the clans too soon. The

Kiradyns have never been at war, but they're beginning to make preparations for it, and their vigilantism may be just enough to force the clans to take up arms."

"So after me, who was next on their list?"

Eileis frowned. "Anyone they'd had problems with in the past. Suspected sinners, fornicators, inverts...pretty much anyone they thought was deviant or strange in the head."

"There couldn't have been many accused then."

"Over a hundred so far."

"*What?*"

"Course there wasn't any proof to back up the claims. The Vestry said there was no need. They sent a ritual of prayer to Daghadar and figured if they were wrong, the Maker'd tell them so."

"So how many were spared?"

"None."

Dayn sank onto the nearby bench.

"Falyn was right to warn you away from Kiradyn, Dayn."

Dayn looked down at Falyn's letter. In truth, she hadn't warned him away at all. She had asked him to meet her at the Well of Wishes, and though it was a long walk from Kiradyn, and even more than that from Haskel's, she obviously wanted to see him.

Eileis stepped closer. "I meant what I said earlier, Dayn. No foolish notions about seeing Falyn, you hear? Lorcan's not a man to be crossed, and with things as they are with the Vestry—"

"Of course not," Dayn said. "No girl's worth getting killed over." *Except maybe this one.* He glanced toward the door. "I think I'd like to turn in now, Eileis. I'm really tired. Shall I escort you back to the dance?"

"No need," she said. "You get some rest. You'll need an early start if you're taking us to the cave."

Dayn nodded. The earlier he took the Chieftains to see the drawings, the earlier they would leave for Kiradyn. With that kind of evidence, they would have little choice but to go to the Vestry, and then Dayn could slip away to meet Falyn. But no matter what plans he set, he knew it was a waiting game. The next several hours would feel like a lifetime, but for one moment alone with Falyn, he would wait an eternity.

◌

# CHAPTER 25: AGAINST THE WALL

Eyan danced till his lungs burned and his legs ached, but he had no intention of stopping. He let out a hoot—he couldn't believe his luck! Just about every girl in the room had joined him on the dance floor tonight, and just about every boy had watched him on account of it. It gave him a sense of satisfaction he didn't understand, but knowing they watched him was all that mattered. For too long he had been invisible. Now he held everyone's attention.

His current dance partner smiled at him, then skipped to her right. Eyan watched as she twirled. The girl was pretty, he thought, with her curls all a-swirl with pink ribbons, and her fingers so dainty and slender. He could not deny that he enjoyed looking at her. For that matter, he could not deny he'd enjoyed looking at all the girls he'd danced with that night. But as he thought on it now, he realized it wasn't enough.

He had been watching the boys all evening, too, observing how they dressed and danced and behaved. One

boy in particular had caught Eyan's eye: the boy from the
Crests that Dayn had pointed out earlier. The boy seemed
well-liked. He was always surrounded by friends; girls vied
for his attention; even the boys followed him around like
lapdogs. He was nicely attired in a quilted tunic of blue,
and appeared to be about Eyan's age, though much taller
and broader in the shoulders. He was an impressive figure, Eyan thought. The perfect model of what he himself
wanted to become.

The boy's name was also handsome: Quillan. Eyan
knew because he had asked one of his dance partners earlier. He'd focused on the boy ever since, noting his man-
nerisms, how he interacted with others, the charm of his
smile, the spark of his personality. Now *there* was someone
to emulate. He was pleased when Quillan's eyes had finally
turned to his, and though the observance had been brief,
Eyan was thrilled the boy had noticed him at all. Why, if
Quillan was as curious about Eyan as he was about him,
they might actually become friends.

The music ended with the thump of a drum and a
friendly call for break. Eyan thanked his dance partner, who
curtsied, then turned and headed for the nearest refreshment table. He grabbed up a mug of cider and plopped
onto a nearby bench. How late was it? he wondered. He
scanned the crowd, searching for Dayn, but his cousin was
nowhere to be seen. Well, no matter, he thought; Dayn
hated these things, though Eyan couldn't imagine why.
Alicine, on the other hand, was still making merry with
a group of friends across the way. Eyan smiled. He liked
seeing her so happy.

He tipped the mug to his lips and took a swig, catching
sight of Quillan just over the rim. Quillan was staring back

at him, he realized, and it sent exhilaration to his belly, but it quickly soured when Quillan's expression turned hostile.

Eyan shifted his gaze and gulped down the contents of his mug. Why had Quillan looked at him like that? he wondered. Perhaps he was annoyed by Eyan's earlier surveillance of him. It probably *was* bad manners to stare at a person like that. But Eyan couldn't help it. Until now, what little he'd learned about boys and girls had been by watching them from the shadows, and he hadn't had much opportunity to do even that. It was only on the rare occasion that company stopped by that he'd had a chance to spy on anyone. All he knew he'd pretty much pieced together; his parents had worked hard to keep him in a constant state of childhood. But he was nineteen now, a man, not a boy. No longer could he simply watch from the sidelines.

He glanced up to see Quillan heading for the door. Urgency built in his throat; what if Quillan really *was* angry with him? Eyan could not bear the thought of it. He rose and set his mug aside, determined to make restitution, then shouldered through the crowd and worked his way toward the exit.

Eyan stepped outside and looked right, then left, catching sight of Quillan's blue tunic rounding the corner of the barn. He hustled after him and soon found himself beyond the security of the light from the party. He thought to call out Quillan's name before the boy got too far, but before he could say a word, Quillan disappeared to the back.

Eyan followed and stepped around the corner, then stopped and retreated a step or two. Quillan, he realized, was but a few feet away, relieving his bladder onto the timbers of the barn.

Eyan pressed his back against the side, attempting to give the boy some privacy, but in what seemed like an instant, a fist grabbed hold of his collar and yanked him around the corner. With a shove, Eyan's cheekbone was slammed against the wall, his left arm twisted painfully at his back. A muscular forearm pressed against his neck.

"You *watchin'* me?" Quillan demanded.

"No," Eyan cried. "I—I was just waitin' for ye."

"Waitin' for me?" The pressure on his neck increased.

"I—I'm sorry," Eyan sputtered. "I was waitin' for ye to finish."

Quillan shoved his full weight against Eyan's body, pinning every limb to the wall. "I know what ye are," Quillan hissed.

Eyan struggled to escape, but he was no match against Quillan. "I don't know what ye mean."

"Ye said you were waitin' for me," Quillan said. "Why?"

"I wanted to—,"

"To *what*?"

"To apologize."

"For what? Workin' your spells on me?"

Eyan's heart flew into a panic. What did Quillan mean, working his spells? Spell work was forbidden. Everyone knew that. "I—I don't know what ye mean," he stammered.

Quillan shoved a knee into Eyan's lower spine. The pain nearly sent Eyan's legs out from under him.

"I've heard what your kind do," Quillan said. "Demons ensorcel people into wanting 'em…that's what I hear. I'm not talkin' the normal kind of want, mind ye. I'm talkin' the forbidden kind, the perverted kind."

Tears pricked Eyan's eyes. He blinked them back.

"You've been castin' your spell on me all evenin', haven't ye," Quillan said. He pressed his lips to Eyan's ear, his warm breath coiling into it. "I'll show ye what happens to demons that look my way."

"Please," Eyan said. "I won't look at ye again. I swear it."

Eyan closed his eyes, tensing for the inevitable blow, but suddenly the weight of Quillan's body evaporated. Eyan opened his eyes to see the boy being lifted by the back of his collar, dangling before him by a man nearly twice his size—Brenainn!

"Now watcha doin' there, tryin' to take advantage of a poor boy who can't be knowin' much about this world, includin' the likes o'you?" Brenainn said.

Quillan struggled until at last Brenainn set him on his feet. But the Chieftain kept a firm grip on his collar.

"I'm not the evil one—he is!" Quillan cried, pointing a shaky finger at Eyan. "He ensorcelled me. He did!"

"D'ya think I was born yesterdee, ye kit!" Brenainn said.

"It's true," Quillan insisted. "He's been givin' me the evil eye all night. I came outside to do my business, is all, and the next thing I know he's ensorcelled me to—to—"

"To *wha'?* Assault him agin' the wall? I seem to recall 'im beggin' ye to stop. Ye do know wha' stop means, don' ye?"

"I swear. It wasn't me! It was—"

"Who? Yer mother's gre' mare?" Brenainn yanked Quillan's face within an inch of his own. "Now I say ye get yeerself on away now an leave this here lad alone. Cos iffen ye don', I'll be payin' yer da a visit right quick. Or better yet, mebe I'll be payin' yon lady Olwyn a visit first."

"You wouldn't!" Quillan said.

"Aye, I would. Just try me an' see." Brenainn released his hold on Quillan's collar, shoving him back a step. "Now off with ye, ye scoundrel, before ye learn wa a *real* man can do." Brenainn grabbed hold of his wide belt buckle and gave it a tug.

Quillan's eyes grew three sizes; he spun and double-stepped around the corner, flinging mulch in his wake.

Brenainn roared with laughter. "Ye wouldin' know what to do with a man my size, ye kit!" he called after him, then laughed even louder than before.

Eyan continued to cower, speechless, against the wall. He had no clue what had just transpired, and was at a complete loss as to how to respond.

Brenainn turned to him. He narrowed his eyes and cocked his head. "So ye ensorcelled the lad, eh?"

"No!" Eyan blurted. "I—I don't know what he means."

"Don' ye?"

"No, I swear, I just wanted to tell him I was sorry, that's all."

"Fer wha?"

Eyan swallowed; his throat had become alarmingly dry. "For starin' at him."

"*Starin'* a him? Are ye not knowin' anythin' at all? Ye don' go starin' at a lad like that and not be expectin' to get somethin' in return fer it."

"What?"

"Ye do know what I'm referrin' to, don' ye?"

"No. I mean...aye. He didn't like how I was lookin' at him."

"So ye *were* givin' him the evil eye."

"What? No!"

Brenainn stroked his beard, deep in thought for a moment. He raised an inquisitive brow. "What do ye know about lads an' lads, boy?"

"What d'ye mean?"

"I mean boys that be liken' boys."

"I don't...understand."

"Gor, ye *were* born yesterdee." Brenainn shook his head. "I think ye need some schoolin'. But I don' think I'm the one to be doin' it. Mebe ye should be askin' your da to explain it."

Eyan ground his teeth. "My father doesn't tell me anythin'. He said I'm not allowed to marry, so there's no sense in me knowin' about things like that."

Brenainn guffawed. "Well, the las' time I looked, boys weren't marryin' boys, so I don' see wha' marriage has to do wi' it. But if your da don' see fit to tell ye, then it ain't my place to be a doin' it."

"Then I guess I'll never know anythin' then."

"Listen, boy. I'll be tellin' ye this: Ye watch how ye look at boys like Quillan. He is wha' he is, an' I'll not deny him his right to it. But assaultin' ye to cover his own fears, well, it's wrong it is. But if ye were to be caught doin' the deed by the Kiradyns, even if ye weren't a wantin' to, things could go bad for ye—a lot worse'n a little pain in the backside, I'll be tellin' ye that."

"Wha—"

Brenainn leaned toward him. "The Vestry's proclaimed it an *abomination*, the damned fools. But bein' as it is, ye could be burned at the stake fer it, an' your partner wi' ye." He straightened his back and put a commanding hand on Eyan's shoulder. "Talk to your da, lad. He'll explain it to ye. Just don' be doin' anythin' ye should'n hear? And if ye ain't sure about it, well, don' do it anyway."

❦

Eyan slipped into the house, closing the door behind him. "Talk to your *da* about it," he muttered. "Like *he'd* tell me anythin'." He walked toward the hearth then stopped. Dayn, he noticed, was asleep on a pallet near the fireplace. Eyan looked around the room. It was dim, but the coals in the hearth illuminated it well enough, and there was a still-lit candle flickering on the kitchen table. None of the adults were in their beds, he noticed, nor was Alicine who would probably be out for hours. Dayn seemed to be the only one home, which suited Eyan just fine; he was in no mood to see his parents at the moment. They could stay gone all night for all he cared, and from the sound of the music in the barn, that was a likely possibility. The dance was obviously back in full swing.

Eyan tiptoed closer to Dayn and stopped to gaze down at him. He would have welcomed some company, but Dayn's eyes were closed and his breathing steady. As Eyan looked down at him, he realized how handsome his cousin was. He had always thought so, but he could not help but wonder why he was currently more aware of it. Surly it was just a casual observation. After all, anyone, boy or girl, would be blind not to see it. Eyan thought of Brenainn's warning about lads and lads. Did his own admiration for his cousin's beauty apply? He analyzed Dayn's features: straight nose, pleasant mouth, but his eyebrows *were* oddly pale. And his hair, so strange, so…golden. Eyan shook his head. Probably too much cider.

He turned and made his way to his own bed, then threw himself upon it. Propping his hands behind his head, he stared at the ceiling. Music vibrated through the walls, reminding him of how promising the evening had begun, only to die a cruel death at the hands of Quillan. He felt like such a fool. Here he'd been thinking he was making a good impression, when everyone was probably laughing at him instead. How many people besides Quillan still believed he was a demon—or worse?

Eyan shifted restlessly. What if he *was* what Quillan said. Was it possible he *had* given the boy the evil eye? Had he really been sending messages that even he didn't understand? Eyan yanked the pillow out from under his head and pulled it over his face. If he could just block out the world and everyone in it—

"Eyan?"

Eyan peeked an eye out from behind the pillow. Dayn, the bottom half of him anyway, could be seen standing next to the bed, candle in hand.

"How was the dance?" Dayn asked, then yawned.

Eyan hugged the pillow closer to his face. "Fine," he mumbled into the feathers.

Eyan felt the weight of the bed give as Dayn sat down beside him. Dayn eased the pillow from Eyan's face. "What hap—" he began, but then his voice grew alarmed. "God, Eyan—what happened to your *face?*"

Eyan lifted his fingers to his tender cheek. He'd almost forgotten his face had been slammed against the barn. "Nothin'," he said, covering the bruise with his hand.

Dayn shoved Eyan's hand aside and moved the candle for a closer look. "Who did this to you?" he insisted. "Did someone hit you?"

"I don't want t' talk about it."

"Well you're *going* to talk about it." Dayn set the candle on the night table next to Eyan's bed. "Let me get some salve," he said, and hurried to the medicinal cabinet across the way.

Dayn returned, a crock of ointment in his hand. He dipped his fingers into the jar and reached out to smear a glob on Eyan's cheek.

Eyan jerked away. "I'm fine."

"Don't be an idiot."

"I'm not an idiot!" Eyan snapped. He rolled over to face the wall. "Or maybe I am."

Dayn laughed softly. "What'd you do, flirt with the wrong girl?"

"No."

Dayn placed his hand on Eyan's shoulder. "What then?"

"I don't understand how everythin' works." Eyan sat up to face him. "There are things I should know, but I don't.

"Like what?"

"Like who I am, where I fit."

Dayn's brow creased in thought. He reached a hand to Eyan's cheek and dabbed the ointment on it. "I know how you feel," he said softly. "I don't fit either."

"At least your parents didn't hide ye away. They didn't try to keep ye a child like mine did."

"No," Dayn said. "But it wasn't any better for me. Mine tried to pretend I was like everyone else. And they wanted everyone else to pretend it, too. But I'm not and never will be." He shrugged. "But I don't care anymore. Now I know where I belong. I'm going back to Tearia, so it doesn't matter what the Kiradyns, or the clans, or anyone else thinks of me."

"That's not true," Eyan said. "Ye just *want* it to be true."

"Why do you say that?"

"Because I know ye care what Falyn thinks. Ye love her, don't ye?"

Dayn nodded.

"So why would ye leave her to go back to Tearia?"

"It's...complicated."

"For you or for her?"

"Her, I guess. For me, it's simple." He forced a laugh. "But since she probably won't have me, I'll likely be going."

Eyan considered it for a moment. "What does it feel like?" he finally asked.

"What? The way I feel about Falyn you mean?"

"Aye." He peered at Dayn with curiosity. "What does that feel like?"

Dayn set the jar aside. "Well..." he began slowly. "I'd say, most of the time it feels good. Like when I think about her, I...well...I guess I tingle or something." He frowned. "But it hurts, too. Because I know I'll probably never have her. Then I have to convince myself all over again that there's still a chance." He paused. "It's like a part of me is missing." He attempted a smile. "Does that make sense?"

"Have ye ever touched her?"

"Touched her?"

"Ye know, like *really* touched her."

Dayn blinked. "You mean like—"

"Like for pleasure. I've been thinking about it, and I think there's more to men and women gettin' together than procreation."

"Well, yes. There is." Dayn's face went red; he released a slow breath. "Maybe you should ask your father to explain it."

Eyan shoved Dayn from the bed. He leapt from the mattress and planted his feet on the floor. "*This* is what I get for all my father's *explanations*!" he said, aiming a finger at his own throbbing cheek. "What does it mean for a boy to like a boy?"

Dayn took a step back. "*What?*" he asked, nearly choking on the word.

"I got this from a boy who thought I was givin' him the evil eye at the dance. I don't know what that means, but *he* sure did!"

"Who? *Who* thought that?"

"It doesn't matter who," Eyan said.

"What did he do to you? Tell me."

"He got as far as slammin' me against the wall and accusin' me o' things I didn't understand, that's what he did. If Brenainn hadn't come along—"

"*Brenainn?*"

"Aye. Brenainn put a stop to it. Then he gave me a warnin'. He said to be careful about things like that because I could be burned at the stake for it!"

Dayn collapsed onto the edge of the bed. "God, Eyan. How could this have happened?"

"I don't know," Eyan replied. "Don't you *understand*? I don't *know*."

Dayn looked up at him. "Who else knows about this?"

"No one. Just me and Brenainn, and—and the other boy."

Dayn rose to his feet and gripped Eyan by the shoulders. "No one else can know about this, Eyan." He gave him a harsh shake. "You understand me? *No one*."

Dayn's tone made the hairs on Eyan's neck rise. "Why? What'll happen?" he asked.

"You heard what Brenainn said. The penalty is death."

"The penalty for *what*?"

"God, didn't Haskel tell you *anything*?" Dayn glanced over his shoulder. "All right, but you'd better sit down."

Eyan sat on the edge of the bed. Dayn paced for a moment, then slowly began the explanation. Eyan nodded with understanding, but then his eyes grew wide. Much of what Dayn said he already knew. But there were some things he had not been expecting. By the time his cousin had finished explaining "the sins of the flesh", Eyan's world felt a little off kilter. It wasn't from the details of what Dayn was telling him. It wasn't even from the anger he felt toward his parents for keeping him in ignorance all these years. No, it was due to fear, but it was a fear unlike anything Eyan had ever experienced. At the beginning of Dayn's speech, Eyan's emotions, his body, his very soul seemed to have awoken, prompting him to ask his cousin question after question. Some answers Dayn had been prepared to give, but the concern in Dayn's expression, coupled with occasional evasiveness, told Eyan that some things were better off not said.

His questions finally stopped, and both he and Dayn grew silent.

Eyan pondered his cousin's words for a moment, then said, "Thank ye for tellin' me. I think I understand now."

"Are you sure? I mean—"

"Yes. Now I know why I felt like I did when I was dancin'." Eyan turned his eyes away. "I'm tired," he said. "I think I'll go to sleep now."

"All right," Dayn said. "See you in the morning, then."

"In the mornin'."

The candlelight moved with Dayn away from Eyan's bed. Eyan climbed under the covers and yanked the pillow back over his face. He stared into the muffled blackness and hugged the pillow tight. But this time it was not to block out the world. It was to hide from it.

∽

# Chapter 26: Divination

As promised, Dayn took the Chieftains to the cave. Eyan refused to go; he felt guilty enough for betraying his father's orders and had disappeared shortly before they left. Alicine insisted on going, of course, as had Eileis and Haskel and even Uncle Nort. Vania stayed behind to see to the needs of her guests, while Morna and Seela remained at the house to offer her their support.

An unusual number of clan folk stopped by the house that morning, hoping for a hint of where the chiefs were going and what they expected to find. Vania and the other women feigned ignorance, though in truth they were not entirely sure what the men would discover. But they refused to give the busybodies any more fodder for gossip, so said it was none of their concern and that they would just have to wait to find out like the rest of them.

It was hours before the expedition returned, but when the group entered the doorway, the looks on their faces revealed more than words could say.

Brenainn plopped down onto one of the kitchen benches. "Ne'er seen anythin' like it," he said.

"What did you see exactly?" Morna asked anxiously, but her focus was on Haskel, not Brenainn.

"Just stories," Haskel replied. "Told in some old drawings on the walls of the cave. Eyan found 'em several months ago and took me to see 'em."

"Stories?" she said. "Why hadn't you mentioned them before?"

"Didn't want to give ye anythin' else to worry about, what with your children gone and all."

"Lord, Haskel. What kind of stories *are* they?"

"Stories of the past," Eileis said. "Maybe even the future."

Haskel bristled.

"You can't deny what you saw, Haskel," Eileis said.

"I don't know what I saw," Haskel replied. "All I know is they dispute the Written Word and the Vestry won't accept 'em lightly, if they accept 'em at all."

"I agree," Peadar interjected. "The images could be the ravings of a heretic or a madman."

"Or a seer," Eileis said.

"Careful," Vania whispered. She crept to the window and peeked out. "Folks have been comin' by all mornin', askin' Morna and me if we know anythin'. That's all we need...for someone to overhear us speakin' of *divination*."

"What do you mean?" Alicine asked.

"The Vestry is apprehending anyone suspected of the art," Eileis said. "But I say the Vestry's nothing but fools. Prophecy is a gift from the Maker. It shouldn't be hidden away as if it's something to be ashamed of!"

"Prophecy is a gift," Alicine said with a tone of authority. "I learned that in Tearia. But with it comes great responsibility."

All eyes turned to her.

"Dayn's cousin Reiv had it," she continued. "He's a Transcendor."

Brenainn leaned in and rested his fist on his thigh. "Watcha be meanin' there, girl—he's a what?"

"A Transcendor. The Word tells us that when we die, if we go to be with Daghadar that is, we gain all knowledge, right?"

Heads nodded in agreement.

"Well, Reiv died."

"Then how can ye be knowin' what he knows, eh?"

Alicine rolled her eyes. "He's not dead *now* of course."

Brenainn threw his arms into the air. "Would ye mind explainin' what it is yer tryin' to explain because I'm sure not understandin' it."

"Reiv drank a potion. It was poison, but he did it to save the life of Kerrik." Faces remained blank. "Kerrik is a boy who lives on the other side of Aredyrah. He had been injured, and legend said that if someone drank the potion and went to the After Place, they could ask the gods for knowledge."

"*Gods?*" Uaine said in his usual curt tone.

"Yes, *gods,*" Alicine said. "So Reiv drank it and died. But he came back to life and when he came back he knew things, all kinds of things. And one of those things was an ingredient that could make a medicinal to save Kerrik."

"Do ye think the body in the cave, assumin' he, or she, was the artist of the drawings, could have been a Transcendor?" Ionhar asked. He had been quiet thus far, but now seemed genuinely intrigued by what Alicine had to say.

"Perhaps," she replied. "The drawings indicate knowledge that we are already aware of, but it also suggests things we don't know, or don't want to know."

"Such as?" Peadar said.

"There's no denying the paintings are old. Yet they show things that happened recently, and some that are happening now."

Uaine scoffed. "I saw nothing in the cave that depicted any such thing."

"What about the people being burned at the stakes?" Dayn said.

"The very same thing happened after the Purge," Uaine countered.

"Aye, tis true," Brenainn said.

"What about the migration of the Tearians to the valley?" Dayn added.

"Who's to say that didn't happen generations ago?" Peadar said. "Those could be demons that crossed over durin' the War o' Konyl."

"But the image showed *Reiv* leading the people there," Alicine said.

"This Reiv person you speak of," Uaine said. "Why are you so certain the image we saw is of *him*? Could it not be someone else? An ancestor perhaps?"

"Could be," Dayn conceded, "but there are images of him all over the walls. Reiv is a Transcendor, which makes him a vessel of Aredyran history. If the person in the cave was a Transcendor also, he would have known about the coming of Reiv. And if Reiv leads our world to greater things, isn't it possible the artist in the cave wanted us to know about it?"

"So what you're sayin' is this Reiv fellow could be headin' our way as we speak?" Brenainn said.

"And bringing demons with him if the images are to be believed," Uaine said.

"I told you," Dayn insisted. "There are no demons. If Reiv is leading people to the valley, then his reasons are peaceful ones."

"Dayn," Alicine asked anxiously. "Do you think something bad has happened in Tearia?"

Dayn shook his head. "I don't know. I hope not, but—"

"Well something bad is happening *here*," Eileis interrupted. "The mountain's awakening, and people are dying for it."

"If something similar is happening in Tearia," Alicine said with concern, "then Reiv and his followers might be trying to escape a similar fate. He knows of the valley; he's the one who told us about it in the first place. Could they be seeking refuge there?"

"When we left, everything was calm," Dayn said thoughtfully. "The Jecta were at peace with Tearia, and all Reiv wanted was to lead a normal life. We haven't been away that long. Could so much have gone wrong in such a short time?"

"They're just drawings!" Uaine stressed.

"And the Written Word is just *words*," Eileis said. "Who's to say there's more truth in one than the other?"

Uaine's face grew stern. "Watch what you say! The Vestry could tie you to the stake for it."

"And who's going to tell them I said it? You?" she countered.

"Enough," Peadar ordered. "It could take decades to interpret those images, just as it took decades to interpret the Written Word."

"Don't forget," Dayn said. "Whether the Written Word was given to us by the Maker or another source, the words were still set to parchment by men. They were interpreted by men and transcribed by men. You know there are passages that were not included in the final texts. There were many versions until the Vestry settled on the one we study now. Who's to say it's the one true version."

"And who's to say the drawings in the cave aren't lies?" Uaine replied.

"No one can say," Eileis agreed. "So that is the point we must argue with the Vestry. We must ask them to open their minds to other possibilities. Our world is changing; the mountain will see to that. And we must change too if we are to survive."

"Reiv told the Tearians the same thing," Dayn said. "It was the Jecta, the outcasts, he told first. They were the ones in the most need of understanding. At first they were skeptical, but before long they knew what he said was true."

"So what you're sayin' is that one fella had enough charisma to spirit his people away from their beliefs?" Brenainn said.

"Charisma. He does have that," Dayn said with a laugh. "Have you ever met someone with hair the color of fire and a tongue to match?"

"Well, I did know a woman once with a temper that would singe the hairs off your balls," Brenainn reminisced, "but—"

"Enough," Eileis said with a wave of her hand. "The Vestry meets tonight. Are the implications in the cave enough to sway them? Probably not, but it might at least give them pause."

"I, for one, am willin' to present to 'em what we found," Peadar said. "And if they wish to see it for themselves, they're welcome to the land of the Aerie, but only for that purpose. With all the clans still gathered here, I doubt they'd try anythin' foolish."

"We'd best be callin' the plenum to order then," Brenainn said, rising from the bench. "Cos if we're gonna settle the issue with the clans *and* reach Kiradyn by night-fall, we'd best be quick about it."

All agreed, though Uaine was skeptical, and headed out to call their clans to the Plenum of Four. Within the hour all were gathered within the circle. The evidence found in the cave was presented, and Dayn's and Alicine's story about their trek to Tearia was revealed in full detail. The topics were hotly debated, but after some time it was agreed that the Chieftains, along with Haskel and Eileis and several bodyguards, would leave immediately for the Vestry. As almost an afterthought, Eyan was accepted as a member of the clan, but throughout it all, Dayn's thoughts were elsewhere—on the Well of Wishes and the girl who would hopefully be waiting for him there.

It was mid afternoon by the time the mounted delegation departed for Kiradyn. Every member of the party was a skilled horseman, but none of them dared ride too swiftly. Eileis was amongst them, and though her spirit may have been as strong as a warrior's, her brittle bones were not.

Dayn had paced the floor until the group finally left. The instant the flank of the last horse disappeared down the road, he grabbed up some flint and one of Eyan's bows from the barn and headed for the woods.

"Dayn!" Eyan called at his back. "Wait. I'll go with ye."

"No," Dayn said over his shoulder. "I think I'll go by myself this time."

Eyan caught up to him. "But if we both go," he said, "we'll bring back more. Mother says we're nearly out o' meat."

"I didn't say you couldn't go hunting, Eyan," Dayn replied impatiently. "I just don't want you to go hunting with *me*."

Eyan's face fell.

"Look, I'm sorry," Dayn said, trying to sound as though he meant it. "I just have a lot on my mind and I want to be by myself, that's all."

"Well, I've a lot on my mind, too," Eyan said crossly. "Or have ye forgotten? It would be nice to have *someone* to talk to."

"Well that someone is not going to be me," Dayn snapped. "Maybe later." Then he marched down the path and toward the forest, leaving Eyan behind.

Dayn veered off the path and into the trees, navigating the woods as quickly as he was able. He knew the tangle of undergrowth would slow his pace for a time, but it was only a temporary decoy. He would detour onto the main road further down, then fork off toward the Well of Wishes.

It was said the well could grant a person's deepest desires. To make a wish, one only had to throw a coin into it. If the coin made a sound when it hit the water, the wish would be granted. But if there was silence, well...better luck next time. The well had once been a place for parties and celebratory gatherings, but over time it had dried up, and few visitors went there now. Dayn had heard rumors that lovers sometimes still met there, but most people stayed away. If wishes were no longer granted, it was just a long walk to yet another pile of rocks.

As Dayn marched in that direction, he wondered what he might wish for if the well still held its magic. At this point, a conversation with Falyn would suffice, but considering the way he usually behaved around her, he would more than likely end up stammering at his boots. It occurred to him that he hadn't stammered at all when he confronted her father that night at the springs. He had, in fact, acted rather bravely, he thought. Falyn, however, might not have thought him brave at all. Perhaps she thought him a fool instead and was inviting him to the well to tell him that very thing. As for her brother—why, he probably hated Dayn more than ever, especially since Dayn had seen him naked and vulnerable. But Sheireadan was not someone Dayn wanted to think of at the moment. He shoved the boy's scowling face from his mind and replaced it with one far more pleasant: Falyn.

He envisioned her standing before him, her almond-shaped eyes staring into his, her lips inviting him for a taste. Would she allow him to kiss her? he wondered. He had only ever kissed one girl, and that had been Jensa. As he thought back on it, he recalled how nice it had felt, but it had also alerted him to how easily a kiss could lead to more. And it was the "more" he truly wished for with Falyn.

He glanced around him. The forest was darkening with elongated shadows. How long had he been walking? He was confident he was on the right path, he had long since forked off the main road, but he had not expected it to take this long. The sun was setting behind the trees now, darkness would soon be upon him, and with no moon to light the night sky, he would have only the stars to guide him. With luck, no clouds would roll in to obscure them, but he had brought flint just in case, and could fashion a torch if need be.

A clearing up ahead caught Dayn's attention, and he realized he was nearly to the well. He could just make it out through the foliage; it was centered on a grassy knoll that was dotted with rocks and tumbled old ruins. But then he realized the area surrounding it was illuminated. He ducked behind a tree and peered around it toward the knoll. A lantern could be seen resting atop a crumbling wall, and next to it someone appeared to be leaning over the well. From where Dayn stood, it was difficult to determine whether they were friend or foe, but when the person straightened up, he realized it was Falyn.

Dayn's insides fluttered like a thousand butterflies. In his eyes, Falyn looked like a fairy in a dream. But surely that was what she was, for never had he seen anything so beautiful. His heart danced with fear and anticipation. This was it—the moment he had been waiting for—the chance to finally tell Falyn how he felt about her. But then a disturbing thought shoved its way in: What if he didn't like her response?

*Courage,* Dayn whispered through gritted teeth. He pulled in a steadying breath, determined not to waste a moment more, but then he realized he should give her a hint of his presence at least. He thought to whisper her

name or clear his throat, but before he could do either,
another worry entered his thoughts. He'd received many
a black eye, or worse, for a single step in Falyn's direction.
Sometimes, if he'd been lucky, he'd have gotten a smile
from her, or *maybe* a word or two. But smiles and words
were no longer enough, his heart demanded more, and if
he failed to convince her tonight, he knew the pain of that
would be far worse than any beating he had ever received.

He watched her for a long moment. She was leaning
over the well again, gazing into its depths. Her long, black
hair had tumbled over her shoulders, obscuring her face.
Dayn felt his hands begin to tremble. How he longed to
run his fingers through that hair, to pull her into his arms
and press his mouth to hers. *Don't be a fool*, he told himself.
*She'll toss you into the well the minute you try.* He thrust his
hands into his pockets and stepped slowly toward her.

Falyn's eyes turned to his. She straightened up and took
a startled step back. "Dayn," she said.

Dayn tilted his head toward the well. "What were you
wishing for?" he asked.

Falyn fingered her skirt nervously. "I was wishing that
you wouldn't come," she said.

Dayn grimaced.

"I didn't mean it like you think, Dayn," she said anxiously.

"How *did* you mean it then?"

She stepped toward him, but Dayn made no move to
tighten the distance. He could not trust himself not to
grab her and pull her into his arms.

Falyn stopped. "I only meant that it was dangerous for
you to come. I should never have asked you."

"There is nothing I wouldn't give you," he said, gathering his courage.

"I know."

"Do you?"

She nodded. "I do."

"So what is it you want?"

Falyn grew quiet, as if playing his question in her mind. Then she said, "I want you to leave and never come back."

Dayn laughed. He couldn't help it. "Not without you."

"You said you would give me anything!" she said, her face reddening.

Dayn's laughter faded. "Do you hate me that much?"

"No. It is because I...*do not* hate you that I am asking you to leave."

"I'm going to need more of an explanation than that."

"Please, Dayn. Father will not rest until he sees you brought to justice. He's talked to the Vestry about it more than once and with each member individually, but tonight is when they will decide what formal action to take against you."

"Against *me*? What action will they take against *him*?"

"None. That is why you have to leave."

Dayn eyed her cautiously. "And just where would you like me to go?"

"To wherever it was you hid before. Otherwise Father will find you."

Dayn felt his anger flare. "I'll not run away like I have something to be ashamed of! If anyone should be ashamed, it's him. He has no right to treat you the way he does."

"You're wrong," Falyn said. "He has every right."

"Then come away with me," Dayn said. "I'll take you to a place where we'll both be safe."

"There is no such place."

"Of course there is," Dayn insisted. "I've been there." Then he hesitated. How in the world was he going to explain Tearia and the valley and all that he had learned since running away all those months ago? Would Falyn think him a liar, or even worse, a heretic? "Falyn, please listen. When I left, I wasn't hiding in the clan lands."

Falyn cocked her head. "Where were you then?"

"Alicine and I went into the cave...it took us beneath the mountains." Falyn gasped, but Dayn continued, the pace of his words quickening. "We got lost and ended up on the other side. There's a whole other world there, Falyn. It's called Tearia. That's where my real parents live...that's where I'm from. I met my cousin Reiv—he was a prince, but was disowned and became a Transcendor–and there were people there called the Jecta and the Shell Seekers and there was a battle and—"

"I don't believe you," Falyn said.

"It's the truth, Falyn. I swear it. You know how the mountain spewed rock and smoke recently? The people in Tearia were affected by it, too. That's why Alicine and I came back; to make sure Mother and Father were all right."

"Father said it was Daghadar punishing the Kiradyns for their wickedness," Falyn insisted. "As soon as everyone began tithing additional coin at Service, it stopped."

"It hasn't stopped," Dayn said.

"But the mountains are calm now. See?" she said, gesturing toward the range.

"Listen to me. They're not calm. When Alicine and I crossed between them, we saw things you couldn't imagine. There were molten rocks and rivers of fire, and charred trees and mudslides. What's happening now–the tainted wells, the dying livestock—they're all because of the mountain and might be signs of something bigger to come."

"How can you know?" Then Falyn's hand flew to her mouth. "Father says *you're* causing the poison, because you are—"

Before Dayn knew what he was doing he grabbed her by the shoulders and shook her. "Now you listen to me. I'm *not* a demon and you know it! Everything I've said is true. You have to believe me."

Falyn tried to wriggle from his grasp, but he pulled her close, his face inches from hers. "I love you, Falyn. You know that. Please. Come away with me. I'll never let anyone hurt you again."

Falyn shoved him back. "I can't, and if you care about me you'll accept it."

Dayn shook his head. "I don't accept it. I'll never accept it."

"You have to," she said firmly, "because I'm not going with you."

Dayn released a slow breath. "Very well," he said. "But before I leave, I ask one thing of you."

Falyn set her chin. "Anything."

"Kiss me."

Falyn backed away, but Dayn matched her step for step. He reached out and yanked her into his arms, his body pressed to hers. "Kiss me," he breathed into her ear. "Or I swear I will die."

Falyn tipped her face to his, her eyes wide. "Dayn," she whispered. But before she could utter another word, Dayn covered her mouth with his.

Falyn pressed her palms against his chest, and Dayn felt sure she was about to rebuke him. But then she threw her arms around his neck and kissed him in return.

Dayn's heart beat wildly. He worked his mouth from her lips to her neck, tasting her skin, breathing her scent. Could this be happening? *Please dear god, let this be happening!*

Suddenly Falyn pushed him away. Dayn reached for her, but she held him back with a thrust of her hand.

"Stop!" she said, panting. "Stop...please."

Dayn stared at her, shaking so hard he could barely speak. "I—I—but—what?" he managed.

"I can't do this, Dayn. I can't!"

Dayn felt consumed with shame. "I have offended you."

"You did not *offend* me, Dayn. I liked it...very much." Falyn's cheeks blushed red. "It's just that we're not married and we should not be touching this way."

Dayn stared at her, realizing her lips and neck were red with the marks his mouth had left there. Was he so desperate to satisfy his own lust that he would sully her reputation and risk losing her forever? He reached out and gently took her hands in his. "Marry me," he said.

Falyn gasped. "What? No—impossible—we're not of age, and according to the law—"

"The law be damned," Dayn said. "Marry me."

Falyn pulled her hands from his. "It's a sin to take a spouse too soon; you know that."

"According to who?"

"According to the Written Word."

Dayn laughed. "Lies, most of it," he said.

Falyn's expression darkened. "Well, if that's what you think, then you had best seek another wife. I'll not be married to a sinner!"

Dayn took her by the waist and drew her near. "We're all sinners," he said. "People just pick different sins, that's all." He brushed his lips across hers. "You're my sin, Falyn," he whispered. "God help me, you are."

Falyn turned her face away. "No, Dayn. I can't."

A knot mushroomed in Dayn's throat, and he released her. "I understand. You do not want me."

"No–I do!" Falyn grabbed his hands in hers. "But I'm too young, and even if I weren't, Father would never agree to it."

"I'll make him agree to it."

"You can't. No one can. Don't you understand?"

"Then come away with me," Dayn said.

"It's not so simple," Falyn replied.

"But it *is*. Just come with me. Right now. My family would welcome you," he hoped, "and–"

"And then what? Do you think my father will let me leave without so much as a fight? He would come after us and–"

"But I know a place where he will never find us–a valley. It's far away, and we would be safe there, safe from him, safe from everything."

For a moment Dayn detected a hint of longing in her eyes. It gave him hope that he might be able to sway her. "You would love it there," he persisted. "I know you would. It's beautiful; there are meadows of flowers, and mountains that sparkle like jewels. There's wildlife and a sea of grasses and a sky so vast you'll be able to see every star in the night sky. I know we could be happy there, Falyn. I know we could."

"It sounds...wonderful," Falyn said. "But even if I *were* to consider it–" She bit her lip. "I can't leave without my brother."

"Your *brother*?" Dayn said, feeling happiness slip from his grasp. He flung her hands from his. "You speak to me of him *now*?"

Falyn reached out for him, but Dayn stepped away, keeping her at arm's length. "For as long as I can remember," he said, "I have loved you. You are the reason for every decision I have ever made, for every beating I ever took!"

"I know, but I want–"

"How can I know *what* you want? Do you want me, do you want freedom, or do you want your brother?"

"I want my father out of my life, Dayn; I'll not deny it. But Sheireadan needs me. If you and I were to leave, I would have to find a way to take him with us. Father has been watching him like a hawk and–"

Dayn looked at her suspiciously. "Why has your father been watching him? What has he done?"

"I—I can't tell you. Please don't ask me to."

"So what makes you think Sheireadan would agree to come with us? He hates me."

"He'll come because he'll want me to be happy. And I'll make sure he knows I *won't* go without him. But that's not all that I want, Dayn."

"What else then?"

"You."

Dayn struggled for reassurances. All he had ever dreamed of was temptingly close. "So if I agree to let your brother come–"

"Then I will go with you."

"Even if you don't love me?"

"But I *do* love you."

Dayn stared into her eyes. How many times had he dreamed of her saying those words? Was it possible she had said them, but more importantly, that she meant them?

"I love you," she repeated.

And that was all he needed to hear.

"When can you meet me again?" he asked.

"I—I don't know." Falyn's brow furrowed as she thought on it. "In two weeks and a day it will be Father's rotation to visit the outlying homesteads, those most affected. A lot of people refuse to leave their farms, but they need food and medicine and fresh water from time to time. So the Vestry's been sending volunteers to help them. It takes a few days to make the rounds." She shook her head. "But Father always takes me and Sheireadan with him."

"Could you make up some kind of excuse not to go?"

"I don't know; I could try."

"Then you and Sheireadan meet me here at high sun on the fifteenth day," he said. "If I'm not here, follow the main road eastward...there." He grabbed up a stick and drew a quick map in the dirt.

"What do you mean, if you're not here?"

"Haskel doesn't want me near Kiradyn any more than your father wants you in the clan lands. Right now my uncle is with the Chieftains, heading for the Vestry meeting."

"He's what?"

"They have information that might convince the Vestry to stop the executions and their demands to turn me over. That's the only reason I was able to slip away tonight."

"The Chieftains will only make them angrier by going," Falyn said. "This is too dangerous, Dayn."

"Not any more dangerous than staying. I'll try to meet you and Sheireadan here, to escort you to the clan lands. But if I can't make it, come on without me." He pointed the stick toward the map, motioning with it. "Don't travel on the road itself; someone might see you. Follow it, but keep to the woods, out of sight. My uncle's homestead is just east of the fork that turns northward; you'll see the fork on the right, but it's easy to miss, so keep an eye out. Don't come straight to the house, though. Hide just past the woodpile near the barn. I'll be looking for you. Do you think you can do that?"

Falyn nodded, but her eyes were filled with worry.

Dayn wrapped her in his arms and pressed his lips to hers, perhaps to seal the agreement, but then an unexpected noise alerted him to a presence in the woods. He spun around and saw two eyes peering at them from the foliage. Dayn stepped toward them and recognized the face behind the eyes—Eyan!

෴

# Chapter 27: Grounded

Eyan burst through the double-doors of the barn, Dayn sprinting after him. "Stop!" Dayn shouted. But it was too late. Eyan disappeared over the edge of the hayloft, taking the ladder with him.

"Eyan! Get down here," Dayn yelled.

No response.

"I swear, if you don't get down here I'll—"

"You'll what?" Alicine asked. She was standing in the doorway at his back, clothed in her nightgown, a shawl wrapped around her shoulders and a lantern clutched in her hand.

"This is none of your concern," Dayn said over his shoulder. "Go back to bed."

Alicine huffed. "I'll do no such thing. What are you carrying on about?"

"Nothing. It's between me and Eyan, that's all."

Alicine looked at him suspiciously. "Why are you getting home so late? Your face is as red as a beet and you're panting like you've been in a race."

"Nothing. I told you—"

"Tell her," Eyan said from the loft. "If it's nothin', then tell her."

Dayn and Alicine tilted their faces upward. Eyan was leaning over the edge of the loft, staring down at them through the lamplight.

Dayn hurriedly scanned the barn. No one else appeared to be there, but if a discussion was to be made, it had to be a private one.

"I'll tell her, but only if you let us come up," Dayn said.

"What'll ye do to me if I do?"

"I just want to talk," Dayn said impatiently. "It's not like I'm going to hit you or something."

Eyan was quiet for a moment, then he eased the ladder over the side. As its legs hit the dirt, Dayn grabbed hold of the rungs and climbed up.

"Thanks so much," Alicine grumbled as she struggled up behind him, the lantern still in her hand.

Dayn stormed toward Eyan, who was now retreating into the corner.

"What did you see?" Dayn demanded.

"Ye know what I saw," Eyan retorted.

"You say it like I was doing something wrong!"

"What are you talking about?" Alicine asked, shaking bits of hay from the hem of her nightgown.

"He went to see Falyn," Eyan said.

"*What*? When?"

"Sshhh! I saw her tonight," Dayn said. "At the Well of Wishes."

"Father said you're not to see her," Eyan said. "It's too dangerous."

"I don't care!" Dayn said. "It was worth the risk."

"No, Dayn. It wasn't," Alicine said.

"Yes. It was," Dayn insisted.

"You had no right to go there."

Dayn steadied his voice. "I had every right. Falyn and I love each other. We have every right to see each other."

"That doesn't make it right," Alicine said.

Dayn felt anger rise in his throat. "Listen, it was *our* choice, our risk—no one else's."

Eyan stepped toward him. "This isn't just about you and Falyn," he said.

"He's right, Dayn," Alicine said. "It's about all of us. If Lorcan were to find out, it could be just the excuse he needs to turn on us once and for all. And tonight of all nights, with our uncles and the Chieftains going to meet with the Vestry. What were you *thinking* Dayn?"

Dayn's mind scrambled, then regained its determination. Maybe he hadn't been thinking clearly at first, but if there was one thing in this world he'd risk anything for it was Falyn. And now that she had agreed to leave with him, nothing else mattered.

"Regardless of whether or not you *approve*," he said, "it's done." He glared at Eyan, daring him to say more.

But Eyan glared right back. "Tell Alicine about the plans."

"What plans?" Dayn asked.

"The ones ye were drawin' in the dirt."

"Those weren't plans, those were—"

"You're *lying*," Alicine said, shock in her voice. "I thought you didn't know how to lie. Guess I was wrong."

Dayn opened his mouth to speak, but the unexpected sound of horses' hooves was suddenly heard thundering toward the house. The three of them looked at each other with surprise, then scurried toward the ladder. The Chieftains couldn't be back from the meeting so soon, could they?

They descended and hurried toward the door, but as they drew near, it was clear the party of Chieftains had returned, and from the lather on their horses, they had ridden hard.

Dayn, Alicine, and Eyan hustled toward the house as the last of the men disappeared inside. The moment Dayn entered through the door, he realized the tension in the room was thick. The men were assembling around the kitchen table, some taking their places on benches, others pacing the floor.

"War," Nort muttered. He glanced around the room and noticed Seela staring at him from a chair by the fireplace. Ben was asleep in her arms.

"Ye'd best take the boy to the wagon," he said to her. "No need of him hearin' any o' this." Seela rose, and with Ben still cradled slipped out the door.

Uaine eyed the others. "It doesn't have to come to war," he said. "Surely a compromise can be made."

"Nay," Brenainn said. "'Tis war they want. And I fer one am willin' to give 'em what they want."

Uaine laughed sarcastically. "What they *want* is Dayn," he said. "Are you willing to give them that?"

"What did they say?" Dayn asked.

Haskel stepped toward him. He placed a hand on his shoulder. "Not to worry, boy. No one has a mind to turn ye over."

"They still believe it's you that's causin' all the problems," Peadar said from the table bench. "A demon's to blame. Might as well be you."

"So they still want me because they think I'm a demon," he said, but in truth he felt somewhat relieved. At least the Vestry's reason had nothing to do with Falyn.

"So what's this all mean then?" Vania asked, setting mugs of hot tea on the table. She looked around. "Where're Eileis and Ionhar?"

"Ionhar and a couple of his men took Eileis home to help her pack," Haskel said. "She's not safe in Kiradyn anymore. The Vestry as much as said so."

"But she's their spiritual leader!"

Brenainn snorted. "Not anymore she 'en."

"Then why didn't you bring her back with ye?" Vania asked. "What if the Vestry followed her home?"

"We tried to tell her," Haskel said, "but she'd have nothin' of it. Said she had some things she couldn't leave behind." Haskel raised his palms in preparation for the argument he knew was coming. "I know...I know. But she insisted. When we told her we'd wait, she about took our heads. Ordered us to head back to warn the clans. Said she wouldn't be long."

"Don' worry, lass," Brenainn said. "Ionhar and his men'll look after her."

"So what else did the Vestry say?" Vania asked.

"Only that there'd be war if we didn't turn the boy over to 'em," Haskel said.

"But didn't you explain about the drawings," Alicine said, "and Tearia, and the Transcendors, and—"

"The fools wouldn't listen," Brenainn replied. "We were barely allowed t' speak a word before they called us *blaspheemers* and threw us out!"

"Threw you out?" Dayn eyeballed the assortment of more-than-adequate weapons at the Chieftains' belts. "How is that even possible?"

"They were ready for us," Peadar said. "They knew we were comin'."

Dayn eased his eyes toward Alicine and Eyan.

"Tell them," Alicine mouthed silently.

Dayn frowned and shook his head. She and Eyan could think what they wanted, but he knew the truth—Falyn would never betray him like that.

Alicine stepped to Dayn's side. "Tell them," she whispered. "Or I will."

"You wouldn't," Dayn whispered back.

Alicine gripped his arm. "These people are risking *war* for you. Don't you think they deserve all the facts?"

Dayn noticed that Eyan was glaring at him, the message in his eyes clear: if Dayn or Alicine didn't say something to the Chieftains, then Eyan would. Dayn ground his teeth, realizing he had little choice. Either he told the men in his own words, or they would be told by someone who could put their own spin on it.

"I have something to say," Dayn announced stiffly. But no one seemed to notice; they were all caught up in discussions of their own. "I said I have something to say," he said more loudly.

The room stilled.

"I met with Falyn tonight."

Voices erupted in shock—Haskel's most of all. "Ye did what?" he bellowed.

"We met at the Well of Wishes," Dayn said.

Haskel turned toward Vania. "I told Eileis not to give him that fool letter!"

Vania waved him off with a sweep of her hand. "Wasn't your decision to make," she said.

"Of course it was my decision to make! Now look what's happened."

Morna stepped from the shadows and approached Dayn. "What *did* happen, son?"

For the first time Dayn felt shame rise to his cheeks. His mother was a devout woman and would never understand. "I..." he began, "I mean, we—" But for some reason the words refused to leave his lips.

"Oh, Dayn," Morna said, judgment in her tone.

Vania approached her and wrapped an arm around her shoulders. "Now, now, dear," she said gently. "Daghadar will be the final judge as to whether or not Dayn did anythin' wrong."

"Did anythin' *wrong?*" Haskel cried. "He disobeyed my orders for one!"

"But I love Falyn," Dayn protested. "It's not right that I can't see her!"

"I don't care whether ye love her or not," Haskel barked. "You'll not be seein' that girl again!"

"You can't order me about!"

Peadar squared his shoulders. "You'll not talk to your elders like that, boy," he said.

Dayn felt his own nerve shrink. Maybe he had gotten away with disrespecting his uncle before, but no one in their right mind would disrespect a Chieftain. "Sorry... sir," he muttered.

"Don't be tellin' me. It's your uncle ye should be apologizin' to. Ye owe him your respect."

Dayn slowly lifted his eyes. "Sorry, uncle."

"I mean it, Dayn," Haskel said. "You're not to see that girl again, ye hear?"

Dayn opened his mouth to retort, but then snapped it shut. Nothing he wanted to say at the moment could be construed as respect.

"And if ye have an idea to dishonor your uncle by sneakin' off again to see her," Peadar added, "you'd best think twice. As Chieftain of the Aeries, I order ye to stay away from Lorcan's daughter. Clearly she's the one that warned the Vestry about us comin'."

"That's not—" Dayn began, but then he adjusted his tone. "Falyn wouldn't do that."

"How did ye know to meet her at the well?" Haskel asked accusingly.

"From her letter," Dayn said.

"And when ye met the girl, did ye by any chance mention that we were headed to the meetin'?"

"Yes, but Falyn wouldn't have had time to tell the Vestry before you got there. She and I were together for a long time. We only left when we saw—" Dayn stopped mid-sentence, realizing it best to leave Eyan out of the conversation. No sense in them drilling his cousin for information that Dayn would just as soon them not know.

"When ye saw what?" Peadar asked.

"When we saw how late it was getting. There's no way she could have told them before you arrived, that's all."

"Regardless," Uaine said. "We need to make preparations. I for one believe the clans should head home first thing in the morning."

"An' do what?" Brenainn asked. "Wait in our cabins 'til the Vestry sends men with torches to burn us out? I say we stay 'n fight!"

"I agree...up to a point," Peadar said. "The women and children must leave of course."

"Why must the women leave?" Vania asked defensively. "There's not a woman amongst us that can't wield a carvin' knife or a pitchfork."

Uaine scoffed. "Very well, *Aerie* women may stay."

Peadar eyed the other Chieftains. "I'll not be askin' any of ye to stay and fight for the Aerie. It's Dayn they want. He's our responsibility."

"The way I see it," Brenainn said, "some of us'll stay and some of us'll go. But if it's yon Dayn they're after, then he needs to be leavin' too."

"No! I won't!" Dayn couldn't believe what he was hearing. "If there's going to be a fight on my account, then I'm staying. I—I—" Suddenly Dayn felt the room tilt and spin. His stomach was churning in one direction while his head was whirling in the other. He fell to his knees, clutching the ground for support.

"Dayn!" Alicine cried, but her voice sounded a thousand miles away.

Dayn's tunic became drenched with sweat. He felt someone place a hand on his back, but it felt like fire against his skin. Heat filled his senses. It singed his throat and flared behind his eyes. "Fire," he gasped.

"What do you mean, boy?" Uaine's distant voice demanded. "Is it the demons? The Vestry? Are they sending fire?"

Dayn felt himself yanked up and shaken.

"Tell us what you know!"

"Leave him be!" Alicine pulled Dayn from Uaine's grip and helped him to a bench.

"What's wrong with him?" Uaine asked. "Is he possessed?"

"No," Alicine said. She wrapped her arms around Dayn protectively. "He gets ill sometimes, that's all. He's not possessed. It'll be over in a minute. You'll see."

Morna rushed to Dayn's side with a damp cloth. "My god, he's burning up!" She held the cloth to his face.

Alicine took it from her. "He'll be fine, Mother. Go get him something cool to drink."

Dayn doubled over and retched onto the floorboards. "And bring another cloth."

When Dayn awoke he was lying on Eyan's bed, a circle of concerned faces leaning over him. He blinked, trying to bring them into focus. "What happened?" he muttered.

"You were ill," Alicine said.

"Ill?" Dayn tried to lift himself onto an elbow, but Alicine pushed him back down.

"How long?" he asked

"Not long. Do you remember anything?"

Dayn closed his eyes as he tried to recall. "Fire," he said. "Something about fire."

"What about it?" Peadar asked him.

"I-I don't know. Maybe the mountain is going to send fire or—"

Uaine stiffened. "Are you claiming divination, boy?"

"Call it what you want," Alicine said. "But when we were in Tearia a similar vision saved thousands of lives."

Haskel looked at her suspiciously. "Explain," he said.

"Dayn would get sick from time to time. When it happened, he would say the earth was moving, but no one else could feel it. Right before the eruption, he got sick, only worse, like now. That time he saw a vision. He saw what was happening under the earth and in the mountain. He warned everyone in the city of Pobu to get out."

"Pobu?"

"Yes," Alicine said. "He told everyone to get out of the city and they did. That morning, the mountain exploded." She narrowed her eyes at Uaine. "If the people hadn't listened to Dayn, they would have died."

Brenainn moved closer to the bed. "So, lad," he said softly. "Is that what yer seein' for *us?*"

Dayn swallowed thickly. "Maybe...I—I don't know. I just saw fire."

Uaine threw up his arms. "This is nonsense."

"No," Peadar said. "It could be a warnin' from Daghadar. An opportunity to save ourselves."

"And if Dayn is wrong?"

"Nothin' lost, nothin' gained," Peadar said. "The Aerie are the closest to the mountain. If it's fire it's sendin', we'll be the first to know it." He turned to the others. "You each have a decision to make: whether to stay and help us against the Vestry, or leave to prepare for the mountain. We don't know that either one'll reach our borders at all, but before ye make your decisions, ye need to tell your folk what Dayn's foreseen, even if it goes against their beliefs."

"The Sandrights will be leaving," Uaine said, then he seemed to reconsider. "But I'm a fair man. I'll give them the choice."

"Very well," Peadar said. He turned to Brenainn. "I'll not ask ye to stay, friend. You've always had our backs, but we may be facin' a fight we can't hope to win."

Brenainn stroked his beard. "Well, I be thinkin' that anyone who leaves is a damned coward—no offense to Uaine here." He slapped his hand on Peadar's shoulder. "Never knew a Basyl to run from a fight. We're wi' ye, all of us, if ye'll have us."

Peadar smiled. "Indeed we will." He then turned his attention to Nort. "Nort, your homestead is the next in line after Haskel's here. Would you be willin' to take some of Brenainn's men to your place to prepare a second line of defense?"

"Aye," Nort said. "I'll leave first thing in the mornin' with Seela and Ben."

"Good enough," Peadar said. "I'll explain to the Aeries what must be done, and I'll speak with Ionhar and Eileis when they return."

The men dispersed to spread the news.

Vania leaned down and felt Dayn's forehead. "How are ye feelin', dear?"

"My stomach's a little queasy, but otherwise I'm fine."

"I'll mix ye up a brew."

"No—no need," Dayn said hastily. "I'll be fine. Really."

Vania nodded, but he could tell by the set of her mouth that she didn't believe him. She turned and took Morna by the shoulders, then guided her to bed. "Let's all of us get some rest," she said. "Big day ahead."

Alicine sat down next to Dayn. Eyan, who had been hovering in the shadows throughout the entire conversation, slipped to their side. "Is what ye say true?" he asked. "Is the mountain really goin' to send fire?"

"Not to worry," Alicine said. "If it is, we've been given plenty of warning, right Dayn?"

"I hope so," Dayn said. "But it seemed different this time."

"How was it different?"

"I don't know, just different." Dayn took stock of their worried faces. "Listen, the Chieftains have agreed to warn the clans, haven't they? That's a lot more time than the Jecta received in Pobu. Everything will be fine, you'll see."

But Dayn wasn't so sure. There was something about this vision that was more disturbing than all the previous ones. This time he had not only *seen* the fire, he had *felt* it. But of even more concern was the fact that he had seen a person standing between it and the mountain. And that person was Reiv.

෬

# PART FOUR

## THE EDGE OF THE ABYSS

# Chapter 28: Into the Black

It had been two weeks since the refugees had left the familiarity of their homeland to follow Reiv into the unknown. At first they had headed northeast, following the coastline until they met a branch of the river that took them due north. Keeping close to the river, they had managed to bypass most areas recently ravaged by the mountain. For a time, all went smoothly. The river provided enough fresh water and fish to sustain them, and it guided them through meadows and forests abundant with edible vegetation and wildlife. Many felt the gods had surely spared these regions for a reason; why not simply choose a place and stay? To this, Reiv reminded them that while the unblemished land did indeed hold many wondrous things, the gods had not spared it for them; it still belonged to Tearia. Best to keep going, he insisted, for they would never find peace in a place that claimed Whyn as its master.

By rights they were still in Tearian territory, but little of the landscape the refugees had traveled thus far resembled the Tearia of their births. For the Shell

Seekers, there were no palm trees, no smell of the sea, no sparkle of sand or shell. For the Jecta, accustomed to mud-brick cities and dusty encampments, the land was greener and more alive than any place they had ever seen. But it did not take long for the geography to take a sudden and disturbing turn. They had reached the border of a region known as The Black.

The Black was an area of Tearia which had been utterly destroyed during the ancient Purge of Aredyrah. At one time, the capitol city had been located there, but liquid fire had consumed it, and the surrounding area was now nothing more than craggy ravines, macabre rock formations, and endless desolation. Reiv had no intention of taking the refugees too far into it; nothing could be gained by leading them through a land that symbolized death. But he knew that in order to reach the mountain pass they would have to at least step into it. He could only pray they would live long enough to step out of it.

The sun was ablaze in the sky, and the cool green forests that had previously shaded them were growing distant at their backs. Since late morning, they had been winding through an area dominated by red-rock formations and a labyrinth of striped canyon walls. The air was dry and hot, and the sun seemed to have grown three sizes since sunrise. As they worked their way through the canyon, Reiv feared he was leading them to a dead end. He honestly didn't know whether or not he was, but there was little choice in the matter. Time was too precious for them to turn back.

He led the caravan onward, but he soon came to feel as if the canyon walls were closing in on them. If the Guard were to follow them, he knew there would be nowhere to run. He gazed up at the cliffs that towered on either side of them. The walls were jagged and patterned in shades of rust and pink and white. So strange, he thought, yet so beautiful. But he quickly redirected his attention when a loud gasp sounded from Jensa who was walking at his side.

"What is it?" Reiv asked anxiously.

Jensa was staring into the distance, her eyes wide and transfixed. "Shells," she said, pointing her finger. "Oh look, Reiv—shells!"

Reiv turned his gaze to where she was pointing, and saw that not far ahead of them the ravine opened onto a vast and arid plateau. Beyond it a massive cluster of pink and white formations outlined the distant horizon.

Reiv smiled, realizing the scallop-shaped hills did indeed resemble giant shells. "I would like to see you put one of those in your basket," he said with a laugh.

"Perhaps we could stay there tonight?" Jensa asked, not taking her eyes off of them.

Reiv squinted up at the sun, then estimated the time and distance it would take for them to reach the formations. The shells were probably not as far as they appeared; more than likely the caravan would reach them well before dark. "We cannot slow our pace," he said. "We have to keep moving."

"Oh please, Reiv," she begged. "We are all so tired..."

"He's right, girl," Gair said at her back. "We'll waste daylight if we linger there."

The blacksmith shifted his grip on the handles of the cart he was pulling, then rolled his neck and shoulders to work the tension from them.

"Don't you think it would do Torin good to rest for a while?" Jensa suggested. "He's been jostled about for days now."

Reiv looked past Gair's cart and toward the horse-drawn transport that carried Torin. Torin, he was pleased to note, was fast asleep, and Kerrik, in a similar state of unconsciousness, was curled up at his side. Cora walked protectively alongside them; she had not let Torin out of her sight since she'd first tended him at the Jecta encampment. "He's doing well," she said in response to Reiv's non-verbal inquiry. "Much better today I think."

Reiv turned his attention back to Jensa. "You see?" he said. "Your brother is fine. No need to worry."

"How can you be sure?" she said. "You know he's not one to complain."

"No, he is not, but…" Reiv lifted an eyebrow.

"Oh," she said in challenge. "But I am?"

Reiv chuckled. "I did not say that."

"Hmmph! You may as well have."

"I promise," Reiv said, "there will be plenty of time to rest when we get to the valley."

Jensa nodded, but Reiv knew she was not happy about it. For the past several days now it seemed she'd been told "no" more often than not. When she'd offered to tend Torin's bandages, Torin had said, "No, Cora will do it." When she'd offered to help Gair pull the cart, he'd dismissed her with a wave of his hand. And when she'd asked if she could join the scouts that kept a lookout for approaching Guards, Reiv had replied "absolutely not." In this, Reiv could not help but feel conflicted. Though he knew Jensa was perfectly capable of climbing trees and high ridges to help keep watch at their backs, for some reason he did not want her amongst the scouts. They were all male. And she was all female.

Now here she was being told "no" again. Was her request really so unreasonable? Perhaps his response had been hasty. The heat and terrain *were* taking their toll. Why, if a man like Gair was showing signs of wear and tear, what must the others be feeling? But what else could Reiv do? He hated the thought of stopping at all, even at night, but in that he had no choice. The journey had been difficult; there were still many sick and injured amongst them. Dozens had died along the trail, but even in that Reiv had never risked a moment of daylight. He'd insisted the dead be buried at night, and had instructed the mourners not to place markers on the graves. If Whyn followed, as Reiv expected he would, it would be foolish to leave additional evidence along the way; their trail was nearly impossible to disguise as it was. No, he reasoned, they would not stop until dark. And that was his final decision.

With little fanfare, Reiv had become the leader of the caravan since the moment it departed Meirla. Even Yustes had warned the people against thinking otherwise. "There can be no conflict in the line of command," he'd told them. "Reiv is leading us to Oonayei; our duty is to follow." Reiv had to admit, he rather liked being in charge. He'd had so little power over anything this past year, it felt good to finally have power over *something* again. As for those he considered family, Brina had not forgotten he was a royal, and Torin was still too weak to argue with him, or anyone else for that matter. Cora held Reiv in high regard for what he had done for them, and the children respected him as a child should any adult. But when it came to Jensa...

He glanced at her, wondering whether or not he should prepare himself for another dose of her temper. Over the past several days, they'd had frequent arguments over his "acting like a fool of a prince," as she put it. But this time she seemed barely aware of his presence at all; she was staring off at the hills, her eyes moist with emotion. She sighed sadly, and Reiv's fortitude went a little soft. Perhaps he could offer her a compromise, or at least let her *think* he was. "Very well," he said. "When we get there, we shall see how much daylight is left. Will that make you happy?"

Jensa smiled her beautiful smile, and Reiv could not help but smile in return. But then he detected a glint of satisfaction in her eye, and his smile all but evaporated. Had she actually tricked him? Even Kerrik was no longer able to do that, and he was the master of manipulation.

"Well, do not count on staying there," Reiv added gruffly. "If there is even a half hour left of daylight, we keep moving."

"Of course," Jensa said, and she kissed him on the cheek.

Reiv felt a flutter in his belly, but he clenched his muscles to tame it back. He refused to be sidetracked by emotions. There were more important destinations to reach.

The plateau proved to be a vast wasteland of black sand and rocky debris. Fist-sized rocks, dark as midnight and pocked with tiny craters, slowed the caravan's pace to nearly nothing. And the sand, unlike anything they had ever seen, crunched and shifted beneath their feet. There was little doubt as to how The Black had come by its name. Carts jerked precariously as the caravan slowly crossed the jagged terrain. The rocks that littered the ground further radiated the afternoon heat, sending many weary travelers to their knees.

Reiv left his position at the front of the line and worked his way back. "This will be the worst of it," he told the people encouragingly as he passed, though he had no idea if it really would be. He knew less about how to get to the valley than he dared let on; he'd only seen snippets of it during his Transcension, and rarely allowed any of the visions to enter his waking mind. He had done well to bury the now, the then, and the maybe. To allow even a hint of them to seep into his consciousness risked a flood of images he did not care to see. For now, he was determined to focus only on that which he knew, that which he had told Dayn and Alicine before they left Meirla: "...follow the river toward the first peak beyond the tallest one... there is a pass between them that will take you into a valley."

As Reiv thought about Dayn and Alicine now, he realized how very much he missed them. Before they had entered his life, he'd had few friends, except for his brother who was now his enemy, and Cinnia who had betrayed his heart. Brina had been his one true constant, though she was more like a mother to him than a friend, but his relationship with Dayn and Alicine had been special, and altogether different. In Dayn, Reiv had found a kindred spirit. He trusted him and could confide his more personal fears and desires. But there were some things he could not tell even Dayn. Some were memories long hidden, memories of things that had happened to him well before he Transcended. One in particular had been buried for so long, he could not be certain it had happened at all. Perhaps it was just a remnant of a childhood dream, or of a childhood nightmare. Recently, it had threatened to seep to the surface, but he had quickly shoved a stopper in it. Over the years, he had become skilled at that. The memory, if that was what it was, had something to do with Crymm, and Crymm was not someone Reiv wished to think of ever again.

He turned his thoughts to Alicine and realized his feelings in her regard were somewhat mixed. He could not deny that he found her attractive; the fact that he had practically taken her on Nannaven's floor was proof enough of that. But he could not shake the realization that she had rebuked him and then had simply left him. Though he understood her concerns for her family, he somehow felt that if she truly loved him, she would have stayed. The moment she had told him she was leaving, he knew: there would not likely be anything more than friendship between them. For a while, the realization had deeply bothered him, but he had finally been able to put things in perspective: Alicine would never share his bed; there was no sense dwelling on it. Best to set his sights elsewhere—like the challenges of the path before him.

He turned his thoughts from his empty heart and toward the shell hills now towering before him. To his surprise, the caravan was nearly there. He glanced up at the sun. It was at least two hours from setting.

He returned to the head of the line, resuming his place at Jensa's side. "You see," he said, feeling victorious. "Much too early to stop."

Jensa didn't say a word, just continued to gaze at the huge formations that looked as much like shells up close as they had from a distance.

Reiv led the caravan around the base of the scalloped hills. The Shell-Seekers stared up at them in awe. Kerrik and the other children laughed and climbed up and down the rocky slopes, sending little avalanches of dirt and gravel bouncing downward. As they rounded the last of the formations, Reiv realized they would soon be at the base of the mountain range itself. He knew where the pass to the valley *should* be, and gauging from where they were in relation to it, he estimated one more day of travel and they would reach it. If they could just make it through the pass, they would be safe from Whyn. He could not imagine his brother or the Guard going into the mountains. That was where the gods dwelt, or so they believed, and it was not likely they would dare tread into such a sacred place.

As for the refugees, Reiv felt certain many of them would become apprehensive once they reached the mountains. Hopefully with Yustes there to encourage and inspire them, there would be no demands to turn back. Everyone knew that in order to reach the valley they would have to enter places previously forbidden. But now, looking up at the monstrous rise of white-capped granite looming in the distance, Reiv could not help but wonder if even he would be tempted to turn back. Though he had recently learned many truths that disputed the beliefs he had been raised on, including the fact that the gods did not dwell in the mountains after all, he had come to realize that some fears were hard to erase. *Doubt is a temptation of evil*, he had been warned as a child. *To doubt the gods is to invite eternal suffering.* As he thought on it now, it seemed to him that those who taught that message had caused more suffering than all the gods put together. But still…if doubt *was* a temptation of evil…

"Hey, Reiv!" Kerrik shouted from the nearby hillside. "You'll not find a bigger shell than *this* one today!"

Reiv grinned. "It is a fine one, Kerrik," came his customary reply.

Reiv watched as Kerrik and the other children skittered from rock to rock, and he began to wonder if the cara-

van already *was* treading on sacred ground. To his knowledge no one had ever traveled so close to the mountains,
except for Brina who had only done so to save the life of her
son Dayn. Were these formations hallowed ground also, he
wondered? And if those who trespassed upon them were
sinners, and thus destined to suffer for all eternity, would
children like Kerrik and Nely and Gem be doomed to suffer also? Surely no god would willingly cause the suffering
of a child, Reiv reasoned. But he called the children down
from the hillside nonetheless.

Reiv directed the caravan along the westernmost corner
of The Black and toward the edge of the mountain range.
From there they continued along its border, until at last
it became dusk and Reiv ordered the line to set up camp.

The area surrounding the campsite was dotted with
pines, and the cool night air was a welcome relief from
the hot, rugged terrain they had recently crossed. Reiv
surveyed the encampment, trying to estimate how many
souls had survived the journey thus far. As was his custom
each night, he walked throughout the encampment, paying his respects, checking to see if there were questions or
needs, or to simply determine the state of the line. During each inspection, he also made a point of speaking with
Yustes, who generally took up the rear. As he worked his
way in that direction, he heard a concerned voice calling
his name. He turned, realizing it belonged to Peyada, a
woman whom he knew to be close to Yustes.

The woman hustled in his direction. "It is Yustes," she
said breathlessly upon reaching him. "He is ill."

An unpleasant feeling gathered in Reiv's belly. "Take
me to him," he said, and soon found himself kneeling next
to the bedroll of the wise old Elder.

Reiv took the man's hand in his. "Yustes," he said.

Yustes opened his eyes and forced a smile. "Reiv," he said weakly. "Not far now, eh?"

"No. Not far." Reiv felt the Elder's forehead. It was clammy, but it did not feel hot, not like those suffering from the fever. "Tell me what ails you."

"Old age," Yustes said, a hint of humor in his voice. A cough spasmed from his lungs.

"Enough of such talk. You are not so old."

The Elder sighed, his breath rattling. "Old enough to know when my time has come."

"Well, your time will have to wait," Reiv said. "We must get you to Oonayei first."

"Dear boy, even if my body does not make it, my spirit will." He turned his fading eyes to Reiv. "You will see that it gets there, won't you?"

"Yes, of course. But...how?" Reiv asked, wondering how he, of all people, could have control over someone else's soul.

"I am...a part of everyone you see around you," Yustes said haltingly. "We are all kindred spirits. If you get my people there...then you get me there."

"I will do what I can."

"I know you will." Yustes swallowed thickly. "Peyada, water...please," he said.

The woman, standing nearby, quickly brought him a water skin. Reiv took it from her and tilted it to Yustes's lips. With Reiv's assistance, the old man was able to lift his head and take a sip. "Tastes sweet," Yustes said. "But the waters of Oonayei will taste even sweeter."

"Yustes," Reiv said hesitantly. "What if the valley is not the place you think it is? What if Oonayei does not exist?"

"It will exist if enough people believe it does."

"One cannot simply wish a place into being," Reiv said.

"Perhaps *one* cannot, but together many can."

"And if I cannot unite them in that belief?"

Yustes smiled. "You already have, my boy. You already have."

Yustes died that night. His loss was immediately felt. He had been a touchstone of hope for many, and Reiv could not help but pray that hope had not died with him. Burial rites were held under the stars. All who could, attended. The Elder was laid to rest beneath a canopy of trees, protected by the shade that their branches offered, blanketed by leaves against the cold of the night. No stone was set to mark his simple grave, but all who knew him would never forget his courage. He had given his people the strength to turn their backs on oppression; he had lifted their souls and had turned their hearts toward freedom. But would that strength last?

The night was quiet and still when Reiv returned to his own bedroll. He lay there, his eyes turned toward a star-studded sky, but all he could see were worst case scenarios blackening his mind. Would the Shell Seekers want to continue their journey now that their spiritual leader was gone? Or would they leave the caravan and stumble their way home by way of the route they had already traveled? The Jecta, he was certain, would not retreat; they would face certain annihilation if they did. But the Shell Seekers had at least been given a chance to survive through servi-

tude to the King. Would they come to regret the choice
they had made?

"What am I doing?" he muttered. "I am such a fool."

He felt someone's presence and looked up to see Jensa
standing next to him.

"You're worried," she said. She settled down beside
him. "What are you thinking?"

"Nothing," Reiv lied. "What are *you* thinking?"

She lay on her side, facing him, her head propped up
by a hand.

The proximity of her body sent an unexpected flutter
to Reiv's chest.

Jensa doodled her finger on the blanket for a moment.
"Well," she said, "I'm thinking that you've spent so much
time seeing to everyone else's needs that no one has seen to
yours."

The rhythm in Reiv's chest quickened. By the gods,
what did she mean by that?

"Tell me, Reiv," she continued. "What do you need?"

Reiv's mind raced toward an obvious conclusion, but
rather than consider the ridiculous possibility of it, he
responded with a burst of laughter instead.

Jensa sat up angrily. "I'm sorry you find me so...so
*amusing*," she said, and moved to rise from the bedroll.

Reiv grabbed her arm and pulled her back down.
"Please; I am not laughing at you," he said. "I am laughing
at me."

"As well you should be," she said.

"Well, I *am* a fool of a prince, am I not?"

"At your convenience."

"Very well," he said. "What I *need* is to get these people
to the valley. That is what I need."

"Well, at least in that you're no fool; you're their savior."

It was then Reiv's turn to sit up. "I am *no* savior. I am—" He stammered, not sure *what* he was exactly.

Jensa rose to her feet. "You're that and more. But I don't think I wish to argue with you about it tonight."

Reiv lay back down and rested his hands behind his head. "Well you were the one that came over here. If you do not wish to argue, I suppose you had best stay away from me."

"Fine," she said, and turned and marched away.

Reiv pulled the blanket over him. The air had become surprisingly cold since Jensa's departure, and for the first time he realized how very much he longed for the warmth of her body next to his.

∽

# Chapter 29: Inch by Inch

Darkness engulfed him; it filled Lyal's every pore. Like a great parasite it wound its way through him, eating his flesh from the outside in, expelling it in pieces from the inside out. It filled his lungs with liquid ice. It coiled into his ears and mouth and nostrils. No part of him was spared the agony that it dealt. It blinded his memories and poisoned his mind; it stole his identity and replaced it with fear. Pain was all that was left to him now; the rest had been devoured, sucked from the marrow of his bones and spewed into the blackness.

He was locked in an abyss, an endless nightmare of darkness and despair. When he had first been cast there, there had been no pain, only silence and fear and endless night. In the beginning, he had prayed for light, thinking it would bring him warmth. When none came, he sought solace in the millions of lights that flickered behind his eyelids. They looked like tiny stars, he thought, like those one might see in a foggy night sky. Gazing at the miniature lights, he tried to imagine that he was lying on the sand, staring up at the heavens, listening to the sea as it stroked the shore, feeling the breeze as it caressed his skin. He had clung to that fantasy for what seemed like a very long time, playing it over and over until the rhythm of it lulled him to sleep. Only then could he call darkness his friend, for when he slept he dreamed, and sometimes the dreams held color and reminders of what it was to be alive. But after a while the stars began to fade, and the dreams grew vague and colorless, and all he was left with was darkness again.

He had never been afraid of the dark, had never really been afraid of anything. But it did not take long for Lyal to wonder if he had simply been left to wither away in it. His body screamed for nourishment and warmth, and the constant sound of his own breathing, the only sound he could hear, was slowly driving him mad. He crawled and crawled along the perimeter of his prison, trying to claw his way out, but there was no escaping it. He prayed and he begged, but the only response he received was the echo of his own voice in his ears. It was then that he became truly afraid. Was this to be his death—to slowly rot away in madness? He implored the gods to release him from his nightmare, for surely that was what this was—a terrible dream from which he would eventually awake. If only the gods would send the sunrise! If only they would rescue him from this damnable night and deposit him into the arms of morning!

An eternity passed, but at last his prayers were answered: light had finally come! A *creak* like that of an opening door filled his ears, and a sudden flash of brilliance blinded his eyes. He scrambled to his knees, awash with joy and gratitude, but he quickly learned he had been betrayed, for the light that came was indeed as bright as the sun, but unlike a sunrise, it brought no warmth or the promise of a new day. It brought cruelty and hate, and with that, unfathomable pain.

The light said not a word as it grabbed him and slammed him onto a hard, cold slab. It asked him no questions as it bound him in chains and tortured him in ways he could not have imagined. It abused him over and over again, without regard to his cries for mercy. Lyal screamed and he raged, but it did no good. It seemed the more he begged, the more his tormentor took delight in it. The light came to him frequently after that, each visit laced with more cruelty than the last, and before long Lyal was praying again. But now he was praying for darkness.

∽

# CHAPTER 30: DARK SAVIOR

The morning sun streamed through the etched-glass windows of Whyn's sprawling room, splashing light onto its colorless walls, and rainbows into Whyn's colorless world. He sat up and shoved back the coverlet that was draped across his legs. Like just about everything else in the room, the coverlet was white, as white as the walls, as white as the satin nightshift he wore, as white as the kingdom that she, through him, was determined to rebuild. He planted his feet on the floor and crossed the marble tiles toward the dressing table, yanking his nightshift over his head. Attendants rushed from out of nowhere to assist him, but he waved them out of the room with a flick of his hand.

Before him stood a gilded mirror that reached from floor to ceiling. Whyn stopped to gaze at his full-length reflection, turning this way and that as he examined his naked body from every angle. For all the physical abuse she had inflicted on him over the past several months, he was pleased to note that his flesh bore no scars, at least none that could be seen in a mirror.

He stepped to the nearby dressing table, then pulled out a stool and sat. A second mirror, equally elaborate but smaller than the first, hung on the wall before him. Leaning toward it, he studied his face. Still handsome, he thought: smooth skin, straight nose, and his eyes—so blue. He eased back, keeping his gaze upon his reflection. How long had it been since his eyes had been so blue?

Glancing at the dressing table, he noted the usual assortment of potions and face paints that littered the surface, as well as the numerous hair ornaments and grooming tools. He picked up a comb and raked it through his sleep-tangled hair, but he did not attempt to braid or adorn it like he usually did. Setting aside the comb, he moved his fingers to a paint brush, then pushed it aside. Today he would apply no paint to his lips or glitter to his eyes. Today he would dress as a king, not the puppet of the entity that so frequently possessed him.

Whyn rose and stepped to a massive wardrobe located along the wall. Turning the latch, he threw back its door. Within the wardrobe were his finest garments. They had, in fact, once been his favorites. There were velvets and satins and silks and brocades, all exquisitely made. Most were dyed in shades of gold and yellow, the traditional colors of his class, but there were a few darker shades amongst them. Most he had worn when he was a prince, but since becoming King, she had not allowed him to touch them; it was a miracle she had let him keep them at all. He fingered the garments, grateful to finally have the freedom to do so, and rested his eyes upon a hunting tunic of emerald green. To wear it would be such relief from the colorless garbs she usually made him wear. Fortunately, today he would enjoy that relief.

He removed the tunic from the wardrobe and brought it to his nose, breathing in the scent of what he used to be. A rush of memories filled his mind, but there was no time to dwell on the past. He pulled the tunic over his head and belted it with a fine chain of gold, then draped a velvet cloak of the same emerald color upon his shoulders. After securing it with a brooch, he pulled on his best deerskin boots and hurriedly exited the room.

Outside the newly-built palace wing that housed Whyn and his personal servants, a guard stood at attention, prepared to escort him to the nearby catacombs. At one time, the catacombs had only housed the remains of the dead. Later, it had imprisoned political enemies as well. But the recent earthquake had very nearly destroyed it. Only recently had it been cleared of enough rubble to bring the tunnels, at least somewhat, to their original state. The catacombs now held a single prisoner, the only one worth keeping, and as was Whyn's daily custom, he was heading to see that prisoner now. But this time his purpose in visiting was far different.

The guard, torch in hand, escorted Whyn through the narrow entrance of the tunnels and down a dark, winding corridor. It did not take long to reach the cell of destination. After securing the torch in a metal bracket on the wall, the guard lifted a ring of keys from a nearby peg. He unlocked the door to the cell and shoved it open, then grabbed the torch and moved to usher Whyn inside.

"Hand me the torch," Whyn said. "Today I go in alone."

The guard hesitated, but knew better than to disobey. "As you wish, my lord," he said.

"And the keys," Whyn said. He snapped his fingers, then took the ring being held out to him. "You may leave, but wait at the entrance. And keep alert should I need you."

The guard bowed and retreated into the shadows.

Whyn held out the torch as he stepped into the musty cell. It was small, and thick with the miasma of human waste and utter despair. A sudden movement and the rattle of chains directed Whyn's attention to the far corner.

"Lyal," Whyn said gently.

Lyal scrabbled along the wall, trying to distance himself from the glaring light turned in his direction. But the chains at his ankles allowed him no retreat.

Whyn reached a hand toward him. "I am not here to harm you," he said.

Lyal recoiled against the wall, his chains stretched as far as they would go. "Stay away from me," he rasped. His eyes, anguished in the glare of the torch, blinked wildly.

"Does the light hurt you?" Whyn asked. "Here, I will move it further away." He placed the torch in the bracket outside the door.

Lyal stared up like an animal caught in a snare. To look at him, one would have thought he was. His hair was filthy and matted, and his once handsome face was swollen with bruises. His body, thin and weak, was caked with his own excrement and infected with the bite marks of the vermin that shared his cell.

Whyn stepped closer. He squatted down and fingered Lyal's tangled hair. Lyal cringed and jerked from Whyn's touch.

"I regret that she did this to you," Whyn said. "But you must understand; it was not me; it was her."

Lyal turned away, cowering against the wall.

"Look at me, Lyal," Whyn said firmly. "I want you to see me as I truly am."

Lyal eased his eyes toward him. "I see only a murderer and a tyrant," he said, then flinched as if expecting a blow.

Whyn sighed. "She is that, and more. But she is gone now."

Lyal's brow furrowed. "What do you mean...gone?"

Whyn rose and turned in a slow circle. He stopped, his hands beseeching Lyal to gaze upon him. "Do you not see? I am all man now; no longer am I man *and* she-witch!"

"How can I...trust you?" Lyal said. "After what you did—"

"After what *she* did," Whyn corrected. He knelt before Lyal. "I swear to you. I have freed myself of her. It was no easy task, but I have done it!"

"What is that to me?" Lyal asked cautiously.

"Freedom."

Lyal's eyes grew wide. "Freedom?"

Whyn held up the ring and *jangled* the keys. "I have come to set you free. But before I release you from your chains, you must promise not to run or to do me harm. An armed guard waits for us at the entrance. He will escort us back to the palace where you will be given a hot bath, clean clothes, and as much food and drink as you desire. I owe you that, and more. But if you betray me in this, Lyal, the only bath you will find yourself in will be that of your own blood. Do you understand?"

Lyal hesitated, then nodded.

"I swear to you on my father's grave," Whyn said. "I only wish to help you." And with that he twisted the key and released the prisoner from his chains.

Lyal followed Whyn toward the palace, every agonizing step a reminder of the abuse he had suffered. At times the guard escorting them had to prop Lyal up and half-carry him. Other times Lyal was left to stumble along on his own. The blinding glare of daylight, coupled with the fogginess in his head, forced him to keep his bearings by training his eyes on the green cape that fluttered before him. The King was but steps in front of him, well within his reach. But even had Lyal possessed the strength to raise a hand to him, for some strange reason he no longer possessed the desire.

Whyn turned and gazed warmly into Lyal's eyes, and Lyal could not help but meet his in return. When Whyn had first presented himself to Lyal shortly after his capture, the King had not seemed human at all. His eyes had been red and demonic, like a beast from another world, and the cruelty in his soul had been etched upon his face, much like the ancient ritual of scarification. But now the young King appeared handsome and gentle and kind. Was it possible that Whyn spoke the truth? Had he truly been possessed by an evil entity, but now was rid of her?

"Here we are," Whyn said as they approached the palace door.

Lyal shifted his gaze to the rose-colored building before them. Though the palace was currently nothing more than a single wing that housed the King and his servants, based on the construction going on around them, it would soon return to its original grandeur.

As Lyal glanced around, he recognized the faces of many of the slaves that toiled in the rubble and rising frameworks of the structure. Most of them were Shell Seekers, though they no longer wore shells around their necks or kohl around their eyes. One by one they stopped their work and watched as Lyal passed. There was pity in their faces, he realized, pity for him. It filled him with humiliation, but then anger rose to take its place. Why should they feel pity for *him*? he seethed. Were *they* not the ones whose backs would soon be striped for stopping their work? Was he not the one who would soon be bathed and fed and pampered by the King himself? He turned his eyes forward, determined to ignore their penetrating stares. He had paid his dues, certainly more than the rest of them. None of them had endured the abuse that he had. Not one of them had been thrown into a dismal cell, their body ravaged and tortured in ways they could not imagine. Only he had suffered that. Only he was due the restitution of the King.

Two guards pushed open the great double doors leading into the palace wing. Whyn entered and Lyal followed. "Prepare a bath for our guest!" Whyn barked to the servants now hustling around them.

Lyal gazed, awestruck, at the cavernous foyer. It was wide and high-ceilinged and decorated in elaborate tapestries and elegant furnishings. Lyal slowed his pace as he drank in the magnificence of the entryway.

"Come...come," Whyn coaxed. "No need to linger in the hall."

Lyal stepped more quickly, but was suddenly aware of the grime that coated his skin and the stench that clouded his body. How could he bring such filth into a place like this? He hunched his shoulders as though, like a turtle, he could hide within himself.

Whyn glanced back, recognizing his discomfort. "Do not feel unworthy, Lyal," he said. "It is not your fault that you are in such a state. You should be proud of the way you stood up to her."

"Proud?" Lyal said. If he had had the stamina, he would have laughed.

Whyn stopped and turned to face him. "You endured much," he said. "I regret I was a party to it, but please know that all the while you were suffering, I was suffering also."

Lyal lowered his gaze and remained silent.

Whyn gathered Lyal's face into his hands, forcing Lyal to look at him. Lyal's first instinct was to jerk away, but as he stared into the endless blue of Whyn's eyes, he found it impossible.

"Do you think I enjoyed tormenting you in that filthy cell?" Whyn asked. "Well, I loathed it. Every moment of it. She made me do those things to you, Lyal. It was my punishment as much as it was yours."

"Your punishment?" Lyal asked, realizing that in a strange way, he was beginning to feel pity for the King.

"Yes, *my* punishment. You see, I said the one word to her that she does not like to hear—'no'. And for that I was forced to abuse you in the muck and the stench of your cell." Whyn released Lyal's face. "But now I shall help you forget the pain and the humiliation you endured. And in so doing, perhaps I shall forget it also."

Whyn turned his attention to a nearby open door. Serving girls scurried in and out of the room beyond it. "Ah," he said. "I believe your bath is ready."

He led Lyal through the doorway and gestured toward a large bathing cask located beneath a window of frosted glass. Thick steam rose from within, beckoning Lyal to the comforts of the tub. But he could only stop and stare.

"Come," Whyn said. "Do not be shy."

Lyal slowly approached the cask. More than anything he longed to strip off his clothes and dive in, to scrub his body free of the grime and the vile memories of the cell. As he drew nearer, he noticed flower petals floating atop the water's surface, adding their essence to the scented candles that glittered the room. On a nearby chair, soft fluffy towels were stacked, and against the wall a large poster bed, thick with comforters and downy pillows, invited him to it.

He was soon surrounded by serving girls who undressed him and led him to the cask, all the while caressing him with gentle hands. Had he been in a better state, he would have enjoyed the attention and risen to the occasion. But as he was now, he felt only shame.

Lyal entered the tub as directed, and slowly rested the back of his head against the rim. He closed his eyes, trying to focus on the comforts of the water and that of the hands now sponging his body from head to toe.

"Drink, good sir," a soft feminine voice said.

Lyal opened his eyes to see a golden goblet suspended before him, held in the delicate hand of a pretty young serving girl. He sat up and took it from her with a nod of thanks, but his hands were shaking so badly he did not know if he could hold it.

"Here, allow me," the girl said. She wrapped her hands around his and tilted the goblet to his lips. "The King wishes you to drink this. It will hasten the healing of your wounds."

The wine tasted sweet on Lyal's tongue, but the after-taste was bitter and strange. It stung his lips and burned his throat as it made its way down, and for a moment he felt the need to retch. But then a cool cloth was placed upon his forehead, held there by caring fingers, while others massaged eucalyptus oil into the tight muscles of his neck and shoulders. Lyal felt his body relax and his mind drift. Again the wine was held to his lips, but this time his body accepted it without complaint.

"Well done, Lyal," Whyn said. "You shall soon feel better."

The voice jerked Lyal back to reality. The King was still in the room, he realized, standing near the cask, watching as the girls massaged the pain and filth from his body. Lyal swallowed thickly. Heat rushed to his cheeks. For a moment he thought to cover himself with his hands, but as he looked at Whyn, he realized he felt no shame or fear toward the handsome young ruler, only gratitude and affection. It was Whyn who had rescued him. It was Whyn who would protect him now. No longer did the King seem like an enemy or an abuser. If anything, he seemed more like his friend. Whatever of Lyal that Whyn wanted, Lyal would give to him, and gladly. Whyn was his savior now. And gods willing, Lyal would be his.

⁂

The banquet table was covered with more food and drink than Lyal had seen in his twenty-something life. As he stood in the doorway, he could not help but gawk at the feast that filled the room before him. The King had said he would be well fed, but never in Lyal's wildest dreams could he have imagined this! Surely others would be attending, he reasoned; this could not be for him alone. But other than the dozen or so servants scurrying about, he appeared to be the only one there.

He was escorted to a massive high-backed chair at one end of the table and invited to sit. A goblet of wine was immediately placed before him, the jeweled decanter from which it was poured well within his reach. An identical chair faced him on the opposite end of the table, and he could not help but pray the King would soon be sitting in it.

Lyal moved his gaze from the empty chair across the way and toward the lavish feast. At the center rested a mound of roasted fowl, cooked to a golden brown. The aroma of it was so enticing, Lyal was certain he could see it wafting through the air. Clusters of fat, purple grapes surrounded it, and on either side red apples and freshly picked figs were arranged in bowls as large as wash basins. There were assorted cheeses in shades of white and yellow and orange, and buttery rolls and braided breads displayed on large polished plates. Chocolate pastries and pastel sweets could also be seen, stacked like miniature castles throughout the lavish spread. The sight and smell of it filled Lyal with such longing, he found himself battling the urge to literally attack the table.

Lyal gripped the arms of the chair, but he could not help but fidget. It was not from the overwhelming desire to eat. It was not even from the abuse his body had recently suffered. It was more from the discomfort of the clothing he had been ordered to wear. He was dressed in a dark, high-collared blouse, hugged at the torso by a pewter-colored vest, his legs wrapped in form-fitting leathers. The outfit was similar to the uniforms worn by the Tearian Guard: dark, stiff, and molded to the body as if cast from metal.

When the clothing had first been presented to him, he had protested; never before had he worn anything so...Tearian. But the serving girls had insisted that he wear them, probably because Whyn had instructed them to do so, and miserable or not, Lyal did not wish to displease the King. And so he had allowed the girls to dress him and paint his eyes and braid his hair, all the while listening to them twitter about how handsome he was. Only then had he begun to feel less self-conscious about the uniform he was wearing.

Lyal ran a finger under his collar, arching his neck to relieve the tightness pressing against his throat. The room was unbearably hot, he thought, no doubt due to the ridiculous amount of clothing he had on. He glanced toward the fire that roared in the fireplace against the far wall. Its heat seemed to permeate the room in shimmering waves, much like that which reflected off the beach at high sun. Throughout the room and scattered across the table, tapered candles flickered, adding more warmth to the aura of heat that filled the room. Lyal grabbed up his wine goblet and drank down its contents, then poured himself another. But all the sweet liquid managed to do was send another flush to his skin.

A lone figure suddenly shadowed the doorway. The servants dropped to their knees and bowed their heads to the floor. Lyal set down his goblet and rose, shoving back the chair with a thrust of his legs. He stepped to the side and, taking the servants' cue, lowered himself to the floor and pressed his forehead to the tiles.

Other than the crackle of the fireplace, the room was quiet as the King strolled toward the banquet table. He stopped before Lyal and bade him rise. "No need for formality," Whyn said. "You are my guest. Sit—eat! Whatever you desire, it is yours." Then he turned and headed for the chair at the opposite end of the table.

Whyn sat, and Lyal followed his lead. A servant filled Whyn's wine goblet and stepped back, decanter in hand. Whyn raised the goblet to Lyal with a smile. "May this humble meal please you," he said, then snapped his fingers to the servants. "Fill this man's plate and be quick about it!"

Lyal's eyes bulged as a plate piled high with food was placed before him, but his insides could not help but clench. It had been so long since he had eaten anything, he did not know if his stomach would tolerate it. But then he recalled the drink the girl had given him, and Whyn's assurances that it would help him heal. Since drinking the potion, he could honestly say he had felt no pain in his body or his mind. In fact, his flesh no longer bore evidence of his abuse, nor did he recall much about it. It was as if he had reverted to what he was before, or perhaps he had been born anew. Regardless, at this moment it was as if none of it had ever happened. The only thing different about him now was that he felt unconditional loyalty toward the man sitting across the table from him.

Lyal dug into the food on his plate, savoring every bite. He did not care if his manners were less than stellar. He did not care if grease trickled down his chin and into his lap. He shoveled in mouthful after mouthful, unaware that he had already polished off two plates and was now starting on a third. All he knew was that he could not stop; he was like a blood-crazed animal burying its face in the kill. He looked up and saw that Whyn was watching him. Lyal set down his utensils, mortified by his own ill manners. The servants would have done better to set a plate for him by the back door.

Whyn rose and slowly walked toward Lyal. "Come. Sit with me by the fire," he said.

Lyal was relieved to see that the King's eyes were filled with amusement rather than disgust. He rose and followed Whyn to two overstuffed chairs by the hearth.

Whyn settled into one and gestured for Lyal to sit in the other. "Did you enjoy the meal?" he asked.

"I did indeed, Sire," Lyal replied. "It was excellent. Thank you."

"It was my pleasure." Whyn cocked his head. "You know, I could find a place for you here. If you wished it."

"A place for me?" Lyal said with astonishment.

"More wine?" Whyn asked, changing the subject. He motioned the wine-bearer over.

"Yes," Lyal replied. But in truth his head was already spinning from the decanter he had drained during the meal.

The servant handed them each a glass of wine, then stepped back.

"Well," Whyn continued, "as you may have noticed when you arrived at the palace, there are many Shell Seekers working on the rebuilding of the city."

"Yes," Lyal said, but strangely he felt no animosity for it.

"You may have also noticed that there were no fish or crustacean included in the meal that you just ate." He took a quiet sip from his glass.

Lyal turned his attention to the table, then back to Whyn. "I—I had not noticed," he said.

Whyn set his wine glass aside and steepled his fingers under his chin. "I regret what happened to your village," he said at last. "It was most…unfortunate."

Lyal nodded.

"I would like to see it rebuilt," Whyn said. He lifted a brow. "Would you be interested in leading the effort?"

"Yes—yes Lord, of course! But—but what of the rebuilding of Tearia? Are the Shell Seekers not needed for the task?"

"Indeed they are, for now. We will not be able to rebuild Meirla until I have enough workers to replace those currently here, of course. Though many are engaged in the construction effort, others have different but equally valuable jobs. The food we just ate took a great deal of effort to secure." Whyn shook his head. "If only she had not allowed so many people to leave with my brother. I would have had more than enough laborers then, and the rest of the Shell Seekers would be free to serve me by hunting the seas as they always have."

Lyal struggled to recall the murky details surrounding the escape of the Jecta with his people. Since his capture, it had all become so confusing. He knew many had left, and that Reiv had played a part in their decision to do so. Anger welled in his breast. It must have shown on his face, for Whyn added, "My brother can be very charismatic. People are frequently misguided by him. It is unfortunate that so many Shell Seekers left with him. Do you know why they elected to do so?"

"Because Reiv is a liar and they are fools," Lyal said.

Whyn laughed. "Well, you have part of it right." He reached for his glass and swallowed down the rest of its contents. "Bring me the special," he barked to the servant waiting nearby. "The one I serve to only my important guests."

He grinned at Lyal. "As I was saying, I would be interested in having you lead the effort to rebuild Meirla. There will, no doubt, be much resentment toward me; your people cannot possibly understand me as you do. You therefore must explain to them the truth of the matter: I was possessed by a demonic witch, but she is gone now. From this day forward, I promise to be a kind and just king, but only to those who are loyal to me in return. Do not misunderstand me, the rebuilding of Tearia is my utmost priority, but I do not wish to do it at the expense of the Shell Seekers. Until recently, we had a very amicable relationship. I see no reason why it should not return to the way it was."

"How may I help?" Lyal asked.

"If there was some way I could persuade the Jecta to return..."

"What of the fever they were carrying?"

"I am pleased to report there have been no new cases here in the city. Cruel as it may sound, I believe the burning of the Jecta encampment stopped the plague from progressing much further. By the time the refugees are found, the illness will likely have run its course. I fear some of your people may have perished during the trek, but I am sure those who survived will be eager to return and resume their normal lives, especially when they learn I will grant them their freedom."

Lyal furrowed his brow in contemplation. There was more to the departure of his people than simply fleeing from the King's servitude. They were going *to* something, not just *away* from it. "I—I do not know if they will wish to return," he said. "They were going to..." Lyal hesitated. Dare he tell the King where they were heading?

Whyn laughed softly. "Do not worry as to whether or not to tell me about Oonayei, Lyal. I am well aware of their planned destination."

Lyal was quiet for a long moment. Whyn leaned toward him. "Lyal," he said gently. "It is for their own good that they return here. There is no hope for their survival in the wilderness, you know that. The place they think they are going to does not exist. I have studied the maps and am certain of the direction they were heading. They did not pass this way, and the gods would never allow them to enter the mountains. The only way they could have gone is toward The Black." He leaned back in his chair. "And you know what that place holds."

"Yes," Lyal said, "but I do not know if I have the power to turn them back."

"Do you not think it worth the effort, though? Surely there is someone amongst them that you care about. A family member perhaps?"

"No, no family."

"Friends, then."

Lyal frowned. Friends? He'd befriended plenty of women, but they could not be counted as *friends*. As for the men, they only pretended to be his friends so they could make a grab for the females he discarded.

"No. No friends," Lyal said bitterly. He held out his glass for another fill. The wine bearer hustled to accommodate him.

"I can see why a man as handsome as you would have few friends," Whyn said. "You were too busy making time with the women. Am I correct?"

The corner of Lyal's mouth lifted. "I did well with the women; that is true. It brought me few friends–and far too many competitors."

"Ah, women," Whyn said with a sigh. "I do love them; I was actually *in* love with one once, but that was. . .another lifetime." He waved off the thought. "But we are not here to talk about me." He ran his finger around the rim of his glass. "Tell me, Lyal; have you ever been in love?"

Lyal felt a catch in his throat as the image of Jensa took shape in his mind. She was the only person he could honestly say he'd ever loved, if he even knew what that meant. By the gods, why had he not fought harder to keep her?

"Ah…" Whyn said. "I see you have felt love's cruel sting."

"That I have," Lyal said. "She was stolen from me by another."

Whyn smiled sadly. "I see." He rose and set his wine glass aside. Facing the hearth, he clasped his hands behind his back and stared at the flames. "Have you ever hated anyone, Lyal?"

Lyal hesitated. "Yes," he said.

Whyn kept his gaze on the flames. "How deep did your hatred go?"

"Deep, Sire."

"And was this person the one that stole the woman from you?"

"He was."

Whyn turned to face him. "Was it my brother perhaps?"

Lyal's tone turned hard. "Indeed it was."

Whyn motioned for the servant to refill both of their glasses. "Then it seems we have a common enemy, my friend. The question is, what do we do about him?"

Lyal rose from the chair and stood to face him. "We find him and bring him back."

"And with him your people."

"And with him my people."

Whyn turned again toward the fire. "How unfortunate you do not think they will return of their own free will. I was so certain you could persuade them."

"I suppose I could try. But..."

Whyn pivoted to face him. "You would do that for me, Lyal?"

"Yes, Lord. But it will not be easy. After all, they believe they are going to Oonayei."

"Tell me of this *Oonayei*."

"It is a place spoken of in the Prophecy of Kalei. A promised land. Some believe Reiv was foreseen to lead them there." Lyal scoffed. "But I think they are wrong."

"Of course they are wrong," Whyn said. He placed a hand on Lyal's shoulder. "But do not blame your people for following my brother. As I said, he can be very charismatic. Surely by now they realize what a pretender he is. More than likely most of them will welcome the news that they are free to return—especially if it were to come from you."

"I'll speak to them, if you wish it," Lyal said. "But how will I find them?"

"Fear not," Whyn said cheerfully. "We have studied every map in the kingdom and know the route they are taking. Scouts are following their trail as we speak, and I have a host of Guard ready to escort you." Whyn laughed. "I am sure your people will not be difficult to find."

"When shall I leave? I am yours to command."

"Right now I command you to take yourself to your room and get some rest. Tomorrow is a new day. We will discuss your departure then."

Lyal set his glass aside. "As you wish, Lord," he said, and in what seemed like an instant a servant was at his side to escort him back to his room.

Whyn returned to his chair by the hearth and picked up his wine glass. After draining it of its contents, he leaned his head back and closed his eyes, but he suddenly doubled over with pain, gasping for breath.

*Oonayei!* she hissed in his mind. *We cannot allow them to reach it!*

"Why?" Whyn managed. "What is so special about this...Oonayei?"

*It is sacred ground.*

"Then surely no Jecta will be allowed to step foot there."

Whyn felt her anger sizzle through his veins. *I cannot risk it. You should not have allowed your brother to live. Your foolishness has opened a chasm that may swallow us whole!*

"But Reiv is nothing—no one," Whyn said. "What does it matter if he has led them on some ridiculous folly? We will have them back here soon enough."

*It is written that when the two tribes meet, they will unite against Tearia—but this will only happen if your brother reaches Oonayei and the prophecy of Kalei is fulfilled. He must be stopped.*

"Then I will dispatch more Guard."

*No. Lyal cannot arrive with a show of force or the Jecta will scatter like rabbits. If he cannot persuade them to return, then a host will be waiting to see it done.*

"Should Lyal be told of this?"

*No need to stir his imagination. Best to let him think you are confident in the job you are giving to him.* She laughed cruelly. *I have enjoyed teaching him how to please me.*

Wynn nodded, but could not help but cringe. "I will summon the Commander to assemble a group of men in the morning," he said stiffly. "Once Lyal has departed, the rest of the forces will be gathered."

A crack of pain twisted through his bones. *Now you listen to me, boy. This time your brother must be destroyed. No evidence can remain of him. Do you understand?*

Whyn grimaced. "Yes. I—I will see it done."

*Indeed you will. For if you do not, your life will be not be worth the living. And believe me when I tell you, Whyn, I will see to it that you live for a very long time.*

౬৩

# Chapter 31: Passage

The caravan traveled for two more days, heading north along the mountain range. Reiv was confident of the pass's location, at least as confident as he could be. Since taking this journey, he had allowed few visions to trespass into his conscious mind, for when he did, unwelcome memories always slipped out with them. But the one directing him to the valley had filtered through long ago, and so he had no need to revisit it.

He gazed upward toward the towering peaks. With luck, they would soon provide passage to a life free of Tearian rule. It occurred to him that had one event in his life not happened, had his hands not been burned, *he* would be the oppressor of the people following him now, not Whyn. The thought made him more anxious than ever to leave the land of his birth behind, to press onward through the darkness if need be, but he knew to travel at night was foolish; the narrow pass was going to be hard enough to find as it was. He sighed, wishing the sun would linger over them a while longer, but it was already settling behind the mountains, and it would not be long before it disappeared altogether.

Reiv raised his hand, signaling for those behind him to stop, but then he realized a wave of shouts was making its way from the rear of the line to the front of it. He turned to see what all the commotion was about, and spotted a Jecta scout sprinting in his direction.

"Tearian Guards!" the scout shouted. "Approaching from the rear." The man came to a halt, barely able to catch his breath.

"How many?" Reiv inquired.

"A hundred on horseback, maybe more."

Reiv focused his eyes in the direction from which the man had run. "How far?" he asked.

"Four leagues," the scout replied. "Maybe less. They had just cleared The Black when we spotted them. We have no way of knowing if they saw us, but. . ."

"They are headed in our direction."

"Aye. And riding fast."

Reiv felt his alarm build. There was no chance of hiding this many people; running was their only hope. Could he lead them to the pass in time? And would the Guard follow them into it if he did?

"Spread the word that unnecessary baggage is to be tossed," he told the scout. "Tell everyone to take only the barest essentials. We must make a run for the pass, and quickly."

Brina, who had been resting in the back of the cart, slid off and stepped toward him. "What is it?" she asked.

"The Guard have found us," Reiv replied. "We must run."

Brina's face, already pale, went even paler. "Run?" she asked. She ran her eyes over the caravan, then turned them back to Reiv. "You cannot ask these people to run, not in the shape they are in."

"What else can I do?" Reiv said. "We cannot simply stay and hope the Guard will pass us by!"

"I—I know, but—"

"But nothing! Now help alert the others." He spun to face Jensa and Gair. "Take only what you can carry. Leave the rest." Reiv rushed toward the horse and the transport being pulled behind it. "Cora!" he said. "Help Torin up. Get him onto the horse." Torin struggled into the sitting position, shrugging Cora's hands away. "Gair will help me, Cora," he insisted. "You go find Kerrik and the girls."

Cora took off full speed, shouting the children's names louder with every step she took.

Reiv ran to the transport and unhitched it, then hurried to the cart and thrust his hands into its contents. He yanked out a bundle wrapped in cloth and handed it to Torin. "Nannaven gave me this," he said. "No matter what happens, do *not* let it fall into Tearian hands." Torin looked at the bundle with curiosity, but asked no questions.

The caravan soon became a hysterical mob as the message sped down the column. People dropped their bags where they stood, screaming and running in various directions. Reiv barked an order for them to stop, to wait and follow him to the pass, but once word spread that the Guard was approaching, survival circumvented all common sense.

Reiv knew he had to get the crowd under control, and the only way he knew to do it was to start the line moving. Gair had already helped Torin onto the horse, and Cora was now hustling toward them with the children in tow. Brina gripped the horse's bridle, clinging as if for dear life.

Jensa stepped in front of Reiv. "How can I help? What do you want me to do?" she asked.

"If the Guard reaches us, I want you to run as hard and as fast as you can. Do not stop, not for me, not for Kerrik, not for anyone."

"What? No!" she sputtered. "I won't!"

Reiv took her face in his hands. "Now you listen to me, and you listen well. It would be better that some of us survive than none. Kerrik and the girls are fast; they could easily slip away. And Gair is strong; he will fight for those of us who cannot. But you—you do not want to know what the Guard would do with a prize like you!"

Jensa reached up and gripped Reiv's hands. "I won't. Reiv... please...."

Reiv wrapped her in his arms and held her tight. "Promise you will run," he whispered. "Please promise... for me."

"I—I promise," she said at last. "I will run. As you say."

"Then do it. Now."

Reiv released her and she sprinted to the horse, grabbing the bridle from Brina's hand. Soon the horse was trotting next to Jensa, Torin and the children bouncing on its back. Gair loped behind it, Brina's hand in his. She looked on the verge of fainting, but Reiv knew that were she to tumble, Gair would be there to pick her up.

Reiv serpentined toward the back, shouting orders for people to drop unnecessary belongings and follow the caravan's lead. Many who had hastened in other directions soon rejoined the group. The line began to advance more and more quickly. Reiv stressed urgency, but as hard as they

were running, their efforts were slow compared to those of
the Guard drawing near.

Reiv regained his place up front. He glanced at the sky.
It was nearly dark, and the incline before them was treacherous. He would have wished for more moonlight, but that
would have further alerted the Guard to their whereabouts.
Even a single torch would have signaled their position.

The people ran as one, not looking back. Their earlier
cries had long since waned. Now all that could be heard
was footsteps pounding the gravel, and the rhythm of lungs
laboring through the encroaching darkness. Reiv kept his
eyes trained toward the mountain. At some point the rocky
wall to his left *had* to merge westward. Where was the pass?
he wondered. Had he missed it? Or had he been wrong about
it all along? "Agneis, help me," he whispered. "I do not know
where to go!"

*You must accept and understand your own heroic path,* her
voice sounded in his head. *Only then can you inspire the changes
in others that will lead to a brighter future.*

Reiv felt his annoyance flare. The goddess had spoken
those words during a time that seemed long ago, but now
they were more like a dream, a figment of his imagination.
"Heroic path indeed," he thought. "I am no hero." But then
he recalled Jensa calling him a savior, and though he had
emphatically denied it, perhaps it was time to accept the
fact that maybe he was one. Were it not for him knowing
of the valley and encouraging the refugees to accompany
him there, they would likely be dead by now, or enslaved
by Whyn. He supposed that in that regard he had indeed
saved them, until now at least. He glanced at the shadowy
throng at his back. After all this time, after all the hard-
ships these people had endured, they were still following

him. He could not let them down now. He would get them through the pass, even if he did not make it through himself.

He rounded a massive tumble of boulders and realized, to his relief, that there was an ample widening between the rocks. The opening looked like a wide alley between two towering buildings, just as he had seen in the vision. Like the labyrinth of canyon walls that had guided them to the plateau and then into The Black, this one would hopefully take them to the valley.

"This is it; I am sure of it," he called to Jensa who was still leading the horse. "Take them in. I will go back and alert the others."

Jensa did not slow her pace. She turned her gaze toward the passage. "In there? But Reiv—"

"Just keep going. The valley is on the other side."

"But you'll be back—before we reach it, I mean."

"I have to see everyone through first." He ran to Brina and briefly grabbed her hand. She was having trouble breathing, and Gair was practically carrying her. "We are almost there, Brina. Just a bit further." She nodded, but even in the darkness she looked as gray as ash.

"You will look after her, Gair?" Reiv added.

"Course I will," Gair said.

Reiv moved back to Torin and the children. Kerrik was in first position on the horse, with Gem and Nely squeezed in behind him. Torin's arms encircled the children from the rear. "No worries," Reiv said as he trotted beside the horse. "We are almost there. I will see you shortly."

"Where are you going?" Kerrik cried, twisting around to face him. "You can't leave us!"

"I must see that everyone gets in. When the last person is through the pass, I will meet you on the other side."

"But what if the Guard comes?" Kerrik asked. "They'll catch you!"

"They'll do no such thing," Cora's panting voice said from the other side of the horse. "Reiv knows what he's doing."

"That is right, Kerrik." Reiv craned his neck to see around the horse. "Thank you, Cora," he said. He gave the horse a slap on the rump and turned and headed in the opposite direction.

Reiv made his way down the line, assuring everyone they would soon be through the pass. Sighs of gratitude were expelled, but no one dared slow their pace. As Reiv watched the last of the caravan go by, he realized how very near they were to safety. He shifted his eyes behind them, searching for the Guard, but he saw no sign of them.

The sky began to deepen from shades of dark lavender to thick charcoal gray. A bank of clouds was creeping across the stars, obscuring what little there was of the light. The wind picked up, sending a whistle into the air. The breeze felt strikingly cool against Reiv's skin. Dayn had told him once that it was much colder in the mountains, and Reiv could not help but shiver at the thought of how much colder it could actually get. He was not dressed for inclement weather, and neither were the refugees who had tossed most of their baggage along the trail.

He looked over his shoulder and down the mountainside. A line of flames was snaking up the slope. The Guard were closing fast, and clearly they were not concerned with detection. Their torches bathed a wide swath of landscape around them.

The last of the caravan began to disappear into the pass. Reiv shouted to a few men who were taking up the rear. "Wait! We have to hide the entrance!" he said. "Help me pry some rocks loose."

"But won't they see where our footprints left off?" one asked hesitantly.

"Perhaps, but it is our only chance."

The men looked doubtful. They glanced from Reiv toward their families who were now melting into the shadows.

"Listen," Reiv said impatiently. "We do not have much time; we must do something, otherwise the Guard will follow us in. If we pry some rocks loose and send them onto the trail, we might not fool them, but we can at least delay them. They will have to move the rocks to get by, will they not? That might give us time to hide or perhaps set up some sort of defense down the way."

The men finally agreed, and soon they were all scrambling up to various locations. The first few boulders they released were not large, but they echoed loudly through the passage as they pounded down the slopes. Smaller rocks bounced in their wake, sending clatters of gravel after them. Reiv winced at the racket they were making; it would surely alert the Guard to their whereabouts.

A rumble more powerful than that of the tumbling rocks suddenly sounded in the corridor. It rose from the ground and seemed to vibrate through the range. The earth shook as more rocks were dislodged from their roosts, raining down the slopes like monstrous hail. Reiv felt his legs go out from under him. He grabbed for the nearest boulder, but it plummeted from his reach, sliding down the slope beneath him at increasing speed. More rocks crashed and bounced around him, showering down from above. He threw his body beneath a shallow overhang, praying it would not collapse from the weight pounding off of it. He heard a scream and saw the body of one of his men tumble like a rag doll, only to be buried beneath a growing pile of rubble. Another man cried out, but Reiv could barely hear his voice over the explosion of granite around him.

The rumbling finally stopped and the landslide stilled. A slow hiss, like that of a viper, filled the air. Putrid steam shot from geysers between the rocks, one close enough for Reiv to feel its scalding mist upon his arm. He scrambled from his hiding place and made his way as best he could through the dust and debris. The rocks beneath his feet were unstable and precarious, and he feared he might vanish into a crevice, swallowed forever by darkness, or worse still, meet a plume of steam, boiled alive where he stood.

He felt something trickle down his forehead and into his eye. He reached up a hand and felt a sting of pain. Looking down at his fingers, he realized they were dark and sticky with blood. He clambered over the rocks, panting with urgency and desperation. There was no way the Guard would follow them into the passage, would they? He glanced over his shoulder, but behind him was nothing but darkness and an occasional glow from rising miasmas of gas.

Reiv tried not to breathe the fumes, but he could not stop his lungs from gulping for air. *Slowly,* he told himself. *Just breathe slowly.*

He turned in the direction the caravan had gone, searching for a sign of light, any sort of movement. Had the refugees made it through before the landslide? he wondered. Or had they perished like the men who had stayed behind to help him? The thought of Brina and Jensa and Kerrik, of all those he loved buried beneath a pile of rocks sent his emotions spinning. He would have screamed had he not feared the echo of his voice would bring down another barrage of rocks upon him.

Reiv began to feel dizzy, disoriented, as if his mind was cloaked in a fog. He stumbled and fell in the darkness, unable to rise to his feet. He lifted an arm and forced his palm forward, then shifted a knee and planted it upon the next rock. But it was no use; he was drained of strength. He crumpled onto the cold granite, unable to go further.

"Reiv!"

The voice jarred him to his senses. "Here," he mumbled.

"There! He is there!" a commotion of voices said.

The hardness of the rock disappeared from beneath him. Reiv felt his body lift as if floating on a cloud.

"Get him out quickly—he needs fresh air!" a familiar voice said. "Reiv! Can you hear me? Talk to me. Open your eyes."

*Open my eyes?*

"Look at me Reiv!"

Reiv forced open his eyelids. Jensa was bending over him, her shadowy face inches from his. "You're with me now," she said. "You're safe."

*Safe?* Reiv coughed violently. "With you, Jensa…no man is safe."

She grinned. "Then you're surely doomed, for after this, I'll not be letting you from my sight."

❧

# CHAPTER 32: PEAKS AND VALLEYS

Reiv blinked open his eyes, trying to make sense of his surroundings. He seemed to recall being lost in darkness, but now all he could see was sunlight. He sat up, realizing a cape of some sort had been draped across him.

"Ah, you are up," Jensa said. She handed him a pouch of rich, red berries and ordered him to eat. "How are you feeling?"

"Fuzzy, but better." Reiv reached into the pouch and grabbed a handful of fruit. "Where did you find these?" he asked between chews.

"There was an entire cliff wall of them," she said. "But the vine is pretty well picked clean now."

"Let us pray they are not poisonous," he said, taking another handful.

"Well if they are, we shall all die happy," she said. "Come let me show you."

Jensa took his arm and helped him up. The air was cool, but beginning to warm, and after a few cleansing coughs, Reiv's lungs began to feel refreshed and his body invigorated. As she led him through the encampment, he realized there did not seem to be as many people as usual.

"Where is everyone?" Reiv asked with alarm. "They did not—"

"No," Jensa assured him. "We only lost a few men."

Reiv slowed his steps. "Those from the back of the line," he said.

"Yes."

Reiv turned his eyes to the ground. If only he had not asked those men to help him; if only he had allowed them to continue on with their families. The landslide would have happened with or without them; stopping had been a waste of time, and life.

"It was not your fault," Jensa said as if reading his mind. "It is said they remained behind to help you barricade the trail."

"Yes."

"You felt it had to be done, did you not?"

Reiv nodded.

"And they willingly stayed to do it. Their families feel their loss, of course, but they are proud of them."

"Those men should be honored as heroes," Reiv said.

"And they will be. When we get home." She smiled and took his hand.

They walked up a path until at last they reached a scenic overview. As they stopped, the sight before them snatched Reiv's breath. As far as he could see, a panoramic landscape stretched, so beautiful that even the After World could not hope to compete with it. It was a valley, draped in patterns of lavender and green and gold, encircled by a ring of burgundy mountains tipped in white. Throughout it, blue streams criss-crossed like ribbons woven through shimmering tapestries of grass. At the base of the mountains, deep green forests could be seen, and dotting the meadows and marshes were elk and deer and other forms of wildlife.

Jensa squeezed his hand. "Oonayei," she said.

People mingled about in silent awe; others sat on the ground and rocky perches, staring out at the scenery, their eyes filled with longing. Many noticed that Reiv was now amongst them and stepped toward him and thanked him. He smiled in response, but felt unsettled somehow. They had reached their destination, but a nagging feeling in the back of his mind left him uneasy.

"Where are Brina and Torin and the others?" he asked.

Jensa glanced around. "There," she said, pointing through the crowd toward a jutting overhang across the way.

Jensa and Reiv wound in that direction. Kerrik bounded toward them. "We're there, Reiv! We're there, we're there!" he proclaimed.

"So we are, sprite." Reiv smiled. "Where are Nely and Gem?"

"Climbing on the rocks," Kerrik said.

"Well tell them to be careful," Reiv said. "Better yet, tell them to get down."

Kerrik scowled. "You're no fun."

"Well, it won't be fun if the girls fall and crack their skulls," Jensa scolded. "Now run along and do as Reiv says."

Kerrik sighed loudly, then turned and headed off.

Jensa and Reiv stepped beside the others. Torin had his arm around Cora's waist. His other arm was still in a sling, and his wounded shoulder was somewhat slumped, but otherwise he seemed in little pain; in fact he looked better than Reiv had seen him in weeks. Brina was standing at Gair's side. His arm was wrapped around her, but Reiv soon realized its purpose was for physical support, not romantic inclinations.

"Brina," Reiv said at her back.

She turned to face him, and it was then that he saw how gray she looked. Dark shadows encircled her eyes, and sweat glistened on her brow.

"You are ill!" Reiv said with alarm.

"Just tired," she responded weakly.

Reiv caught a glimpse of Gair's worried expression. Clearly the blacksmith knew Brina was more than just tired, but he dared not say it in front of Brina. He had probably learned, as all men eventually did, that she was not the sort of woman to argue with.

"Well, we obviously do not have far to travel," Reiv said. "And with little to pack, there is no sense in lingering. The sooner we are in the valley, the sooner you can rest."

The others agreed and they turned to walk back toward the make-do encampment. But before they had taken more than a few steps, Brina collapsed. Gair caught her in his arms and lowered her to the ground. Reiv knelt beside her and felt her forehead. "She is burning up!" he cried.

"It's the fever," Cora said gently. "We suspected it two days ago, but she insisted you not be told."

"Not be told!" Reiv leapt to his feet. "Why not?"

"She did not want you to slow the caravan down on her account," Torin said.

"That should have been my decision, not hers!"

"Reiv, if you had stopped the caravan every time some-one grew ill, we would still be in Meirla."

"But—" Reiv sputtered. "She is not just someone!"

"Think what you are saying," Jensa said. "You cannot risk the lives of hundreds for the life of one. Brina would not want you to do that, and you wouldn't want to do it either."

Reiv shook his head. "I know, but—"

"But nothing. We would have been caught by the Guard had we lingered. Brina's silence is what probably saved us."

Reiv felt a great lump in his throat. "Can you carry her, Gair?"

"Course I can," Gair said, and reached down and swooped her up.

"Cora, gather the children," Reiv said. "We leave for Oonayei. Now."

It took half the day to reach the valley floor. By the time they arrived, the afternoon temperatures had warmed considerably. The first order of business was to select the best location to set up the encampment. The Shell Seekers wanted to settle next to the streams, as being near water was their nature. But after realizing the risks for potential flooding, and the fact that the open terrain would make for easier viewing by predators, it was decided that the best place to settle would be at the edge of the forest. The materials needed for constructing huts, temporary ones at first, more permanent ones later, were more readily available from the resources of the woods, but the reeds and grasses of the marshes and meadows could be also utilized.

Within days, small huts framed with saplings and reeds and covered with leafy branches had been constructed. Built according to the size and needs of each individual family, most structures could accommodate four or more persons, but height and width were kept to a minimum in order to maintain warmth inside. All cooking was done outside over campfires, most of which were communal. The Jecta men immediately took to the forests and marshes to hunt, and in no time at all the Shell Seekers had harvested a great many fish from the streams. The waters were nothing like those of the sea, they were shallow and contained no salt, but the biggest adjustment was to their icy temperatures. The Shell Seekers quickly learned that spears and nets were more reasonable, and less chilling, methods for fishing.

Quantities of game were brought back daily from the hunts, the forests and meadows were well-stocked with wildlife, and their carcasses were stripped, the meat and hides hung to dry. Most of the refugees had arrived with only the clothing on their backs and knew that the cooler temperatures, something they were not used to, were only going to get worse. Winter was nearly upon them, and though the changes in seasons were barely noticeable on the Tearian side of the mountains, Reiv assured them it would be far different here. He had not forgotten what his cousin had told him, nor how Dayn and Alicine had been dressed when he had first met them. Every limb on their bodies had been covered in thick clothing; even their collars had reached all the way to their chins. On top of that, Dayn had worn a coat, so heavy and cumbersome that at the time Reiv could not imagine the purpose of such a thing. But now he was beginning to more fully appreciate

Kiradyn fashion, and regretted he did not have a coat like Dayn's.

Brina was moved into a hut as soon as Gair and Reiv, with some assistance from Torin, were able to construct one. Reiv had insisted they build two: one for Brina and himself, the other for the rest of the family. Though he knew everyone had already been exposed to the fever, he felt more comfortable having her quarantined, especially from the children. He had stayed with her day and night ever since they had arrived five days prior, and though she was not getting worse, she was not getting better either.

On the sixth day, having had little sleep, Reiv felt the overwhelming need for fresh air and sunshine. Brina had slept most of the morning, and for now showed little sign of waking. He rose and stepped through the low portal of the hut, disappointed to see a sky gray with clouds. It was only mid-day, and the breeze felt warm against his skin, but that did not mean colder air was not being ushered in behind it. He eyed the pelts hanging nearby. They were not yet cured, but if the weather grew bleak, there would be little choice but to wear them.

Jensa approached. "How is Brina today?" she asked.

"The same," he replied.

"I brought her some broth," she said, nodding to a gourd she was holding.

"I will take it to her," Reiv said.

"No. You need to get out for a while. I'll take it."

"I would rather you not go in there."

Jensa huffed. "I was around her for days before you even knew she was ill. If I am going to get the fever, then I probably already have."

Reiv frowned and held out his hand, but Jensa moved the gourd from his reach. "I said I will take it."

"Do not be ridiculous," Reiv said.

"Listen," Jensa said, attempting a reasonable tone. "There were others sick when we arrived, but not near as many as when we left Meirla. Most are already up and walking about. I think the fever has run its course. I'm sure Brina will be well in no time."

"I cannot take that chance."

"Well, I can!" Jensa said. And with that she stepped away from him and ducked into the hut.

Reiv's shoulders tensed, then slumped with resignation. In truth, he was too tired to argue with her or anyone else. He gazed toward the trees rising along the slope beyond the hut and headed in that direction. Before long he found himself in a small clearing nestled beneath an overhang of firs. It was dotted with decaying tree stumps, but it was also blanketed with golden grasses and yellow wildflowers. He walked amongst them, examining each one, hoping to find Frusensias or something similar. Since arriving, he had asked everyone to keep an eye out for the white flowering herb. If he could just find a handful, perhaps it would be enough to concoct a potion similar to the one that Alicine and Nannaven had made for Kerrik. Thus far, no Frusensias had been found, but even if they had, Nannaven was dead and Alicine was gone. And only they knew the formula for such a brew.

He plopped upon the grass and leaned his back against an old tree trunk, pondering the tribulations he had been through, and those which Brina was going through still. He could not bear the thought of her suffering, could not fathom the idea of losing her. Ever since he had been little, she had been his ally. When his own mother had given him no love, Brina had provided him with more than he deserved. As a result, she was more to him than an aunt, more to him than a friend. She was his mother in all but the biological sense of the word. He knew there was only one way to save her. But to do so meant he would have to leave her. Did he possess the strength to go through with it? And was it the right thing to do? He closed his eyes, playing various plans over and over in his mind. Something had to be done. Something...

He was awakened by light flickering behind his eyelids and the tantalizing smell of broth under his nose. He squinted at the ball of fire hovering over him, then raised an arm to block the glare.

"I'm sorry to wake you," Jensa said quietly. She leaned the torch against a rock. "I brought you a blanket and something to eat."

"Why? What time is it?" Reiv mumbled, realizing he was curled up on the grass.

"After dark."

Reiv sat up with a start. "Brina?" he asked.

"The same. No worse."

"Reiv moved to rise, but Jensa's commanding hand pushed him back down.

"You'll eat first," she ordered. "Brina is sleeping, and Cora's outside the hut, listening for any sign of her waking."

Reiv heaved a sigh. He grabbed the gourd from her hand and took a sip of broth.

"All of it," Jensa said, circumventing his next move, which was to hand it back to her.

"It is hot."

"And you're cold."

Reiv realized it must be very late. The sky was pitch black now, the moon and stars veiled behind a thick layer of clouds. Even the temperature had dropped considerably. He was clothed in only a tunic that reached from his shoulders to his knees, and he could not deny that something warm in his belly would do him good.

Jensa draped the blanket around his shoulders. The warmth felt pleasant against his skin. "Where did you get this?" he asked, studying it.

"A woman brought it as a gift, for you."

"For me?"

"She said her husband had no more need of it."

Reiv's eyes shot to hers. "Was it—"

"No."

Reiv nodded and clutched the blanket under his chin with his free hand, then noticed that Jensa, still standing, was clothed in little more than that which she usually wore.

"Would you like to share it with me?" he asked, then realized the implications. To his surprise, she sat down beside him and pulled a corner of the blanket around her shoulders.

Reiv kept his eyes forward as he continued to sip. The warmth of Jensa's arm, as well as her pleasant scent, was quickly usurping that of the soup.

She snuggled closer. "This feels nice."

"Um-hmm," Reiv responded, and tossed back a swig.

"Are you warm enough?" Jensa asked, running her fingers down his leg.

Reiv bit back a gasp, nearly dropping the bowl. Jensa laughed. "You'll warm up in a hurry if you spill that into your lap," she teased.

Reiv gripped the gourd tighter. He honestly no longer felt cold, but goose bumps were marching across his skin nonetheless.

Jensa ran her fingertips along the tiny bumps that were forcing the hairs on his leg to stand at attention. "You *are* cold," she said. "Here, let me warm you."

Before Reiv could utter a word of protest, she moved to his back, draping the blanket around the both of them, her arms encircling his. She rubbed her hands vigorously up and down his arms, then his torso, all the while blowing warm gentle breaths upon his neck and into his ears. It sent a quake through Reiv's limbs and forbidden thoughts to his head.

Reiv set the gourd aside and grabbed her hands. "I am quite warm now," he said. "Thank you."

"Very well," Jensa replied, but she sounded disappointed.

Reiv felt like a fool. He would have liked her to continue, any male with an ounce of sense would, but still, in all good conscience, he could not allow it without first telling her what was on his mind.

"Sit beside me," he said. "There is something I must tell you."

Jensa sank down at his side. "You do not have to say it," she muttered. "You do not want me."

Reiv could not help but laugh. "I thought you said I was *the worst*."

"What?" she asked.

"That day on the beach, when you and Lyal were arguing; you said I was the worst."

"The worst what?"

"That when people thought we were mates, they were thinking the worst."

"You *remember* that?"

Reiv shrugged. "It is not every day that I am labeled as such. Of course I remember it."

"I was only disputing Lyal's accusations," she said defensively. "I didn't mean it the way it sounded."

"Well, I *will* be the worst if I do not find a way to help Brina. I have searched for Frusensias. I have searched for anything that even resembles them."

"To make the medicinal that Alicine knew of."

"Yes. But I have not found a single one, and even if I had, who amongst us knows how to make the brew? Nannaven is dead, and Alicine in Kirador. I cannot risk Brina dying, Jensa. I must find a way to save her."

"But how?"

"By leaving...tomorrow."

"What!" Jensa said, drawing the simple question into an exclamation. "No; you can't. We've only just arrived."

"I must go find—"

"Alicine," she said curtly. "You go to find Alicine."

"She is the only one who can help. Regardless, we do not know how to survive a winter in these mountains. We need someone to guide us. Perhaps Dayn will agree to come back also."

Jensa remained silent.

Through the flicker of torchlight, Reiv realized her eyes were misting. "I will be back," he assured her. "I promise, I will. I only go to find help for Brina."

Jensa nodded as if she understood, but she turned her face away. "So, you'll bring Alicine back with you," she said.

Reiv was not sure how to respond. She clearly did not want Alicine here, but Nannaven had taught Alicine everything she knew. If anyone could help Brina, Alicine could. And if Dayn came also, who better to teach the refugees about surviving in the mountains? But would either of them agree to it?

"I do not know if she, or Dayn, will want to return with me," he said.

"Do you wish it?"

"I do not know what I wish anymore, only that Brina get well. But if Alicine and Dayn do come back, I think it would be a fine thing. Do you not agree?"

Jensa leaned against him, pulling the blanket tighter. "I'm frightened."

"Of what?"

"That you will not return." Jensa raised her eyes to him.

"Of course I will return."

"And if Alicine asks you to stay with her in Kirador?"

Reiv took Jensa's hand in his. "I have affection for Alicine. I do not deny it. But if she felt the same for me, she never would have left."

"I would never leave you," Jensa said. She rose to her knees to face him. "Because I love you."

Reiv drew a sharp breath, his mind stuttering with confusion. Jensa loved him? As in *loved* him? He cared for her too, of course, but in his suddenly muddled state, he could not be certain it was the same thing. His thoughts darted back and forth, searching for an answer to her unexpected announcement. But as he turned his focus back to her, he realized the answer was kneeling right in front of him.

Jensa leaned toward him and planted her lips on his, and for a moment Reiv thought to put a stop to it. He had, after all, only just learned of Jensa's feelings, and he hadn't had time to even consider his own. But then his body responded, and any thoughts he had of waylaying her advances slipped entirely away.

Reiv's heart raced with anticipation. He wrapped his arms around her, returning her kiss with one of his own. Then Jensa's passion increased, and she pressed him to the ground, working her lips from his mouth to his chest. Reiv gripped the grass, desiring nothing more than to roll the girl over and return the favor. Without warning, Alicine's face barged into his consciousness, sending a painful catch to his throat. His mind grew confused with desire and conflict. He loved Alicine, he was sure of it, but she had rejected him—hadn't she? Reiv gasped as Jensa ran her hand under his tunic. *The past be damned*, he decided. He flung Alicine from his thoughts, and Jensa onto her back.

Reiv traced his fingers over Jensa's body, exploring as much as he dared. He could barely feel her due to the damage to his hands, but he hoped his touch would at least bring her some pleasure. But then an embarrassing thought entered his head: he had no real experience in matters such as this, but Jensa obviously did. And it would soon be all too clear that he was still pure in that regard.

Jensa gasped, and Reiv snatched back his hand. Gods, he was so clumsy! Had he harmed her in some way?

"Don't stop," she panted. But then she opened her eyes to him. "What is it?"

Reiv hesitated, then said, "I do not wish to...displease you."

"You could never displease me." Jensa studied his face, then her eyes grew wide. "Am I...your first?"

Heat flared to Reiv's cheeks. "Yes," he said. "In this regard, yes."

Jensa smiled. "I think we'll manage," she said. She drew his body to hers, and it was then that Reiv knew beyond all doubt: whether this was right or whether this was wrong, regardless of the consequences, their lives were now united, bound forever by this single moment in time.

෴

# PART FIVE

## PENANCE

# Chapter 33: Into the Pit

"Are your things not gathered *yet?*" Lorcan asked crossly. He eyed the half-packed satchel that rested atop Falyn's bed and the assortment of clothing still draped across the coverlet.

"I can't decide what to bring, Father," Falyn said. "We are, after all, going to be away for three days." She folded a nightgown into her luggage, then stepped toward the dresser, determined to keep her back to her father as much as possible. Over the years he had become skilled at reading her eyes, and she could not risk him reading what would surely be written in them today.

"Where's Sheireadan?" he asked. "It is our rotation to visit the outlying homesteads, and we would not be setting a good example if we were to arrive late."

"I don't know," Falyn said. She bit her lip. She knew full well where her brother was, but she also knew better than to confess it. If Lorcan learned where Sheireadan had gone, the consequences would be severe.

Falyn could feel the heat of her father's temper building. "Shall I go and find him?" she asked, risking a turn in
his direction.

Lorcan scowled. "No need. I'll find him myself."

"Shall I pack for him?" she asked as if in afterthought.

Lorcan stepped across the hallway toward Sheireadan's
room and glanced inside. "He appears to have already done
it," he said. "Well, at least the can do *something* right." He
stormed toward the front door, his boots pounding the
floorboards.

"You might try the apothecary," Falyn called after him.
"He said something earlier about his stomach."

The front door slammed, sending a vibration to the
windowpanes and a tinkle to the crystals dangling from
the lampshade. Falyn stepped to her bedroom window and
eased back the curtain, watching as her father disappeared
down the lane. The apothecary was not far, a ten minute
stride from the house at most. Perhaps Lorcan would find
his son there, perhaps not. And it was the "perhaps not"
that Falyn was most concerned about.

The back door suddenly opened, but before it could
close, Falyn rushed toward it.

Sheireadan stepped through the doorway and stopped,
startled to see her fast approaching.

"Hurry," she said impatiently. "We don't have much
time."

"Time for what?" Sheireadan asked. "I'm already
packed."

"Father is looking for you. And he's *not* happy."

Sheireadan flinched, but then he reached into the
pocket of his trousers and pulled out a package. "I got the

medicinal like you suggested. You told him to check the apothecary, right?"

"Yes, but you know as well as I do where he'll look next if he doesn't find you there. And if anyone saw you with Caryl—"

"Well, nobody did," Sheireadan said with annoyance. "So there's nothing to worry about."

Falyn turned and headed back to her room. Sheireadan followed at her heels.

"Get your bag," she said over her shoulder. "We need to be out of here before Father returns." She shoved one last piece of clothing into her satchel and secured it.

"What are you talking about?"

Falyn brushed past him and into the hallway, suitcase in hand. "I'll explain later," she said, gesturing for him to follow.

"What haven't you told me?" Sheireadan asked.

"I'll tell you on the way," she replied.

Sheireadan halted. "On the way to *where?*" he demanded.

Falyn set her expression to firm, then turned to face him. "We are going to meet Dayn."

Sheireadan took a startled step back. "We're *what?*"

"We're going to the clan lands. Now get your bag."

"Have you lost your senses? We can't just—"

"Of course we can. It's all been arranged."

Sheireadan threw his hands into the air. "*Arranged?*" he cried. "By whom?"

"By Dayn. He has invited us to live with him. I didn't tell you sooner because I was afraid you'd do something foolish."

Sheireadan gaped at Falyn as if she had grown a second head. "Is this some sort of joke?"

"No. We're to meet him at the Well of Wishes at high sun. He'll escort us on to the clan lands from there."

Sheireadan guffawed. "I'm not going anywhere with that—that—"

Falyn slammed her bag to the ground. "Now you listen to me," she said, poking his chest with her index finger. "If you love Caryl, you'll do as I say. Because if you don't, you know what will happen."

Sheireadan turned his attention toward the front door. "I can't just *leave*. Caryl would never understand."

"You'd be doing this for him as well as yourself."

"But Caryl wouldn't know that!"

"Of course he would. He's seen what happens to those accused of the act the two of you have been stupid enough to commit."

Sheireadan huffed. "What makes you think Father would risk anyone knowing? If Caryl went to trial, then I would, too, wouldn't I?"

"Not if Father found a way to keep your name out of it. I wouldn't put it past him to make an example of Caryl anyway."

Sheireadan's nostrils flared. "Let him try!"

"Watch your words or you just might find yourself next to him on an execution pyre!" Falyn placed a commanding hand on his arm. "You have to leave, Sheireadan. It's the only way."

Sheireadan grew quiet as he worked to digest her argument. At last he nodded, then blinked as if coming to his senses. "No. Absolutely not. I'll not have you giving yourself to a demon to save my skin or anyone else's."

"I'm not giving myself to a demon—I'm giving it to Dayn. Besides, I'm not just doing it for you. I'm doing it for me." Falyn turned her eyes to her feet, then back to her brother. "I love him."

Sheireadan's eyes nearly bulged from his skull. "You *what*?"

"Don't you dare judge me," Falyn snapped.

"*Judge* you?" Sheireadan said sarcastically. "Why in the world would I judge you? After all, you've only just told me you're in love with a demon."

"And *you're* in love with a man!" Falyn retorted. "At least *my* crime isn't punishable by death. Yet."

Sheireadan's jaw dropped, but no sound escaped.

Falyn lifted her chin. "So? Are you going to get your bag or not?"

Sheireadan held his ground for a determined moment more, then stomped to his room and grabbed his satchel off the bed.

They walked toward the front door, Falyn leading the way, but then she realized Sheireadan was no longer following. She turned to see him staring at the floorboards.

"Sheireadan," she said gently. "This doesn't mean you'll never see Caryl again. Once we get settled, we can send for him."

Sheireadan shook his head. "You know as well as I do that will never happen."

Falyn stepped toward him and set her bag at her feet. She took him by the shoulders and gave him a determined shake. "No matter what happens, you will always have me. You are my brother, and I love you."

Sheireadan smiled painfully. "I know, but you can't give me the kind of love that I need. You'll have Dayn. Who will I have?"

Falyn did not know how to respond. She had no way of knowing whether or not the clans would accept her brother for what he was. For that matter, she didn't know if Dayn would either. Sheireadan had made Dayn's life a misery for years, ever since her father had caught her and Dayn talking over the fence that ran along their front yard. From that moment on, it had been Sheireadan's assigned duty to keep Dayn away from her, and he had done his duty well.

"I can't make you any promises," she said at last. "We're both going into the unknown. But isn't that better that living with what we *do* know—that I will be forced to wed Zared and you will never be free of Father's fist?"

Sheireadan's eyes grew distant, as if he were recalling all the times he had been bullied and abused by his father. Lorcan had always been hard on him, but hard had turned to cruel when Sheireadan had reached the age to court. His father had introduced him to many prominent daughters, but after steadfastly rejecting all of them, it soon became clear that Sheireadan's interests ran in a different direction. And for that, Lorcan hated him.

"You're right," Sheireadan said. "I will always be what I am, no matter how many times Father tries to beat it out of me."

Sheireadan picked up Falyn's satchel and handed it to her. "At least I won't have to damage my knuckles on Dayn's face anymore." His expression turned grim. "I'm no better than Father, am I."

"You're nothing like Father, at least not on the inside," Falyn said. "Your actions toward Dayn, however, were becoming a rather good imitation of him."

Sheireadan smirked. "And what of *your* imitation—that of the perfect daughter."

"You're right," Falyn said. "I've gotten good at hiding that part of myself I could not allow Father to see."

"Which is?"

"The part that is in love with Dayn." Falyn smiled, then took Sheireadan by the hand, pulling him toward the door. But in that instant the door burst open, stopping them both in their tracks.

Lorcan grabbed Sheireadan by the front of his tunic and shoved him against the nearby china cabinet. Dishes toppled behind glass casements, some spinning, others crashing from shelves being knocked from their brackets.

"What did I tell you about seeing that boy?" Lorcan shouted, his face bulging with fury.

"I—I don't know what you're talking about," Sheireadan stammered.

Lorcan backhanded him across the face, sending Sheireadan sprawling. "Don't lie to me!"

Sheireadan gained his footing and scrambled across the room. "I'm not lying, Father. I swear it!"

"Don't you dare run from me, boy," Lorcan bellowed. He grabbed up the walking cane he kept propped by the door. It was carved from dark wood, with a brass handle molded into the shape of an elk's head. But it was seldom used for walking.

Lorcan marched toward his son, chairs and lamps flying as he swept them aside.

"Father, no!" Falyn screamed. She rushed toward him, grappling for his arm, but he shoved her away.

"You'll take what's coming to you," Lorcan yelled. "And you'll take it like the man I raised you to be."

Sheireadan inched along the wall, his eyes wide with terror. For a moment he looked more like a child than a young man, but what else could he be when every ounce of self-respect had been beaten out of him.

"Please, Father. I—I only went to the apothecary, I swear!"

"Lies!"

Lorcan drew back the cane, then swept it down. Sheireadan raised his arm to stop the blow, but it did no good. Wood met bone, and Sheireadan fell, slumped against the wall, cradling his elbow.

Falyn leapt toward him just as Lorcan was raising the cane for another go. She planted herself in front of her brother, positioning her body in a protective stance. "Don't you *dare* touch him again!" she threatened through her teeth.

Lorcan froze, the cane still raised. For a moment his eyes held a look of disbelief, but then they grew dark. "Step aside, daughter, or you'll be next."

Falyn felt her body trembling and prayed her father did not notice. But she could not remain silent. "If you're going to hit me, Father, then you had best get on with it. I'll not let you touch him again."

Lorcan lowered the cane slowly, but Falyn knew better than to let down her guard. Though her father might not use the cane on her, he had other methods of keeping her in her place.

Lorcan stared hard at her. "It is the Maker's will that children respect their parents," he said firmly.

Falyn quailed at the speech she knew was coming.

"The Written Word speaks of it," Lorcan continued, "in verse after verse. When I took your mother into my bed, I did not take my duty as her husband lightly. And what did I get for my devotion?" He turned his smoldering gaze to Sheireadan. "A son corrupted by the worst of all possible sins." Then to Falyn. "And a daughter who condones it."

He moved toward Falyn and shoved her aside, the strength of his arm knocking her to the floor. With a sudden grab he had Sheireadan by the hair and was yanking him to his feet. Sheireadan grimaced as Lorcan shoved him toward the door, but he made no attempt to escape. His arm was still cradled against his chest, and his spirit was too damaged to run.

"No, Father!" Falyn cried.

"By all that is mighty, girl, I will cure this family of its ills!" Lorcan bellowed. "It began with your brother and it will end with him. If the threat of pyres and eternal brimstone are not enough to cleanse his soul, then I will purge it myself!"

Lorcan shoved open the door, and with Sheireadan's hair still in his hand dragged him through it. Falyn scrambled up and ran after them, demanding that her father stop. But Lorcan ignored her and continued toward the woods behind the house.

It did not take long for them to reach the pit. An odorous fog hovered over it, blanketing its long, jagged opening. The crevice was not wide, but it was large enough for a full-sized man to disappear into.

Lorcan yanked Sheireadan toward the edge, forcing him to look down. "You see this, boy? The heat of this is nothing compared to the flames that will be licking your boots if you don't mend your ways." He jerked him closer. "How long were you in here the last time?"

"A day and a night," Sheireadan's barely audible voice said.

"Obviously not long enough." Lorcan shoved Sheireadan in.

Sheireadan cried out as he plunged into the darkness.

"No!" Falyn rushed to the edge, gazing down at the shadowy figure of her brother sprawled upon the rocks below. She spun to face her father. "He won't survive down there!"

Lorcan looked at her, his expression strangely void of emotion. "He does not come out until he is cleansed."

"And if he can't be cleansed?"

"Then he dies." Lorcan turned away. "Come daughter," he said. "There are families awaiting our aid."

But Falyn did not follow her father's instructions. She gathered her skirts and plowed past him, running as fast as she could toward the house. She knew Lorcan would stroll home, expecting to find her curled up on her bed, crying into her pillow as she usually did. But this time would be different: her bed would be empty, and so would the stall that housed her father's fastest horse.

෴

Dayn paced by the well, nervously eyeing the sky. A fast-moving bank of clouds was obscuring the sun, turning its former brightness to a milky haze of gray. When he'd left home that morning, the sky had been blue and the weather promising. He'd gathered his bow and saddled his horse, casually announcing a sudden desire to go hunting. Much to his surprise, there had been no protests. Two weeks prior, his uncle would have strictly forbidden him to go. Haskel had kept a close eye on Dayn ever since learning of his earlier rendezvous with Falyn.

Since then, Dayn had worked hard to regain his uncle's trust. He'd accompanied Haskel to numerous homesteads, helping those families who wished to leave, and preparing defenses for those who wished to stay. Haskel's homestead, being the closest to Kiradyn, was the first in the line of defense should the Vestry decide to attack, but even though it was at the greatest risk from both the Vestry and the mountain, hundreds of clansmen had stayed on after the Gathering to lend their support.

A gust of wind ruffled the branches of the trees, sending a shower of leaves spiraling to the ground. Dayn prayed a storm wasn't brewing, but then a flash of lightning flitted across the sky, followed by a long, deep rumble of thunder. The air became noticeably cooler as the wind whipped through the trees. Dayn pulled his collar around his neck and flicked a shock of hair from his face. If only the rain would wait a while longer, he lamented, at least until he and Falyn were safely on their way. Another rumble sounded, but this time Dayn realized it wasn't thunder; it was the sound of pounding hooves.

A horse and rider suddenly tore into the clearing. Dayn's heart raced—it was Falyn, flying like a tempest toward him, her skirts and long, dark hair billowing at her back. Dayn stepped into the clearing, his hopes riding high. But they dropped like a stone when he saw the distress lining her face.

Falyn leapt off the horse and ran toward him, her eyes swollen with tears. Dayn gathered her into his arms. "What is it?" he asked, praying she had not come to say goodbye.

"Please, Dayn," she sobbed. "You have to help me. Father cast him into the pit and—"

"Who? What are you talking about?"

Falyn wiped the tears from her face. "Father was angry at Sheireadan. He hit him and threw him into the pit."

"What do you mean…pit?"

"A chasm, in the woods near our house."

Dayn's eyes widened. "A chasm?"

"Yes. It opened up a few months ago and–"

"But why would your father throw Sheireadan into it?"

"Father says it will purge Sheireadan's sins." Falyn grabbed Dayn's arms. "Please. You have to help me get him out!"

Dayn gulped, realizing the repercussions if they attempted rescue and were caught by Lorcan. He had every intention of telling her no, that it was too dangerous, but then the voice in his head reminded him that he couldn't just leave Sheireadan to die. Falyn would never forgive him, and he would never forgive himself.

"All right," he said reluctantly. "But we leave for the valley right after. Agreed?"

"The valley? I thought we were going to your aunt's and uncle's first."

Dayn frowned. "They told me I'm not allowed to see you. If I bring you there, they'll probably take you and Sheireadan back to your father. Are you willing to risk that?"

Falyn shook her head. "No."

"Then we get Sheireadan and head out of Kirador. No turning back. All right?"

"All right."

Thunder exploded overhead, followed by a flash of lightning. Raindrops began to pelt the ground. Dayn grabbed Falyn's hand in his. "Come on then," he said. "Let's go save your brother."

∾

# Chapter 34: Betrayal

Dayn and Falyn dismounted their horses and tethered them far enough from the chasm so as not to be seen. Dayn grabbed the rope that was draped across the pommel of his saddle. He always carried it when he hunted; today would be no different. With caution he and Falyn worked their way through the woods and toward the rocks, careful not to snap a branch or make any noise that might announce their presence.

Falyn stopped and put a commanding hand on Dayn's arm, nodding her head toward the rocky hillside nearby. A billow of steam could be seen rising from the ground, dissipating into the cool, damp air.

Dayn shivered, realizing how cold he was. He was soaked to the bone from the recent downpour, but at least the storm had moved on toward the east. Falyn was equally wet, her dress plastered against her body, her long hair coiled in wet tendrils down her back. Dayn could not help but run his eyes over her. Even wet as a fish she still looked beautiful.

He turned his attention toward the chasm. "How deep do you think it is?" he whispered.

"I don't know," she replied. "I have a rope hidden in the rocks; I used it the last time to lower him food and water."

"You mean he's been down there *before*?"

"Yes. But the rope barely reached the bottom, and the pit looked so much deeper this time."

"We can tie it to this," Dayn said, indicating the rope in his hand. "Hopefully that will give us the length we need."

Falyn nodded and guided him toward the rocks, the two of them ducking behind trees and bushes as they worked their way toward their destination. At last they reached a tumble of boulders. Falyn crouched down, then pulled a coil of rope from between them. Dayn squatted and tied the ropes together while Falyn kept watch.

Dayn eased his gaze over the boulder. The pit was on the other side of the rocks, not far, but far enough that they would have to step into the open to rescue Sheireadan. No one else appeared to be in the area, but that didn't mean someone wouldn't show up.

He ducked back down, pulling Falyn with him. "All right. When we get there, I'll lower the rope and you stand behind me. It'll take both of us to pull him up."

They slid from behind the rocks and crept toward the crevice, keeping their eyes and ears attuned. When they reached the pit, they stared into its depths, but could see nothing more than a dark, roiling haze of steam.

"Are you sure he's down there?" Dayn asked.

"Yes. I saw Father push him in and I saw him lying on the bottom."

"Was he..." Dayn hesitated. "Was he conscious?"

"No." Falyn's voice faltered. "He fell hard."

Dayn felt anger well in his breast. What sort of monster would do such a thing to his own son? It was then that Dayn realized how fortunate he had been to have a father like Gorman, regardless of the man's lies. But Dayn also realized how fortunate Eyan was to have Haskel. Even though Haskel had hidden Eyan away all these years, at least it had been to protect him from monsters like Lorcan.

"If Sheireadan is too injured to tie the rope around himself, we'll have to secure it to something so I can climb down and help him," Dayn said.

"What? No...you can't go down there. It's too dangerous!"

"Well, I'm sure not letting *you* go down there."

"And just how do you expect me to pull you both out?" Falyn asked.

Dayn glanced toward the trees. "Listen, we could tie one end of the rope around me and the other to one of the horses. Then the horse could pull us both out."

Falyn bit her lip. "All right," she said.

"Let's see if we can see him first," Dayn said. "I'd hate to climb down only to discover he's already made it out." He got down on his knees and leaned over the edge, squinting his eyes to see through the steam. Falyn knelt beside him, her long hair dangling.

"Come away, Falyn," an unexpected voice commanded at their backs.

Dayn and Falyn swiveled their heads, horrified to realize Lorcan was standing but steps away. Behind him stood a group of at least two dozen men. Some were dressed in dark brown robes and caps, members of the Vestry. But others were dressed in everyday attire, burly sorts, there to lend their muscle to whatever dirty work Lorcan had in mind.

Dayn scrambled to his feet, pulling Falyn up with him. He wrapped a protective arm around her.

Lorcan eyed Dayn's hand upon his daughter with distain. "Get your hands off of her," he ordered.

Before Dayn could utter a word, Falyn was yanked from his hold. Hands grabbed him from both sides, catching him off guard. He had been so focused on Lorcan, he hadn't noticed the goons approaching from the side. Dayn struggled to get free of them, but it was no use. The men were strong, and he was outnumbered.

Lorcan's lip curled into a snarl. "You see, citizens?" he said. "The demon was about to take my daughter into the fiery depths with him!"

The men uttered their disgust.

"That's not true!" Dayn cried. "I was only trying to rescue Sheireadan from the pit that *you* threw him into!"

Lorcan's eyes widened with feigned surprise. "Surely you do not expect anyone here to believe such a tale," he said. He turned to address the Vestry. "Do not be fooled by the trickery of his words, gentlemen. A demon wouldn't know the truth if it reached out and bit him on the hand."

"Dayn's not lying!" Falyn shouted. She tried to release her arm from the man who had pulled her from Dayn's side, but his hands gripped her like a vise.

Lorcan stepped toward Falyn. She stopped her struggles, but did not quail. She lifted her chin defiantly. "It is you who is the liar, Father."

Lorcan ran his fingers lightly down her cheek. "My poor dear girl," he said sympathetically. "But do not worry. You are safe now."

Falyn jerked from his touch. "I will never be safe as long as I'm with you," she spat.

Her father sighed. "I forgive you, child. After all, none of this was your doing. You have clearly been ensorcelled, but we will soon see you purged of the demon. Once the fires consume him, you will be free of his taint, as will the rest of us."

"No!" Falyn screamed. She turned her eyes to the Vestry. "My brother is down there!" Suddenly Sheireadan emerged from the crowd.

"You're—you're all right?" Falyn cried. Her eyes darted to her father, then back to her brother. "Tell them, Sheireadan! Tell them what happened."

Sheireadan tightened his jaw and said not a word.

Dayn strained against the arms still holding him. "Sheireadan, tell them!" he said.

Sheireadan glanced at his father, then back to Dayn. "I fell from my horse because of the spell *you* conjured to keep me from protecting my sister."

"*What?*" Dayn couldn't believe his ears. Was Sheireadan actually throwing him to the wolves? But then Dayn realized it should have come as no surprise. The boy had hated him for as long as he could remember. Why should it be any different now?

"Take him to Vestry Hall," Lorcan instructed the men surrounding Dayn. "He must be tried before he can work any more mischief."

"Tried?" Dayn shouted. "For what?"

"For black magic, of course," Lorcan said.

"No!" Falyn screamed, writhing to escape the man still holding her.

Lorcan snapped his fingers, and a second man went to the other's aid. "Escort her home," Lorcan ordered them. "And lock her in the cellar until I arrive." The men grinned as they dragged Falyn, kicking and screaming, away from the crowd.

Dayn was yanked off his feet and half carried, half shoved through the throng. Shouts of "demon" and threats of execution sounded in his ears. He searched the faces that surrounded him—surely there was *someone* who didn't believe him a demon! Then his eyes met Sheireadan's, and he realized the earlier hostility in the boy's expression had somehow melted away. Instead of hatred, there was shock, but there was also something else: fear.

Dayn scrabbled for the right words to say in his own defense. Perhaps there was still time to persuade Sheireadan to tell the truth about Lorcan. As Dayn was dragged past him, he twisted his head, desperate to keep Sheireadan in his sights for a moment longer. But all he could say was, "Don't let him hurt her, Sheireadan. Please."

Sheireadan held Dayn in his stare until the mob folded around him. Then he turned and disappeared into the crowd.

❦

# CHAPTER 35:
## ACROSS THE DIVIDE

It had been seven days since Reiv had left the valley, and he was beginning to doubt his ability to find that which he was seeking: a cure for Brina. He had yet to come across a single Frusensia. Chances were, they did not grow on this side of the mountains. But Alicine had mentioned a similar herb that thrived in the higher meadows of Kirador, so he hoped to at least find some of those. Of course, that still did not solve the problem of how to concoct the remedy. For that he would need Alicine.

He glanced at the sky. Dark clouds had rolled in from the northwest, threatening to cut his day's travel short. "Just what I need," he grumbled.

He wrapped his fox cape more securely around him. The fur was soft and warm, but the leather was stiff and cold. It had not been treated well enough to be pliant, but no matter; at least he had a cloak around his shoulders, boots on his feet, and pants on his legs, thanks to the generosity of the Jecta. Reiv squirmed in the saddle, a necessity for such a long ride. He was not used to having so much material pressed against his skin, but neither was he used to being so cold. In hindsight, he couldn't even remember the last time he had been warm. Perhaps it had been in The Black, but then he realized, no; it had been that night with Jensa. He sighed, resolved to the fact that he would just have to endure until he was in her arms again.

The wind picked up, followed by the *plop plop* of raindrops falling on the forest's leafy canopy. Reiv scrutinized the surrounding landscape, searching for any sign of shelter, but all he saw was a shallow overhang of rock fronted by a few scruffy cedars. He steered Gitta toward it, then dismounted, grabbing his bedroll and satchel from her back. He tossed his belongings beneath the overhang, then tied the horse's reins to the nearest tree.

"Sorry, girl," he said. "But I do not think you will fit."

He turned and climbed beneath the overhang and sat, instantly banging his head against the rock. "Gods," he groused, rubbing his skull. He rolled out the bedroll and lay upon it, curling himself beneath the cloak.

Reiv stared out at the soggy landscape, his teeth chattering. A fire would be nice, but considering the deluge, and the shallowness of his shelter, it wasn't possible. He closed his eyes, listening to the pounding of the rain, and turned his thoughts to Dayn and Alicine. The moment could not come soon enough when he would see their smiling faces again.

☙

# CHAPTER 36: TRIALS AND TRIBULATIONS

Dayn's trial was swift. Lorcan had seen to it. Time was of the essence, he'd insisted; they could not risk the demon working any more mischief. Lorcan had ordered that Dayn be locked in a storage room during the proceedings. The Vestry had to be protected from the threat of any spell work. Some members suggested that normal protocol should be followed, at least somewhat. Could the demon not have *some* semblance of a say in his own behalf? But Lorcan was swift in his rebuttal: "Have not enough wells dried up and crops withered? Have not enough innocent children died from the poisons hanging in the air?" With those words, most readily agreed to Dayn's absence. As for the rest, Lorcan snuffed any remaining doubts by reminding them that Dayn had tried to spirit Falyn into the fiery depths–and every man there had been a witness to it.

The mock trial proceeded with the only witnesses to Dayn's crimes the Vestry itself, and of course Sheireadan, who had been forced by his father to speak against the defendant. The trial was over in less than a heartbeat, at least that was how it seemed to Sheireadan. What the Vestry was doing was unjust, even he knew that, and though he'd been raised to hate Dayn with every fiber of his being, for some reason this felt...wrong. Without thinking, Sheireadan had risen from his seat when the verdict was reached—guilty. But he had very nearly fallen back into it when the punishment was read—death. At that moment, his stomach had felt as though it was being swept into a whirlpool, but when his father announced, "Death by fire...at high sun...with all the eyes of Kiradyn as witness...," it was as if his soul had been swept in with it.

Sheireadan staggered out the door of the Hall and into the cold evening air. His body felt feverish but at the same time bathed in chills. He swallowed in an attempt to calm his churning insides. If he hadn't left the room as quickly as he had, he was sure he would have vomited the contents of his stomach onto his boots. He leaned his forehead against the side of the building, beads of sweat trickling down his neck. Death by fire—an agonizing way to die, even for a demon. But was that was Dayn was, a demon? Though Sheireadan had always believed it, a nagging voice in the back of his head insisted that Dayn was innocent, and that nagging voice was Falyn.

Sheireadan stared blindly at his feet. *How am I going to tell her? When she learns I spoke against Dayn...* He groaned and closed his eyes, replaying his father's lies as well as his own, and the verdict that had resulted because of them. Falyn would never forgive him, of that he was certain. But what could he do? There was no way to challenge the verdict now; were he to retract his words, he might very well find himself on the pyre next to Dayn. As for the punishment, the Vestry had no choice. Fire was the only way to purge evil. The Written Word said so.

Sheireadan shook his head. If only he and Falyn had left before their father had come home, where might they be now? In those dreadful clan lands, no doubt, but at least there they would be safe. If Lorcan had gone after them, he wouldn't have stood a chance against the clansmen. Sheireadan straightened his back. The clansmen! If he could get word to Dayn's family...to the clans! He spun from the wall and ran full speed down the road that led home, his mind racing with a plan. Falyn knew the way to Haskel's homestead; Dayn had drawn her a map. She was a swift rider and...

The house came into view; Sheireadan slowed his pace. Falyn would be in the cellar around back, and probably well-guarded by his father's men. He stopped at the side of the house, gulping to catch his breath, then peeked around the corner. As predicted, two men were lingering near the cellar door.

Sheireadan pulled in a steadying breath and strode toward them. "Gentlemen," he said casually.

"Ah...Lorcan's boy," the two said in greeting. "How fares the meeting?"

"Well. But slow." Sheireadan nodded toward the cellar. "Has my sister given you any trouble?"

One of the men chuckled. "Just entertainment."

Sheireadan felt fury bubble in his throat. "What do you mean *entertainment?*" he demanded.

The man stammered, "I—I—nothing...I mean, she had a slew of words for us, is all."

The other guard's head bobbed in agreement. "Just words. She has a temper, that one."

Sheireadan eyed them threateningly. "Indeed she does. But my father's is far worse."

The men's faces blanched.

"Well," Sheireadan said. "You'll not have to listen to my sister's temper any more tonight. My father has sent me to escort her to her room."

The men hesitated. "We were given orders to keep her confined until your pa came back."

"And I was given orders to get her to her bed." Sheireadan folded his arms across his chest. "I left the Hall but moments ago, gentlemen. The sentence has been announced, no surprise there, but my father now must oversee the construction of the pyre and–"

The men snorted. "Bout time we had a real demon at the roast," one of them said.

"At any rate," Sheireadan said with forced control, "my father does not wish his daughter to sleep in a cold damp hole when a nice warm bed is but steps away."

The men shifted their stance. "Well, I dunno," one said.

Sheireadan curled his lip. "You doubt me? Very well. Whose name shall I give my father when I tell him you denied my sister her bed *and* risked her health over it?"

The men glanced at each other. "Risk her health... but... we mean...all right," one of them grumbled at last. "We don't want the girl gettin' *sick*, after all."

"But you'd best be tellin' your father that, ye hear?" the other added. He scowled, then nudged the other man to follow him to the road.

Sheireadan waited until he was sure the men were gone. He slid out the board securing the cellar door and tossed it to the ground, then lifted it open with a *creak*.

In the farthest reaches of the cellar an oil lamp flickered. Sheireadan made his way down the steps toward it, taking them slowly and cautiously. His feet were big, and the stones were narrow and slick, but that wasn't the reason he descended with trepidation. He paused, attempting to gather his wits, and wiped his clammy hands down his pants. The musty smell of the cellar always filled him with fear and loathing.

"Falyn," he said shakily. If only he could get her to come up the steps, rather than him having to go down them. "Falyn." But there was no response.

Sheireadan forced his feet downward until at last he reached the bottom. He shivered and wrapped his arms around himself. The walls felt as though they were closing in around him. The cellar was a dismal space, he thought, with its cobwebs and slimy walls, and the horrific memories it always brought him. For some reason, Lorcan had always gravitated to placing his children in dark holes when punishing them. Maybe someday someone would place *him* in a hole.

Sheireadan surveyed the shadowy recesses, noting the familiar shelves lined with canned goods and the wooden barrels filled with grain and assorted sundries. But he saw no sign of Falyn. He stepped toward a stack of crates in the far corner. The lantern was sitting atop them; perhaps that was where he would find her. Leaning around the crates, he was relieved, but saddened, to see his sister curled up on a pile of burlap bags. It had once been Sheireadan's own corner of solitude, if you could call it that, offering him a place to hide from the monsters in the cellar, and the real-life one that lived in the house above.

He stepped around and squatted next to Falyn. The lantern threw flickering patterns upon her face, revealing the traces of tears that had no doubt lulled her to sleep. He placed a hand on her shoulder. "Falyn," he said. "Wake up."

Her eyes shot open, and she blinked them into focus.

"It's all right. I've come to take you out."

Falyn sat up with a start. "What happened to Dayn?" she asked anxiously. Then her eyes grew stormy. "How could you have lied about him like that!"

"Later. Let's get out of here first," Sheireadan said, guiding her up by an arm.

He grabbed up the lantern and helped her navigate the steps, then closed the door quietly behind them. Snuffing the light, he directed his eyes to the house. The windows were dark, a good sign their father was not yet home.

Sheireadan motioned for Falyn to follow him.

"Where are we going?" she asked.

Sheireadan lifted a finger to his lips. "Sshhh," he whispered. "The barn." Falyn looked puzzled, but followed as instructed.

When they reached the barn, Sheireadan glanced back at the house, then eased open the barn door just wide enough for the two of them to enter.

All of the horses were in their stalls, except for the one Falyn had taken earlier and that Lorcan had ridden to Vestry Hall. Sheireadan set the lantern down, then grabbed a blanket and a saddle and threw them on the back of the nearest horse. He secured the straps beneath its belly, then attached the bridle and reins.

He lifted a riding cape from a nail by the door, then took Falyn by the arm and pulled her toward the horse. "Get on," he ordered.

"What? Why?" Falyn asked. "Where am I going?"

Sheireadan threw the cape around her shoulders and fastened it beneath her chin. Then he lifted her onto the horse. "Do you remember the directions Dayn gave you to his uncle's place?"

"Of course, but—"

"That's where you're going." Sheireadan picked up the lantern and hooked it onto the pommel of the saddle, then tossed a saddlebag next to it.

"But...but what about Dayn?"

"He's to be executed in the morning."

Falyn raised a hand to her throat, her eyes wide with terror.

Sheireadan snatched some fire sticks from a nearby box and shoved them into the saddlebag. "You have to get help, Falyn. You're the only one who can do it. The clans won't let the Vestry get away with this. The minute they hear of it, they'll ride in to save him."

"What if there's not enough time?" Falyn asked desperately. "What if—"

"There won't be if you don't leave now." Sheireadan led the horse to the barn door. He peeked out, then pushed it open.

"It'll be dark before you reach the clan lands," he said. "But you've got the lantern."

A cold breeze ruffled Sheireadan's hair, sending a chill down his spine. Falyn reached out a hand to him. "When Father learns you let me out of the cellar–"

Sheireadan took her hand in his and forced a smile. "Don't worry about me. I'll be fine. You just save Dayn, all right?"

Falyn nodded, and Sheireadan slapped the horse's flank, launching the animal and its rider off into the night.

☙

# CHAPTER 37:
## DANGERS IN THE NIGHT

The sound of horse's hooves thundered down the road, sending mud flying and the sound of urgency raging through the forest. The sky was still heavy with clouds, obliterating a full moon that should have been bathing the landscape in silvery light. Falyn glanced at the darkening trees on either side of her. Their distorted shapes looked like charred skeletons, she thought, reminding her of those that had littered the pyres. She kicked in her heels. "Hyah!" she screamed, spurring the horse on faster.

The tree line to her right was a dizzying blur, but she kept her eyes trained on it nonetheless. It was there, somewhere, that she would find the road leading to Haskel's place, that is if she hadn't already passed it. Dayn had told her it would be an easy miss; it was far less traveled than the main road she was currently on. So far, she had seen nothing even resembling a fork, and though speed was of the essence, she realized she might miss it altogether if she didn't slow down. She tightened her hold on the reins, forcing the horse to ease its pace.

Falyn scanned the forest, searching for even the slightest break in the trees, but all she saw was an endless maze of vines and foliage. Something caught her eye, adding more worry to her already pounding heart. A thick fog was creeping along the forest floor, blanketing everything it touched.

Her surroundings soon became cloaked in gray, reducing Falyn's range of vision to nearly nothing. She brought the horse to a stop and dismounted. Mist swirled at her ankles as her boots hit the dirt. Tugging the reins, she slowly walked, fanning her skirt as she coaxed the fog from her path. She had not gone far when she halted and unhooked the lantern to light it. Disturbing noises were beginning to sound in the woods around her, no doubt creatures of the night rousing for the hunt.

The horse snorted and neighed nervously. Falyn placed a calming hand on its neck. "It's all right," she cajoled. "We'll be there soon." But in truth she was beginning to lose faith that she would ever find the turnoff.

The lantern, now lit, sent out an orb of light, bathing the fog in eerie shades of green. Falyn's hands began to tremble. Courage, girl, she told herself. A pair of glowing eyes blinked at her from the shadows. She jumped and thrust out the lantern toward them, but they vanished into the darkness.

Falyn pushed her shaking legs forward, but she soon realized she was hopelessly lost. It seemed as if she had been traveling for hours—had she missed the fork? She glanced behind her, not sure what she should do. Should she retrace her steps, or continue in the direction she was heading?

Suddenly a sound screeched through the trees. Falyn froze, her eyes darting back and forth. She lifted the lantern just as a large, shadowy form rushed past.

"Who—who's there?" Falyn asked. But she was met by only silence.

"I—I'm looking for the homestead of Haskel of the Aerie clan," she continued, praying she was addressing a clansman and not something far worse. "Could you tell me how to get there?" She paused and listened, but again there was no response. She continued to study the spot where she was sure she had seen the shadow, but she saw no further movement. Determined her mind was playing tricks, Falyn took a step, but then a dark shape emerged onto the road.

Falyn drew a startled breath. Whatever was standing before her was beyond the reach of the light, but judging by its silhouette, it appeared to at least be human. "Please, sir," she said. "I—I need help. I must reach the clan lands."

The figure did not say a word, but cocked its head as if studying her.

Falyn felt panic stir in her breast, but she dared not let on. "Very well," she said, forcing composure into her voice. "If you cannot help me, I will be on my way."

The stranger made a bizarre noise, like a deep primitive rumble in the depths of its throat. Was he toying with her? she wondered. Her annoyance flared. Well, if that was the case, she had no time for games.

Falyn jerked the horse's reins, intent on heading in the opposite direction, but before she had taken two steps, the man leapt in front of her, quick as a cat.

The stranger's features were now strikingly clear in the orb of the lantern. Falyn took a startled step back. The stranger was like no creature she had ever seen, nor could have imagined. He was a young man, tall and muscular, with thick black hair spiked around his head. His eyes were dark and outlined in lines of kohl that continued down the sides of his nose, making him look more feral than human. His lips were painted black, and the leathers that clung to his barely clad body were beaded with claws and animal teeth.

The cat-like man looked her up and down, then reached out and fingered her hair. Falyn's insides clenched as she realized what he probably meant to do with her. But then he flashed her a smile so warm, it was clear he meant her no harm.

A crash sounded through the brush as three more men dressed in similar attire stepped into the light. Falyn's eyes darted amongst them, realizing their expressions held none of the kindness of that of the first. "Do—do you know where I might find H-Haskel of the A-Aerie clan?" she managed.

One of the men, an older one, argued with the first, but the words he spoke were not a language Falyn had ever heard. Voices soon escalated as the other two men joined in the fray, and it was not long before Falyn realized she did not need to understand their words, their tones were clear enough: They were arguing over her.

The young man stepped between her and the others, hissing as if daring them to step closer to the girl now quailing at his back. Three pairs of eyes glowered at him in response. One of the men approached him but was met with a shove and a flash of blade.

Falyn retreated slowly. Blade or no, the young man now protecting her was outnumbered and likely to lose.

In a moment of quick thinking, she threw the lantern to the ground, smashing the glass and sending oil into the dirt. The oil flared for a moment, catching the men off guard. As they leapt from the reach of shattered glass and sputtering flames, Falyn flew onto the horse and kicked in her heels. Screams from the men ensued, followed by hands grappling at her skirts. She thrust out a foot, knocking one of them down, then swept past the rest, daring not a glance back. She plunged the horse into the darkness, not knowing whether she was still on the road or lumbering into the forest. But at this point she did not care. All she knew was that she had to get away from the cat-men, and quickly.

She had not gone far when the horse skidded and lurched, nearly throwing her from the saddle. Before her, a huge shape was rising from the shadows. The horse whinnied and struggled to retreat, but its legs were tangled in a snare of briars, and all it could do was twist in a heightened state of frenzy. Falyn yanked the reins and kicked in her heels, but it did no good. The horse was thoroughly trapped.

The horse screamed and reared on its hind legs. Falyn clung desperately to its back, but a sudden wrench sent her sailing through the air. She hit the ground with a *thud*, ramming her spine and jarring her skull. She would have groaned had there been an ounce of air left in her lungs.

Fighting for breath, Falyn felt herself lifted from the ground. A bristle of coarse fur tickled her cheek as two massive arms held her against a rock-hard chest. She clawed against the brute with all her might, but swirling darkness was sapping her strength.

*This is the end,* she thought weakly. *I am about to die. Oh...Dayn...Dayn...*

The last thing she heard before she plunged into oblivion was a deep timbre voice.

"Now whatcha be doin' out on a night like this, lass?" it said. "Tis naw safe for a girl such as y'self ye know."

～

The thud of boot steps sounded on Haskel's porch, sending its inhabitants scrambling toward the door. Alicine swung it open. "Did you find him?" she cried.

Brenainn shouldered his way in, Falyn draped in his arms, and made his way to the nearest bed. "Naw, but I did find this," he said, laying the unconscious girl onto the mattress. "She was in a real tizzy. Don' know what she was doin' out there in the middle o' the night, but—"

"Was Dayn with her?" Alicine asked anxiously.

Brenainn shook his head. "Saw no sign of 'em. But never ye worry. There's plenty o' men still lookin' fer 'em."

Morna began to wring her hands. "Oh why didn't we realize he was missing sooner?"

Vania put an arm around her shoulders. "Now, dear, ye know the boys often come in after dark when the huntin's good. He probably lost track o' time and decided to camp somewhere. He'll be fine, ye'll see, and probably cartin' plenty o' game with him when he returns."

Alicine stepped to the bed and frowned down at Falyn. She knew as well as Vania did that Dayn's absence was not due to a successful hunt.

"Wake her," Alicine said. "She'll know where Dayn is."

"Do you think she does?" Morna asked.

"Why else would she be here?" Alicine said. "She and Dayn were obviously planning to meet."

Morna's lips compressed. "He was *strictly* forbidden to see her," she said firmly. "I seriously doubt he would–"

"Oh, Mother. Do open your eyes," Alicine said. "Of course he would." Alicine shook Falyn's shoulder roughly. "Falyn. Wake up, do ye hear?"

Vania rushed over with a damp cloth. "Gentle, now. She might be bad hurt."

"She's going to be worse than that when I get through with her," Alicine said. She shook her again.

Vania brushed Alicine aside and pressed the cloth to Falyn's brow. The girl moaned and reached a hand to her head, then sat up with a start. "Wha—where—"

"Where's Dayn," Alicine demanded.

Falyn's eyes darted around, resting momentarily on the concerned faces staring down at her from around the bed. "Dayn," she whispered. *"Dayn!"* She leapt from the bed, swaying on her feet. Brenainn grabbed her by the shoulders, attempting to steady her. One look at his burly face and she screeched in terror. "You—you—"

"Rescued yer tail is what I did. Now tell us, lass. Do ye know where Dayn is?"

Falyn blinked, seeming to realize she was safe, at least for the time being.

Alicine yanked Falyn from Brenainn's hold and spun the girl to face her. "Where's my brother," she said.

Falyn burst into tears. "He's in Kiradyn. He was taken by the Vestry."

*"Taken?"* voices cried.

The front door suddenly burst open and Haskel stormed in. "I got word ye found an injured girl in the woods," he said. Then his eyes fell on Falyn. "By the Maker—"

Falyn ran toward him. "Please. You have to help Dayn!"

"Help him? Aye I'll help him—to a good whippin'," Haskel growled.

"No—please–you don't understand," Falyn said. "My father—he and the Vestry took him—Dayn's to be executed at high sun!"

Morna screamed, then collapsed onto the bed. She covered her face with her hands and began to sob. Vania and Alicine rushed forward.

Haskel's face went gray. "*Executed?*"

"Yes. Please," Falyn begged. "He's to be burned at the stake. You have to—"

"I'll gather the men," Brenainn said, marching for the door. "I'll have me Lorcan's *head* I will!"

"I'm coming, too!" Alicine said.

"No. Ye'll stay here with your mother," Haskel ordered. He headed to a nearby trunk and threw back the lid, then lifted out a dirk wrapped in a sheath of dark leather. After securing it at his waist, he hurried to the door.

Alicine grabbed her coat. "I said I'm coming!" she said, and marched after him.

"You'll do no such thing," Vania said.

"I will! And you can't stop me!"

Haskel wheeled to face her. "Now you listen to me—"

"No, you listen to *me*. I have something that can prove Dayn's innocence!" Alicine rushed to the trinket box she kept under her bed and pulled out the amethyst brooch she had hidden there. She dashed back to Haskel and thrust it under his nose. "This is evidence that Tearia exists," she said. "When the Vestry sees it, they'll have to believe us."

Haskel's eyes widened. Never had a jewel the size of this one been seen in Kirador, and certainly not one with this quality of craftsmanship. Perhaps the ornament would prove Tearia existed, perhaps not, but knowing Lorcan, it might at least serve as a bribe.

"All right," Haskel said. "But I'll be the one takin' it to the Vestry, not you."

He reached for it, but Alicine slipped it down the front of her dress. "Take it from me then...if you dare," she said.

Haskel stammered for a moment, then hissed, "Fool girl. Very well, if ye *insist* on goin'..."

"No!" Morna cried. She sprang from the bed.

"Husband, no," Vania said. "Ye can't let the child go. If ye don't make it in time, there's no tellin' what she might see. Are ye willin' to risk that?"

"It's a risk I'll have to take. Lorcan might agree to take the jewel as a bribe, but without her tellin' him and the Vestry all she knows about Tearia, they'll be back after Dayn in a heartbeat."

He turned his eyes to Alicine, and for the first time Alicine saw fear there. "Ye understand what your aunt is sayin', don't ye?" Haskel said grimly.

Alicine set her jaw. "I do."

"All right then. Let's go."

They headed out the door. A host of clansmen, including Peadar, Brenainn, and at least fifty more, were waiting for them. All were armed with knives and swords and an assortment of fighting gear. Haskel leapt onto his horse and swept Alicine into the saddle behind him. With a warlike cry the posse exploded from the scene, leaving Vania, Morna, and Falyn trembling in the doorway.

꧁꧂

# Chapter 38: Demon on the Mountain

Reiv awoke, surprised to discover the rain had stopped and the morning sun was beginning to glow behind the trees. He yawned and blinked his eyes awake, then groaned. Why had he allowed himself to sleep so long? he lamented. Rain or no rain, he should have covered more distance the day before.

He rolled out from beneath the overhang and staggered to his feet. His bones ached from the cold, and his joints were stiff from the bitter ground he'd slept on. Clutching his cloak around his shoulders, he surveyed his surroundings. The landscape was draped in morning shades of green and gold, and the damp, earthy forest smelled pungent and sweet. Reiv pulled the air through his nostrils, then released it with a sigh. He had to admit, it *was* beautiful on this side of the mountains. If only it wasn't so blasted cold.

He stepped toward a nearby bush to relieve his bladder, then turned to gaze toward the sky. The sun was low on the eastern horizon, he realized. At least the day was still young. The storm may have cost him time, but there was no sense heading off with frozen fingers and an empty belly.

He ducked beneath the overhang and opened his satchel. From within it he pulled out a snare, some flint, and a pouch of rags. The rags were greased with animal fat, a trick Gair had taught him, and would at least get a small fire started if little dry kindling could be found.

From the nearby tree where she was tethered, Gitta neighed with annoyance. Reiv worked his way to her and released the reins. "Thirsty, girl?" he said as he led her toward a stream that could be heard nearby. Down the slope, not far from where he had slept, Reiv found the rain-swollen creek. It was moving fast, splashing noisily over sand bars and mossy rocks, but did not appear deep. He led Gitta along its shore, looking for a spot where the currents ran gently, until at last he found a place that would suffice.

Reiv let go his hold on the reins. He stripped off his gloves, then squatted beside the horse as she drank. Cupping his hands toward the water, he noticed his own reflection staring back at him. The sight of it caught him off guard. Though he recognized his own violet eyes staring back at him, that was about the only thing he did recognize. His hair was a wild, disorderly mess, and his face was streaked with dirt. He scowled. "Is this how you would go meeting Alicine after all this time?" he muttered. But then he realized: What did it matter? Alicine was no longer his to impress. He had already given himself to Jensa.

He dipped his hands into the stream, obliterating his reflection, and took a drink. After several more sips, he brought one last handful to his face and scrubbed it clean. He ran his fingers through his tangled hair, but without a comb there was little more he could do with it. For a moment he thought to bind it at his back like he used to, but he knew it would be much warmer draped across his shoulders and down his back, and so he left it to hang there.

Reiv straightened up and reached for the horse's reins, but the sudden snap of a branch stopped him short. Heat coursed through his veins as he quickly scanned the landscape. But he saw no sign of danger. He slanted his eyes toward Gitta and realized her gaze was equally focused. Clearly he was not the only one on alert.

Eyan crouched, well-hidden by a thick hedge of forest foliage. His tunic was of a similar green, the perfect camouflage, and the soles of his deer-skin boots were perfect for stalking. Unfortunately, they'd just snapped a branch so loudly, his presence had been shouted from one end of the mountain range to the other. Eyan gritted his teeth, praying his prey had not bolted on account of it.

He had left home pre-dawn to search for Dayn. No one in the household had realized Dayn was missing until well past midnight, something even Eyan felt guilty for. Since beginning his search, he had visited every location the two of them had ever hunted together, but there was still no sign of him.

As Eyan crouched in the shrubbery, he held his bow and arrow ready. Though he had not left home with the intention of hunting game, there was no sense in letting an opportunity pass. Moments before, he had spotted what appeared to be a fox near the stream, and though a fox would not make good eating, it would certainly provide a fine pelt.

Eyan crept cautiously toward the flash of red he had spotted on the opposite bank of the stream. As he drew closer, he realized the creature, though still barely visible, was much larger than a fox. He also realized there was more brown to its coat than red. A buck perhaps? Eyan's mouth watered. He had not come across one of those in months. Now that would be a catch!

He notched the arrow and eased through the branches. As the leaves parted before him, he took aim, prepared to fire the instant the animal was clearly in his sights. *Nearly there*, he whispered to himself. *Steady now.*

He took a step closer, keeping his eyes trained on the far bank of the stream. With arrow notched, he pushed aside the last branch and prepared to shoot, but in that instant he realized the animal was no buck. It was a horse, and next to it was—

A creature that looked barely human rose to face him, its glowing eyes turned in Eyan's direction. A beam of sunlight broke through the trees, igniting its hair into fiery tendrils of red.

Eyan took a startled step back. It could be only one thing—demon!

The beast moved toward him, its clawed hand extended. "Wait," it growled.

But Eyan did not wait. The moment the creature spoke, Eyan felt the arrow leave his bow and sail through the air. It hit its mark and the demon tumbled, and Eyan, horrified, turned and crashed through the woods in the opposite direction.

❦

Eyan slammed open the door and tore into the house. "Demon!" he screamed. "There—there's a demon in the woods!" Vania and Morna leapt up from their places at the table. Beside them Falyn rose, gasping at the sight of the young man who had just exploded into the room.

Eyan gawked in Falyn's direction. "Wha—what's she—"

Vania rushed toward him. "What? *A demon?* Where!"

Eyan swung his attention from Falyn to his mother. He gulped a breath into his rasping lungs. "In–in the woods, near the stream. I shot it."

Vania did a double-take. "You *what?*"

Eyan looked frantically around the room. "Where's Father; is he back? It–it might not be dead!"

Vania hurried to retrieve her cloak. "Your father's not home," she said, fastening the clasp beneath her chin. She grabbed up an ax that was kept by the door. "Take me to it," she commanded.

"Bu—but mother," Eyan stammered. "Ye can't!"

"Of course I can. Now go." Vania stepped through the exit, ax in hand, then paused to address Morna and Falyn. "You two stay here," she said over her shoulder. "Don't worry. We won't be long."

"Vania, please," Morna said. "It's too dangerous."

"We'll be fine," Vania insisted. "Ye want to be here when Dayn gets back, don't ye?"

Morna blinked. "Yes, when Dayn gets back," she said. But her words sounded as if they had been spoken in a trance.

Falyn moved to Morna's side. "I'll look after her," she said. "Go. We'll be fine."

Eyan looked at Morna and Falyn with confusion, something was definitely going on, but before he could ask a single question, his mother was hustling him off the porch and toward the woods.

It did not take long for them to reach the area where Eyan had seen the demon. As they approached, they slowed their pace, Vania with ax at the ready, Eyan with arrow notched.   Eyan nodded toward the shore. "There," he whispered. Vania gripped the ax more tightly, then slowly stepped in that direction.

Upon the opposite shoreline, a brown horse with a black mane stood, staring at the two of them as if daring them to come closer. At its feet lay a bundle of what appeared to be leathers, but from where Eyan and Vania stood, it was hard to tell exactly what it was. One of Eyan's arrows, however, was clearly imbedded in it.

Vania narrowed her eyes. "Are ye sure it was a demon?" she asked suspiciously. "I never heard of a demon ridin' a horse before, and a saddled one at that."

Eyan felt doubt rumble in his belly. Had he been too hasty?

"But—but its hair was on *fire*, Mother," he insisted. "And its eyes—"

"Well, we won't find out standin' here, now will we?" Vania waded into the stream, and with Eyan at her side, picked her way over the rocks and rushing waters. Her long skirts swirled around her ankles, then billowed on the surface as the water rose to her calves. Eyan stayed close as they slogged to the opposite shore.

The horse was but feet from them now, standing protectively between them and the demon on the ground. The horse snorted and stomped a hoof.

"There there, girl," Vania said gently. "We're only here t' help."

The horse eyed her warily, keeping itself between the strangers and its injured master. Vania laid the ax upon the ground, then held up her hands. "Ye see, girl? No harm." She reached out, then stroked the horse's velvety nose. The horse calmed, but its eyes remained on Eyan.

Eyan stepped toward the victim that was lying on the other side of the horse, but he kept his distance, deciding to stand at the demon's feet so as not to be ensorcelled by its eyes. Vania, on the other hand, seemed to have no fear of the thing. She rounded the horse and moved toward the demon's head, then knelt down beside it.

"Not so close," Eyan warned.

"Shush!" Vania said. She leaned in closer to the demon, examining it, then grunted. "On *fire*, ye say?" She brushed the long red hair away from the demon's face. "Looks like a boy with red hair to me."

Eyan gaped at the unconscious stranger. "I swear, Mother. He looked like a demon."

Vania clucked her disapproval as she examined the arrow protruding from the boy's cape. She breathed a sigh. "Just grazed his shoulder," she said with relief. She lifted the edge of her skirt, still wet from being dragged through the stream, and dabbed the wound. The laceration was bleeding, but it wasn't deep, definitely not life-threatening.

The boy moaned and raised a hand to his shoulder.

Eyan jumped at the sight of the scarred hand that Vania was now swatting away from the wound. As Eyan stared at the mottled fingers, he realized the hand wasn't a claw as he had first imagined. It had obviously been burned.

Recognition smacked him in the face. "Ye don't suppose this is—"

"Reiv," Vania said.

The strange boy's eyes fluttered open. They were violet—just like Dayn and Alicine had described—just like the image of the boy in the cave that—

The boy blinked up at them, then at the arrow embedded in the ground next to him. "Gods, are you trying to kill me?" he groused. He struggled to rise, but Vania pressed him back down.

"I'm sorry," Eyan said. "I thought ye were a demon."

The boy glared. "What is with you people?" he muttered.

"Not to worry, Reiv," Vania said. "We'll have ye mended in no time."

The boy's face took on a look of surprise. "You *know* me?"

"Only of ye. Dayn and Alicine—"

"Dayn and Alicine?" Reiv scrambled to his feet. Eyan grabbed his elbow to steady him.

"Lands, child," Vania said, taking Reiv by the other arm. "Ye need to stay put."

But Reiv ignored her. "They are here?" he asked anxiously. "Tell me!"

"Aye," Eyan said, feeling his own excitement rise. "They're—"

"Relatives," Vania added hastily. "You'll see 'em soon enough. Let's get ye to the house and tend that shoulder of yours first." She guided him to the horse. "Eyan, help him up, will ye?"

"It is only a scratch, and I am perfectly capable of mounting a horse," Reiv said. "It is not like your boy there has much skill with a bow."

Eyan's spirits fell. For some reason he wanted Reiv to like him. And his skills as a hunter were about the only thing he had going for him. "I'm usually much more accurate," he said defensively.

"Is that so," Reiv replied. "Well thank the gods *this* time you were not."

Vania shook her head. "Alicine said ye had a pride about ye."

"She should know," he said with a laugh.

"Well, pride or no pride, I'd rather ye let Eyan help ye," Vania said. "Ye hit your head when ye fell; might be dizzy for a spell."

Reiv acquiesced, too muddled to argue the point, and moved to mount the horse. "Oh, my things," he said, turning toward the hillside at their backs. "I left them up there, beneath an overhang. The storm—"

"I'll get 'em," Eyan said.

Eyan bent over and cupped his hands for Reiv to step into, then hoisted him up and into the saddle. Once Reiv was settled, Eyan darted up the hillside to gather the rest of the belongings. But when he arrived, he realized there wasn't much to retrieve. There was one ratty bedroll and a leather bag with a few oily rags, but very little food. As for tools and weapons, there was a dirk tucked beneath the blanket and that was it. *He must be starving*, he thought. He turned his gaze down the hillside toward the proud young man sitting on the horse. *Someday I'll prove to ye my aim's not so bad,* Eyan decided. *Ye'll see.*

༄

# CHAPTER 39:
# SEEING THE LIGHT

Dayn lay curled up in the darkness, shivering. His clothes were still damp from the drenching they had received earlier, and he had been given neither blanket nor cloak to help keep him warm. He could not imagine how long he had been lying there; there were no windows to help him judge the time by sunlight or moonlight, or for that matter, any other light. Still, it seemed as though he had been there a very long time.

The door creaked open, sending a stab of light to his eyes. He raised a hand to shield them, then squinted up at the light. He quickly realized a lantern was entering the room, and behind it was the dark shape of Lorcan.

Dayn scrambled up from the floor. He clenched his fists at his side. "You can't keep me here," he said. "I've done nothing wrong."

"Oh, you will not be here for long," Lorcan said smugly. "As for the other, a verdict has already been reached."

"What do you mean, verdict?"

"The one determined at your trial, of course."

Dayn's jaw dropped. *"Trial?* Should I not have been allowed to speak in my own defense?"

Lorcan set the lantern on a nearby barrel, then pulled up a crate. "Sit, Dayn," he said. "Let us discuss your sentence."

Dayn felt his legs begin to shake. "Sentence? What sentence?"

"Sit, if you wish to hear it," Lorcan replied. "If you're lucky, I might even make you an offer."

Dayn sank down onto the crate. He knew he was about to hear some terrible news, and wished he had the courage to hear it standing on his feet.

"You are to be executed at high sun," Lorcan said matter-of-factly. He watched Dayn closely, hoping to relish a response, but Dayn found himself unable to give one.

"Do you wish to know the method?" Lorcan continued.

"I assume it will be at the stake," Dayn said. For some reason he felt no panic; his mind had moved him into a temporary state of denial.

"I regret your death is to be so painful," Lorcan said with feigned sympathy, "but you do realize there is no other way. Evil can only be purged by fire."

"So I understand," Dayn replied. "Will you be joining me there?"

Lorcan's eyes flashed with hatred, then he calmed, though with obvious effort. "I mentioned earlier that I might be willing to make you an offer. Will you listen?"

For a moment Dayn's hopes lifted, but then he realized any offer Lorcan made would probably not be worth the taking. Still, he could not help but ask, "What sort of offer?"

"First, give me the names of all those you have corrupted. Second, free my son and daughter from your spells. If you do, I will see to it that your heart stops before the flames lick your boots. "

Dayn jerked his head in bafflement. "*What?*" he said.

Lorcan stepped toward him threateningly. "No point denying it. You know as well as I do that you ensorcelled them. Why else would Falyn agree to go with you? Why else would my son be what he is?"

Dayn stood to face him. "What makes you think I won't ensorcel *you* right now?"

Lorcan scoffed. "I'm immune to your black magic, boy. Do your best. You'll not work your spells on me."

"You're right," Dayn shot back. "Because I don't know *how* to."

"Oh, but you do." Lorcan's eyes narrowed. "Now, as I said, tell me the names."

"There are no names!"

Lorcan grabbed Dayn by the front of his tunic and shoved him against the nearest wall. In the blink of an eye he had whipped a blade beneath Dayn's chin.

Dayn froze, his survival instincts sapping all ability to move.

"Have you ever seen someone die at the stake, Dayn?" Lorcan asked. "*No?* Well let me enlighten you. First you will be tied to a post atop the pyre for all to see. The square will be filled with spectators: men, women…even children. Some will pelt you with rotted fruit, others will taunt and laugh at you. At first you will feel only humiliation. After all, the pyre is not yet lit; your flesh is not suffering; you still harbor an element of hope. But soon the executioner will arrive with the torch. It is then that you will realize true terror. Your eyes will search for rescue. But alas, there will be none.

"The executioner will turn to face you, making sure you are witness to the moment he touches the torch to the wood piled around you. At first the pyre will only smoke, then a telltale crackle of flames will reach your ears. The crowd will cheer. You will struggle. And then the smoke will thicken. Tears will begin to sting your eyes; your chest will struggle for want of air. The flames will rise around you. Soon they will lick your boots, melting the leather to your feet. The pain will be horrendous, Dayn, but nothing compared to the agony you will feel as the flames creep up your trousers, then your shirt, then your face. You will writhe and scream. You will pray for death. But you will still be alive—a pillar of fire, yes. But still alive.

"Some in the crowd will turn away, no longer having the stomach for it. But most will stay, for they know your death will bring them life. No longer will you poison their air and taint their wells. No longer will you kill their crops and destroy their homes. But more importantly, no longer will you possess their children."

Lorcan eased the knife from Dayn's chin. He rotated the blade, considering it for a moment.

"Now, boy, as I was saying. If you give me the names of those you have corrupted, I will see that you are dead before the flames reach you. A knife thrown to the heart, an arrow shot to the head. It is no matter to me; I give you the choice."

Dayn's mind raced. "But—but I told you," he managed. "There are no names, and I can't release anyone from a spell I didn't conjure!"

Lorcan curled his lip, then walked toward the door. He paused, turning to face Dayn one last time. "As you wish, demon—die in agony. But know this: When the flames eat your flesh, I will see to it that my daughter is a witness to your screams."

# Chapter 40: Race for Time

The ride to Vania's and Eyan's cabin was not a long one. In no time at all Reiv found himself being led into a clearing and toward a small timber dwelling located in the center of it. Around the clearing and scattered amongst the trees were campsites occupied by rugged-looking men and not-so-genteel women. Most were dressed in forest greens, much like the color Dayn had worn, but others were clothed in shades of blue or burnt sienna. The most intimidating amongst them, however, were those in browns with plaids of red, clearly the alphas of the group. As Reiv glanced at the well-armed men and women staring at him as he passed, a nagging sense of dread began to weave its way into his thoughts. He could not be certain, but judging by the weapons, and the expressions of the people carrying them, a conflict was in the making.

At last he and his escorts arrived at the cabin. Reiv dismounted and looped the horse's reins over a nearby post. Eyan assured him he would tend the animal as soon as Reiv was settled inside. Vania stepped onto the porch and opened the door. Reiv entered behind her, his hopes riding high at the possibility that Dayn and Alicine might be inside. To his profound disappointment, the only persons he saw were a frail-looking woman and an attractive girl about Alicine's age. The two of them rose immediately from their places at the table, gaping at Reiv in obvious alarm. Reiv felt annoyed by their reaction, but he dampened it down. He didn't appreciate their less than friendly greeting, but could he blame them? Even had he been in a better state, his Tearian features would have still screamed demon.

"Morna. Fetch me some cloth and a bowl of fresh water," Vania said. She pulled off her cloak and hung it by the door, then took Reiv's from his shoulders and did the same. "Oh, and bring the medicinal in the amber bottle there," she added. "The boy's shoulder needs tendin'."

The woman nodded and made her way to a cabinet in the nearby kitchen. The girl scurried to the woman's side, working to keep a wide distance between herself and the monster that had just entered the room.

Vania motioned Reiv to the table. "Sit," she said.

Reiv did as instructed, all the while surveying his surroundings. The interior of the cabin, he noted, was one large room, crowded but cozy. The table where he sat could accommodate at least a dozen people and stretched from one side of the room to the other. Numerous pegs lined the wall near the front door, most of them covered with an assortment of cloaks, his own included. Reiv scanned them, looking for a hint of the coat he had once seen Dayn wear. But there was no sign of it. He moved his eyes to the far wall. Several beds could be seen, each with a trunk located at the end of it. It soon became clear that a rather large family was living in a rather small space. He could only pray that Dayn and Alicine were amongst them.

"Falyn dear," Vania began.

"Falyn?" Reiv leapt from the bench and turned his attention to the girl still standing in the kitchen. "You are Falyn?" He rounded the table and stepped toward her, grinning, but she backed away.

Reiv halted his approach. "Dayn told me much of you. I am Reiv—his cousin."

Falyn gave a little gasp. "Reiv?"

Morna spun from the sink where she had been drawing water from the pump. She dropped the bowl with a *clank* and a loud splash of water.

Reiv narrowed his eyes at Vania. "What is it you are not telling me?"

Vania turned to Eyan. "Go tend to Reiv's horse," she said.

"*Now?*" Eyan asked. But one look at her face and he knew there would be no debating it. "Fine," he said with a scowl. He turned and stomped toward the door, then shoved it open with his foot. "Why am I always left out of everythin'," he groused, slamming the door behind him.

"I think ye'd better sit, dear," Vania said to Reiv. Then to Morna, "Water?"

Morna picked up the bowl to refill it.

Falyn stepped timidly toward the table where Reiv had retaken his seat. "You're Dayn's cousin?" she asked. She managed a feeble smile, but there was no disguising the worry in her eyes.

Reiv swung his attention back to Vania. "Where are Dayn and Alicine?"

Vania reached for the bowl that Morna was now handing her and the cloth draped across her arm. "Let's tend that shoulder of yours first."

Reiv rose from the bench. "No," he said, "I think I would rather have my question answered if you do not mind."

Vania set the supplies on the table and folded her hands. "Very well. Dayn is in Kiradyn, and Alicine has gone with Haskel and some clansmen to rescue him."

"*Rescue* him? From what?"

Morna turned away, her hand covering her mouth.

"He's been tried and sentenced to die at high sun," Vania said.

"*What?*" Reiv cried. "By the gods, what did he do?"

"He didn't do anything," Falyn said. "But the Vestry blames him for the eruption of the mountain and just about everything bad that's happened since. They say it's black magic—Dayn's black magic."

"You must be joking," Reiv said. "Other than his sensitivity to earth tremors, and his uncanny ability to predict them, Dayn possesses no mystical abilities."

"Of course he doesn't," Vania agreed, "but there's more to it than that."

"Such as?"

"Falyn's father never took keenly to Dayn's interest in her," Vania continued. "When Dayn faced him down recently...well...let's just say Lorcan went out of his way to plant the idea that Dayn's the cause of everyone's problems."

"So that is why there are armed men camped outside your home?"

"There's goin' to be war over it, no doubt. Especially if Dayn's executed."

Reiv straightened his spine. "How do I get to Kiradyn?" he said.

"Don't be foolish," Vania replied. "There's nothin' ye can do."

But Reiv refused to believe it. He brushed past her and marched to the door, then threw it open in time to see Eyan disappearing into the barn with Gitta. "Eyan," he hollered, "bring back the horse!"

Reiv stepped onto the porch, but Vania grabbed his arm. "Reiv, ye can't! If ye were to show up there—"

Eyan returned with the horse in tow. Reiv pulled his arm from Vania's hold and hurried out to meet them. He reached into the pack that was still secured to the saddle and removed his dirk, then shoved it into his waistband. "Eyan," he said. "Tell me how to get to Kiradyn."

Eyan looked at him, dumbfounded. "Why in the world would ye want to go *there*?" he asked.

Falyn rushed forward. "I'll tell you how to get there," she said.

"Falyn, no," Vania insisted, following at her heels. "It's too risky. Let Haskel and the Chieftains handle it."

"What's goin' on?" Eyan asked with confusion. "What do ye mean, handle it?"

Falyn pointed in the direction of the road leading into the forest. "Head that way and follow the road for several miles," she said. "Eventually you'll come to a main road. Go left and—"

"Dayn's in *Kiradyn*?" Eyan cried, piecing it together. "Why's he—"

"I'll tell ye later," Vania said.

"No! Tell me now!" he ordered.

Vania's expression tightened, then she said, "He's been arrested and tried for witchery. He's to be executed at high sun. Your father and a group o' clansmen have gone to fetch him."

Reiv leapt onto the horse and gripped the reins.

"I'm goin' with ye," Eyan insisted.

"No, Eyan. There's no time," Reiv said. He turned his attention to Falyn. "From the main road, then what?"

"It will lead you directly into Kiradyn, but you'll have to ride fast," she said. "Once you reach the city, make your way to the center of it."

"Is there a particular building I should look for?"

"No. The execution will happen out of doors, in the town square. You'll see a crowd. There's always a throng of spectators when the stake is involved."

"The *stake?*"

"Yes," Falyn said anxiously. "Dayn's to be burned at the stake." She glanced at the sun. "Please Reiv, there's not much time!"

Reiv swung the horse in the direction of the road, but Eyan rushed toward him. "Take these at least," he said, pulling his bow and quiver from his back. "Ye might need 'em."

Reiv took Eyan's offering with a word of thanks, then swung the quiver and bow over his shoulder. With one last look at Falyn and the others, he jabbed his heels into the horse's ribs and bolted toward the road.

༝

The posse of clansmen rode like a cyclone through the forest, their long black hair mingling with the clan-colored cloaks billowing at their backs. At their sides and attached to their saddles, weaponry clanked–swords and axes, maces and daggers–but it was the men's brutal determination that would be their greatest ally.

From out of nowhere a deafening roar sounded. The ground began to ripple like waves in a stormy sea. The horses twisted and lurched; the men fought them with kicks and shouts and yanks on their reins. Alicine clung to Haskel's waist as the horse they were riding bucked, threatening to toss them. But Haskel refused to be tossed. He jerked the horse's reins with such force, the animal had no choice but to obey. The rumbling stopped almost as quickly as it had started.

The clansmen spurred their horses onward, but they had not gone far when the ground began to rumble again. But this time the men managed to keep their mounts advancing. Trees teetered around them. Some crashed to the ground, others slammed into those swaying next to them. Alicine buried her face in Haskel's back, then felt her stomach flip as their horse sailed over a fallen branch. Her body lifted from the saddle, then dropped in a spine-crushing jolt. She risked a look over her shoulder, relieved to see the rest of the horsemen still behind them.

With a shout, Haskel suddenly reined his horse to a halt. The rest of the pack stopped in a frenzy of confusion at his back.

"By the Maker," Haskel said, staring at the road ahead.

Curses sounded, and Alicine leaned around to see what held her uncle's attention. She gasped. A steaming fissure could be seen straddling the road, stretching as far as the eye could see.

Peadar and Brenainn urged their horses next to Haskel's. "There'll be no jumpin' over *tha*," Brenainn said.

"Then we go around it," Peadar replied.

Haskel glanced at the sun. "We're runnin' out of time."

"So are the Aeries," Brenainn reminded him. "If Dayn was right, and it's seemin' to me that he was, then we'd better get him in a hurry if we've any hope o' gettin' back."

Without a word, Haskel kicked in his heels and reined his horse toward the chasm and the maze of fallen trees that would hopefully lead them around it.

∾

Footsteps sounded then stopped outside the door to the room where Dayn was imprisoned. Muffled voices could be heard, followed by the tell-tale *click* of a key in the lock.

The door swung open, sending a swath of light across the floorboards. The shape of someone holding a lantern entered, but this time Dayn was unable to determine who it was. He scrambled from the floor, praying it wasn't Lorcan, or the executioner.

"I brought you something to eat," a voice said, closing the door behind him.

Dayn realized it was Sheireadan. Fury bubbled in his throat. "How could you have turned me over to the wolves like that!" he demanded, taking a step toward him.

"I didn't have any choice," Sheireadan said. He turned and set the lantern and a plate of food on a nearby barrel.

Dayn grabbed Sheireadan by an arm and spun him around to face him. "Of course you had a choice! You did it to save your own skin."

"No. I didn't," Sheireadan said, jerking his arm away. "I did it to save someone else's."

"Whose? Falyn's?" Dayn asked.

"No."

"Then whose?"

"A person whose name my father said you gave him," Sheireadan said.

Dayn was taken aback. "I didn't give your father any names. How could I? There aren't any names to give."

Sheireadan nodded. "I figured you didn't, but I wanted to hear it from you anyway."

"Well, you've heard it. Now what?"

"Now nothing."

"Well thank you very much," Dayn said. "I'm sure your sister will thank you too when she's watching me burn alive in the town square!"

"I won't let that happen," Sheireadan said.

"What, the sister part, or the burning part?"

"The sister part."

Dayn felt relieved, at least for that. "Thank you," he said.

Sheireadan stared at the floor for a long awkward moment, then stepped toward the door. "I'd better go. I'm not supposed to be here."

"Wait," Dayn said. "Why did you *really* come?"

Sheireadan shrugged, but did not turn to face him. "To clear my conscience, I guess. But it's probably too late for that."

"The only one who has to worry about "too lates" is me," Dayn said.

"No," Sheireadan replied. "Not just you." He picked up the lantern and placed a hand on the latch. "Don't lose faith, Dayn," he said quietly. "It's all you've got left." Then he exited the room, leaving Dayn in darkness again.

Dayn stepped toward the plate of food Sheireadan had left, realizing he might as well take one last meal, though he had no appetite for it. But the floorboards beneath his feet suddenly lifted and fell, sending a wave of nausea to his gut. He dropped to his knees, gripping the floor as swirls of light flickered behind his eyelids.

A vision formed in his brain, sending new dread to his heart. The mountain was awakening, and judging by the looks of it, he wasn't the only one who would be meeting their fate this day.

◦～๏

Reiv rode like a madman, dodging piles of forest debris, soaring over trees that had crashed to the road. The ground rumbled, opening steamy chasms through the tangle of woods on either side of him. But he refused to turn back. No matter the risk, he had to reach Dayn before it was too late.

He cursed his own stupidity. Why had he not paid heed to the visions Agneis had given him? They were roadmaps of events, he now realized, each one leading to a different future. He had possessed the ability to study them all along, but instead of recognizing them for what they were, he had suppressed them. The goddess had told him he had to understand his own destiny before he could inspire a brighter future for others. If only he had listened! But he hadn't. Instead he had jumped from one path to another, never choosing, always going where others willed him to go. And it was because of this that Dayn was in the predicament he was now.

Reiv spurred the horse on faster, but then he spotted a wide chasm straddling the road ahead. Common sense told him to stop, but the urgency of his mission refused to consider it. Reiv leaned into the horse and screamed it onward. He closed his eyes. *Please, dear gods, give us wings.*

The horse took a sudden leap, and for a moment Reiv thought they truly had sprouted wings. The air whistled past his ears, the pounding of hooves momentarily silenced. Reiv kept his head down, waiting for the landing that seemed to take forever. At last the horse's hooves hit the dirt, nearly jarring him from her back, but she galloped on, barely breaking stride. Reiv pressed his cheek to her neck, whispering a prayer of gratitude.

༄

Dayn was yanked from the floor and shoved toward the door. He hadn't heard anyone enter the room; he had been too ill to think of anything but his roiling stomach and spinning head. He was thrust into daylight. The pain of it sent his senses reeling. Rough hands grabbed him as if to steady him, but he quickly found himself shoved to the ground instead.

Dayn struggled to his knees, but he could not gain his balance. He dry-heaved into the dirt.

Laughter sounded around him. "Scared as a rabbit," an amused voice said.

Dayn spat the foul taste of bile from his mouth and again attempted to rise. A hand jerked him up. "Get on with ye," its owner said.

Dayn glanced at the group of ruffians that surrounded him, then at the alleyway just ahead. He knew it would lead him directly to the town square, and from there, the stake. A drone funneled down the passageway toward him, the voices of a thousand people waiting for his death.

With a gruff command Dayn was ordered to walk. He shuffled his feet forward, but his legs felt as if they had turned to liquid. He drew a calming breath, trying to muster his strength, then lifted his head and straightened his spine. His legs may have felt like jelly, but he would meet his accusers walking like a man.

The alleyway was long and narrow. As Dayn neared the end of it, the noise from the square became almost deafening. Spectators turned in Dayn's direction, then let out a *whoop*. A wave of cheers echoed through the crowd. Over the sea of heads looming before him, Dayn could just make out the tip of the stake where he would soon be tied. For a moment he thought to turn and bolt, but he knew such an attempt would be futile. With walls at his side and goons at his back, there was no place to run.

As he stepped into the square, spectators heckled him and shuffled aside, opening a narrow pathway to the pyre. Dayn made his way slowly down it, keeping his eyes ahead of him rather than on the hostile faces lining the walkway. But as he stared forward, a far worse sight met his eyes: the stake. The horrid thing was tall and dark and surrounded by a massive pile of split wood and dried kindling. *Don't look at it*, he told himself. *Anywhere but there*. He forced his gaze past the stake, but found himself staring into the faces of those who had ordered him there instead. On a viewing platform, close enough to enjoy the show, but a safe distance from the impending flames, sat the brown-robed members of the Vestry. At their sides and behind them, an assortment of religious elders and upper-class dignitaries could be seen. Lorcan was there, of course, his dark eyes glistening with anticipation. Sheireadan sat next to him, but clearly he did not share his father's sentiment; his face was as gray and motionless as a statue. Dayn scanned the rest of the spectators on the platform. To his profound relief, there was no sign of Falyn.

The crowd jostling on either side of him sneered and spat as he continued toward the pyre, but from within the confusion he detected a familiar voice raised in his defense.

"Let the boy go, ye fools!" it shouted. "He's committed no sin. It's the rest of ye that will have Daghadar to answer to!"

Dayn turned his eyes in time to see Jorge, the blacksmith, shouldering his way through the crowd. The smith broke through the line and hurried to Dayn's side.

"Jorge," Dayn said. "Oh, Jorge." Tears welled in Dayn's eyes. Over the years, Jorge had been his one true friend in Kiradyn. The man had offered Dayn sanctuary in his blacksmith shop on more than one occasion, and had never failed to offer Dayn kindness and advice when no one else would.

Jorge grabbed Dayn's shoulder and gave it a squeeze. "I'm here for ye boy," he said. "I'm here for ye."

The men at Dayn's back tried to move Jorge aside, but the tough old smith would have nothing of it. "Get your stinkin' hands off me," he growled, "or ye'll find your head across my anvil and your horses lame for want o' shoes."

The guards relented, but whether it was fear of the anvil, or the fact that the only smith in town was threatening to deny them future services, was not clear.

Dayn glanced at Jorge from the corner of his eye. "What am I going to do, Jorge? What am I going to do?"

"Don't know there's much ye can do," Jorge said grimly. "They're fools, all of 'em."

A rotted piece of fruit sailed from the crowd, pelting Dayn on the side of the head. He raised his hand to the sting, but kept his eyes forward, pretending not to care. Jorge, however, was incensed. "What 'er ye doin!'" he hollered at the assailant, but the only response he received was increased agitation from the mob around them. More and more vegetation flew in Dayn's direction, but when rocks started being hurled, Dayn became more concerned for Jorge's welfare than his own.

"Jorge. Go," he insisted. "It's not safe for you here."

Jorge started to protest, but Dayn stopped in his tracks and gave him a shove. "I said go! I don't want you here!"

Jorge looked hurt, but then he seemed to understand. "I'll not let Kiradyn forget the terrible injustice they did to ye today, boy. I swear it."

Dayn felt a lump in his throat. "Go, Jorge. Please"

Jorge nodded, then turned and was swallowed by the crowd.

꩜

# CHAPTER 41: FIRE AND BRIMSTONE

The clansmen tore down the hillside, the silhouette of the city at last in their sights. No hint of smoke was rising over the rooftops, but the sun was high, and there was still much ground to cover before they reached the square.

The roadblocks the rescue party had met during their frenzied journey had cost them valuable time. The chasm that straddled the road had proved to be too long to go around, and so they had been forced to abandon the road and go cross-country instead. It had slowed their pace considerably; the forest was thick and tangled and difficult to navigate. But still they had pressed on. At last they broke through the trees and into an open meadow, and that was where they were now, careening down its slope toward Kiradyn.

Alicine peeked around her uncle's back toward the city looming before her, and could not help but recall the last time she had seen it. It had been on their way to the Summer Fires Festival, and she and her family had stopped on the hillside to take in the view. That was to have been a happy day, she realized, but fate had dealt them a blow instead. But before she could ponder the fates further, the mountain range at their backs sent up a deafening roar. As one, she and the clansmen swiveled their heads to see a billow of smoke rising from the tallest peak.

"The mountain's erupting!" Alicine cried. "We'll never reach him in time!"

"The hell we won't," Haskel said, and screamed the horse onward.

⟆

Shrieks of shock and terror ricocheted throughout the town square as all eyes shot toward the mountains. Smoke could be seen mushrooming from the tallest summit, expanding in every direction as it billowed into the atmosphere. Lighting crackled within dark, roiling clouds; thunder split the air then rumbled across the land.

Dayn turned with the rest of the crowd to gawk at the terrible sight. Though his illness had given him warning, seeing it with his eyes was so much worse than seeing it with his mind. People began to panic, shoving him this way and that as they scrambled past him. For a moment he thought the pandemonium might offer him an escape from the pyre, but a voice suddenly boomed, stopping everyone in their tracks.

"Be still!" the voice commanded. "Be still I say!"

Dayn's hopes fell as he, along with everyone else, turned to the face behind the voice: Lorcan. The man was standing like a god on the viewing platform, his hands raised.

"My friends. Hear me," he shouted.

The hysteria of the crowd began to subside, but waves of anxious voices still rolled throughout.

"Do you not see?" he said. "It is but a scare tactic, a last-minute attempt by the demon to escape his fate!"

Attentions shot from Lorcan to Dayn, who was now standing, unprotected, in their midst. Voices rose around him. "Yes, he's the cause of this! Quick! Get him to the fire!"

Dayn felt himself being grabbed from all sides and shoved toward the pyre, but this time he had no intention of going without a fight. He kicked his feet and swung his fists. He cursed and dug in his heels. But it did no good. A sudden blow to his gut sent him doubled over and plummeting to the ground. Before he could think, what felt like a hundred arms lifted him up and passed him over the heads of the crowd toward the pyre.

"Burn him...burn him...burn him!" people chanted. "Destroy the demon!" others cried.

Dayn was dragged up a scaffold of steps and down a short boardwalk leading to the pyre. He tried to twist away, but his back was quickly slammed against the stake. Ropes were tied to his wrists and bound behind him. He jerked and yanked, but more ropes were brought, binding him at the ankles, waist, and neck. Before long, he could barely move at all.

Dayn's eyes darted toward the wood piled beneath his feet, then at the mountain smoking in the distance. "I haven't done anything!" he screamed. "Listen to me! The mountain is going to erupt whether I'm dead or not." But no one was of a mind to listen; they were too busy chanting his death.

"Executioner, bring the torch," Lorcan commanded above the roar.

Dayn strained in an attempt to see Lorcan, but the ropes at his neck made it impossible.

The executioner, cloaked and hooded in black, stepped between the pyre and the crowd. A flaming torch was in his hand. He held it high for all to see. But then the earth rumbled again, sending chunks of buildings tumbling to the cobbled streets below. Screams resonated throughout the square. A few people grabbed their children and began shoving their way toward the exits, but the majority pressed closer in a heightened state of hysteria.

"Do it now!" Lorcan shouted at the executioner. "Before it's too late!"

The man in black plunged the fiery torch into the base of the pyre. The wood began to smoke and crackle. Several people rushed forward and grabbed sticks from the pile, touching them to the flames and flinging them at Dayn.

Jorge broke through the mob, shoving and swinging his fists at those closest to the pyre.

"Jorge, no!" Dayn shouted. "You have to get out of here!"

Jorge hesitated and looked up at Dayn, but a blow to the smith's face sent him spinning in the other direction.

Dayn stared at the flames now rising. Waves of heat were beginning to bake his face and clothes. Smoke spiraled around him, its sting blinding him to the chaos below. "Jorge," he screamed. "If you can hear me, get out! Go north, then east past the mountains. You have to get out of Kiradyn."

The wind picked up, fanning the flames. The smoke parted for a moment, just long enough for Dayn to see

Jorge's bloodied face staring up at him from the base of the pyre. An explosion of fire leaped between them, sending Dayn a burst of indescribable heat. He writhed and yanked at the ropes, coughing and rasping for air. *This can't be happening…this can't be happening…*

A dizzying whirlwind of images churned in his skull: friends… enemies…good times…bad. Some he knew to be memories, but others he did not recognize at all. It was all so confusing. Why was he seeing them now? But then Falyn's face swam into view, and everything became clear. She would never be his wife; they would never have children or grow old together. But she loved him, and not even the fire could take that away from him.

The flames crept closer, the heat and smoke unbearable. Dayn clenched his teeth to keep from screaming. *Control your mind! Control your fear!* he told himself. But then the fire reached his boots, and unfathomable pain consumed his feet. *Don't scream…don't scream…don't scream…don't scream—*

Dayn screamed. And all went black.

The posse of clansmen burst into the square with a vengeance that rivaled that of the mountain itself. Spectators scattered from their path. Those who hesitated were trampled beneath a brutal battering of hooves. Screams shattered the air as the clansmen slashed their way toward the pyre, their weapons leaving a swath of blood and dismemberment in their wake.

Haskel charged his horse toward the pyre and leaped onto the scaffold leading to it. In an instant he reached the stake. Flames were all around it but had not yet risen beyond Dayn's feet. Haskel grabbed a branch that was untouched by flames and shoved the burning wood as far from Dayn as he could. He yanked his knife from his waist-band and reached down to cut the ropes.

A shout of warning redirected his attention. "Haskel," Alicine screamed. "Behind you!"

Haskel turned to see Lorcan rushing toward him, a flashing blade in his hand.

Alicine gripped the reins as she struggled to control Haskel's frenzied horse, but then she felt an unexpected yank on the bridle. She looked down to see Sheireadan commanding the animal to calm, but his eyes were not on the horse, they were on the scaffold leading to the pyre. Alicine followed his gaze to Haskel and Lorcan who were now battling on the boardwalk.

She leapt off the horse, intent on sprinting to the pyre to pull Dayn from it, but Sheireadan grabbed hold of her and jerked her to a halt.

"Let go of me!" she cried. "I have to save Dayn!"

"I'll get him," Sheireadan said.

Alicine shoved him away and staggered back. "I don't believe you!" But Sheireadan grabbed her again.

"I said I'll get him," he said between clenched teeth. "You can't carry him. I can."

Alicine turned her eyes frantically toward the fire that was burning its way toward Dayn, then to Haskel and Lorcan still fighting on the platform. Past them, all around the pyre and throughout the square, the other clansmen were beyond her reach, caught up in clashes of their own.

Alicine grabbed Sheireadan's tunic in her fist. "I swear if you're lying, I'll kill you."

The muscles in Sheireadan's jaw tightened. "I'm not lying," he said. "Not this time." He pulled away and spun toward the steps, taking them three at a time as he dashed onto the narrow boardwalk leading to the pyre. Lorcan and Haskel were in his path, still battling it out, but Sheireadan sprinted past them. He leapt toward Dayn, then pulled out his pocketknife to release the ropes. Dayn slumped forward as the last bond was cut, but Sheireadan was ready for it and quickly rounded the stake to grab him.

Alicine watched breathlessly as Sheireadan clambered with Dayn in tow over the pyre and toward the platform. Just then, Haskel threw Lorcan a punch that sent him sprawling. Momentarily free, Haskel rushed to help Sheireadan. The instant Sheireadan's feet hit the boards, Haskel lifted Dayn into his arms. "It's all right, son," he said. "You're safe now."

Alicine breathed a sigh of relief, but then something happened that seemed to play in slow motion. Lorcan unfolded from his stupor, rising like a viper to his feet. With an echoing scream, he moved toward Haskel. But Haskel could only stare as if frozen at the crazed man now moving in his direction. It was then that Sheireadan stepped out to meet his father, and with a great lift of his arms, Sheireadan had Lorcan flying through the air and straight toward the pyre. The man hit the post and crumpled beneath it.

A great wind suddenly swept the courtyard, speeding up time as it sent a funnel of flames spiraling up the pyre and around the writhing form of Lorcan. Alicine threw a hand over her mouth to stifle her scream, then turned with a start as a loud clattering of hooves stopped at her back.

Peadar leapt from his horse. "Get to my horse, girl," he said. "Your uncle's goin' to need room for your brother."

Haskel lumbered down the steps of the scaffold and toward the waiting horse. With assistance from Peadar, he got Dayn into the saddle, then settled in behind him.

He grabbed up the reins and turned his attention to the burning stake. Sheireadan was still standing on the platform next to it, watching as the flames consumed his father.

The mountain rumbled more violently than before, sending people scurrying in every direction. With the mob momentarily distracted, the clansmen hastened in the direction of Haskel and Peadar.

"We've got what we came for," Peadar called to the men. "Time to head out."

"Wha' about *him*," Brenainn said, lifting his chin toward Sheireadan.

"What about him?" Peadar asked impatiently.

"Well, it seems to me tha' since he cut Dayn's ropes *and* took care o' a certain fella fer us, we might be wantin' to take 'em with us."

Peadar looked at the boy still staring motionless into the fire. "Ye do realize that's Lorcan's son, don't ye?"

"Aye. All the more reason. Poor lad."

Peadar snorted. "Very well...but be quick about it. And *you're* responsible for him, ye hear?"

Brenainn scowled. "I din say I wanted to *adopt* him," he muttered. Then he dismounted his horse and thundered up the steps and onto the platform.

"Boy," Brenainn said when he reached Sheireadan. "Come away now."

Sheireadan turned slowly toward him. Tears were streaming down his face.

"I know it's a loss to ye," Brenainn said gently. "But yer welcome to come with us if ye want."

Sheireadan looked surprised by the invitation, but then he gazed into the crowd, worry clouding his expression.

"Nothin' ye can do fer 'em," Brenainn said. He glanced toward the mountain. "Well, if yer comin' ye'd better get on with it. The mountain's got no patience for them who wait." The Chieftain turned and Sheireadan followed, but his eyes continued to scan the crowd.

Brenainn reached his horse and mounted it. He held out his hand to Sheireadan. "Ye'll have to ride with me. Not much room, but we'll manage."

"I—have a friend," Sheireadan said. "If I find him, can he come, too?"

"No time," Brenainn said. "We have t' go."

"But—" Sheireadan looked around frantically.

"Let's go men," Peadar ordered, and spurred his horse northward. The clansmen followed.

Brenainn lingered a moment more, his hand still extended. "This is yer crossroad, boy. Which road ye gonna take?"

"I—I don't know."

"Seems to me ye do. Ye saved an innocent boy's life today, din ye?"

Sheireadan looked one last time at the tumult of people in the courtyard, then he grabbed Brenainn's hand and swung into the saddle behind him.

ര_

Reiv exploded into the square and barreled through the crowd. Eyes widened and voices shrieked at the sight of the fiery-haired creature now charging into their midst. Threats sounded, but Reiv paid them no heed. His only thoughts were on the billowing smoke and flaming pyre across the way.

He galloped full speed toward it, then reined his horse to a staggering halt. A charred corpse could be seen crumpled amongst the flames, and for a moment Reiv could only stare in disbelief. Pain built in his chest, clenching his heart like a brutal fist. Had he arrived too late? No—he refused to believe it. That could not *possibly* be Dayn, he reasoned. But then he realized, it could be no one else.

A scream of anguish tore from Reiv's lungs. He reeled toward the maddening crowd, a reckless rage coursing through him. Hatred flashed in his eyes. His hair whipped around his head like a fire storm. If ever there was a demon, these monsters were about to meet one!

Reiv slid his dirk from his waistband, and with a cry of fury lifted it into the air. People cowered, then began to back away. "Butchers!" he screamed. "Murderers—all of you!" He kicked in his heels and charged into the mob, his blade swinging.

Reiv's anger blazed white hot. No one was safe from his blade or his wrath. He hacked his way through, regardless of who or what was in his path. Blood spilled; bodies fell. But Reiv was aware of only one thing: They would pay for what they had done. They would pay!

Another explosion sounded from the mountain, sending brick and mortar raining into the streets. Some members of the crowd scattered, but others froze in their tracks, watching as a massive cloud imploded down the mountainside.

Reiv reined his horse to a halt and stared at the thunderous plume descending upon them. His instincts told him to flee, but for some reason he did not have the will to do it. It was then that he realized his arm was still suspended, his bloody weapon clenched in his fist. He tore his eyes from the dirk and scanned the courtyard around him. Bodies lay everywhere—men, women, even children!

*Gods, what have I done?* he whispered.

A chill stole over him. His heart filled with despair. He was no better than the rest of them! His eyes shot toward the avalanche of hot gasses speeding toward the city, then to the confusion of people stumbling around him. They were all going to die, every one of them. And he was going to die with them.

Reiv closed his eyes as the roar of the monstrous cloud drew nearer. But then the courtyard became strangely quiet. He opened his eyes and realized everyone had gone. *No, not everyone,* he reminded himself. He steered his horse around the bodies and worked his way toward the pyre. Sorrow mushroomed in his throat; tears stung his eyes. How poor Dayn must have suffered. Did he himself deserve to suffer any less?

Cobblestones began to dance at his feet. The horse skittered nervously. Reiv glanced at the approaching cloud at his back, then toward the exit at the opposite side of the courtyard. Should he stay or should he go? To stay meant instant death. To leave meant years of guilt and restitution. He stared at the body one last time. "Forgive me, Dayn," Reiv said, then he kicked in his heels and galloped out of the courtyard.

∾

# CHAPTER 42: LOST

Dayn was jostled awake by searing pain in his feet. He moaned, fighting to lift his head, but an arm tightened around him. "I've got ye," Haskel said. "Be still now."

Dayn blinked open his eyes. Scenery swam past in a blur of trees. "Where are we?" he croaked.

"Headin' north," Haskel said. "The mountain erupted. Couldn't go back the way we came."

Dayn coughed, the taste of smoke lingering in his mouth. "What–about Kiradyn?" he managed.

"Gone."

The pain in Dayn's feet intensified. He grimaced and tried to reach for them, but Haskel tightened his grip.

"Stop," Dayn said. "Please. Can we stop?"

Haskel slowed the horse, and the clansmen at his back did the same.

"The boy needs to rest," Haskel called to them. "I think we're far enough out that we can stop for a bit."

Dayn held onto the pommel as Haskel dismounted. His head felt groggy. What had happened? Why was he here? Then he remembered—the pyre. He turned his eyes toward the men now milling about and realized their clothes were splattered with blood.

"Uncle, what—" he asked with alarm.

"Let's get ye down first," Haskel said.

Haskel helped Dayn from the horse and laid him on a nearby grassy patch. Alicine approached with a water skin.

Dayn gasped at the sight of her. "What—what are *you* doing here?"

She knelt down beside him. "You didn't think I'd let them go without me, did you?"

"But how did you know where I was?"

"Falyn told us."

Dayn attempted to sit up. "Falyn? She's safe?"

"Yes," Alicine said, pressing him back down. "Now, enough talk. We need to get these off." She looked at his boots and furrowed her brow.

Haskel knelt on the other side of Dayn. He pulled a flask from his jacket and held it to Dayn's lips. "Here, drink," he said. "It'll help ease the pain."

Dayn did not bother to ask what the flask contained. He took it in his shaking hand and gulped the contents down.

He handed the flask back to Haskel. Haskel eyed its empty contents. "Well, that should do it," he said with amusement.

The alcohol immediately warmed Dayn's veins. His limbs began to relax. "Might as well get on with it," he said to Alicine.

Alicine began to gently work a boot from his foot. Dayn cried out, then coughed violently. "W—wait!" he said. He gripped the grass, panting with distress. "Just—just give me a minute."

"I think we'll need to cut the boots off," Alicine said.

Haskel pulled out his knife. "I'll do it. Just hold him still." He grasped the top of Dayn's boot, then slowly worked the blade of his knife down it. After a few inches, he gently peeled back the leather, but stopped when he realized Dayn's blistered skin was adhered to it. He shook his head. "This is goin' to take more skill than we can offer here."

Alicine bit her lip. "He's going to need treatment soon if we're to avoid infection."

Dayn struggled to his elbows. "Let's go, then," he said, but then his eyes fell on Sheireadan standing a short distance away. Dayn scowled. He could not help but feel resentment toward the boy whose lies had helped send him to the stake. "What's *he* doing here?" he grumbled.

Haskel glanced at Sheireadan, who turned his eyes away. No doubt he could feel the sting of Dayn's glare.

"He was invited," Haskel said.

"*Invited?*"

"Yes," Alicine replied. "He saved your life."

"What?"

Brenainn stepped up beside them. "How's the lad doin'?" he asked, staring down at Dayn. He winced at the boots. "Gor, *that's* gotta hurt."

Haskel rose. "We can't do anythin' for him here. We'll have to wait until we can get him to Eileis."

"Hopefully tha' won't take long," Brenainn said.

"If the clans moved in the direction Dayn told 'em to, we should meet up with 'em by nightfall."

"*If* the clans moved in the direction Dayn told 'em to," Brenainn added.

"They'd have been fools not to. The first rumble of the mountain would've alerted 'em. And that happened hours ago."

"Yer right," Brenainn concurred. "They've been pre-parin' for the possibility of it fer weeks. Wouldn't make sense fer 'em to ignore the signs."

Peadar walked toward them, then stopped and squatted next to Dayn. He grabbed Dayn's hand. "How are ye feelin', lad?" he asked. "Ye well enough to travel?"

"Yes," Dayn replied.

"Gather the men," Haskel said to Peadar. "I'll get Dayn settled."

Suddenly there was a commotion behind them. The pounding of horse's hooves could be heard in the distance, galloping full speed in their direction. The clansmen pulled out their weapons and planted their feet. They hadn't gotten this far to be stopped by a Kiradyn vigilante.

The rider appeared over the horizon of the road and slowed his pace but did not stop. Whoever it was was clearly not afraid of the well-armed clansmen standing in his path. As the stranger drew nearer, Dayn realized that this was no vigilante. "Jorge!" he cried with joy.

Jorge dismounted and rushed toward him.

"Thank god you're all right!" the old man said. He ran his eyes over Dayn, then settled them on the charred boots. "Ye'll be needin' a new pair o' boots I see."

"I never liked these anyway."

"Good thing."

"We were just leavin'," Haskel said. "We need to make time while there's still daylight."

"Reckon it's time I rejoined my clansmen. Figured ye wouldn't mind," Jorge said. He tilted his head toward Sheireadan, who was waiting by Brenainn's horse. "Seein' as you're takin' in strays and all."

Peadar smiled. "We'd be happy to have ye."

They did not meet up with their kin by sunset as they had hoped. At first they were concerned that the Aeries and the clans that had stayed with them had not evacuated at all. But they held out hope and camped for the night, determined to continue in the agreed upon direction in the morning. At the rise of the sun they headed out, and before long they came upon a rarely used mountain road. It was rutted by horses' hooves and wagon wheels—a sure sign that they were on the right track. They hastened on, and by late morning found the caravan within their sites.

Shouts of joy resonated down the line as word spread of the approaching clansmen. Wagons stopped. Women rushed to embrace their returning husbands. Children tugged at their father's pants legs, clambering to hear of their victory.

Vania hustled toward Haskel who was riding toward her. Falyn was at her side, Dayn realized, and his heart nearly leapt from his chest.

"Oh Dayn...Dayn," Falyn cried upon reaching them. She grabbed his leg, then leaned her forehead against it and wept.

Dayn reached down and stroked her hair. "I'm all right," he said. "Just need to get these cursed boots off, that's all."

Falyn looked at the boots and began to cry even harder.

"Brought ye somethin' that might cheer ye up a bit, girl," Brenainn said, approaching.

Falyn looked up to see Sheireadan walking at Brenainn's side. She flew into his arms. "You're all right," she cried. Then she realized the somber expression on his face. "What happened to—"

"See to Dayn first," Sheireadan said quietly. "He's the one that needs you right now." He turned and walked away.

Haskel helped Dayn from the horse and lifted him onto the bed of the wagon. "Where's Eileis?" he asked Vania. "The boy needs tendin'."

"She's at the front of the line. Morna's gone to fetch her." She looked toward the reunion of clansmen and their families, then stood on tiptoes, her eyes searching.

"Not to worry," Haskel said to her. "Everyone made it back. Even brought a couple o' extras with us."

Vania sighed with relief. "He found ye then," she said.

"Who?" Haskel asked.

"Reiv," she replied.

"*Reiv?*" Dayn and Alicine cried. Dayn struggled from the wagon bed and landed on his feet, but the pain forced him to sit back down. He gripped the side, trying to regain his breath.

Vania's face grew worried. "He didn't find ye then?"

Alicine rushed toward her. "He was here?" she asked anxiously. "Reiv was here?"

"Well, not *here*," Vania said. "Eyan found him in the forest this mornin'. Thought he was a demon." She laughed nervously. "Anyway, to make a long story short, we brought him to the cabin and it was then that he learned about Dayn."

"And?" Alicine pressed.

"Well, when he learned you and the others had gone to fetch him, he tore out to help."

Dayn gasped. "He—he went to *Kiradyn?*"

"We have to find him!" Alicine said. She wheeled toward Haskel's horse, but Haskel stopped her short. "Don't be a fool, girl," he said. "Kiradyn's gone."

Dayn slid from the bed of the wagon and hobbled a few steps toward him, biting back the pain in his feet. "Just because the city's gone doesn't mean Reiv is!" he insisted.

"Dayn," Haskel said firmly. "Ye know as well as I do that if the boy made it there, he *didn't* make it out. If the mob didn't get him, the mountain did."

"No!" Dayn shouted. "I refuse to believe it! I'm going to find him, with or without your help."

"So am I!" Alicine said.

Haskel nodded toward Brenainn who was standing nearby. Brenainn walked up to Dayn and with a great lift deposited him in the back of the wagon. "Yer uncle says ye'll be stayin', so that's what ye'll be doin'."

Alicine was tossed in next to her brother. They opened their mouths to argue, but Haskel and Brenainn stood their ground.

"Now you listen to me, the both of ye," Haskel said. He motioned to the mountain behind him. "Ye see that?"

Dayn and Alicine turned their eyes reluctantly toward it.

"That there's the sister of the peak that's havin' the temper fit. And if one siblin's riled, the one next to it's probably riled, too." He glanced between the two of them.

"Now as ye well know, right as we hightailed it out of Kiradyn, the mountain sent a cloud movin' straight for it. We escaped only because we had a moment's head start. If

Reiv arrived in the city, he arrived after we left. Otherwise we would've seen him. And if he didn't arrive, then he was still on the road headin' in that direction. Either way, there's no way the boy escaped."

Alicine buried her face in her hands.

"I'm sorry," Haskel said. "But there's nothin' you or anyone else can do for him."

Morna hurried toward them. "Eileis will be here shortly," she said. She stepped toward Dayn and gave him a grateful hug.

Dayn turned his face away. "Let's just go," he said bitterly.

Vania climbed into the driver's seat of the wagon. "Come, Morna," she said softly, and Morna settled in beside her. Falyn, who had already slipped into the back, wrapped her arms around Dayn. Haskel mounted his horse and positioned himself behind the wagon, no doubt to prevent Dayn and Alicine from trying anything foolish. Sheireadan, however, was nowhere to be seen. And neither was Eyan.

"Where's Eyan?" Dayn asked, realizing he had not yet seen him.

"Oh, he's here...somewhere," Vania said, looking around. "Don't worry." She flicked the reins.

Dayn and Alicine swayed in their misery as the wagon lurched forward. Falyn leaned her head on Dayn's shoulder. "I'm sorry for all that's happened, Dayn," she said sadly. "I'm to blame for most of it, especially Reiv."

"What do you mean, especially Reiv?" Alicine asked.

Falyn lowered her eyes. "Vania didn't want him to go to Kiradyn. She wouldn't tell him how to get there. So I did."

Alicine scrambled to her knees. For a moment it looked as though she were going to strike the girl. "You told him how to get there? How could you be so—so—*stupid*!"

Falyn's eyes flashed. "I did it because I love Dayn!"

"And I love Reiv!" Alicine shot back.

Alicine looked at Dayn guiltily. "I love you, too," she said. "You know that." She huddled next to him and wept into his shirt.

Dayn reached for his sister's hand and gave it a squeeze. He hated seeing her cry, but seeing her do so now made him want to weep with her. He turned his eyes to Kiradyn, grieving for Reiv and for the role he himself had played in leading him there. But then his heart filled with determination.

He wrapped his arm around Alicine. "Don't worry," he said. "I'll find him. No matter how long it takes...no matter how far I have to go, I promise you, I *will* find him."

End of Book Three
The Saga Continues in
*The Shifting of the Stars: Book Four of the Souls of Aredyrah Series*

# GLOSSARY

**Aeries** (*AIR-eez*)—Clan located in the southeastern region of Kirador along the mountain range. Clan color is green. Chieftain is Peadar.

**Aredyrah** *(Air-uh-DEER-uh)*—An ancient island world, divided by mysticism and a forbidden range of volcanic mountains.

**Agneis** *(AG-nee-us)*—Goddess of Purity. Supreme deity of Tearian culture.

**Alicine** *(AL-uh-seen)*—of the Aerie clan. Daughter of Gorman and Morna of the Aerie clan. Sister of Dayn.

**Basyls** *(BAZZ-uls)*—Rugged clan located in the northeastern region of Kirador along the mountain range. Clan colors are red and brown. Chieftain is Brenainn.

**Ben**—of the Aerie clan; Seela's son; adopted son of Nort.

**Brenainn** *(BREN-un)*—Chieftain of the Basyl clan.

**Brina***(BREE-nuh)*—Tearian. Sister of Queen Isola. Birth mother of Dayn. Maternal aunt of Ruairi (Reiv) and Whyn. Widowed wife of Mahon who was the Commander of the Tearian Guard.

**Cinnia** *(SIN-ee-uh)*—Tearian. Deceased. Former queen and wife of Whyn.

**Cora** *(KOR-uh)*—Shell Seeker; young woman who befriends Reiv.

**Crests** *(KRESTS)*—Clan located in the northwestern coastal region of Kirador. Clan color is blue. Chieftain is Ionhar.

**Crymm** *(KRIM)*—Tearian. Deceased. Former body-guard to Ruairi.

**Daghadar** *(DAG-huh-dar)*—Also called the Maker. The one true God of the people of Kirador.

**Dayn** *(DANE)*—of the Aerie clan; also Tearian and Jecta. Adopted son of Gorman and Morna of the Aerie Clan of Kirador. Brother of Alicine. Only child of Brina and Mahon of Tearia. Cousin of Reiv and Whyn. Believed by some in Tearia to be "The Light" of the first Prophecy.

**Eben** *(EH-ben)*—Jecta. Deceased. Childhood friend of Jensa and Torin. Former husband of Mya. Father of Farris, Nely, and Gem.

**Eileis** *(EYE-luss)*—Kiradyn. The Spirit Keeper (healer and spiritual guide) of Kirador.

**Eyan** *(EE-yun)*—of the Aerie clan. Son of Haskel and Vania.

**Falyn** *(FAL-un)*—Kiradyn. Daughter of Lorcan. Sister of Sheireadan.

**Farris** *(FARE-iss)*—Jecta. Son of Mya and Eben; brother of Nely and Gem.

**Gair** *(GARE)*—Jecta. Blacksmith of Pobu.

**Gem** *(JIM)*—Jecta. Daughter of Mya and Eben. Sister of Nely and Farris.

**Gitta** *(JIT-uh)*—Reiv's horse.

**Gorman** *(GOR-mun)*—Of the Aerie clan. Deceased. Adopted father of Dayn. Father of Alicine. Husband of Morna.

**Haskel** (HASS-kuhl)—of the Aerie clan. Brother of Mahon. Husband of Vania. Father of Eyan.

**Ionhar** *(EYE-o-nar)*—Chieftain of the Crests clan.

**Isola** *(Iss-O-luh)*—Tearian. Deceased. Wife of King Sedric. Mother of Ruairi and Whyn. Sister of Brina.

**Jecta** *(JEK-tuh)*—The name given by the Tearians to anyone considered "impure." The Jecta primarily live in the city of Pobu, but many work within the walls of Tearia as slaves or servants. Their impurities include (but are not limited to) dark coloring, scars or other bodily imperfections, tainted blood, family ties, and criminal activity.

**Jensa** *(JEN-suh)*—Shell Seeker. Sister of Torin and Kerrik.

**Jorge** *(JORGE)*—Kiradyn. Blacksmith in the city of Kiradyn.

**Keefe** *(KEEF)*—Dayn's Tearian birth name.

**Kerrik** *(KARE-ik)*—Shell Seeker. Adopted younger brother of Jensa and Torin.

**Kirador** *(KEER-uh-dore)*—Region northwest of the mountains on the island of Aredyrah. Home of four clan regions and the city of Kiradyn.

**Kiradyn** *(KEER-uh-din)*—Primary city in the region of Kirador. Also refers to any person living in Kirador.

**Konyl** *(KON-ul)*—a hero of ancient clan lore; believed to have saved Kirador from demonic invaders.

**Labhras** *(LAB-russ)*—Tearian. Wealthy land owner. Father of Cinnia. Best friend of King Sedric.

**Lorcan** *(LORE-kun)*—Kiradyn; father of Falyn and Sheireadan; Head of the Vestry, the governing board of Kiradyn.

**Lyal** *(Lile)*—Shell Seeker; former love interest of Jensa.

**Mahon** *(MAN)*—Tearian. Deceased. Former husband of Brina. Uncle of Ruairi and Whyn. Birth father of Dayn (Keefe). Was Commander of the Guard.

**Meirla** *(MEER-luh)*—Shell Seeker village on the southern coast of Aredyrah.

**Memory Keeper**—A historian. The term generally refers to members of a covert group that came into being after the Purge which banned all documents belonging to the Jecta. The Memory Keepers are dedicated to preserving all forms of writing.

**Morna** *(MORE-nuh)*—of the Aerie clan. Dayn's adopted mother. Alicine's birth mother. Wife of Gorman.

**Mya** *(MY-uh)*—Jecta. Widow of Eben. Friend of Jensa and Torin. Mother of Farris, Gem, and Nely.

**Nannaven** *(NAN-uh-vin)*—Jecta. Elderly Spirit Keeper of Pobu. Was the daughter of a Memory Keeper.

**Nely** *(NELL-ee)*—Jecta. Youngest daughter of Mya and Eben. Sister of Gem and Farris.

**Nort**—of the Aerie clan; brother of Gorman and Haskel.

**Olwyn** *(ALL-win)*—of the Sandrights clan; daughter of Uaine (chieftain of the clan.)

**Oonayei** (*EW-nie-ay*)—promised land spoken of in the Jecta prophecy of Kalei.

**Peadar** (*PAY-uh-dar*)—Chieftain of the Aerie clan.

**Plenum of Four**—the official gathering of the four clan Chieftains for the purpose of business.

**Pobu** (*PO-boo*)—Jecta city to the south of Tearia.

**Priestess**—Title of the supreme leader of the Temple. Known by no other name. The Priestess is the true power of Tearia.

**Quillan** (*KWILL-un*)—of the Crests clan; courting Olwyn.

**Reiv** (*REEV*)—Jecta. Name given to Ruairi when he was disowned by his family.

**Ruairi** (*Rue-AW-ree*)—Tearian. Reiv's birth name. Means "Red King." Was believed to be the second coming of a king of old who carried out the first Purge. Ruairi's name was taken from him when he was disinherited.

**Sandrights** (*SAND-rites*)—Clan located in the west-central region of Kirador. Clan color is burnt sienna. Chieftain is Uaine.

**Sedric** (*SED-rik*)—Deceased King of Tearia. Husband of Isola. Father of Ruairi and Whyn.

**Seek**—The term used for hunting shells beneath the waters.

**Seela** (*SEE-luh*)—of the Aerie clan; Nort's common-law wife; mother of Ben.

**Seirgotha** *(Seer-GOTH-uh)*—Legendary sea serpent. The Shell Seekers believe the slayer of Seirgotha will gain great knowledge from the gods.

**She**—formerly known as the Priestess; an evil parasitic entity that has been in control of Tearia since the reign of the Red King.

**Sheireadan** *(SHARE-uh-den)*—Kiradyn. Dayn's nemesis in Kirador. Son of Lorcan. Brother of Falyn.

**Shell Seekers**—A community of Jecta who live in the coastal village of Meirla. The Shell Seekers are known for their skills at diving and hunting the waters for food and shells. They are also excellent craftsman, using shells to make jewelry and decorative vessels.

**Spirit Keeper**—Title given to a healer and spiritual advisor. This title is consistently used by all the residents of Aredyrah.

**Taubastets** *(TOUW-bas-tets)*—a tribe of "cat people" driven out of the mountains during the War of Konyl.

**Tearia** *(Tee-AIR-ee-uh)*—Great city-state to the south of the mountain range of Aredyrah. All navigable land on this side of the island is known as Tearia. The city itself is a walled metropolis of elegant architecture, fountains, colorful gardens, and art. It is home to a race of people who strive for purity, as dictated by their gods and defined by Temple law.

**Tenzy** *(TIN-zee)*—Jecta. Deceased. Was the daughter of a Memory Keeper and the sister of Nannaven. Was imprisoned by the Priestess to interpret forbidden texts.

**Torin** *(TORE-un)*—Shell Seeker. Older brother of Jensa and Kerrik.

**Uaine** *(EW-ane)*—Chieftain of the Sandrights Clan; Olwyn's father.

**Unnamed One**—Person spoken of in the Prophecy. Depending on the interpretation, he can be either savior or threat. Once believed to be Reiv. Now believed to be Dayn.

**Vania** *(VAN-yuh)*—of the Aerie clan; wife of Haskel; mother of Eyan.

**Vestry**—the political and religious council of Kiradyn.

**Whyn** *(Win)*—Tearian. Fraternal twin brother of Ruairi. King of Tearia. Son of King Sedric and Queen Isola (deceased.) Former husband of Cinnia (deceased.)

**Will of Agneis**—The Tearian term that refers to the custom of killing infants who are not considered pure.

**Yustes** (*YOU-stus*)—Religious Elder of the Shell Seekers.

**Zared** (*ZARE-ud*)—Kiradyn; member of the Vestry who has been promised the hand of Falyn.

# ABOUT THE AUTHOR

Tracy A. Akers is both a teacher and an author. She grew up in Arlington, Texas, but currently lives in the rolling hills of Pasco County, Florida. She graduated from the University of South Florida with a degree in Education, and has taught in both public and private schools. She currently divides her time between teaching, writing, lecturing, and spending time with her family.

Ms. Akers has won numerous awards for her *Souls of Aredyrah Series*, and was acknowledged for her contribution to young adult literature by the Governor of Florida during the 2008 Florida Heritage Month Awards Ceremony. Books One and Two of the Aredyrah Series are included in the Florida Department of Education's 2008 *Just Read Families Recommended Summer Reading List*. In addition, Ms. Akers has been an invited guest author at major book events and writers' conferences, a panelist at fantasy and science fiction conventions, and was a member of the steering committee for Celebration of the Story, a literary event held at Saint Leo University.

As an active participant in the Florida Writers Association, Ms. Akers helped develop and lead writers groups for both adults and young writers. She is frequently invited to speak at middle schools and high schools, and works every day to incorporate her passion for story telling into the classroom setting.

*The Souls of Aredyrah Series* is Ms. Akers' first series of novels for young adults.

For character illustrations and additional information about the series, please visit her website at www.soulsofaredyrah.com.

8889701R0

Made in the USA
Charleston, SC
23 July 2011